Moloch's Garden

An Eamon Tauk Space Odyssey - Book 2

J.E. Park

Contents

BLURB

The League had given Eamon Tauk a cause to die for, but it was a woman who had given him a reason to live. He was going to desert the Corps for her. They were supposed to flee to some distant corner of the known galaxy and spend the rest of their days together.

Then a Narman insurgent murdered her in front of his very eyes.

With his beloved now gone, Tauk is freshly committed to his mission. He will help the Corps cleanse Kanaris of hostile forces – just so long as he can avenge his loss in the process.

As Tauk's Marines and their Narman enemies become entangled in a war of ever-escalating cruelty, it is not long before Eamon is left questioning whether he is the hero or the villain in this conflict. Unfortunately, his superiors are wondering the same thing and doubting his commitment to the cause. By the time Tauk realizes some of his commanders want to take his life as badly as his adversaries do, he has half a mind to give it to them.

But not without taking as many of them with him as he can.

Moloch's Garden is an action-packed, heart-pumping sci-fi thriller that will leave you breathless!

Trigger Warning

Look, I'm just going to come right out and say it: This can be a dark novel. I wish I could tell you that what you are about to read was solely a product of my wonderfully twisted mind, but the truth is that very little of this was pulled from my imagination. At this stage in the Eamon Tauk saga, the man is at war and I wrote that aspect of his tale as a horror story, as human conflict invariably ends up being, even to the victors.

To inspire the feel of these passages, I read about the atrocities of World War II. I watched graphic videos of the current war in Ukraine. To do justice to some of the more unfathomable aspects of the human condition, I tried to capture the essence of the savagery we inflict upon one another when we make that decision to dehumanize our fellow man and kill him *en masse*.

While my intention was not to create an epic work of gore porn, and I don't think that I did, if you finish parts of this novel and are not left wondering with a bit of distress about how you might act in an indescribably horrific situation, I failed in what I was trying to do.

Other than that, I hope you enjoy the story!

Chapter 1

PAIN AND PRAISE

Despite knowing I would have to face him at some point, I was not expecting Gunny Malcolm to be the first person I encountered once I stepped off the dropship. Like me, he was in his dress greens, standing in the unrelenting Kanarisian rain, getting soaked to his bones while flanked by a pair of military police officers.

I was surprised to see that Malcolm had decided against getting his eye fixed. He greeted me with a black patch covering his empty socket, a pair of shackles in his grip, and a grin on his face that radiated genuine warmth. The man greeted me like an old friend. I found that odd considering what he was about to do to me.

"Welcome back to Kanaris, Cadet Tauk," the old Marine told me as he extended his right hand.

Smiling back at my former platoon sergeant, I clasped his paw and shook it. "Thank you, Gunny," I said, my eyes locked onto the restraints he was holding. "I presume those are for me?"

Malcolm nodded. "I'm afraid so. How are you feeling? Your orders say you're fully recovered. Is that right?"

The last time Gunny Malcolm saw me, I was dying. I had been shot twice and was surrounded by an army of medics trying to plug my leaks. That was six months earlier. I had come a long way since then. "I think I'm as good as I'm ever going to be."

"You positive?" Gunny asked, showing me the chains he was holding. "Are you sure you're up to this?"

I let out a long sigh. "I wouldn't be here if I didn't believe I was. I have to admit, though, I didn't think this would happen the instant I stepped off the transport."

Malcolm shrugged. "It's best to get it over with. The quicker we put all this shit behind us, the faster we can move forward. It's better for the Corps, it's better for me, and though it may not seem like it right now, it's best for you, too."

I nodded in resignation. "I understand. You don't need the cuffs, though."

"I know I don't," Gunny agreed. "But it's part of the process. Let me see your hands."

After I stuck my arms out in front of me, Gunny Malcolm clasped the shackles around my wrists. The military police also stepped forward and chained my legs together. When they finished, the gunnery sergeant turned to me and asked, "You ready?"

"I guess I'm as ready as I can possibly be."

"Then let's do this. For-warrrrd...March!"

One of the MPs called cadence as we trudged off the landing pad, but the leg irons made it impossible for me to march in step. The best I could manage was an awkward shuffle as I tried to keep up.

Had I been a typical prisoner, I would have been transported to my hearing in a command vehicle. Because I was credited with taking the life of the Butcher of Deraghun, I was paraded through the streets for three blocks to the ceremonial grounds of the Corps' headquarters. My arrival had been announced beforehand, so the curbsides were lined by those who had not been invited to the official proceedings. Along the entire way, people pointed at me and asked, "Is that the guy who killed Gori Dravidas?"

Trying my best to ignore the gawkers, I turned to Gunny and mused, "The colonel really wanted to make a spectacle out of this thing, didn't he?"

Malcolm nodded. "Yeah, he wants to send a message to the troops that nobody's above the reach of military justice. Not even our heroes."

I chuckled. "If he wanted them to actually believe that, maybe he should be doing this to one of the Samaari highborn under his command."

Gunny spat on the road. "Ain't that the fuckin' truth."

Narman's Pyke was no longer considered a combat zone, so the three hundred officers and NCOs gathered to watch the brigade commander pass judgment on me wore their dress greens, not armor. It was going to be a lot of work for those troops to get their uniforms back into inspection condition once the rain was finished with them, but I had little sympathy for those in attendance. I figured it served them right for seeking entertainment in my suffering.

As Gunny Malcolm and our MP escorts led me to the stage, Colonel Dalton Palkrait took his place behind the podium in front of us. Rank had its privileges, so instead of getting soaked like the rest of us, the colonel stood beneath an awning that kept him dry and comfortable. His uniform was going to be just fine.

Once I was in position before Palkrait, Malcolm marched off to the right to take his place at the far end of the stage. The two MPs stood fast at my shoulders.

"Cadet Eamon Tauk," Palkrait said, once I was presented to him. "The Disciplinary Review Board has concluded that you are guilty of willful insubordination for actions taken on the seventh day of the tenth month, four hundred and forty-two years *aetate explorationis*. According to the account of Gunnery Sergeant Konor Malcolm, you returned to the wreckage of *Wasp-Three* against the direct orders of your immediate superior. The DRB also concluded that you abandoned your assignment, which was to guard the battalion's guide, and were derelict in your assigned duties."

The colonel paused and stared at me for dramatic effect. "Cadet Tauk, there's also the matter of Vernor Blyte's death. Yes, as a squad leader, you had the authority to execute a Class Zero convict for being unable or unwilling to perform his duties, but that doesn't mean the Space Corps is encouraging its junior NCOs to casually commit acts of random cruelty. Blyte may have been a Class Zero convict, but by all accounts, he was a useful and productive military asset. Your actions in regard to Blyte deprived the Corps of a valuable resource. Do you understand that?"

"Yes, sir," I answered. "I do."

Palkrait sighed. "Cadet Tauk, would you care to explain your actions on the day *Wasp-Three* crashed on the beach just off the Buvalla Sea?"

"Yes, sir," I replied, surprised to learn the body of water where we had crashed actually had a name. "After escaping the disabled dropship with Jella Duverii and Corporal Harlund Merik, we nearly drowned crawling over a massive mud flat, which we later discovered to be a type of trap laid by a sizeable carnivore. This sludge was claiming our troops by the dozens because they were trying to cross it with their battle packs still on.

Their rucks, averaging about forty kilos apiece, were the difference between making it to the tree line and dying in quicksand.

"Knowing that many more Marines would perish if they were not warned to drop their gear, I ensured Dr. Duverii was in capable hands, then returned to *Wasp-Three* to warn the others."

"Did anyone try to stop you?" Colonel Palkrait asked, even though he knew the answer to that question.

"Yes, sir. Gunny Malcolm ordered me to return to the tree line."

"And you disobeyed him?"

"Yes, sir."

"Why?"

"Because of my mission, sir," I told the colonel. "I did not think I could get Jella Duverii to Narman's Pyke alive by myself. I needed Marines, sir. We were already down to less than a third of our allotted troops after our other two dropships were destroyed. If we lost half of what remained, we would be even more vulnerable than we already were."

"Did you realize you were disobeying a direct order from Gunny Malcolm?"

"Yes, sir."

"And did you know the consequences of disobeying that order?"

With a single nod, I said, "I did, sir."

"And you did it anyway?"

"Sir," I started. "I had to weigh the rewards versus the consequences. If I had to sacrifice some skin off my back to save Marine lives and complete my mission, so be it. Gunny Malcolm gave me a lawful order, and I disobeyed it. The order was sound, but from my point of view, I did not think he was considering the big picture when he issued it."

"So you disobeyed his order because you disagreed with it? You, a recent Citadel graduate on your first combat mission, thought you knew better than a veteran gunnery sergeant with more than two decades of experience? You didn't think you'd come to regret that?"

"Oh, I was certain I'd regret it," I admitted to Colonel Palkrait. "I also knew that I could save hundreds of Marines and that I'd regret letting them all drown even more."

The look on Colonel Palkrait's face suggested he did not really know how to respond to that. The fact that he decided to go on to another topic all but confirmed it. "Let's move on to the matter of Vernor Blyte. Why did you think it necessary to execute a man being medically evacuated from a wrecked dropship?"

"Again," I told the colonel. "It came down to priorities. Chief Warrant Officer Je'Sikka Albarn was an incredible pilot who saved not only our lives, but our mission. Her spine was broken and we needed a self-propelled stretcher to get her to safety. The only stretcher I had access to was one occupied by a convict laborer. I did not know Vernor Blyte. All I was aware of at the time was that he was a Class Zero convict, a true irredeemable, who'd been crippled by the eels in the seawater that was flooding our dropship's wreckage. The Corps does not typically fix Zeros who've had the flesh gnawed off their legs from their ankles to their knees, so I figured they'd just euthanize him anyway. Having him on that stretcher was a wasted resource. I put him out of his misery so his SPS could be used to evacuate Albarn."

Palkrait seemed to agree with my point of view. "Okay. I see. Well...."

"Sir," I said, unwisely interrupting a senior officer. "If I may, I would like to add that I do truly regret taking Blyte's life. Everything I heard about him since his death suggests that he probably did not deserve to be a Class Zero in the first place, and even if he had, he'd made amends and turned himself around. He became a skilled medic and had a reputation for risking his life to save others. In fact, doing that was exactly what landed him on that stretcher. If there's one thing I could take back about that day, Colonel, it's that."

Our brigade commander stared at me for several moments, taking in what I had said. He then cleared his throat. "Do you have anything else you would like to say about the accusations levied against you?"

Shaking my head, I said, "No, sir."

"Okay then. I've reviewed the charges and the DRB's recommendations. I've listened to your explanation of events and found nothing in your statements that would justify the mitigation of your sentence. You do not appear to be appealing for leniency, nor am I inclined to give it. Are you prepared to receive your punishment?"

I stiffened as close to the position of attention as my shackles would allow. "Yes, sir."

"For the charge of disobeying a direct order, I sentence you to ten lashes. For blatant insubordination, I sentence you to another ten. For willful dereliction of duty, ten more. Fifteen for abandoning your post."

I swallowed hard. I knew I had a flogging coming to me, but being whipped forty-five times could prove crippling. It could even be deadly.

The colonel seemed to savor the look of terror on my face. He let me stew for a couple of moments, then said, "For risking your own life and safety to protect your fellow Marines, however, I remove fifteen lashes off your sentence. I also understand that you performed admirably during the mutiny that occurred behind these walls and that you played a major role in keeping your commander from being killed by insurgents. Considering how unworthy that man was of your efforts...."

Palkrait himself had sentenced Captain Briggund to death and had him hung like a common criminal not far from where I was standing. Despite what was in store for me, I smiled thinking about that.

"...and how hard you must have struggled to not just let the rebels have their way with that son-of-a-bitch, I reduce your sentence by another fifteen lashes. Gunny Malcolm!"

"Yes, SIR!" called my former platoon sergeant, marching three steps toward center stage with a bullwhip in hand.

"Fifteen lashes, this prisoner has earned!" the colonel proclaimed.

"Then fifteen lashes that prisoner will receive!" Malcolm called back.

As Gunny marched my way, one of the MPs tied a line to the chain that tethered my wrists together. The other pulled a dagger from his belt, then cut my tunic and striped undershirt off, exposing my bare back. The two of them then led me to the whipping post, a large, heavy horizontal log lifted off the ground high enough to reach the chest of an average Marine. My feet were tied to a pair of rings sticking out of the deck while my arms were pulled over the trunk, stretching me tightly against it.

When he was satisfied I was entirely immobilized, Gunny Malcolm stepped beside me. Pulling a piece of thick leather from a pocket on his tunic, he said, "Open your mouth and bite down on this."

I shook my head and looked at him as defiantly as I could. "I don't need that."

"As a man who's been in your position several times myself," Malcolm growled, "I'm telling you to put that thing between your fuckin' teeth. This's going to hurt worse than anything you've ever experienced before. That strap will keep you from shattering your pearly whites or biting your tongue off when you clench your jaw."

Not willing to question Gunny Malcolm's experience, I gave him a nod and opened my mouth. As the one-eyed Marine shoved the leather between my teeth, he said, "Try not to scream until the third or fourth lash. By then, your body will have come to terms with what's happening, and you won't have to bite down so much. Fifteen lashes mean about ninety seconds of agony. It'll be the longest ninety seconds of your life, but it's still only a minute and a half. There's no shame in anything you do up here to get through it. Besides, you're a blooded academy Marine," Malcolm reminded me as he turned his chin toward my audience. "You think any of those candy asses out there have the balls to call you out for whatever you do up here?"

Even though I was drenched by the rain, Malcolm could see how much I was sweating. "You're going to be all right, son," he reassured me. "See you on the other side of this shit."

CRACK!

I was expecting pain, but *nothing* like that. The whip cut me from the top of my right shoulder, diagonally across my spine, to a spot just above my left hip bone. The sensation was electric, and every muscle of my body tensed up rock hard. It took my breath away.

CRACK!

Just as Gunny said it would, the second lash forced my jaw to clench shut so hard that it popped. I tried to whimper, but there was not enough wind inside of me to get it out. Even though I knew it was futile, I started fighting to get out of my restraints.

CRACK!

My eyes instantly welled up the third time I was struck. I fought against my shackles even harder.

CRACK!

I screamed, spitting out the leather bite guard. Then I got sick.

CRACK!

I tried to shriek once more and pleaded for someone to help me, but I inhaled some of my vomit and began coughing as I wailed. I could feel the warmth of the blood pouring out of the wounds Gunny was slicing into my hide.

CRACK!

Snot blew violently out of my nose while thick red saliva oozed out from over my lips. My body went limp. I noticed my wrists were bleeding from trying to rip my hands from their cuffs.

CRACK!

I wet myself.

CRACK! CRACK! CRACK! CRACK! CRACK! CRACK! CRACK! CRACK!

The pain became so intense that I almost grew numb to it. My mind drifted off into some ether realm where it felt like Malcolm was whipping someone else. Then it stopped, and I did not even realize it.

Before I knew it, Gunny was whispering in my ear. "Can you stand?"

"I don't know," I sobbed.

Gunny ordered the MPs to remove the shackles from my feet. After he thought I could support my own weight, he had them release my handcuffs. I immediately fell backward into Malcolm's arms, bleeding profusely all over his uniform.

"Bring him here," ordered Colonel Palkrait.

Malcolm dragged me back toward the center of the stage. When we stopped, each MP grabbed one of my arms and propped me up in front of our brigade commander.

"Cadet Tauk," Palkrait told me. "It doesn't matter what your intentions were; good order and discipline demand that no act of insubordination goes unpunished. Letting you get away with what you did would send a very bad message to the rank and file. Orders are not suggestions, Marine. You knew what the consequences of your actions would be, yet you did them anyway. In the process, you likely saved hundreds of Marine lives, not to mention that of a heroic young pilot. You've paid for your transgressions; now it's time to be recognized for your selfless dedication to duty. For risking your life crossing the Buvalla mud flats, an action leading to the safe evacuation of a downed landing craft, your command has seen fit to award you the Nova Cross, Second Degree."

The audience broke into a round of polite applause as the colonel approached to hand me a box containing the prestigious medal. I was too weak to accept it and was not wearing a tunic to pin it on, so Gunny took it for me, slipping it into his pocket.

Taking my chin in his hand, Palkrait lifted my head to look into my eyes. "I'd also like to let you know that General Duuq has approved your graduation from cadet status. Once you've recovered enough to return to service, you'll be coming back as a second lieutenant. Congratulations, son. On a personal level, I'm happy to see that you survived everything that went down on Toranad...."

Colonel Palkrait was with me when I got shot.

"...and I'd like to express my condolences for what happened to Dr. Duverii. I understand that the two of you were, uh, close."

I tried to thank the colonel for his sympathetic words but was afraid I would not be able to speak without losing my composure. It might have been six months since Jella died, but the old wounds reopened by my memory of her hurt worse than the fresh ones scourged upon my back. It took everything I had just to nod my gratitude.

Palkrait understood, quickly dismissing the formation so the medics could get to work on me. As we waited for the corpsmen to arrive with a stretcher, my voice returned just enough to weakly ask Malcolm, "Did I just get flogged, awarded, and promoted for the exact same behavior?"

"It appears that you did, sir," Malcolm said. I was honored that he was the first Marine ever to address me as a commissioned officer.

"What kind of twisted outfit would do something that stupid?"

The gunnery sergeant grinned. "Who else but the goddamned Marine Corps, sir?"

Chapter 2

SPIRITS

When I opened my eyes in the infirmary, Gunny Malcolm was sitting bedside, dressed in a brand new uniform and sucking Sukka Brandy out of a pocket flask. "Don't you have Marines to attend to?" I weakly asked.

Malcolm scoffed. "I'm between platoons at the moment."

"Still?" I asked in disbelief. "It's been six months since we liberated Narman's Pyke. They haven't given you a new platoon yet?"

After taking a quick sip from his flask, Gunny used his sleeve to wipe his lips off. "I'm not 'still' between platoons, sir. I'm between platoons 'again.' While you've been back on the mothership getting manicures and sponge baths, I've been down here killing shit." Malcolm paused to take another drink. "More like getting killed by shit, actually."

I shifted my weight to make myself comfortable, only to have the wounds on my back remind me of why I was under medical care. "Holy shit! That frickin' hurts! How do I get some pain meds around here?"

Gunny laughed. "They ain't going to give you anything for your discomfort, sir. That would defeat the whole purpose of flogging your ass." The gunnery sergeant held his flask out toward me. "You want a drink?"

Academy Marines were not supposed to consume alcohol. But then again, we were not supposed to get flogged, either. I took Gunny Malcolm's flask and downed half of it in one pull. "What are you doing here?" I asked as I handed Gunny back his booze.

"I'm here to celebrate, sir. To congratulate you on being awarded your commission. Despite all the skin I ripped off your hide, I like you, Tauk. I think you're going to be a good officer. I haven't had to work with many Academy Marines, but the few I've been around have all been fanatics. They've been tough, smart, and resourceful, but way too zealous for my liking. They tend to burn through Marines like there's no tomorrow. Our grunts should get hazard pay just for serving under you Citadel pukes."

I nodded, wincing as I tried to roll from my stomach to my side. "Yeah, well, the academy spent a lot of effort trying to hammer the concept of integrity into our heads. 'A Marine officer is honest above all,' they liked to tell us. Dishonesty was a cardinal sin. Ever since I've left the Citadel, all I've seen the bastards do is lie. That kind of dulls the edge off the company line I'm supposed to toe."

Malcolm grinned. "A bit disillusioned, are you?"

"Aren't you after that shit show we lived through hiking up here? Six thousand of us left the mothership. How many of us survived to be rescued? A hundred if we include our wounded?"

Gunny shook his head. "Closer to eighty."

"I had eighteen people under me. When it was all over, there were only four left. Two of them were convicts. The worst part is that most of those Marines were killed because of Samaari incompetence, not the enemy."

"I can't argue with you there," Gunny told me. "But Palkrait did hold Briggund responsible for what he did to us. The colonel hung his sorry ass in the courtyard. You saw that. The system worked."

"If the system worked," I countered. "That prick never would've been in charge of us to begin with."

Malcolm chuckled. "Ah, the idealism of youth! Is that why you came back to Kanaris, sir? To singlehandedly transform the Space Corps?"

Shaking my head, I told Gunny, "I'd have to be elected Chief Minister to transform the League first. Because of them, the Corps's gone so rotten I wouldn't even know where to begin. I didn't come back here for any of that. I came for Deena Vulk."

"Who the hell's that?" Malcolm asked as he raised his flask to his lips once more.

"The bitch that killed Jella Duverii."

Gunny lowered his drink and hardened his expression. "You came back for vengeance?"

I nodded.

Malcolm's face twisted as if he were readying to smack me like he used to. Now that I was being commissioned, however, that would've resulted in his arrest. "Do you not remember that conversation we had after the mutiny, sir? Huh? Revenge is like the hydra from the ancient earthly myths. If you slice off one head, it'll only be replaced by two more. Mark my words, sir, when you're at war, you will *never* run out of people you want to hurt. Unless you want to end up as the next Butcher of Deraghun, you take that rage and anger you got inside and focus it on the enemy standing between you and your objective. Don't waste it on personal scores. That's a great way to lose the hearts and minds of the Marines you lead, not to mention their lives."

"You saying our Marines don't want blood?"

Gunny turned red. "Of course, they want blood! Now that we've had our asses handed to us a few times, they want it more than ever! You've got to understand your Marines, though, Tauk! Less than thirty percent of our ranks are CITRECs, white-striped true believers in The Cause! The rest are either conscripts or prisoners, people who've had the League come into their homes and force them into the military at gunpoint. Many have been on the receiving end of the weapons we wield. You go in there and start putting civilians to the sword looking for this woman, and they'll begin relating more to the enemy than to those of us issuing them their orders. Sir, we've already got people defecting to the Narmans here on Kanaris. In one case, enough of them switched sides to turn a Corps victory into a devastating defeat. I barely escaped that one. One of your people, Mazada Duum, didn't."

"Duum's KIA?"

The gunnery sergeant shrugged. "Yeah, he's gone. Damned shame, too. He was turning out to be a bona fide killer."

I could believe that. Duum was an insufferable prick with the biggest chip on his shoulder I had ever seen, but he was dependable in a fight. The Corps would feel his loss. "You have any idea where the rest of my people are?"

Malcolm gave me a nod. "I got Akkam Lumuk a billet providing security to the medics. He's worthless in combat, but he's got some solid protective instincts. That man's incapable of harming another human being, but he'll run through the gates of Hell to rescue one. I figured he'd do better there."

Nodding in agreement, I said, "So do I."

"Barone Parsons, one of your convicts, fought well against the Quarakai. I also found out he was once a Marine corporal. I sent him down to the motor pool. I figured he'd earned himself a safe and cushy assignment to ride out the rest of his sentence in."

"I'm sure he appreciated that. I worked out some stuff for him, too. While I was convalescing in orbit. What about Ritza Xi?"

Malcolm let out a long sigh and lowered his head. "She was a little trickier. Xi's a Class Zero, sir. She's convicted of killing children...."

"We both know she didn't do that, Gunny."

"It doesn't matter what we know, sir," Malcolm snapped at me. "It only matters what's in her record."

I let out a long sigh. Zeros had no rights. They were slaves in all but name and could be used in any way that a Marine saw fit. I knew where most female Zeros ended up, and my stomach turned thinking of where Ritza Xi probably was. "Where is she, Gunny?"

"You already know," Malcolm answered, unable to bring himself to say it out loud.

"As an Academy Marine, I get to hand-pick my first platoon, right?"

Gunny nodded. "Right."

"Do you think I can pick her as one of my Zeros?"

Malcolm thought about that for a moment, then shrugged. "I've never heard of an officer requesting a specific Zero before, but I don't see why you couldn't."

"Then I'm getting her out of there."

Gunny smirked. "What're you going to do with her?"

"Make her one of my praetorians."

Malcolm laughed at my suggestion to turn her into a bodyguard, but I was not joking. I did not think Ritza Xi murdered her children, but that did not mean she lacked a killer's instincts. Quite the contrary, actually. Not only did the League railroad her for a crime she did not commit, but they also sterilized her, abused her, and did everything they could to work her to death. And now, the Corps had turned her into a comfort woman. The Marines had taken a housewife and, after years of maltreatment, transformed her into a monster.

Xi was full of unbridled rage, a fury that allowed her to slaughter four combat veterans that tried to rape her during the mutiny against Captain Briggund. I was forbidden to slip so much as a butter knife into a Zero's palm, but I could train her so that anything else she got her hands on could prove just as lethal.

13

"Maybe you should make her your platoon sergeant," Gunny joked.

"Actually," I told Malcolm. "That was a job I was planning on offering to you."

"Not a fucking chance," Gunny said before raising his flask to his lips once more. He took a drink and passed it to me again. "You can go ahead and finish it off. Look, sir, I submitted that report chit on you the minute you made clear to me that you were willfully disobeying my orders and returning to *Wasp-Three*. If I could've rescinded it, I would have. Since I was going to rip your hide, I tried to make it up to you by taking care of your people. I did what I could for them. We're even.

"Now, I'm flattered you want me as your number two, but it'd be a disservice to both of us if I accepted the offer. A word of advice to you: don't ever let yourself serve under someone you've once commanded. It's too hard to suppress the former dynamic. No matter how much you may trust in their abilities, you'll always see them as some green new guy who needs to have their mistakes corrected."

"That's exactly why I want you at my side, Gunny. I want you to correct my mistakes."

"No," Malcolm insisted. "You won't. Not when it counts."

"I could order you to."

Gunny shook his head. "No, sir, you couldn't. The command, your superiors, will back me up on this. Even if I wanted to, and I don't, Colonel Palkrait would never allow it."

"So, you're going to leave me high and dry?"

"No, I'm not," Malcolm assured me. "My last gift to you in honor of your commissioning is my recommendation for your choice of platoon sergeant. I know a gal who's also between platoons at the moment. Gunnery Sergeant Shai Brumit. We served together on Portuna."

"With Gori Dravidas?"

Malcolm nodded. "Yep. He was there, too."

"Does she know I killed that guy?"

"She does."

"I take it she wasn't a fan of the man, then?"

"Gunny Brumit was far closer to Dravidas than I was. They were friends."

I finished Malcolm's liquor and passed his flask back to him. "You giving her a chance to avenge her buddy?"

Gunny shook his head. "Like I told you before, things were nasty on Portuna. All sides of that conflict treated each other with a level of barbarism that defies comprehension.

Gori and I gave in to it. We did things we thought ourselves incapable of. Shai didn't. She resisted us every time we gave in to our darker natures. When we left Portuna, it's safe to say both me and Gori hated that bitch's guts. We refused to deal with her for years. We weren't alone, either. The woman was something of a pariah. She still is, kind of."

Out of habit, Malcolm paused to take another drink before realizing his flask was empty. "It took me years to realize the woman was right, sir. I was too ashamed of what I'd done to tell her that, though. What happened on Portuna tortured Dravidas so badly that he sought Brumit out to confide in her, to let someone know he was sorry for what he'd done. Of course, she can never admit it, but I suspect Brumit might have been the one who persuaded Gori to atone for the atrocities he'd committed by bringing them to light and letting the public know what happens when they send people out to kill on their behalf."

I was getting the impression that Gunny Brumit might have been a bit conservative for me. "I want a hard charger as my number two, Gunny. I'm not looking to go out there and commit war crimes, but I don't want someone who'll run to the chain of command if something goes awry, either."

"Brumit's no snitch," Malcolm assured me. "She never told a soul what went down on Portuna. I just suspect she convinced Dravidas to spill the beans. Of course, when all that nastiness came to light, they took the only Marine to express regret about what he'd done and publicized his crimes so they could discredit him and lead the man to slaughter. Look, sir, make no mistake about it. Brumit's a killer. She's a solid tactician, knows how to keep Marines disciplined and motivated, and you'll be hard-pressed to find a more experienced combat veteran in the entire Expeditionary Force."

"I could say that about almost every gunny sergeant in Narman's Pyke. What would Brumit bring to the table that you can't?"

"Restraint," Gunny answered. "Unlike back when we were on Portuna, the League's under a lot of tension these days. The Samaaris have us so divided that half our Marines feel more animosity toward their own leadership than they do for the enemy."

Malcolm pointed out the window of my hospital room, toward the jungle. "When people have good reasons to see their own government as the source of their suffering, they're much more receptive to believing the forces we fight just might be the better cause. We also have to reckon with the fact that the Narmans and their alien allies are not the pushovers we thought they were. Back home, folks have been told that we're up against a technologically superior species with the potential to wipe humanity right out of the galaxy. That's eased some of our fissures and pulled us closer together for the moment. Corps recruitment is up back home. That's a good indicator we're uniting against a common foe."

Gunny dropped his arm and directed his finger to the deck. "Here on Kanaris, though? Where our Marines have heard what went down and know what we're up against? Well, many of our troops've been thinking, 'If you can't beat 'em, join 'em.' They're mutinying. Surrendering. Defecting. If you're going to be successful out there, Tauk, you need to drill into the minds of your Marines that *we* are the good guys. Your best shot of doing that is to give up this vendetta bullshit and have someone like Gunny Brumit acting as a check valve against your baser instincts. Understand?"

I nodded as Gunny stood up to take his leave. Receptive to heeding at least half of his advice, I said, "I'll take Brumit if she's willing."

"She's willing. I've already spoken to her." Holding out his hand, Malcolm then said, "It's been an honor, sir. You did well out there, hiking up here to Narman's Pyke. I wish you the best."

Despite the pain it caused me, I reached out and shook his hand. "Thank you, Gunny. For everything. What're you going to do now?"

Malcolm sighed. "If history is any judge? Probably all the shit I just told you not to."

I laughed a little, which hurt, too. "Have you seen them, Gunny?"

Malcolm paused. "Who?"

"The aliens."

"The Morghul?" Malcolm shook his head. "No. Not personally. I've been on the wrong end of their weaponry, but no, I've never actually laid eyes on them. That's a good thing, though."

"How?" I asked.

"Well, the way I understand it, sir, is that if you're close enough to see them, they're close enough to see you. And once they see you, you're dead."

Chapter 3

PUSTOV

Captain Feliks Pustov did not look like a Marine Recon officer. He had the pale complexion of a man who was not overly fond of the outdoors and the build of someone with a debilitating eating disorder. I heard talk that he had picked up a parasite in the swamps of Terris Mor that had wreaked havoc upon his digestive tract, preventing him from putting on weight.

Pustov also lacked the bravado typical among infantry officers and carried himself with an aura of humility that many mistook as being submissive. His demeanor begged people to underestimate him, and legend had it that those who took the bait quickly regretted it. A master martial artist, the captain's hands were as quick as his wit, and he was eager to rise to any challenge to his authority, be it by brains or by brawn. Though he could keep pace with the toughest Marines, it was his mind that the Corps valued most and the reason he was chosen to rebuild the Recon Battalion after the disastrous trek to Narman's Pyke seven months prior. I was glad to have drawn him as my new company commander.

After Pustov's orderly let me into his office, I marched to the captain's desk, put myself at attention, and rendered him a crisp salute. "Second Lieutenant Eamon Tauk reporting for duty, sir!"

My new commander seemed bemused by my theatrics. He smiled at me, returned my salute, then casually waved his hand at the chair in front of his desk. "Lieutenant, I know the academy takes great pride in pomp and formalities, so I hope you're not offended by my somewhat lackadaisical approach to it. My experience is that excesses in formality often impede the free flow of ideas and information. In front of our Marines, I do expect strict adherence to all military protocols. When it's just us officers and senior NCOs, though, I prefer to focus our energy on problem-solving instead of military ceremonies. Is that okay with you?"

"It's perfect, sir," I told the captain as I took my seat.

"How's your back?"

It had been three weeks since my flogging. "It's still a little tender, but it's healing fast. I'm anxious to get back to work, sir."

"I bet you are," Pustov mused. "You've been out of action for quite some time."

I nodded. "Seven months, sir."

My captain shook his head. "That's unfortunate. I heard about what you had to endure to get to Narman's Pyke. It was disgraceful, to say the least. Six thousand Marines left the mothership, and when it was all said and done, there were but thirty of you left standing. What was there, about eighty survivors here in the Pyke altogether?"

"Yes, sir," I answered. "Plus a couple hundred Marines that never left the beach."

"That's right. I understand you had a hand in their survival as well."

"My contribution was accidental at best. Dmitri Naktada deserves all the credit for that."

"Dmitri deserves most of it, yes. Not all, though. Had you not directed him to recover that cockpit video, he'd probably be among the Marines rotting in the Kanarisian Hot Zone right now. If the Corps knew the entire truth about how he ended up staying behind with the wreckage of *Wasp-Three*, he'd probably have been court-martialed for desertion and flogged right beside you."

"What do you think happened out there, sir?" I asked suspiciously.

Pustov laughed. "Relax, Tauk. Dmitri told me everything. He and I are from the same settlement back on Klepsis-4. My best friend back home is one of his cousins. Shai Brumit, the woman filling your platoon sergeant slot, is also a Klepto. She's from an agricultural settlement not far from mine. Her mother was a Marine. She used to run our Space Explorer guild."

"You make it sound like everyone on Klepsis knows each other."

Pustov nodded. "Well, it's a dead planet. It's too distant from its star to be terraformed into any sort of Replicant Earth Environment, so there's only a few bio-dome settlements on it. Considering how few of us Kleptos go into the military, yeah, it does seem like we've all at least heard of each other. We're known for our scientific accomplishments, not military glory. In fact, back home, the Space Corps is regarded as a refuge for Klepsis's intellectual underachievers."

As Pustov talked, he pulled two mugs from a drawer in his desk and filled them with coffee from a pot behind him. Passing one of the cups my way, the captain asked, "So, what brings you back to Recon, Tauk? Didn't you get enough punishment the last time you were down here?"

After taking a sip of java, I answered, "I like the autonomy, sir. I get a charge going out into the unknown, being the tip of the spear, as they say."

The captain understood what I was saying. "I agree. It's going to be a while before we get back to that, though. I've been tasked with rebuilding the Expeditionary Force's Recon capabilities, but right now, it's all hands on deck trying to break the Narmans."

To relieve some of his nervous energy, the captain stood to pace behind his desk. "You know, I was told that the reasoning behind having academy cadets serve as enlisted at the start of their careers was not just to familiarize themselves with various Marine roles at the platoon level. It was also supposed to allow them to network, to get a feel for the warriors they wanted to serve in their first platoon. When I heard I was getting an academy lieutenant, I assumed you'd be arriving with a cadre of proven veterans at your side."

Shaking my head, I told the captain, "Most of the Marines I would've wanted never made it to the planet's surface, sir."

"How many have you got?"

"Right now, I've only got Gunny Brumit. I haven't yet asked anyone on my list, sir."

Pustov took a sip from his mug. "And how many people have you got on that list?"

"Four." My face turned a little red. I was embarrassed by the answer.

"I take it these are crack troops?"

I thought of Akkam Lumuk, who was probably the biggest coward of the entire expeditionary force. "They all survived the march to Narman's Pyke. I wouldn't consider them elite in the traditional sense, but I have a role for each of them."

Pustov gave me a sympathetic nod. "Assuming all four agree to join you, how are you going to fill the other eighty-one open billets you have in your platoon?"

I shrugged. "I don't really have much of a choice other than relying on Gunny Brumit to put people in my open slots."

The captain nodded. "That's probably best. The two of you need to speed that process up. At most, you've got three months to get yourself staffed and your troops trained to an acceptable level before we see combat. It could be much shorter if the enemy goes on the offensive."

"Offensive?" I asked, surprised to hear the captain use such a word when discussing insurgents. "Have the Narmans got the resources to attack us now that we're on the ground in force?"

"I have no idea," Pustov confessed. "We don't know a whole lot about them, except that they're full of surprises."

The captain walked over to the screen that took up an entire wall of his office and pulled up a map of the vicinity of Narman's Pyke. He pointed to a mountain range at the edge of the display, several hundred kilometers to the west.

"We know there's a lot of Narmans guarding the base of the Satapadaya Ranges," Pustov told me. "And by 'Narmans,' I mean former Marines. Apparently, once you switch sides, the enemy demands proof of your allegiance by sending you to the front to fight your former comrades. Of these troops, of course, we know quite a lot. They're trained and equipped just like us. Militarily speaking, we're on equal footing."

The captain tapped his finger on the map. "But they have some things we don't. For instance, they have Narman guides, who know the terrain and fauna better than we do. You ever hear of a 'naypeto?'"

I shook my head.

Pustov asked the computer to show a picture of one, "It's a creature that stands about two and a half meters high. It has long hair covering its body except for its head, hands, and feet. A type of green mold grows on its fur, which helps keep it camouflaged in the forest. It runs around on two legs, leaving its arms free to fight. Each hand has three fingers and a thumb, while a set of razor-sharp, retractable claws can be deployed from just behind its knuckles. Two long tusks grow upward out of its lower jaw."

Walking back toward his desk, the captain said, "These things are pretty goddamned scary on their own, yet the Narmans domesticated them. They ride them around the forest. Unfortunately, since our sensor array is designed to pick up vehicles, not animals, we can't detect them. They can detect us, though. Those friggin' things can smell us from twenty kilometers away and sneak right up our asses. We can't get within a kilometer of them unless they want us to, however."

Pustov laughed without humor. "We got all this weaponry, all this technology, and we can't seem to contend with an animal equipped with a brain smaller than my nutsack. What about an 'ubati?' You know what that is?"

I had to shake my head again.

"It's a four-legged creature, but instead of fur, they're covered in layers of bony scales. They have long snouts with two massive canines that come out of the upper jaw and two longer tusks that protrude from the lower. They stand about waist high and live in packs of up to a hundred animals. We've learned that the ubati are the most feared creature in the Kanarisian forest. And my god, do they stink! These things spray a type of oily musk so noxious that it'll make it almost impossible to breathe without your helmet filter working on overdrive. Once that smell is in the air, you don't have to worry about anything dangerous coming anywhere near you. Well, the Narmans domesticated those, too. It's why they can live out in the bush without worrying about any other predators bothering them."

"Are they still using quarakai?" I asked.

Pustov pursed his lips. "Yeah, they are, but we don't really consider them animals anymore. We now call them 'the' Quarakai. They're not quite as smart as we are, but they're not that far off. They're bright enough to be regarded as an intelligent life form, albeit a primitive one. They don't seem to have the finger dexterity or fine motor skills to wield firearms, but it appears the Morghul are trying to develop armor and weaponry for them. Fortunately, the Quarakai are not very comfortable with their equipment. It restricts their movement and severely limits their agility. Hell, I've seen the poor bastards fall right out of the trees while trying to sneak up on us in their new gear."

I sighed. "I fought Quarakai that had no equipment. They're too fast to outrun, it takes about thirty rounds to put one down, and they're strong enough that if they get their hands on you, they'll rip you in half. I can't imagine what they'd be like armed."

"They're clumsy," Pustov told me. "So far, anyway."

The captain walked over to a table and picked up a cylinder that was more than sixty centimeters long and large enough in diameter that my commander had to hold it in both hands. "We got a couple of these from some of the Quarks that practically fell on top of us."

Pustov swung the device, which extended a telescopic rod nearly two meters long. "We took the power source out of this one, but when it's energized, the element is charged with a plasma field that'll cut through our armor like a hot knife through butter. The thing works like a fencing foil. I can't tell you how happy I am that those bruins haven't perfected the art of using them yet."

Looking at the device in Pustov's hands, I said, "You know, they tried to drown us by building a dam, letting it fill with rain runoff, then blowing it when we got close. The trees they used looked like they were cut down with laser beams. I bet they used one of those things."

My captain looked at the weapon and nodded his head. "I bet they did. The Narmans call these 'seibaras.' Your man Naktada has reverse-engineered one and is putting the finishing touches on a human-sized version. There are undoubtedly useful applications for these things in close-quarters combat."

Throwing the seibara back on the table, Pustov told me, "That's the kind of stuff we need to be doing out in the field. Collecting Morghul technology. Capturing aliens. Figuring out where all the Narman settlements are."

"And we're not going to be doing that?"

"Not for a while." Pustov pulled the map back up on the wall monitor. Pointing at the mountains to the west, he said, "We chased the Narmans out of the Pyke. They retreated a couple of hundred kilometers west, luring us into the Nimnaya Valley where they were already dug into the high ground. They waited for an entire brigade to enter the kill zone, then hit us with everything they had."

My captain shook his head. "The commander of that brigade was Colonel Muusta, another Samaari who rose through the ranks on the coattails of his family's connections. A competent colonel would have never led those Marines into that situation in the first place, but once they were there, Muusta only made things worse. Knowing he was going to get them all killed, the conscripts switched sides, fragged their officers, and killed most of the senior NCOs. The Narmans faced the League head-on in the Nimnaya Valley, and when the fighting was over, the rebels left the battlefield with three times as many fighters as they started with."

Pustov sighed. "It cost us an entire division, more than 21,000 Marines, to take the valley back. After we accomplished that objective, we chased the bastards west, over the Kula River and along the north bank of the Yuddaya, all the way to the Satapadaya Ranges. They stopped us there, and we haven't been able to advance since. We think that's where the bulk of the Narmans live. We believe the Morghul are somewhere in there also."

"There were ten thousand people at Narman's Pyke. You saying we can't find any trace of them?" I asked.

"Yes, I am," Pustov said. "The canopy's too thick to spot them from above. Because of the Harnillium interference, our recon drones only have a four-kilometer range. Not that they even get that far before the Narmans destroy them."

"And we can't get a Long Range Recon Patrol in there to see what's going on?"

"Oh, we can get LRRPs into the Satapadaya. They just never come out again. That's Morghul country. Our aircraft can't get within a hundred clicks of it without getting destroyed by an alien plasma blast. Since we can't communicate directly with the mothership because of the Harnillium interference, we can't even nuke them from space. Whenever our comm rockets go up, the Narmans go underground. They know our limitations and play them perfectly."

"We can't hit them with artillery?" I asked.

"We probably could if we knew what to aim at," Pustov replied. "The problem is we never see the sons-of-bitches. We got numbers, but they got everything else."

I sighed. "It sounds like what they have the most of is intel. They know where we are; we have no idea where they are. We can't figure out how to leverage the local life forms against them like they can against us. They know all about our weapons and capabilities; we know next to nothing about theirs. You said before that you're rebuilding our recon capabilities, but you made it sound like we wouldn't be doing any recon stuff. Did I understand that correctly?"

"You did. The command thinks that if they had a battalion of special forces storm the front line, they'd break the impasse."

I could not believe Pustov said that with a straight face. "Don't tell me. That's the Battalion Commander's line of thinking, isn't it?"

Pustov grinned and shook his head. "Lieutenant Colonel Baakarad may be Samaari, but she defies convention. She's actually a brilliant officer who's quite good at her job. She knows better."

"This certainly can't be Palkrait's idea."

My captain grinned. "No, this goes way up the chain. It's General Kuolaada's concept."

Of course. He's Samaari, too, I thought to myself. "So, my job's going to be forming a Recon platoon, training it to Recon standards, then using it as cannon fodder?"

Pustov grinned. "Officially, it would appear so."

I squinted at the captain. "Unofficially?"

"I'm relying upon your Citadel training to figure us a way out of it. Tauk, I read your file. You have a reputation for thinking independently. They said you were good at coming up with unconventional solutions to seemingly insurmountable problems. One of your instructors noted that though he considered you one of the toughest cadets he'd ever trained, your mind was your most lethal attribute."

"I wish I agreed with that," I told Pustov. "If I was so brilliant, I wouldn't have gotten myself flogged."

"I was at your hearing, Tauk," Pustov told me. "And I spoke with Gunny Malcolm. What you did to get yourself whipped was no lapse in judgment. It was a deliberate act. You knew what the consequences would be, yet you decided to sacrifice the skin off your back to save Marines."

Pustov returned to his desk, taking his seat directly across from me. "We're going to the front, Tauk. There's nothing I can do about it. I have no idea how long we'll be there before they order us to attack, but before they do that, I need you to figure out how to get us some intel so that when we cross no man's land, we're not dying for nothing."

The captain took another sip of coffee. "Gunny Brumit's an infantry gal. There's no one I can think of who's better equipped to train Marines to attack enemy lines...."

"Any idiot can storm a position," I said, interrupting my company commander. "I need my troops trained for stealth, not suicide missions."

"Brumit can do both," Pustov assured me. "Let her train your Marines. You figure out how to get me the intel I need to break that line."

"What kind of resources can I expect?" I asked.

"Whatever you need." The captain answered.

I smiled. "Good. In that case, can you tell me where I can find your boy Naktada? I need someone out there who's smarter than me."

Chapter 4

Remnants

"How did it go?" Gunny Brumit asked. She had been waiting outside the Battalion HQ and pounced as I left my meeting with our company commander. "Did you get Naktada?"

I nodded. "As long as he's willing to join us."

Brumit looked surprised. "Pustov gave him up that easily?"

Shaking my head, I said, "Trust me, it wasn't easy. Neither Pustov nor Lieutenant Colonel Baakarad were willing to give him up. I had to appeal to Palkrait himself."

Brumit did not seem surprised. "I knew they'd resist. Naktada's working wonders reverse engineering the gear they've turned over to him. He just made a human-sized version of a weapon the Quarakai were trying to use against us."

"The seibara. Pustov told me about that. You think it'll be of any use to us? It's basically a fancy sword."

Brumit nodded. "Aye, but a sword that can easily slice a Quarakai in half. Look, when you've got those damned things charging at you across an open field, you can make pretty short work of them with machine guns and explosives. The problem is that they never charge across an open field. They drop out of the trees. Before you even know they're in the area, they're in your trenches. We can't use our M2117s or grenades in that close of quarters. We'd kill more of our own than of our adversaries. The seibaras would be a perfect alternative in that sort of situation. It's much quicker to take out a Quark with a single swing of a seibara than to shoot one thirty times with an M72 battle rifle."

Having fought the Quarakai before, I agreed with Brumit. "Well, we got Naktada until someone comes up with an alien plasma blaster. If that happens, he'll be returned to the Weapons Development Section."

Brumit scoffed. "We'll only have to return him if we can actually get him out of there to begin with."

"You don't think he'd jump at the chance to risk his life with us?" I joked.

My platoon sergeant grinned. "You know, growing up in a biosphere made me claustrophobic. I got sick of the sterile, manufactured air, the bland food, and the lack of natural sunlight. I couldn't wait to escape that place and breathe free, like humans were supposed to. Dimi, on the other hand, was used to it. He doesn't do well outdoors. I'm not calling the man a coward by any means. It's just that, for him, having his senses so hyper-aware at all times is exhausting. It wears him down. He's just more comfortable inside."

"I could see that," I told Brumit. "Who do you think would have better luck convincing him to join us? Me or you?"

Brumit sighed. "Probably me. I've known him longer. You got anything to sweeten the pot with?"

I nodded. "He's not going to be repairing our exo-systems attached to a squad. I want to make him the Tech Warfare Specialist attached to platoon staff. He'll be promoted to E-6 as well."

"That should help considerably."

"Good," I said, slapping Gunny on the shoulder. "Go dangle that bait in front of him and see if he bites."

"Aye aye, sir," Brumit said as I turned to walk in the other direction. "Where are you going?"

"To see if I can sucker a couple of other people I know into joining my platoon."

Before he was a convict, Barone Parsons had been a Marine. He instinctively saluted once he saw the butter bars on my epaulets. "I'm glad to see you made it, sir. The last I heard, you weren't doing so well."

"From what I understand, it was touch and go for a little while. I'm back at a hundred percent now, though."

"The wonders of modern medicine, eh?" Parsons said.

"Indeed."

As the two of us spoke, a massive Combat Crawler lumbered into the motor pool. Standing ten meters tall and seven wide, the CC-54 got around on several sets of tracked wheels. As far as transportation went, the Crawler was slow and cumbersome, but virtually impregnable. It was designed to carry heavy cargo, but the command used them to transport goods through the Nimnaya Valley, where they hoped Narman bandits would fire upon the vehicles and betray their positions.

Lifting his hands to show the Crawler's pilot the navigation torches he was holding, Parsons directed the vehicle to a parking spot where security could check the cargo.

"Seems like a pretty good gig you got here," I told him.

Parsons smiled as he followed the Crawler on foot. "It sure beats humping shit through a few hundred kilometers of hostile alien jungle."

"I bet it does," I said, jogging to keep up with the prisoner. "Any chance I can convince you to come back and work with me?"

Parsons scoffed. "As a porter? You gotta be fucking kidding me."

"Not as a porter," I told him. "As a squad leader. A sergeant. With a clean record, your crimes completely expunged, and your convictions thrown out. It'd be like you never even went to trial. I'd put a rider in your contract stipulating that your obligation to the Corps would end once the 247th Marine Expeditionary Force's mission to Kanaris is over."

"That could take a mighty long time, Lieutenant." The fact that Parsons did not even slow his pace suggested he was not even remotely interested in my offer.

"Or it could end next week," I countered. "If the powers back on Kyper decide General Kroaht's not doing the job fast enough and choose to relieve him with someone they think could do better."

Parsons shook his head. "Next week, next month, it doesn't matter. The life span of a Marine operating around the base of the Satapadaya Ranges is expressed in hours sometimes. My crystal clear criminal record isn't going to be worth anything to me if I'm dead, sir."

"But if you survive, between your initial Marine enlistment and us making your incarceration count as time in service, you could extend for two years and retire with a pension. You could start over."

The prisoner stopped and turned toward me. "I think I told you my situation already, Lieutenant. I don't plan on starting over. Once I've finished my time, I plan on actually committing the crime they convicted me of."

"But if you change your mind...."

"I'm not changing my mind," Parsons snapped. Turning his back on me, the convict stepped up to the Crawler's pilot, who was climbing out of the vehicle's cockpit. "How are you doing, Corporal?"

The Marine appeared dazed as she looked around the staging lot. "I...I...I'm glad to be back."

Parsons nodded in understanding and patted the grunt on the shoulder. "You're safe now. We haven't taken fire here in months. Once you get your cargo to its designated offload location, find your way back to the lot shack. There's a master sergeant there who likes to offer those returning from the front some home-brewed hooch. It'll take the edge off your anxiety for a few hours and help you sleep. What've you got in back?"

The corporal looked at Parsons with haunted eyes and handed him her paperwork. "Code forty-four."

Parsons sighed and dialed up the security team on his commlink. "Skip the lot check. I got a Crawler loaded with forty-fours. Intercept it at the hot box."

"Roger that," the security detail said in return.

Passing the driver's manifest back to her, Parsons asked, "You know where the incinerator is?"

The corporal nodded and started marching back to her vehicle. As she walked away, Parsons turned to me and said, "Follow me, sir. I want to show you something."

The prisoner led me to the back of the Crawler and pointed at a steady stream of dark fluid flowing from the hull onto one of the back tracks.

I shrugged. "It's leaking."

"It's not leaking," the convict corrected me. "It's bleeding."

"What?" I asked, stepping forward to take a closer look. The fluid looked dark under the low light, but once I got closer, I could see it was actually a deep hue of red. As the vehicle kicked into gear, more poured from the gap at the bottom of the liftgate.

"Crawlers were designed not to let liquids into the interior," Parsons informed me. "In the event that some did, however, they made these things so they would easily drain. Code 44 is the logistics designation for corpses, Lieutenant. Do you have any idea how many must be packed into that thing to make so much blood pool up in back?"

I shook my head.

"I don't either," the convict admitted. "I only know it's a lot. Lieutenant Tauk, I don't have anything against you. You always treated me fairly despite my being a prisoner and all. I have a purpose to fulfill, though. It's something I can't do if I end up like the poor bastards in the back of that Crawler."

"What if I could bring that purpose to you?" I asked.

This grabbed Parsons's attention. "What do you mean by that?"

"As you might expect, news of us making first contact with an intelligent alien race is big news back home. People are scared that we're face to face with a threat to our very existence. It's whipping the masses into a patriotic fervor, and people from all walks of life are mobbing Space Corps recruiting offices to join the fight. Your home planet of Apalashu is no exception."

I took a step closer to Parsons and lowered my voice. "While I was recovering, I looked into your case. I also went through channels and requested that Section 356 get involved. They had an agent ask around about what happened to your people, and just that little hint of having a Kyperion investigator mentioning your family set off something of a panic. All of a sudden, several officers immediately put in for transfers. Several others retired. Among them was Mathu Pulayne, the man who tried to take advantage of your daughter."

Parsons swallowed hard. "And you can get him here?"

I shook my head. "No. He's too old for military service. I do know where he lives now, though."

"That doesn't do me any good." Parsons scoffed.

"Not while you're a prisoner," I admitted. "But as a sergeant, you'd be eligible for leave. You could take care of him then."

"But I thought you said you were bringing them to me."

"Do you know Luuk Bukki?"

Parsons shook his head.

29

"He was Pulayne's partner. He didn't have the seniority to transfer and was obviously too young to retire. To avoid getting caught up in the investigation, he decided to quit the police and join the Space Corps. Bukki's a fit guy who got himself recon-qualified. Since I get to choose the Marines of my first platoon, all you have to do is say the word, and I'll bring him into my unit. You can do whatever you want to him."

The prisoner sighed. "What happened was seven years ago. This Bukki guy wouldn't have been around back then."

"True," I said. "But my understanding is that this guy's just as corrupt as Pulayne. He probably knows all about what happened to you. I'm sure he's got all kinds of info about the shit that guy was involved in."

Barone Parsons stood there contemplating my offer for a few moments. "Why me?" he finally asked. "Yeah, I was a Marine, but I was just a standard ground-pounder. I never did anything to warrant a special offer like this."

"I trust you," I told him.

"Trust me?" Parsons asked. "To do what?"

"To watch my back if I watch yours. Look, the way I understand things is that the Narmans are kicking our asses with our own people. They're playing upon our divisions and stoking our discontented into mutiny. Facing an enemy across no man's land is tough. It's even tougher when you have to face them in the foxhole beside you, too."

Parsons laughed. "And you think I'm capable of making our conscripts believe that the League has their best interests at heart?"

"No," I answered. "I think you're the guy who could convince them that *I* have their best interests at heart. You're a convict with a damned good reason to hate everything the League stands for. You'll have a ton of street cred among the conscripts. If you tell them I'm a man of my word, they'll believe I'm one of the good guys. Maybe they won't shoot me in the face before they run off to join the Narmans."

"Maybe they will. Maybe they won't." The prisoner glared at me for several seconds. "And if I do this, you'll have my record cleared?"

"Actually," I told him. "I'm having your record cleared anyway. Section 356 has already found a mess of corruption among Apalashu's law enforcement entities. I had them submit your case to the office of the Kyperion Court. Look, man, it's obvious you got railroaded. The right thing to do is clear your name whether you join me or not. That's already in motion, no strings attached."

"Seriously?" Parsons asked.

"Seriously," I answered.

"You know, by saying you're working to exonerate me no matter what I decide, you're undermining your leverage."

"Yep, but it's the right thing to do." I patted Parsons on the shoulder. "Look, go ahead and sleep on this. Let me know within a couple of days what you decide."

Before I took two steps, the prisoner called out. "And I'll get leave?"

I turned around and nodded. "You'll be leave eligible. That doesn't mean you'll get it right away."

Parsons nervously nodded a couple of times. "Okay, I'll do it. I have one more condition, though."

"And what would that be?"

"Do you know where Ritza Xi is?"

I nodded sadly. "I do."

"My condition is that we get her out of there and take her with us."

As a smile crept across my face, I said, "Then let's go get her."

That was going to be my next stop anyway.

Chapter 5

Xi

"You know," I said to the sergeant whose nose I had just broken. "I had a guy on my last squad, a man named Orgo Yisht, who worked security for a brothel. He wasn't a pimp or anything. He just borrowed money from the wrong people to feed his family. He messed up the goons who tried to collect one of his daughters as payment, so the bosses offered him a job. He got ten years as a Class One laborer after the authorities broke up the organization that employed him."

I hauled off and punched the rank on the Marine's shoulder. "And the Corps made you a sergeant for doing the exact same thing!"

Another Marine who had tried to throw Parsons out of the Morale Center was crawling on the ground, looking for one of his teeth. "He was just doing his job!" the injured infantryman yelled, spitting blood from his mouth. "You ain't got no right to do this! Who the fuck do you think you are?"

Turning my back on the sergeant, I marched over to the beaten trooper and wrenched him to his feet by the hair. I then threw him against the wall and wrapped my fingers around his throat. "I'm the guy who killed Gori Dravidas, you little prick. I'm also an officer, so I can do pretty much anything I want. I could probably even get away with snapping your measly little neck. You want to test me?"

"No," the Marine croaked, shaking his head as much as I would allow. I let go and dropped him onto the deck.

Shifting my attention back to the man working the desk, I yelled, "For the last time, Sergeant! What room are you keeping Ritza Xi in?"

Before he could answer, a commotion broke out in the hallway to my left. Barone Parsons yelled out a long litany of venomous obscenities. Another man was screaming as well, but out of pain instead of rage. "Never mind," I told the sergeant. "It looks like we found her."

As I walked to Xi's room, I watched Parsons emerge from an open doorway. His left arm was wrapped around the neck of a naked rifleman. His right hand clutched the Marine's testicles from behind in a grip so tight I feared one of them would pop off before Parsons got his victim to the door. It seemed like an awkward way to carry a man, but I was confident Parsons' discomfort paled in comparison to that of the poor sap he was transporting.

"M-m-my uniform...!" the struggling leatherneck pled through clenched teeth.

"You got another one back at your barracks," Barone growled. "Go get it."

I stepped into Xi's room as she finished slipping into her last client's undershirt. She was startled to see me, but not nearly as startled as I was as I laid eyes upon her.

Ritza Xi had once been a very attractive woman. Sergeant Kyker and his men had nearly beaten her to death during the mutiny, however, and her face had taken the brunt of their fury. The medics patched her up enough to be functional, but Kyker had left her disfigured. Her nose was still crooked and askew. Her mouth was full of chipped, broken, and missing teeth. Her right eye would only open about halfway, and stitch marks could be seen all over her cheeks and forehead. The Space Corps had the ability to make Ritza Xi pretty again, but they were not going to pour those kinds of resources into fixing a convicted child killer.

"Tauk," Xi said, looking surprised to see me. "What are you doing here?"

Parsons stepped back into the room and closed the door behind him. "We came to get you," he told her.

"For what?" Xi asked.

"I've been commissioned," I let her know. "Academy cadets get to hand-pick our first platoons. I want you in mine."

Xi scoffed. "You want me in your platoon?"

I nodded.

"Really? You want me to go out into combat with you, hauling a forty-kilo load through the jungle, and risk getting shot, blown up, eaten by some giant bug, or captured by aliens? As bad as it is here, being forced to hump filthy Marines too pathetic to find a date among their peers is better than humping all your shit through Moloch's Garden."

"I don't want you as a porter, Xi."

"Then what do you want me for?" the Zero asked. "Your girlfriend?"

I shook my head. "You're a killer. Officially, you'll be my orderly, but in reality, I want you as part of my security detail."

"A praetorian?" Xi asked. "Your bodyguard?"

I nodded. "In a way, yes. Obviously, I can't put a gun in your hand, but I can teach you to be deadly with plenty of other things you *are* allowed to carry. Also, you'll not be my personal bodyguard. Instead, you'll be protecting the integrity of the platoon itself."

Xi looked confused. "I don't understand."

I tried to clarify. "Look, from what I understand, the enemy on Kanaris has done an excellent job of getting into the heads of our disgruntled Marines and convincing them that the Morghul are the good guys in this fight. Xi, you survived that march to Narman's Pyke. You saw what they did to our airborne troops. The savages sliced them all open, nipple-to-nipple and groin-to-neck, peeling back their skin as if they were dissecting the poor bastards. And they did it while they were still alive."

"And you want me to sign up with you so they can do the same thing to me?"

"Trust me, I'm not planning on ending up that way," I assured her. "Nor will I let that happen to any of my people without one hell of a fight."

"But here, I'm not at risk of having that happen to me at all."

"Unless Narman's Pyke falls," Parsons told her.

Xi looked at her fellow convict in disbelief. "You think that's possible?"

Parsons nodded. "If the Narmans can convince enough Marines to switch sides? Absolutely. The enemy's no match for us in a direct fight, but seventy percent of our Marines are either conscripts or people forced into the Corps because they were starving. If the Narmans turn all those troops to their side, it'll be us who don't stand a chance against them. The League's a tinderbox. They have a real shot of taking us from the inside."

"You're a Class Zero convict," I reminded Xi. "No one has more reason to hate the League than you. Your primary mission will be to keep your finger on the pulse of my Marines and let me know what I need to do to keep them loyal. And to give me fair warning if they're going to mutiny no matter what I do."

"You want me to be your rat?" Xi sneered.

I nodded. "That's exactly what I want."

"And how do you know the Narmans aren't better than the League?" Ritza asked.

"Because they ordered the Quarakai to kill mutineers trying to surrender when we first got to Narman's Pyke," Parsons answered. "That suggests the aliens are more interested in culling humans than converting them. When they have the advantage in numbers, they'll slaughter us. They only seem to want us to switch sides when we outnumber them."

Xi shrugged. "So, I'm doomed no matter what I do. I don't see how signing up with you guys benefits me."

"I know you're innocent," I told the convict. "I'm already working on trying to get you cleared. By the way, that effort will continue whether or not you choose to join me. It's the right thing to do. What I can offer you on top of that is training. Xi, I can't guarantee you'll live through your stint in my platoon, but I can assure you that I can mold you into somebody who will never be a victim again. Of anybody."

Xi turned her gaze toward Parsons. "Why are you following him?"

"I told you before how I ended up a convict. This is my quickest way to get out of my sentence and back to Apalashu so I can wrap up my unfinished business there."

"I have unfinished business on Kyan-Noa." Xi whispered it so softly it sounded as if she was talking to herself.

The Zero sat silently on the edge of her bed as she contemplated my offer. Finally, she looked up and said, "Why are you asking me to do this? You're an officer. You could order me into your unit."

I shook my head. "If I respect you enough to be under my command, I need to be able to trust you enough to make your own decisions. I don't *need* you in my unit, Xi. I *want* you there. I want to make up for whichever ways I may have wronged you and give you a chance to regain control over your own destiny."

Though she fought hard to restrain it, I saw Ritza's bottom lip quiver. She seemed overwhelmed to be treated as a human again. She also appeared anxious to test me. "I'll join your platoon on one condition," she told me.

"What would that be?" I asked.

Xi pointed at the wall to her left. "Margi Gul works the room next to me. She's from Terrakand. Convicted of terrorism and murder. I want her to come with us."

Pointing toward the ceiling, Xi then said, "Zubi Jenich works upstairs. She was captured with rebel forces on Portuna. She comes, too."

35

"I can't give them the same job as you," I told Xi. "I can take them, but they'd be regular porters."

Xi shook her head. "They won't care as long as it gets them out of here."

I nodded. "Do we have a deal?"

Ritza Xi held out her hand so we could shake on it. "I believe we do."

Chapter 6

Kleptos

When I returned to my command tent, Gunny Brumit was waiting for me with my new Tech Warfare Specialist. As I brushed the rain off my tunic, Dmitri Naktada walked toward me with a big grin on his face and his arms opened wide. Before I could warn him against showing improper familiarity to a commissioned officer, he wrapped me in a bear hug and lifted me right off my feet. "Cadet Tauk!" he laughed. "Man, am I glad to see you! I heard you were a goner!"

"It's *Lieutenant* Tauk, Naktada," Brumit snapped. "You're supposed to salute the man, not feel him up."

Suddenly cognizant of his *faux pas*, the armorer released me. He then stiffened up and rendered a comically proper Marine salute. Referring to himself in the third person, he barked, "Sergeant Naktada apologizes for his exuberance, SIR! The poor bastard never could contain his excitement! We're all lucky he didn't end up tinkling on the deck!"

Laughing, I returned the salute before grabbing Naktada's hand and shaking it profusely. "I'm glad to see you, too, Sergeant. We never did get to have a proper conversation about what you did on the beach and how much I owe you for that."

The armorer dismissed my praise with a wave of his hand. "It's me that owes you, sir. They decorated me for what I did back at the wreckage of *Wasp-Three*. If things had worked out differently, I'd be considered a deserter instead of a hero."

"You're right," I agreed. "You would've. I take it you've decided to accept my offer to make you my TWS?"

Naktada nodded. "Damned straight. I appreciate the promotion, too, sir." Reaching behind his back, my armorer pulled out a cylindrical device and tossed it to me. "I brought you a gift."

Catching the contraption, I turned it over several times in my hands. It looked like something I had seen in Pustov's office, but was significantly smaller. "Is this what I think it is?"

"It's a seibara," Naktada answered. "It's what the aliens are trying to arm the Quarakai with. Fortunately, this technology's not a natural fit for such a primitive being. The Quarks are far more likely to hurt themselves with it than us. In our hands, though, it could wreak havoc on the bastards. I've heard of those pricks taking thirty bullets before going down. A single swipe with one of these will slice them right in half."

Pulling another seibara from behind his back, Naktada tossed it to Brumit. "There you go, Gunny. I brought you one, too."

"How many of these do you have?" I asked.

Naktada shrugged. "Right now? About a half dozen. Once you figure out what makes them tick, they're not that hard to put together."

"You think you could make about eighty more?"

The armorer grinned. "You want to equip the whole platoon?"

I nodded.

Naktada grimaced. "I'm not sure that's a good idea. Not without a lot of training or some way to protect our Marines from someone swinging one right beside them. If everyone's wielding seibaras in the trenches, you'll hack each other to pieces."

Brumit snapped her wrist and extended the telescopic blade from the device's handle. Listening to it hum, the gunny sergeant asked, "What's this thing powered with?"

"The same shit that's been wreaking havoc with our communications down here."

"Harnillium?" I asked.

My armorer nodded. "Harnillium. That shit's a game-changer, sir. Hey, you know that custom magnetic system you rigged up in your old exo-armor?"

"Yeah," I answered. "I lost it after I was evacuated, though."

"You didn't lose it. I got it. You know, Harnillium fields tend to react in some rather extreme ways with magnetism. Do you know the common element between virtually every living planet we've ever discovered?"

"Water?"

Naktada sighed. "Yeah, but that's not what I was thinking. I was talking about an iron core. All that molten metal generates a geomagnetic field that deflects solar radiation and keeps it from burning off the atmosphere and cooking us alive. Harnillium reacts very strongly to magnetism, and if you can focus its field the right way, you can actually levitate."

"You're turning my shell into a flying suit?"

My armorer laughed. "No, we're not quite there yet, but we know it's a theoretical possibility. On a smaller scale, I've tricked out your concept a bit. You know how you could use your magnetic gloves to make your sidearm fly out of your holster and land in the palm of your hand?"

"Yeah."

"Well, I'm tweaking it with Harnillium. I exponentially increased its power and refined it to give you better control. I have some other improvements in mind, but the Weapons Development Section lacks the imagination to give them the consideration they deserve. It's a pretty low priority."

"What's higher?" asked Gunny Brumit.

"Number one is that alien plasma blaster. After reverse engineering the seibara, I have a pretty good idea of what the basic concept is behind that weapon. Still, I need a working model to find a practical solution. Number two is their cloaking technology. It appears they've figured out a way to bend light around them, almost perfectly concealing their soldiers."

"'Almost' is the key word there," I told Naktada. "I saw it atop Mount Toranad. It looks like heat shimmer. When you shoot through it, it sends ripples throughout the field, almost as if you're dropping pebbles into a pond. It's not perfect, but it's light years beyond anything we have."

"You saw the Morghul?" Naktada gasped. "The aliens?"

I shrugged. "Not their physical features, but, yeah, I saw them. They were wearing hooded cloaks that obscured their faces, so I couldn't describe them to you."

"Then how do you know they were aliens?" asked Gunny Brumit.

"I saw one turn its head one hundred and eighty degrees around to speak to its partner. Then it opened up and shot our Raptor with one of those plasma blaster things."

"Holy shit," gasped Naktada as he covered his mouth. "You actually saw them."

"Yep," I told him. "And if things go our way, I hope to see them again really soon. You still in?"

My TWS nodded. "Sure. Do you already have a mission?"

I shook my head. "No. Right now, the powers that be want to use our highly trained Recon Marines to punch through the lines at the base of the Satapadaya Ranges."

Naktada scoffed. "Are you serious?!? Don't tell me. That's a Samaari idea, isn't it?"

"Of course," I said. "Made by someone who obviously doesn't understand what we can bring to the table. My goal is to make them see the value in recon work before they give us the order to charge across some firey stretch of no man's land. We're going to find the aliens, Naktada."

My armorer shrugged. "The Marine Expeditionary Force has been looking for aliens since we landed. We know they're out there because we've been on the receiving end of some pretty nasty armament. We haven't seen them, though. No one has. Besides you, anyway."

"We've seen them," I told Naktada. "So has Palkrait and Section 615. They were with me on Toranad. We'll find them eventually. We just need to keep looking."

"We have been looking," Brumit assured me. "We've sent patrol after patrol into the Satapadaya. The ones that return come back without running into anything. Those that run into something, well, they just don't come back."

I let out a long sigh. "Did they go out there with any idea what they were looking for?"

Brumit shook her head. "No."

I threw my hands up in the air. "Then what did they expect to happen?"

"Do *you* know what you're looking for?" Naktada asked me.

"As a matter of fact, I do." I reached into my pocket and pulled out my tablet. "Reading the battlefield assessments, I know that the Satapadaya Front is manned mainly by Marine deserters. Us. They're getting orders from Narman officers positioned far to the rear."

Naktada scoffed. "Fucking cowards."

"That's not cowardice," I corrected my armorer. "That's brains. The closer the Narmans are to the front, the bigger the risk of us capturing them. They think their biggest weapon is our ignorance, and they're right."

As I punched the keys on the screen of my tablet, I said, "I have no intention of wandering aimlessly through the Kanarisian rainforest looking for aliens. Odds are the jungle will just swallow us up. Or worse, the aliens will run into us before we run into them. My strategy is to start an active campaign to get our hands on some Marines that've switched sides. Sooner or later, one of them will know where we find the Narmans. Once we grab the Narmans, we'll eventually get one that can tell us where to find the aliens."

I paused to show Brumit and Naktada the picture on my tablet. "Or we find this woman. Her name is Deena Vulk. This picture is from her colonial ID, so it's a bit old. Half of her face is burned off now, so she doesn't look much like this anymore. Regardless, she was with the aliens on Toranad when I was shot. She knows where the Morghul are. If we find her, we find them."

Gunny Brumit shook his head. "We've captured Narman prisoners before, sir. They don't give up much."

"Don't worry about that, Gunny," I told my number two. "I'll make that bitch talk."

Chapter 7

MOTT PEELI

When I walked into Captain Pustov's office, I caught him conferring with a first lieutenant who did not seem very pleased to see me. The younger officer glared at me from the moment I opened the door and followed me with his steely gaze until I stopped at the company commander's desk. For that matter, it appeared that Pustov's mood had soured since the last time I saw him also.

"How's the staffing of your platoon going, Tauk?" asked my captain.

"It's progressing, sir," I answered.

"So I hear. You have your staff billets filled?"

I nodded. "I just finished speaking with my new battlefield intel specialist, Sergeant Hariana Espiya. Brumit's worked with her before and highly recommended her to me. I was impressed with her also. I think she's going to be a good fit."

Pustov nodded. "I would hope so. Major Kasius at battalion intel was pretty pissed about you poaching her from him. He raged at me for damned near an hour to get her back."

"I hear he rages a lot, sir," I said. "Thanks for not letting him take her."

"No need to thank me. If I had the authority to reverse your choice, I would have just to get that insufferable prick off the line. Who else do you have?"

"Sergeant Terivenda Sotalain as my senior medic."

"I've heard that name before," Pustov said.

"She was awarded the Corps Cross a couple of months ago for heroism. You might have been at the ceremony."

"Yeah, I seem to be attending a lot of those lately."

"Dmitri Naktada...."

Pustov sighed. "The major in charge of tech intel chewed my ass on that one also. I tend to agree with him. Naktada's a very gifted armorer. He is much more of an asset back at FTRC than he is in the field." FTRC stood for Field Technological Research Command. It was where the Corps put all the smart guys to analyze unfamiliar gear recovered from the battlefield.

"Naktada would be an asset wherever he went," I told my captain. "He'll do us proud in my platoon also. Sir, I apologize for the grief I may be causing you with my candidates, but my intention is to build the best platoon in the expeditionary force. I can't do that drafting second-best Marines."

"That why you're taking the best whores, too?" asked the other lieutenant in the room.

"Excuse me?"

"You heard me," the young officer sneered. "You're expected to fight out in the field, Tauk. Not fuck. So why are you filling your Zero billets with whores?"

Not inclined to dignify the lieutenant's question with an answer, I turned to Captain Pustov and asked, "Why does this guy think that's any of his business?"

My company commander leaned back in his seat and clasped his hands behind his head. "Actually, Tauk, I'm kind of curious about that myself. Unlike Lieutenant Peeli here, I'm not making assumptions. I've heard academy Marines tend to think outside the box, so I'm genuinely curious about your line of reasoning here. Why'd you break a morale sergeant's nose and throw one of our First Platoon comrades out into the street by his ball sack?"

"And without his uniform," added Peeli.

I grinned at the memory, trying not to bust out laughing. "Well, had those Marines remembered how to obey the commands of a commissioned officer, they wouldn't have been injured."

"PFC Diyana was assaulted by a Class One convict," Peeli snarled.

"No," I corrected the lieutenant. "Barone Parsons is a sergeant. He's one of my squad leaders."

Peeli looked ready to argue, but Pustov waved him off. "Gentlemen, let's not get off track. Why whores, Tauk?"

I sighed. "Ritza Xi survived the trek from the wreckage of *Wasp-Three* to Narman's Pyke. From my viewpoint, Xi was convicted unfairly and subjected to all kinds of abuse and degradation as a Class Zero convict. My troops will know she has every reason to hate the Corps and the League. They'll likely try to recruit her if they plan on mutinying. She owes me her life, and I trust her. That's why I want her in my platoon."

"And what about the other two?" asked Peeli.

"One's a POW from Portuna. The other's been convicted of terrorism and murder. Again, they have a well-known hatred for everything we stand for."

"Yet they trust you?"

I shook my head. "No, but they trust Xi. They could prove an even more effective bellwether of the attitude of my Marines."

"That's bullshit," Peeli scoffed. "You need to put them back."

I laughed. "I got an intel sergeant and an armorer over the protests of majors, Peeli. You think I'm giving back my Zeros just because some first lieutenant said to?"

Peeli bristled as the color rushed into his face. As a Samaari, he was used to people jumping when he spoke, despite the fact he was a junior officer. "Do you have any idea who I...?"

"Oh, knock it off!" snapped Pustov as he sat up and shoved his finger in Peeli's face. "If I ever hear you try to pull that 'Do you have any idea who I am?' shit again, I'll bounce your ass right out of Recon. Do you understand me?"

The lieutenant snapped his head around and glared at the captain, obviously not appreciating the commander's tone. That propelled Pustov right out of his chair. "Do you understand me?!?" he yelled.

"Yes, sir." The Samaari officer peeled his glare off the captain and turned it on me. "You know, if an officer has any idea how to lead his Marines, he doesn't need to recruit whores to spy on them."

"What business is it of yours how I run my platoon anyway?" I asked Peeli.

"I make it my business when my Marines get abused."

"Since when did the Samaaris start giving a shit about the plebes?" I laughed. Before the lieutenant could answer, I added, "You're sweet on one of them, ain't you?"

The color rushing into Peeli's face suggested I had struck a nerve and made me laugh again. "That's it, isn't it? Which one?"

"I...uh...no, I...."

"Just so we're clear," I told the lieutenant. "I will snap the dick off any of my Marines who lays a finger on one of my female Zeros. I know you Samaaris aren't used to being told 'no,' so let me assure you that if you feel you're entitled to take liberties with my convicts, I'll snap yours off, too, and stick it right up your ass."

Peeli looked at Pustov as if he expected him to intervene. "You going to let him get away with that? Are we giving our Zero whores more protection than officers in your company, Captain?"

Pustov sighed. "Tauk, we don't threaten other officers in my company. Is that understood?"

"Yes, sir," I answered.

"You can wipe that smug smile off your face, Peeli," our commander told the Samaari. "Because I also expect my officers to behave like gentlemen. If I hear any hint of you cavorting with the comfort women at the Morale Center again, I'll cut your epaulets off in front of your men and have you sent back to the mothership in disgrace. You got that?"

Peeli looked at our commander in shock.

"Answer me, Lieutenant," Pustov growled.

"Aye aye, sir."

"Good. You can go, Lieutenant Peeli."

Since the captain did not dismiss me by name, I stayed behind as the Samaari stormed out of Pustov's office. "I take it that's one of my fellow platoon leaders?" I asked.

My commander nodded. "Yep. That's Mott Peeli, the grandson of a Tahnabaht Conglomerate executive. The Samaaris gotta have someone keeping an eye on Recon."

"If you ever need that eye blinded, Captain, just say the word."

Pustov grinned and shook his head. "I'm not going to need you to kill that shitstain, Tauk. I've got a forty-credit wager going with Captain Dairik in Alpha Company that Peeli will get iced by his own Marines before I have to do anything to the prick."

Chapter 8

KILLBILLIES

There were not many civilians in Narman's Pyke, but there were some. The League had sent a few government officials to determine how to reinvigorate the colony and make it fit for repopulation. Additionally, the Tahnebaht Conglomerate had a contingent on the ground to assess what was needed to get the Harnillium mines going again. I had also seen civil engineers behind the walls designing fortifications and strengthening the settlement's defenses. If there was a commonality among them, it was that they were almost all professionals. They were intelligent, clean, highly educated, polite, and sophisticated.

The men Gunny Brumit and I caught harassing Akkam Lumuk at the medical center were not. They were dressed in ragged, dirty coveralls and wore their hair soiled and unkempt. It appeared they resisted shaving to store leftover food in their beards. They spoke in simple sentences saturated in profanity and seemed to find amusement in random acts of cruelty. And though they appeared too poor to afford soap, each one was equipped with an arsenal worth more than a Marine sergeant could make in a year.

"Who the hell are those people?" I asked my platoon sergeant as I witnessed a half-dozen of them jeering the gentle giant from Gorsu Qat. Lumuk was so focused on his tormentors that he did not notice us watching from afar.

Brumit spat into the mud in disgust. "Death squads. Those men are from Qilkoraan. We call them 'Killbillies.' Believe it or not, they worship the Samaaris."

I choked. "What? For real?"

Gunny laughed. "I'm not even exaggerating. They literally believe the Samaaris are their gods' chosen people and if they serve them well, doing whatever the Samaaris tell them, they'll be reincarnated as one of those prissy fucks in the next life."

"How can they possibly believe that shit after seeing how pathetic the Samaaris are in combat?!?"

Brumit snorted. "Sir, there is absolutely no shortage of the garbage people will believe as long as you start drilling it into their heads as babies. When you get to them young, you can convince them that if they ever question the line of shit they're being fed, they'll be tormented forever."

"Huh. Kind of like what the academy did to me. Luckily, it didn't stick."

Brumit shrugged. "Maybe it would have had they thrown in the concept of eternal damnation."

"So that's how the Qilkorians do it?" I asked. "They threaten them with hell to scare them away from thinking?"

My number two shook her head. "The funny thing is, to these Killbillies, hell is being reincarnated back into a Qilkorian after they die. They mourn their births instead of celebrating them. Even they know what miserable little pricks they are."

"Unbelievable," I said, shaking my head. "What are they doing here?"

Brumit shrugged. "They have their uses. Since they see Samaari officers as prophets, every command they're given is considered a mandate from the gods, no matter how barbaric it may be. Killing, raping, torturing, pillaging – it's all holy labor to them. Every atrocity they commit brings them closer to paradise."

"So they're here to do the things considered too nasty for the Marines?"

"Among other things," the gunnery sergeant told me. "Qilkoraan lacks resources, but is rich in life. There isn't much in the way of industry there, so folks tend to live off the land, growing their food, raising livestock, and hunting for meat. They're known for being expert trackers. They also seem able to domesticate virtually any alien creature that can be tamed."

Up until that point, the Kilbillies had been tormenting Lumuk verbally. It looked like that was about to change when a morbidly obese one unslung his weapon from his back and handed it to a cohort. It was a Farisi AVHE-38. A true hand cannon, the AVHE fired 17mm high explosive rounds that could punch fist-sized holes into the side of a Combat

Crawler. It was one of the most powerful firearms produced and required a man of great strength, not to mention mass, to wield it.

"Where do they get the credits for all that hardware?" I asked Brumit.

"Dope," Gunny answered. "If you ever need to score yourself some KQR, find yourself a Killbilly."

"KQR?" I asked. "What the hell's that?"

Brumit laughed. "I forgot you academy Marines grew up somewhat sheltered from the real world. KQR is Kan Qui Radix. Sometimes it's called 'Demon Root,' 'Kan Qui,' or just 'Radix.' It's a powerful hallucinogenic that grows wild on Qilkoraan."

"Is it legal?" I asked.

"Not even remotely," Brumit scoffed. "For a while, vets were swearing it was a miracle cure for combat stress. Even the League conceded it was effective in about sixty percent of the former Marines that took it. For a third of them, though, it didn't work at all. The problem was it drove the remaining seven percent of its users into a state of psychosis so extreme they'd shoot up stadiums or try to eat their neighbors. That's why it's illegal. Oddly enough, Killbillies use it habitually with no real consequences other than getting brain damaged enough to believe Samaaris are divine."

The freshly disarmed Killbilly put up his fists, challenging Lumuk to fight him. In response, Lumuk shook his head and turned the palms of his hands toward his tormentor, emphasizing he was not looking for trouble.

I sighed. "You know, you would think that guy's size would make the galaxy's malcontents think twice about picking on him. Instead, it seems to draw them in like bugs to light."

"Nothing makes a small man feel bigger than beating someone twice their size," Brumit told me. "And Lumuk's got a reputation for cowardice. That makes him an easy target."

"Yeah, I know," I said as I started marching toward the disturbance. Brumit came with me.

"C'mon, big boy!" I heard the obese Killbilly jeer. "It'll be fun! Try to hit me! I dare you!"

"Naw, sir," Lumuk pleaded. "I don't wanna hit nobody. I just wanna go inside and do my job!"

"I'll hit you, fat man," Brumit said as she strolled into the circle of simpletons surrounding the giant. "If that's what you want so bad."

With a condescending smile on his face showing how amused he was to be challenged by a woman, the Killbilly turned to Brumit and said, "I ain't got nothin' against no real Marine, Gunny. We just havin' ourselves a little fun and tryin' tuh toughen up da big guy is all."

"I don't think it's your job to train Marines," I announced as I crept up on the gathering from behind. "That would be mine."

"Who be you?" asked one of the thinner cretins.

"I'm the guy who killed Gori Dravidas."

"Who da fuck is dat?" asked another.

Brumit laughed at the look on my face. Everywhere I went, people asked if I was the guy who iced the Butcher of Deraghun. I was not particularly proud of it, but revealing what I did was an effective way to intimidate people into doing what I wanted. Coming across men who had never heard of Dravidas threw me off my game. I did not know how to react.

"Killbillies aren't known for having their fingers on the pulse of current events, sir," my gunnery sergeant informed me.

"We're Qilkorians," the obese one told Brumit. "We don't like being called Killbillies. It's offensive."

"I couldn't care less," Gunny responded, daring him to do something about it.

The Qilkorian did. Unable to tolerate a female showing him disrespect, he lashed out and back-handed Brumit across the face.

I had learned long ago that Akkam Lumuk was utterly incapable of lifting a finger in his own defense. When it came to protecting others, however, he acted from instinct. Before Brumit could respond to the slap by gouging one of the Qilkorian's eyes out, Lumuk bent down, wrapped his massive arms around the Killbilly's waist and wrenched him off his feet. It was a blast of instant karma that taught the man how unwise it was to strike a woman in the giant's presence, no matter how insanely proficient she may have been of defending herself.

Akkam Lumuk had a poor reckoning of his own strength. I was sure his intent was only to put distance between the Killbilly and Gunny Brumit, but he was dangerously close to squeezing the man to death. The Qilkorian's eyes looked ready to pop out of his skull. "Auuuughh!" he gasped. "Put me down! I can't breathe!"

"You heard him!" the skinny man next to me shouted as he dropped the AVHE-38 he was holding. It might have been handy, but it was far too heavy for someone his size. Instead, he reached for the Syntek automatic shotgun slung around his back. Before he could grab it, I seized the weapon by the stock and barrel, then spun it so that the sling ripped itself over the man's arm and tightened around his neck, cutting off his air supply. I then swept his feet out from beneath him and took the Qilkorian to the ground, leaving him to choke while I pulled a pistol from the holster on his hip and pointed it at the others.

"Stop!" the obese Killbilly cried out. His face had turned a deep shade of red while veins began popping up from under the skin of his forehead. "You're...killing...me!"

Seeing the Qilkorians reaching for their weapons spooked Lumuk. Without realizing it, he tightened his hold around the Killbilly's waist even harder. The man could no longer beg for mercy. All he could do was grunt and gasp until he eventually released one of the loudest blasts of flatulence any of us had ever heard.

Despite the tension of the situation, Gunny and I began laughing. So did a couple of the Killbillies. When a stream of wet feces started pouring from the leg of one of the obese man's coveralls, we roared even harder. Once he realized what was happening, Lumuk finally let go and dropped his tormentor into the mess he had made, reducing us all into hysterics. Even the skinny guy I nearly choked out cracked up once he worked his way out of his sling enough to breathe.

Lumuk's victim was the only one not amused. Rolling over in his own excrement, he panted for air and whimpered, "I think I shit myself."

Gunny roared. "You pissed yourself, too!"

The commotion drew an audience. Marines coming in and leaving the medical center stopped to see the spectacle, as did troops passing by. Before long, the Killbillies had a couple of dozen people laughing at them. The situation quickly lost its humor as they realized they were rising to meet Qilkorian stereotypes. They looked like rubes, and being the butt of ridicule stoked their inferiority complexes. The smiles fell from their faces and they hung their heads as they tried to help their portly comrade to his feet.

When he could finally stand under his own power, the soiled Killbilly looked over the Marines taunting him and tried to carry himself with as much dignity as a man covered in his own waste could muster. He was seething. Knowing Lumuk would never have dared touch him had Brumit and I not been present, the Qilkorian blamed us for his public humiliation. He was smart enough to know that targeting an officer and a gunnery sergeant would invite the wrath of the entire Marine Expeditionary Force. He seemed willing to gamble that the command would not bother dedicating many resources to avenge a lowly private, however.

Lifting his chin in the air, he turned to the giant from Gorsu Qat and said, "In the name of his holiness, Pomo Vaaleteleva, I condemn you for the outrage of my honor. I give your name the Mark of the Tuuk."

The Qilkorians seemed to stiffen a bit at the proclamation. They turned to stare at Lumuk for a couple of moments as if committing his face to memory before one of them whipped out an old Corps-issued tablet and snapped a picture of the lumbering farm boy.

"What the hell is a 'Mark of the Tuuk?'" I asked the Killbilly I had nearly choked out.

Despite laughing along with us a few moments before, the skinny man's eyes were now all business as he turned toward me and said, "Death."

Chapter 9

CONFIDENCE

"They called President Vaaleteleva 'his *holiness*?'" Parsons laughed when I told him what had happened. "Have they ever actually seen the guy? Or even heard about him? The man's the epitome of every shortcoming the Samaaris are famous for."

Shaking my head, I said, "Like Gunny Brumit told me, if you start pumping a person's mind full of bullshit at birth and keep doing it throughout their entire lives, they'll believe damned near anything." I took a sip of liquor from the bottle Parsons handed me. "I grew up in the Citadel. Judging by what I thought when I left that place, I can tell you that is an irrefutable truth."

Ritza Xi looked up at me. "And you don't believe any of that stuff anymore? What changed your mind?"

"Killing Gori Dravidas," I answered. "It gave me a firsthand look behind the façade and showed me that what our leaders do and what they say are two entirely different things. I was in denial about it when we first landed on Kanaris. After marching through Moloch's Garden with a commander willing to sacrifice hundreds of good Marines to protect the reputation of a dead coward, however, I saw myself for what I really was."

"And what's that?" asked Sergeant Parsons.

"The defender of a regime that's unworthy of being defended." Parson's tent was not even remotely soundproof, so I lowered my voice after taking another drink of brandy and passing the bottle to Xi.

"I was going to leave the Corps with Jella Duverii," I confessed. "We were going to run away and find some world beyond the Kyperion frontier to start a new life. I'm still leaving, but I need to make some things right first."

I pointed at Parsons and Xi. "I know the two of you have scores to settle at home. I fully intend to get both of you out of here to chase the justice you deserve. I can't leave until I've settled my own scores, though."

Parsons looked surprised. "Briggund's dead. Who else is left here that you could be so upset with?"

I pulled out my tablet and called up the photograph of a Narman colonist. Handing the device to Xi, I said, "That's Deena Vulk. She's the bitch that killed Jella. You help me get my hands on her, and I'll help you get the vengeance you two are craving. Deal?"

"Deal," Xi said without hesitation. That was not surprising. As a Class Zero convict, my offer was her only hope of ever escaping the Corps alive.

Parsons did not have many options, either. "You know," he told me. "I'm taking on the entire law enforcement apparatus, police, prosecutors, and judges, of a medium-sized city. I'm under no illusions that my quest is anything other than a suicide mission. Are you really willing to go that far?"

"Jella's death freed up my calendar," I assured the squad leader. "Honestly, getting killed helping the two of you pursue your vendettas is the best offer I've got at the moment."

"And what about this stuff with Lumuk?" Xi asked.

I sighed. "From what I was told, this 'Mark of the Tuuk' thing is pretty serious. It's a blood feud. Killbillies can lose a brawl and retain their honor as long as they've fought well. Allowing one of their own to be humiliated and ridiculed, though, is unforgivable. From the Qilkorian point of view, Lumuk disgraced them all by what he did to...."

"Wait," Parsons pleaded, interrupting me. "You're telling me that six of those pricks can gang up on Akkam and humiliate him all they want, but when he finally sticks up for himself, he's disgraced every Killbilly in Narman's Pyke?"

"That about sums it up."

"That's ridiculous," the sergeant snapped. "I say we kill them all."

"We don't need to," I told Parsons. "We only have to kill Wooster Mikkaine. He's the fat ass who put that shit on our man."

Turning to Xi, I said, "I want you to get to know these Killbilly pricks. Find out who they are, where they live, and what they do. I want you to be able to recognize them so we can deal with the bastards if they show their faces around here. I'm working on getting a picture of Mikkaine so you can identify him if we ever cross paths again. If we ice that fucking moron, the mark on Lumuk evaporates."

"That sounds easy enough," Parsons said. "I'll go kill the man right now. Where can I find these assholes?"

I grinned. "Mikkaine knew we'd be coming for him. I got word that as soon as he cleaned himself up, he caught the first transport to the Satapadaya Front."

Xi laughed. "He's more afraid of you than the Narmans?"

"Seems so," I said. "The prick's gone to a place I'm not willing to send people looking for him. Meanwhile, all his cronies are after our Marine. I'm pulling Lumuk into our platoon so we can protect him."

"Seriously?" Parsons asked. "We're a fighting unit, sir. We all know Lumuk's not equipped for combat."

Shaking my head, I said, "That doesn't mean he's without his uses. He's the man who ripped a set of venomous fangs off a giant centipede. Remember? I agree; the man's worthless in a direct fight. Defensively, however, he could prove a real asset. Besides, who else are we going to call when we want to squeeze shit out of an annoying Killbilly like he's a human pastry bag?"

Parsons laughed at the visual. "Yeah, he did carry that pilot halfway to Narman's Pyke, didn't he?"

I nodded at the sergeant. "Look, Lumuk's a good man. He, you, and Xi got a raw deal to end up in the Corps, and I realize I'm part of the apparatus that put you here. I no longer have any desire to perpetuate a system that grinds people to dust in its gears. I want to make this right."

"Then why don't you just join the Narmans?" Xi asked.

"You saw what they did to our psycho pixies," I answered. "It looked like they were vivisected. Operated on while they were still alive as part of some macabre science experiment. Then they massacred our prisoners when they attacked us at Narman's Pyke."

"Hell," Parsons said. "Why's that such a big deal? Had we not been so outnumbered by Quarakai, we would've slaughtered them ourselves."

"It's a big deal because it shows what we're up against is just as nasty, if not more so, than we are. I'm not deserting the evil I know only to propagate the one I don't. The two of you need to put some thought into this. We're up against an alien menace here, something that could very well wipe us out. All of us."

Parsons shrugged. "Maybe that's not their intention. Maybe they're just defending their homeland."

I sighed. "Have either of you ever studied the history of ancient earth?"

Both Parsons and Xi nodded.

"Do you remember what happened every time a technologically advanced civilization encountered a more primitive one?"

I took their silence to mean they had either forgotten their lessons or did not want to say what happened out loud. I had to answer for them. "The weaker side was vanquished. Slaughtered. Sold into slavery. Some of them were completely exterminated. Taking into account what little alien armament I've been exposed to so far, I'm under no illusions about what side of that technological divide we're currently sitting on."

Reaching for the bottle of brandy, I said, "I know the aliens, the Morghul, are here, but I don't think they're on Kanaris in force yet. If they were, they'd have already destroyed us. If we don't get this thing put down in time to prepare to take on significant numbers of these bastards...."

I paused to take a drink of liquor.

"...then this will probably be the beginning of the end for the human race."

Chapter 10

VAYIPAR

Despite all my misgivings about the League and the Space Corps, I got a lump in my throat when the Sitaara Raptor Assault Ship touched down on the landing pad at Camp Vayipar to unload my Marines. In the academy, I was conditioned to view each and every one of them as little more than tools to be utilized to complete my mission. It would not matter if I led them all to their deaths; as long as I achieved my objective, my endeavors would be considered a success.

Once I realized that Space Corps missions were designed to protect nothing more than Samaari affluence, I began to see my troops differently. They were human beings. Each had a story, people somewhere they loved, and folks who loved them back. Those Marines were not objects; they were a responsibility. *My* responsibility. The anxiety I had about whether my subordinates would let me down was replaced by the abject terror that it would be *I* who failed *them*.

I waited for my warriors at the head of the Third Platoon marshaling area in what passed as Camp Vayipar's parade ground. Located a few hundred kilometers due east of Narman's Pyke, Vayipar was little more than a clearing in the rainforest where Marines were taught to operate, navigate, and survive in the Kanarisian rainforest. In addition to reinforcing skill sets critical to reconnaissance craft and intelligence gathering, the facility was where we would familiarize our troops with situations unique to Kanaris.

For Marines fresh off the mothership with no idea of what to expect on such an unforgiving planet, Vayipar was a terrifying place. For those of us that hiked hundreds of kilometers from the wreckage of *Wasp-Three* to Narman's Pyke, it was even more so. The fact that we were wiser and more experienced was little consolation. The only thing that could make us feel reasonably safe and secure would be the concrete walls of Narman's Pyke. Vayipar did not even have a fence.

What it did have was a group of Killbillies patrolling the perimeter. Adopting a trick from our Narman adversaries, they slaughtered a horde of ubati, fearsome four-legged beasts with tusks as long as my forearm, and harvested the pups. It was not that ubati juveniles were particularly dangerous. It was that they had an unrelenting stench that made Kanarisian predators think twice about getting too close to us. That left me wondering what I could use to convince the Qilkorian contingent to keep their distance as well.

Once the battalion had marched from the transports and formed up by companies, Lieutenant Colonel Arva Baakarad marched out into the rain to address them. Like the last battalion commander I served under, Baakarad was a Samaari, but that is where all similarities ended to my previous CO. Unlike Captain Briggund, Baakarad was motivated, capable, resourceful, and universally respected. The medals on her chest, as well as a scar that ran from the corner of her mouth to her left ear lobe, advertised her active participation in multiple high-intensity combat operations. Her courage was above reproach, as were her abilities.

Unlike most Samaaris, Baakarad did not seem to mind the unrelenting Kanarisian rain. Nor did she care about the mud. Nor fear the creatures lying in wait to ambush her in the bush. If she was uncomfortable with anything, it was public speaking. Her speech to the newly reformed Recon Battalion was short and sweet. In less than three minutes, she conveyed to her troops that they would not look back at their time at Vayipar with fond memories. She assured them she was going to take a personal interest in seeing them suffer and promised that she would be right beside them for their entire three-month stay, sharing in their misery. Baakarad made it clear that the intent of their training was education, not sadism, but they would all be hard-pressed to tell the difference.

After Baakarad turned the troops over to their company commanders, Captain Pustov gave his people a rundown of what could be expected at Vayipar. They were going to start with two weeks of twenty-hour days filled with continuous physical conditioning.

"It's never going to get easier, Marines!" he told us. "This program was designed so that every day is twice as hard as the previous one. You thought Recon School was tough? Wait until you see what Vayipar has in store for you!"

After the fitness portion of their training had been completed, the physical regimen would be reduced to four hours daily, with ten hours of classroom training filling up the void. The second month would be consumed by continuous Long Range Reconnaissance Patrols designed not to find the enemy, but to familiarize our troops with Kanarisian flora and fauna. It was here where they would teach my Marines how to live off the land and keep the local wildlife from living off of them.

"The final month," Pustov told us. "Will be spent on tactical methods optimized for success in this environment. Stealth. Camouflage. Tenacity. Marines, let me tell you something. There is no graduation to this orientation course. There's no final exam. No crucible to endure to prove you're worthy of being a recon Marine in this hell hole. The only way to fail this course is to get yourself killed while participating in it. This evolution is strictly to give you all the tools and information available so you can survive your tour here. That's it. You'll get out of it what you put into it. If you want to glide through this shit and half-ass it, you can probably get away with it. All of us, including me, will be too damned tired to give a shit."

Pustov paused to point at the nearest tree line, barely visible through the torrential rain. "As bad as it's going to get here, it ain't nothing like what you'll experience once we reach the Satapadaya Front. And that's where we're all headed after finishing this course. So pay attention, Marines! You better hang on every word your instructors tell you as if your life depends upon it."

Turning so that all of his troops could see the seriousness on his face, our company commander punctuated his speech with, "Because let me assure you, it does."

Once Pustov finished his remarks and turned control of the Marines over to their platoon leaders, I leaned toward Gunny Brumit and said, "Have them remove their helmets. I want to see their faces."

"THIRD PLATOON!" Brumit screamed. "UNCOVERRRRRRRRRR...TO!"

In unison, seventy-six Marines unsnapped the airtight seals that kept their helmets secured to their neck plates and removed their headgear with their left hand. They then lifted their covers off their heads and tucked them beneath their right arms in one fluid motion. It was well executed and reassured me that Brumit had picked our platoon well.

"Third Platoon!" I shouted at my troops. "I know most of you have never met me! I am Second Lieutenant Eamon Tauk, your new platoon leader! And just to get it out of the way, yes, I am the man who killed Gori Dravidas!"

Turning to the four people gathered behind me, I introduced my staff. "You already know Gunny Brumit. In fact, it is my understanding that you all probably know her better than I do. This woman comes to us with unparalleled expertise, so if she says something, you better listen to every goddamned word she says! I know I will!"

Turning to the mocha-skinned woman at the far left of the line at my rear, I shouted, "This is Sergeant Hariana Espiya! She's a veteran of Sivma-11, which is quite impressive considering how few survivors emerged from that battle. Sergeant Espiya is our Battlefield Intel specialist, the Marine that'll be keeping tabs on enemy activity in our immediate sector. If you see anything amiss, that's the woman you notify! Understood?"

"AYE AYE, SIR!" the platoon shouted. They seemed motivated. I liked that.

Next to Espiya stood our TWS. "Staff Sergeant Dmitri Naktada is our Technical Warfare Specialist! He's also the reason we're all here! Had he not spent weeks in the wreckage of *Wasp-Three* trying to piece together the drop ship's video feed, our landing ships would've been blown out of the sky the moment they breached the atmosphere! He's the best of the best, Marines! You're to treat him accordingly!"

"AYE AYE, SIR!"

The following person in line was our senior medic, a tall woman with dark skin and piercing green eyes from the Dipryal System. "Sergeant Terivenda Sotalain is in charge of our corpsmen. She's already done a rotation along the Satapadaya Front and was awarded the Corps Cross for the uncommon courage she displayed under fire there! That was her third award! Military etiquette demands that she salutes me, but rest assured that if salutes were based upon merit and accomplishments instead of rank, it would be me saluting her!"

A racket rose out of my platoon as my troops began beating upon their breastplates to show their appreciation. Applause was impossible for a Marine holding a helmet in their hands.

Finally, I stepped up to a short young woman with a pale complexion, jet-black hair, and lashes so thick it looked like there were rings around her eyes. "This is my praetorian," I told the troops. I expected someone to laugh at the fact that I had chosen someone so small as my bodyguard, but everyone standing before me knew her. "Nila Chisek hails from Praminat, a system home to one of the most deadly martial arts known to the explored galaxy."

And one that she has already begun to train Ritza Xi in.

"Lance Corporal Chisek may look dainty and fragile, but let me assure you that I doubt there is a grunt in the battalion who could take her. She has also been the reigning marksman of 3rd Brigade for four years running. In addition to that, Chisek beat me three out of four times in a quick draw competition we held in the command tent before you all arrived. She's a badass. Marines, if Lance Corporal Chisek tells you something, you can safely assume that it is coming from me and act accordingly. Is that clear?"

"YES, SIR!"

I acknowledged my troops' enthusiasm with a single nod. "I would like to take this opportunity to let you know I do things differently than most platoons, especially regarding our convict laborers! To my squad leaders, yes, you are authorized by the Space Corps to execute any Class Zero convict that is unable, or unwilling, to carry out their duties. In my platoon, however, you have to obtain my permission first! Understood?"

"Yes, sir!" shouted my four rifle squad sergeants.

"For the men of this outfit!" I continued. "We have three Class Zero females among us! You're to keep your hands off of them! If I catch you trying to molest one, I will ensure that you're charged with felony sexual misconduct so you end up a Zero yourself! Then I'll pull every string I can to send your sorry ass to one of the comfort houses to see how you like it. Understood?"

"YES, SIR!" shouted my platoon's male Marines.

"Good! In this platoon, our convicts are Marines! No, they will not fight! But they will march and train right alongside us, even here at Camp Vayipar!"

I cupped my hands around my mouth to project my voice to the prisoners in the back of the formation. "To my convicts! This is your opportunity to be treated human again! With dignity and respect! Do NOT abuse it! Serving under my command earns you a little leeway, but any misbehavior from you will be met with harsh discipline and an immediate transfer to another unit where you can be abused at will! Am I clear?"

"Yes, sir!" the prisoners shouted back.

"Good!" I took a moment to choose my next words with care. "Marines, it is my understanding that when we get to the front, we will not be used in a reconnaissance function! Some in our chain of command consider us elite troops and think we could best serve the effort in a direct assault upon the enemy!"

No one said anything, nor did anyone move. Still, I could feel the energy get sapped right out of my platoon by the realization they were going to be wasted as cannon fodder. "You can rest assured that I'm going to do everything in my power to convince Division Staff that our capabilities are better served collecting intel. DO NOT count on my powers of persuasion, though! Your results will speak volumes more than my words ever will! As we go through this evolution, I need you to focus on how we can apply this to our skill set and collect the type of data we need to break the stalemate out there! You got that?"

"AYE AYE, SIR!"

"Great! That's all I have for now! Squad leaders! Collect your Marines and get them and their gear to their quarters! Chow is at eighteen hundred hours, and reveille will commence at oh three hundred! This is the most sleep you're going to get for the next three months, people! Enjoy every bit of it that you can! DISMISSED!"

As the sergeants took control of their squads, Gunny Brumit walked up beside me. "What do you think?"

"About our Marines?" I asked, lifting an eyebrow. "They seem like a highly motivated group of killers. Well done, Gunny."

"Any questions, sir?"

I nodded. "Yeah. We got Killbillies patrolling the camps perimeter. Do you think we have to worry about them?"

Brumit sighed. "Probably. Lumuk stands out like a sore thumb out there. The second tallest man in the platoon doesn't even come up to that son-of-a-bitch's collarbones."

I saw that, too. "Normally, I'd tell Lumuk to keep a low profile, but that's physically impossible for a man his size."

Brumit agreed. "It certainly is."

"You got any suggestions on how to handle this?"

My platoon sergeant grinned. "I always got ideas, sir. I suggest we pay the Qilkorians a little visit. You know, set the tone and make sure we ain't got no misunderstandings."

Satisfied we were on the same page, I slapped Brumit on the shoulder. "I agree. Find out where they're at and we'll sneak in and...."

"Sir," Gunny interrupted. "We aren't sneaking up on Killbillies. They're really good at detecting shit like that. They'll make us out in nothing flat. We have to walk in like we don't have a care in the world."

"We're Recon, Shai. You don't think we could get to them unnoticed?"

"Sir, I'm not usually one to root against the home team, but what those people can do defies comprehension. It can't be taught. It comes from being raised on a world where humans die if they can't detect something prowling up on them. After several generations of not quite being at the top of the food chain, they've developed senses that even they struggle to describe. Yeah, they're poorly educated and ignorant, but they've carved out a niche in this galaxy, and they fit into it really well. If we want to talk to the Killbillies, sir, we gotta stroll into their domain loud and proud."

Gunny Brumit turned away from me and spit into the mud. "We also gotta hope they're sober enough to care about the consequences of taking a shot at a Marine officer."

Chapter 11

CUPID

The Qilkorian sentries lived in a compound just beyond the tree line on the southeast edge of the camp. Since it was located in the brush, their quarters could not be seen from Camp Vayipar's facilities, though one could easily hear it. Their outpost sounded like some sort of farm or zoo, filled with all the noises we could typically hear in the Kanarisian rainforest, but concentrated within a tiny parcel of land. From about a hundred meters out, we could smell it.

Not wanting to be seen as a threat, neither Gunny Brumit nor I were dressed in battle gear. We were both carrying weapons, as camp protocol required us to be able to defend ourselves at all times, but both of us opted to wear fatigues instead of armor. That meant we had no helmet to filter out the odor.

Suppressing a gag, I turned to Brumit and gasped, "What the hell is that smell?"

Before Gunny could answer, a voice coming out of the darkness behind us said, "That'd be the ubatis, boss."

Brumit was right. There was no creeping up on a Killbilly, but they appeared able to sneak up on us at will. Startled, my platoon sergeant spun around and asked, "What?"

The man who spoke to us was big, bald, and brawny, carrying a Gatling rig that could spit out more firepower than an entire Marine rifle squad equipped with M72s. "Ubatis. That smell. It's the ubatis. They ain't but runts compared to the big 'uns, but they pack all o' the stink. You fellers lost or sumthin'?"

"No," I told the bruin.

"You out fer a stroll? In this place? Look, yers shouldn't be out here. We's patrollin' and the ubati stink be keepin' a lot of the nasty critters aways, but sometimes shit still be sneakin' through. Yers ain't even got your helmets on with your night eyes. How you gonna see shit in the dark?"

"Actually, we're looking to talk to you guys. You wouldn't be in charge of perimeter security, would you?"

"Naw," the big man said. "But I can take you to 'im. Foller me."

As the big man led us into the rainforest, Brumit told him, "That's some serious hardware you're carrying. I've never seen anything like it. Where'd you find something like that?"

The Killbilly grinned with pride. "Took this off a wrecked hover pod we found junked on Terrakand. Made this here rig myself. At first, it was just a fun gun, but this here beauty works wonders on them anwar things."

Looking over the sentry's rig once more, I imagined it would have. I thought it would be the perfect weapon for Akkam Lumuk. Something that powerful could make up for his military shortcomings. "You mind if I have one of my guys look at that thing? I think it could be a game changer on the Satapadaya Front."

"Yep. Sure could be if yers got someone big enough to control it."

"Yeah," Gunny Brumit said. "We certainly got one of those." I could see my platoon sergeant was thinking the same thing I was.

Once we crossed the tree line, we were confronted with a corral filled with small snaggle-toothed creatures. None were more than calf high, while the smallest stood just above my ankles. They were covered in light brown boney plates that the beasts wore like armor. A couple of the smaller ones, unsure yet of what to make of the humans that held them captive, curled into a ball as we approached, shielding their softer underbellies. "I take it those are the ubatis?" I asked our guide. I could tell by the odor.

"Uh-huh," the Killbilly answered. "They's some pretty int'restin' critters. They's some of the meanest things on Kanaris, but they's social animals, so they bond right quick with the first things they sees when they hatch."

"Hatch?" Gunny asked. "Like from eggs?"

"Uh-huh."

"So they're reptiles?" I asked.

The Qilkorian shrugged. "I dunno. They don't look like reptiles, but they is cold-blooded. They don't act like no reptiles, either. They's pretty smart and train real easy. They also like to play as pups and is real affectionate."

Brumit chuckled. "They sound like dogs."

"Ain't never had no dogs on Qilkoraan, so I ain't spend much time around 'em. Some lady from an REE planet told me these things act more like pigs, though." REE was the acronym for a Replicant Earth Environment. That meant the planet was terraformed to produce a biological facsimile of the rock that originally spawned humanity. Or, at least, as it was before our ancestors killed it.

Kanaris was considered a NEE world. Near Earth Environment. So was the planet from which our escort hailed. "We ain't had no pigs on Qilkoraan, either," he told us. "So I can't really tell yers for sure."

Most permanent buildings on Kanaris were circular, domed, and constructed of concrete. The Qilkorian shelter at Camp Vayipar was square and made of wood. It had electrical power, but other than that, the structure was relatively primitive. And crowded. When we walked inside, we were met by a dozen people gathered around a central hearth, dishing up their evening meal. Though our escort seemed nice enough, the others did not appreciate our intrusion. Excepting the Samaaris, Killbillies proved naturally distrustful of outsiders.

When we entered their abode, no one greeted us. Instead, they stared as if waiting for whatever excuse we had for invading their haven. "Do any of you know who I am?" I asked.

The cook dishing out the gruel shrugged his shoulders. "Should we?"

"Well, considering one of your people put a hit out on one of my Marines...."

"The Mawk of the Tuuk?" asked a man seated in a dark corner near the back of the shelter. He had a speech impediment that made his "Rs" sound like "Ws."

I nodded. "Yeah, that one."

Setting his food down, the Qilkorian in the back stood up to face us. "We ain't put no mawk on no one. That's voodoo shit. Fwom the squads."

"I thought all of you Killbillies were death squad people," Brumit said, managing to offend the entire room in one stroke.

With a long sigh, the man stood up and walked into the light. He had thick black hair he kept cropped close to his head. The sleeves of his coveralls were rolled up past his elbows, revealing forearms full of tattoos. Unlike his cohorts, he had a mouth full of pearly white teeth that looked well cared for. "Weally? The two of you awe gonna walk into ouw home and insult us without even intwoducing you'selves?"

I nodded. The man had a point. "I'm Lieutenant...."

"I don't give a fuck who you awe. Get out."

"Okay," I told him. "Just let me make sure we're clear. If you seriously have no intention of causing harm to any of my Marines, we'll get along just fine. If any of you decide to kill my guy to satisfy your honor vendetta, though, rest assured that we'll kill ten of you for every one of us you get."

The group's spokesman scoffed. "You'll twy."

Brumit did not like being challenged. "I've got eighty killers that...." Gunny was interrupted by the sound of the man who led us there chambering a round into his Gatling rig, threatening to rip us to shreds on full auto.

"Easy, Klyde," the leader told him. "Ain't no weason fo' anyone to get huwt." The Qilkorian chief walked over to the wall and took an automatic rail gun from the rack. "These Mawines awe just leavin'. I'll walk 'em back to wheyeva' they belong."

"We can find our way back," I told him.

The chief shook his head. "While you' in Camp Vayipaw, you' safety's my wesponsibility. Whethah you walk with me o' not's you's choice, but I ain't getting blamed fo' eithah of you getting huwt on the way back to you' tent. Now, get moving."

Neither Gunny Brumit nor I appreciated being ordered around by a civilian. Still, we were outgunned by the Gatling rig alone, not to mention the other weapons the Killbillies had at their disposal. After scowling at the crew one last time to ensure they knew I meant business, I turned on my heel and marched out the door.

When we were at the far end of the ubati corral, safely out of earshot of the rest of the Qilkorian contingent, our escort stopped us. "Hey!" he called out to me. "Hold on a minute. Just so you know, not all o' us awe killahs, Lieutenant. We also don't like being called 'Killbillies.' You unde'stand that?"

Spinning around to face the Qilkorian, I asked, "So you ain't bound by this Tuuk shit?"

"We's Wansairs," he answered. Realizing the limitations of his speech impediment, he added. "Spelled with an 'awe.'"

"An 'R?'" I asked, trying to clarify. "Ransairs?"

The Qilkorian nodded. "Yeah. We animal people. We tame 'em. O' hunt 'em. We' not intewested in hu'ting you o' you Mawines. That don't mean we gonna let you hu't us eithah. You get that? I unduhstand you coming heya to pwotect you's Mawines, but you need to unde'stand that I'm going to pwotect my men just as much as you pwotect you's. If you come to my house and thweaten my people again, we gonna have BIG pwoblems. Okay? You have issues with my people, you come to me and we'll settle it. You appwoach anyone else, and I pwomise that you' gonna get hu't. We good on that point?"

I nodded, understanding the man's position. Holding out my hand, I looked the Qilkorian chief in the eye and apologetically said, "If you're genuinely on your best behavior, then I may have been a bit heavy-handed. My apologies. I'm Lieutenant Tauk."

At first, the chief eyed me with suspicion, but eventually he took my mitt and shook it. "Bufo't Gwaym." After saying his name, he took the time to spell it for us. Bufort Graym. "Evewyone heya calls me Buffy, though. It's a bitch not being able to pwonounce you's own name cowwectly."

Graym's admission cracked both Gunny and me up, significantly lightening the mood. Hoping to capitalize on the decreased tension, I nodded toward the ubatis in the corral. "So these things are the keys to keeping us all safe on this planet, eh?"

Buffy nodded. "Yep. They get pwetty big, pwetty fast. They twavel in packs that sometimes have hundweds of animals. I think these things awe why the Quawakai live up in the canopy and not on the gwound. They can smell them vewy easy, and they keep they's distance."

"You know," I told Buffy. "I hiked to Narman's Pyke from the ocean. I'm surprised we never came across any of these things."

"You su'vived the w'eck of *Wasp-Thwee*?" After I nodded, Graym let out a low whistle. "You was walkin' mainly in the Hot Zone then. I don't think ubatis like the heat much. They pwefuh a mild climate. The animals between the heat layuhs may be similuh, but they evolved diffewently to su'vive in the cooluh climate. At this elevation, they awe still anwah and sowoquids, but the ones heya have twouble living in the awea below us."

After a particularly pungent waft of air drifted past Gunny Brumit's nose, she grimaced and asked, "How the hell can those things hunt while smelling that bad?"

"They can tu'n they stink off. When they huntin', they all quiet and oduh fwee. Nothing evah sees them coming."

Brumit looked almost ready to gag again. "How do you guys deal with this stench?"

Buffy pointed at his schnoz. If you stand out heya fo' a few minutes, you go nose-blind. Aftuh a while, you don't even notice it any mo'.'"

Something caught the Qilkorian's eye, and he walked over to a crate full of large eggs. Picking one up, he tossed it to me. "Catch!"

Laughing as I leapt to grab the egg before it hit the ground, Buffy said, "That one's getting weady to hatch." Reaching down, the Qilkorian picked up a kryptid, snapped its head off, and pitched it to Gunny. "Can you pop that one fo' me?"

Over the next ten minutes, we watched an ubati pup gnaw its way out of its shell until it ruptured and spilled a thick, yolk-like liquid all over my hand. It then opened its eyes and chirped in a voice almost too high-pitched to be registered with human ears. Buffy ripped off a piece of cooked kryptid flesh and passed it to me so I could drop it into the animal's mouth. As the ubati devoured its first meal, the Qilkorian said, "That one's you's, now."

"What?" I gasped. "I don't want one of these things!"

"Doesn't mattuh," Buffy told me. "You couldn't get wid of that thing now even if you wanted to. It's gonna follow you all ovuh the place. All you offisuhs awe going to get one of these. Evewyone fwom the wank of captain to co'powal."

"How are we supposed to take care of them?" I asked.

Buffy shrugged. "Fo' the fust few weeks, they just lay in a box waiting to be fed once a day. Kwyptids awe fine. Aftuh that, they go out and hunt on they own."

Brumit shook her head in disgust. "What if we don't want one?"

"You wathuh stay awake at night and wonduh if a giant centipede gonna come out of the dahk and dwag you' ass scweaming back to its nest?"

When Gunny did not answer, Buffy grinned and said, "I didn't think so. C'mon. It's late. Let's get you and you's new pet back home."

Once we were back at our camp, I found a crate in my tent that looked explicitly built for an ubati pup. As I was laying the animal inside it with what was left of the popped kryptid, Gunny Brumit asked, "You going to name it?"

I shrugged. "You think I should?"

"I don't know how you'll train it to come to you if it doesn't have a name."

I looked at the creature and wondered what moniker it should go by. I had never owned a pet before. "I don't know, Gunny. What do you call a thing that ugly?"

Brumit shrugged. "What did you call your mother?"

I cast a side-eye glare at my platoon sergeant. She blushed, having forgotten that as an academy Marine, I never had a mother. "No, seriously, what would be a good name for this thing?"

Gunny cocked her head to the side as she took in the little beast in all its heinous glory. She then shrugged.

"Cupid?"

Chapter 12

THE SUCK

Had I landed in Camp Vayipar eight months earlier, the first two weeks of conditioning would have been a breeze. After six months of recuperation and a few weeks of building my platoon, however, I had gotten soft. I was still leading my Marines in our evolutions, but it was killing me to keep up.

Every day started three hours before dawn. We were awakened by automatic gunfire and formed up to exercise until the sun rose. Sprints. Mountain Climbers. Squats. Thrusts. Push-ups. Crunches. Planks. All of it was done without armor and in the rain for maximum discomfort.

We were allowed a half hour for breakfast, which was a third of a ration. Once our morning meal was complete, we were ordered to stand at attention in the rain to wash the mud off. After the instructors deemed us clean enough, we were to suit up in full armor, grab our weapons, and proceed to what we called the "muck ruck." That was a stretch of calf-deep muddy earth nearly two kilometers long that we had to run across, then crawl back through.

Lunch was a half ration that we were given no more than fifteen minutes to eat. After that, we were marched off into the rainforest to hike fifteen kilometers out, then fifteen kilometers back. Finally, we were treated to one more muck ruck before dinner.

Our troops were allowed a complete ration for their evening meal, then given one hour to clean and square away their equipment. After our gear was returned to an acceptable state of readiness, it was stored in each warrior's tent. The Marines themselves slept outside in the rain, covered only by a poncho. Our class was luckier than most, as we were blessed with four entire nights of zero precipitation during that initial stretch of training.

I had slept rough for a couple of months during the march to take Narman's Pyke, so I had little trouble resting through the rain. What I was not used to was having an infant ubati snuggling next to me every time I returned home. I assumed that the Killbillies made passes through the camp on a daily basis to feed our pups while we were out in the field. It was the only way I could explain how Cupid nearly doubled in size over the first fourteen days I had her.

Our first day of practical instruction began with a feast. Each platoon was paraded past a succession of tables piled high with edible items pulled from the forest around us. Standing on the other side of them was the Qilkorian cook I had seen manning the hearth when Brumit and I invaded their lodge. "My name is Hirshel Coopa," he told us. "I been on this planet 'bout six months trying to figure out what we can eat around here and what we best leave alone."

Coopa waddled over to a table filled with hundreds of small melons. "Today, I encourage yers to walk through and sample whatever ya see up front here. Get a taste for what ya like and what ya don't. Starting tomorrow, we gonna be takin' yers out in the field and showin' ya how to find these things and safely harvest them."

The cook picked up a black fruit accentuated with orange stripes. "Take this here. This's one of the tastiest things I ever sink my teeth in, but ya can't just go in and grab one. It grows in a thorny bush that'll sting ya if yers ain't bein' careful. One sting hurts like hellfire and burns just as hot twenty hours after it hit ya as it did during the first twenty seconds. If ya get hit with five of those thorns at once, which ain't hard to do, yers is gonna be losin' your mind for a couple o' day. You're gonna be feverish, hallucinatin,' shittin' yourself, and pukin' all over the place. Ten thorns gonna leave ya in a state of paralysis for 'bout a week. Fifteen's gonna make ya nothin' but a memory."

The Qilkorian picked up another item that looked like a blue pear covered with green spikes. "This one here looks even worse than the last thing I showed ya, but it's harmless. The blades aren't meant to keep animals from eatin' it, but to help it hitch a ride to another locale. Use yers gloves for sure, but you can break it in half pretty easy. The insides have a citrus flavor and are full of vitamins."

"Do any of these things have protein in them?" asked Dina Tiago, the sergeant in charge of my second rifle squad.

"Not much," Coopa answered. "Kanaris is crawling with kryptids, though. They's loaded with protein and all kinds of other nutrients."

Tiago grimaced. "I don't like eating bugs."

The Killbilly chuckled. "I don't reckon that the bugs like being eaten, either. But we do what we can to survive."

"Aren't there animals out there we can hunt?"

Coopa nodded. "There's plenty of game around. Kanaris is full of life. There's critters around everywhere you look. We've tried huntin' a bunch of 'em, but truth be told, it ain't worth the effort. The creatures here gots thick hides and dense bone protectin' they's vital organs. Takes a lot o' ammo to bring 'em down, and even then, they's ain't tastin' half as good as no kryptid. Nor is they any more nutritious.

"Speakin' of kryptids, yers know they come in different shades, right? Is there any color out there you shouldn't be eatin'?'"

Akkam Lumuk raised his hand. After Coopa called on him, my giant said, "The green ones?"

The Killbilly cook nodded in agreement. "That's right! You should never eat the green ones. Yers know why?"

Lumuk nodded but bashfully looked at his comrades like he was too embarrassed to shout out the answer. As if it were a secret, Lumuk whispered, "They give you the shits."

My platoon might have chuckled at Lumuk's answer, but Coopa laughed out loud. "That's right. Green kryptids are nature's laxatives. If yers is feeling all backed up, eat yourselves one of those green babies. You better clear your schedule for a couple o' days first, though. One of those things cost me three pairs of coveralls when I first got here. Didn't even try to clean 'em. All I could do was chuck 'em in the fire!"

This brought out another round of laughter from my troops, during which Coopa looked Lumuk up and down. "You's a big one, ain't ya?" the Qilkorian asked after it got quiet again. "You must be Akkam Lumuk."

"Uh-huh," our giant said as Gunny Brumit and I exchanged suspicious nods. A second or two after that, I heard my platoon sergeant's voice come over the commlink and warn, "Don't eat anything that man tries to feed you, Lumuk. You understand that?"

I got up early the following morning to hike over to the Qilkorian camp before the day got started. Cupid was on my heels, snorting and squealing in exuberance. It was as if she knew I was paying a visit to the people that feed her. Before I reached the tree line, I spotted the entire Killbilly contingent on their knees, chanting in the direction of the rising sun. Curious about what was going on, I stopped and stared at them. "What the...?"

"I wouldn't go fu'thuh than that," said a voice from the darkness behind me. The speech impediment told me it was Buffy Graym. "They at pwayuh."

"Prayer?" I asked. "That's what that is?"

"Uh-huh," Buffy answered.

Among the developed worlds, religion was a rarity. It was considered a sort of collective madness and was the providence of primitive peoples that had no access to modern education. I myself found the concept absurd, and from what Gunny Brumit had told me about Qilkorian dogma, their beliefs were far more bizarre than most. "Do you really worship the Samaaris?" I asked the foreman.

"No," Buffy sighed. "We wo'ship ou' gods. You know, about fifty yea's ago, the League came to Qilkowan. They think we's pwetty backwa'd so they fo'ce us fwom ou' homes and into schools. They twy to ewase ou' twaditions, ou' cultu'e, and ou' whole way of life. They twied to mold us into them, which was something we ain't wanna be."

Spitting onto the ground, Buffy then told me, "So we pwayed to ou' gods to send us help. To save us fwom being wiped out by the League. Ou' gods answe'ed ou' pwayuhs by sending us the Samaawis. They pulled the League off Qilkowan and wetuhned ou' people to us."

I found it interesting that the Samaaris abandoned Qilkoraan. The planet must have been almost entirely devoid of natural resources for the Guilds to ignore it.

Buffy pointed his chin at all the men kneeling in the mud. "They's not wo'shipping the Samaawis, Lieutenant. They's thanking the gods fo' sending them to save us."

"Why aren't you praying with them?" I asked.

The Qilkorian shrugged. "The Samaawis might have saved us once, Lieutenant, but they been cowwupting us evuh since. Befo'e the League came, we was a peaceful people living peaceful lives with a peaceful weligion on a peaceful planet. The League wobbed us of that, which made us angwy. Qilkowians awe not vewy sophisticated, so the Samaawis we'e able to take advantage of ou' faith in them. They manipulated ou' gwatitude and tu'ned some of us into killuhs."

"So you left your religion?"

"No," Buffy said. "My weligion left me. The pweists tell us we supposed to do what the Samaawis want because they awe the gods' chosen people. The Samaawis don't even believe in gods. And what they want us to do ain't vewy god-like."

"So I've heard," I told the Qilkorian. "You know, Buffy, one of your men took an interest in that guy of mine that got the mark put on him. He knew my Marine's name."

Buffy Graym shrugged. "So do I. We all do. The contwact's been distwibuted all ovuh ou' netwo'ks. Howevah, you' battalion commanduh, Colonel Baakawaad, she commanded us to dwop the contwact. She's a Samaawi, so huh autho'ity is highuh than some stupid Killbilly like Woostuh Mikkaine."

"I thought you guys didn't like that word."

"Fo' some of us, they's no bettuh descwiption."

"So, my man's safe now?" I asked Buffy.

The Qilkorian foreman pointed at the men chanting in the mud. "Fwom them? You ain't got anything to wowwy about fwom my men, Lieutenant. The guys in the squads, though? That's a diffewent stowy. They twy to make killing you' man about weligion, but it's weally about saving face. Akkam Lumuk made them look widiculous. They need to kill him so they can wegain they honah. Until they do, the othuh squads not gonna wespect them. They even gave Woostuh Mikkaine a nickname because Lumuk made him shit himself."

"A nickname?" I asked. "What're they calling him?"

"Puddin'."

I busted out laughing so hard that some of the Qilkorians paused their chanting to glower at me. I raised my hand and bowed my head in apology, still struggling to regain my composure. Only when all of their eyes were glaring at me did I finally become uncomfortable enough to force myself back under control.

Lowering my voice, I turned to Buffy and asked, "So, in other words, I need to kill Puddin' to keep my man safe?"

Buffy answered with a single nod. "That's what I'd do."

Chapter 13

Pedes

Humans had been inhabiting Kanaris for several decades by the time I landed there. During that short period, the planet's most dangerous predators were taught they were no match for our weaponry. They learned not to come within one hundred kilometers of Narman's Pyke. Those lacking the intelligence to accept that people were not prey ended up being exterminated. As a result, the immediate vicinity of the colony was safe enough for a single person to take a walk in the woods alone, though the command still prohibited it.

Camp Vayipar was far removed from the Pyke's safe zone, and during the sixth week of our training, we were on a Long Range Reconnaissance Patrol, a LRRP mission, that had us far removed from Camp Vayipar. We were so far into the bush that when night fell, we started seeing soroquids again.

The sergeant in charge of Fourth Squad, Jasirat Kal-Xati, was not on *Wasp-Three*, so she had never seen a soroquid before. She had her entire squad drop into the kneeling position and take aim at the creature menacing them from their front. "Lieutenant Tauk!" she shouted over the platoon network. "I've got a giant fucking centipede in front of us! The goddamned thing's gotta be three meters long!"

"Don't let it distract you," I told her. "Have your machine gunner draw a bead on it and aim for the head. There's going to be more sneaking up on you from behind. Have the rest of the squad do an about-face and...."

I was interrupted by a long burst of gunfire from my left, the area where First Platoon was supposed to be. It was followed by human screams and even more gunfire. Then I heard Kal-Xati's squad open up.

"Parsons!" I shouted into the commlink. "Grab your squad and form a line perpendicular to Kal-Xati's position to defend her left flank! Demangel!"

"Yes, sir!" my Third Squad leader yelled back.

"You're right flank! Mind your fire discipline! I don't want stray bullets hitting First Platoon! Sergeant Tiago!"

"I'm in motion!" My Third Squad leader called back. "We're covering Kal-Xati's rear!"

I grinned. *Of course, she is. Initiative and intuition. That woman's a badass.*

So was Gunny Brumit. Before I could say anything, she was already screaming orders to the platoon staff. "We're circling the wagons! Get in the center and make sure everybody's got what they need! Move it! Go! Go! Go! Go! Go!"

Within seconds, we had set our perimeter and decorated its boundaries with the carcasses of a dozen giant centipedes. When the firing stopped, I marched over and slapped Kal-Xati across the top of the helmet. "Those are soroquids!" I snapped at her. "We went over this! We told you how they hunt and how to react to them! You're out here acting like you've never even heard of them before!"

"I know! I'm sorry, sir! I just...I just...well, seeing them for real is a lot different than hearing people talk about them. The pictures don't do the fuckers justice!"

I took a moment to glare at the sergeant. *She took responsibility and offered no excuses. Good.*

I remembered the first time I had come face-to-face with a soroquid. I was probably more rattled than Kal-Xati was.

"You're right," I told her. "The pictures don't do the fuckers justice. Trust me, none of the pictures do. You can't let yourself be surprised by the shit out here. When you see a threat, you need to react to it and issue your squad the proper orders to mitigate it! You do that first and *then* get on the horn to tell me you got a giant three-meter-long centipede in front of you! Understood?"

"Yes, sir!" Kal-Xati told me. "It won't happen again!"

I know it won't. Kal-Xati's a damned good Marine. Even if she was startled, she still got her squad through it without any casualties.

The sound of gunfire was still coming from Lieutenant Peeli's position. I heard several people screaming for medics.

That's more than I could say for First Platoon.

After the firing had died down and the soroquids had retreated, the voice of Second Lieutenant Kita Nuzuri, the leader of Fourth Platoon, popped through my earpiece. "Tauk! Are you guys okay?"

"We're fine," I told her. "How about you?"

"Fourth Platoon is at one hundred percent. No casualties."

"Same here. You hear how Second Platoon made out?"

"They're good, too," Nuzuri said to me. "First Platoon got spanked."

"Yeah, I heard them. You get any word on a casualty count?"

"Yep. One dead. Four wounded."

I shook my head in disbelief. "That's ridiculous. We know how to deal with soroquids. When they attack in small groups, there's no excuse to suffer one casualty, let alone five."

"There was only one casualty to the soroquids. One of their riflemen strolled to the side to take a piss and practically stepped on one. It got him in the kidneys and pumped him full of venom. The medic said the shit practically liquified the poor bastard's insides."

"What about the other four?"

"Friendly fire. It looks like the 'pedes rushed First Platoon before they could set a perimeter, and some of Peeli's Marines got caught in the crossfire."

"You've got to be kidding me."

"Nope," Nuzuri assured me. "Pustov's *pissed*. He's chewing chunks off of Peeli's ass right now."

"I bet he is," I said. I was going to say more, but one of our Killbilly guides came running toward our perimeter. I stood up to yell at my Marines to hold their fire.

Buda Grein looked excited. "We got one!" he told me.

I shrugged and pointed at the carcasses ringing our perimeter. "Okay. We got a dozen."

"No, we got one alive!"

"You captured one?" I asked. "Why?"

Buda shook his head. "So we can take out its nest with the Doom Method! I need a few grenadiers and a breech mine!"

Wait! What? What the hell's the Doom Method?"

"We had a guy come through Camp Vayipar a couple of classes ago who survived the hike through the hot zone...."

A light bulb went off in my head. "Oh, shit! Not 'Doom!' You mean 'Duum!' Mazada Duum!"

Buda nodded. "Yeah, man! He was with a bunch o' yers that blew away a whole nest of them things when they got forced into the jungle by a flood! The 'pedes dragged some poor fucker down their burrow who had a breech mine in his pack. They set it off with a Spaz Rocket and wiped out damned near half of 'em!"

"What about the other half?"

Buda grinned mischievously. "Well, them Marines probably would've had an easier night if they'd waited for all the critters to turn in 'fore they sealed the entrance to their hole. As it was, your Marines ended up stuck outside with the bugs who couldn't get home. It's my understandin' Duum was the only one who survived that little miscalculation."

I remembered Duum rejoining the battalion after the flood. He came back to us completely empty-handed. No rifle, pistol, grenades, or even any of his cherished knives. There was not so much as a single bullet left in that man's arsenal. All he had left was a haunted look in his eyes.

"Yeah," Buda mused. "These things ain't much in small groups, but they get to be quite a handful when ya gotta deal with 'em by the hundreds. It's best we take 'em all out. When they's sleeping."

Giving Buda a nod, I said, "I tend to agree."

The big bald Killbilly with the Gatling rig I met on our first night at Camp Vayipar turned out to be the man credited with capturing the soroquid. According to the tale they told us, the 'pede ambushed him as he was walking point. The beast hit him at an awkward angle, and instead of sinking its fangs into its prey, it wrapped them around the Qilkorian's oversized weapon. Klyde managed to grab hold of the 'pede's massive mandibles and hold them apart while his partners rushed in to wrangle the creature into submission. It was an act of incredible skill and bravery. Because of it, I gained a newfound respect for Camp Vayipar's Killbillies.

The captive soroquid drew quite an audience. Every Marine not manning the defensive perimeter took turns watching our guides tie breech mines to its back. When the beast was ready to go, the Killbillies assembled the crowd close to its rear flank. "These things awe pwetty smaht," Buffy told us. "It knows it's weally outnumbe'ed, so it's gonna wun in the opposite diwection. And we gonna let it go."

"Who's going to follow it home?" asked Captain Pustov.

"They need a grenadier to blow the mines and a sapper to seal the entrance to the nest," I told the company's commander. "I was going to send my second squad with them." Sergeant Dina Tiago was standing beside me when I said that. I caught her puffing her chest out in pride when she heard me recommend her for the mission.

Pustov nodded. "So be it." Turning to the Qilkorian foreman, he asked, "Should we camp here for the night then?"

Buffy shook his head. "No, that'd put you too fa' behind to make the battalion wendezvous point. My guys know a sho'tcut. They'll catch up."

"Okay," Pustov said. "Have it your way." Dialing up the platoon leaders' network, he then ordered everybody to move on out.

As my second squad marched off with Klyde and Buda, Barone Parsons stepped beside me. "Are we good?" he asked.

I turned toward the sergeant in charge of First Squad and said, "You'd be the first to know if we weren't. What makes you ask me that?"

"I was just wondering why you didn't trust me enough to send First Squad after the soroquid nest."

I placed my hand on Parson's shoulder. "I trust you more than anyone else in this entire platoon. I need you close. Get used to it."

Chapter 14

The Ubati

We were on the tail end of our last LRRP when Grim Jitilin, one of the Qilko-rian guides, approached us on the back of a naypeto. We had crossed paths with a couple of naypeto herds during our patrols, but we never saw one so close. They were impressive creatures. The one Jitilin rode in on was almost three meters tall and bore long black fur saturated with green moss. It was an effective camouflage scheme.

Naypetos were bipedal, running about on two muscular hind legs. Their arms looked small in relation to their bodies, but they were still much longer and stronger than ours. The creature had razor-sharp claws that retracted behind its knuckles and a pair of tusks that protruded from its lower jaw. Despite all the sharp points on these animals, naypetos were not predators. They were scavengers. The weaponry was strictly for defense.

"Holy shit," I said to Jitilin as I approached his mount. "I heard the Narmans had domesticated these things, but I didn't know you guys had, too."

"We didn't domesticate this big ole' boy," the Qilkorian told me. "We captured 'im. I don't think it was the Narmans that figured out how to tame these things, either. Pulling the reigns to spin the massive beast around, Jitlin showed me the saddle, pointing to runes stamped onto the riding rig. "Them ain't no letters anybody ever seen before back at the command. We's thinkin' this's alien shit. The Morghuls. We're bettin' they's the one who figured out how to turn naypetos into ridin' animals."

The creature craned its long neck to get a better look at me. I noticed it had serpent eyes that looked positively evil. "How's its temperament?" I gulped.

Jitilin shrugged. "I'm still gettin' the hang of it, but he ain't given me all that much trouble yet. As far as I can tell, as long as you ain't aggressive with these big boys, they ain't gonna show much aggression toward you."

The naypeto reared up a little, showing us it was getting antsy. Jitilin stroked its neck to calm it down. "Trust me, sir, I could talk about my new pet all day, but this ain't the animal I'm here about. You know, we gave yers a bunch o' ubati pups so that yers could get used to them."

I nodded at the guide. "Yeah, I know. Oddly enough, I kind of miss mine now that I've been gone so long."

Jitilin grinned. "Yeah, I bet she misses you, too. Anyways, you and your Marines should be pretty familiar with ubatis when they're on your side. It's 'bout time we give you a taste o' what yers up against in case they ain't."

"Come again?" I had been around the Killbillies for several weeks but still found them difficult to understand.

"We gonna show ya why everything else in these woods here are afraid of them damned things. There's a corral five clicks due east of the Ransair compound at Vayipar. You can't miss the trail. Take your platoon up that path until you see me. Savvy?"

"Savvy."

As Jitilin rode off to the east, I turned to my Marines. "We got a little detour to go on...."

I was interrupted by the groaning of my troops. We had hiked nearly fifty kilometers that day, and they did not want to walk even a centimeter more.

"Hey!" Gunny Brumit screamed at our people. "Knock it off! We're Recon! When the lieutenant talks, you listen! You don't bitch! Just for that, after we see what the Killbillies want to show us, we're all going on a little muck ruck! What do you all think about that!"

"It sucks!" snarled PFC Slai Huurling under his breath. No one would have heard him, but his commlink was incorrectly set, and he accidentally broadcast it to the entire platoon.

"Except you, Huurling!" Brumit responded in kind. "You're going to ruck that fucking muck twice!"

A fully grown ubati was a terrifying sight. The Qilkorians had one trapped in a pit, a hole carefully measured to deny the animal the running start it needed to leap out. Even so, our guides should have dug deeper. The damned thing could still jump high enough to get the tip of its snout above ground level. It was carrying on like a demon possessed, shrieking and snarling at us, showing us that its singular obsession was to rip every one of us to bloody shreds. None of us doubted that, had it climbed out of that enclosure, that was precisely what it would have done. We could see it had little interest in retreat. All it wanted was murder.

"Come on in close," Buffy told us. "I want you to gathuh wound and take a good look at this beauty. He's a big one, ain't he?"

He sure was. If I were to stand in the pit next to the animal, I figured its shoulder would reach as high as my nipples. With the extra height added by its massive head, the beast could look me square in the eye without even raising its chin. The creature was not at all happy about being the center of our attention and let out several ear-splitting shrieks that sounded like a cross between an enraged pig and a dropship initiating a vertical take-off. Looking into its eyes, I could sense nothing but evil intentions. It was hard for me to fathom that this thing and Cupid were the same species.

Patting Buffy on the shoulder, Grim Jitilin took over speaking. Between the Qilkorian accent and the foreman's speech impediment, Jitilin was a little easier to understand. "As yers can see, this animal's covered in boney scales from its head to its ass." Jitilin pulled a government-issued M88 off his hip and fired it at the animal's back. The bullet cracked one of its protective plates, but the ubati barely acknowledged it. It did not even flinch.

Jitilin held his weapon up, showing it to us all. "Your pistol ain't worth shit to one of these things. It's a non-entity. It ain't gonna wound it, ain't gonna slow it down, and it ain't even gonna piss it off. A fully grown ubati ain't even gonna notice it unless you shove that barrel up one of its nostrils before you pull the trigger. You mays well be blowin' it kisses than tryin' to use one of these peashooters against a monster like this."

After dropping his sidearm back into his holster, Jitilin scanned the crowd until he laid eyes on Sergeant Tiago. By all accounts, she had performed with excellence while taking down the soroquid nest and had become something of a favorite among the Qilkorian contingent. "Dina, would you mind taking a shot at that thing with your M72?"

"No problem," Tiago said as she unslung her weapon, took aim, and fired a round off at the beast's midsection. One of the creature's scales shattered, but the bullet was deflected into the next plate, from which it ricocheted and buried itself into the side of the hole. The ubati flinched at the impact but did not seem much more irritated than it was before it got shot.

"Again," Jitilin ordered.

BLAM! The second bullet hit a few centimeters to the left of the first and had the same effect, which was not much at all.

"Again."

BLAM!

"Again."

BLAM! The animal squealed that time but seemed more irritated by the noise than from the discomfort of being shot.

"Again."

BLAM!

Jitilin had my sergeant fire three more times. After seven shots, the captive ubati seemed no worse for wear.

"Marines," the Qilkorian said. "If yers can shoot one of these things four times in the EXACT same spot, you can get through they's armor and break they's skin. Ubatis got theyselves some thick, dense muscle to get through that's gonna slow that bullet down quite a bit before it hits bone. Then it's gonna take you 'bout two or three more bullets to get through that."

Reaching his hand out to one of my riflemen, Private Salwati Wat, Jitilin asked, "You mind if I borrow that weapon for a second?"

After I nodded my approval, Wat untethered his M72 and handed it to the guide. Jitilin checked to ensure the weapon had a full magazine, then opened fire at the animal on full auto. Scales shattered into shards and dust while the ubati was sent into a manic frenzy, pinballing itself around the pit as it tried to seek shelter from the attack. When Jitilin exhausted his ammunition, though, the ubati was still standing. It was wounded and bleeding, but its injuries were largely superficial.

Handing the M72 back to Private Wat, Jitilin said, "Yers assault rifle might be good enough to distract an ubati and send it running for an easier victim, but that's 'bout all it's gonna do. Best not to even waste yers ammo."

Jitilin paused to scan the faces of the Marines surrounding the ubati pit. "Look at this animal," he told us. "He's heavier than yers. He's stronger. He's faster. He's meaner.

There's just two things this beast can't do. He can't climb, and he can't swim. If you got some of these in your area, yers best off pullin' yourself up a tree and takin' your chances with the Quarakai, or finding a lake to get yourselves neck deep in."

"Can anything stop them?" asked Arnaud Demangel, the leader of my third rifle squad.

"Yeah, I was just gettin' to that." Jitilin motioned to the lance corporal standing to Demangel's right, Idris Jatmika. She was one of my M2117 machine gunners. "Miss, would you mind loading explosive rounds into that there rig you're holding? When you're finished, put a twelve-round burst into our friend down there."

The ubati must have sensed what was coming. It became even more unhinged, wailing in fury and unfathomable hatred, frustrated that it was being denied the blood it craved.

After her assistant helped her change ammo cartridges, Jatmika did as she was asked. When the three-second barrage of machine gun fire ended, the ubati was on its side in the water at the bottom of the pit, missing a limb and its tail. It was shrieking in agony now instead of fury. I could even say it was weeping. In a weird sort of way, I felt sorry for it.

"An M2117 with explosive rounds is about the only thing you can use to stop one of these critters!" Jitilin informed us, yelling to be heard over the animal's cries. "Grenades don't even work unless the damned thing practically lies on top of one before it goes off!"

Turning toward Jatmika again, Jitilin nodded and said, "You can go ahead and finish it off."

"No! Wait!" I shouted before Jatmika could raise her weapon. Pulling the seibara Naktada had given me, I deployed the blade and jumped into the pit, reassured by the hum of invisible energy.

Leaping at the opportunity to exact revenge against the fiends tormenting it, the dying ubati rolled over and tried scooting itself toward me, snapping ferociously at my legs with the four rapier tusks protruding from its jaws. When it got close enough, I swung the seibara and hit the beast right between the eyes. Its head instantly erupted into a fountain of flame and sparks as the plasma blade effortlessly sliced through the animal's protective plates, bone, and flesh. The demon creature died in an instant, its skull cleaved neatly in two, exposing the beast's brain matter, still sizzling as if it had been served to me on a hot skillet.

I looked at Naktada's creation in disbelief, amazed by the efficiency of its killing power. It did in a split second what dozens of rounds could not.

With the ubati out of its misery, I retracted the seibara's blade, clipped the weapon back to my belt, and looked up at Staff Sergeant Naktada. "I need you to get on the horn to whatever buddies you have at Narman's Pyke and tell them that we need more of these seibara things."

As I looked up at the walls of the pit and wondered how I would get back topside, I added, "A lot more of them."

●●•◄►•●•◄►•●●

Chapter 15

SLAI

Aside from accidentally conveying his true feelings over the platoon network and earning himself an extra tour of the muck ruck, PFC Slai Huurling did not make mistakes often. When he did, however, he tended to compound them.

Throughout our acclimatization course at Camp Vayipar, Huurling had been among my platoon's top performers. He paid attention during the coursework and retained everything, often reinforcing the lessons to his comrades to keep them from hurting themselves in the bush. He displayed excellent attention to detail. I had heard Gunny Brumit remark several times that it was proving impossible to find things to gig the young man on during inspections. During team exercises, Huurling was one of the Marines Sergeant Kal-Xati depended upon to keep her squad performing better than all the others. During individual contests, such as cross-country runs, the PFC regularly finished in the platoon's top five.

Slai Huurling was one of the Marines I had my eye on. Even after his little outburst over the commlink, I had every intention of promoting him to Lance Corporal if a platoon billet opened up. When I formulated my succession plan, I had him on the short list of candidates to move into an assistant squad leader slot if one of my corporals became a casualty. But that was before Gunny Brumit broke him in the mud.

Like the rest of my troops, Huurling was exhausted when we returned from our final LRRP. He was looking forward to shedding his armor, getting a hot meal, and catching up on some desperately needed sleep. Then came the detour to learn about the ubati. Then the muck ruck with the platoon. Then the second muck ruck with the extra attention of my platoon sergeant. Gunny Brumit worked that man over hard. And long. By the time they returned, the chow line had been secured and most of the Marines were preparing to turn in for the night.

It had been weeks since Huurling had enjoyed a hot meal. It would likely be weeks before he would have a chance to enjoy another. Missing that one minor treat proved to be the straw that broke the camel's back. Robbed of the joy of fresh food, Huurling decided to seek his comfort from another source.

Though I had issued orders that my platoon's Zeros were not to be abused, they were still outcasts and slept in a collection of spartan tents on the edge of our camp. They participated in the same training my Marines did, but when our instructional evolutions were completed, they separated themselves from the regular troops. Huurling's tent was right next to the Zero bivouac and as he passed through it, the PFC caught sight of Margi Gul, a woman whose company he had often enjoyed at the Pyke's morale center. As he marched past her, Huurling grabbed Gul by the bicep. "Come on, Margi. You're coming with me."

Gul ripped her arm out of the Marine's grip. "What do you mean I'm coming with you? For what?"

Huurling glared at her as if that had been the stupidest question he had ever heard. Then he seized her again. "What do you think? We're going to do what we used to."

"The fuck we are," Gul scoffed as she struggled to free herself from Huurling's grasp. "The lieutenant said I didn't have to do that stuff anymore and...."

"You're not doing this because you have to," the young Marine snarled at her. "You're doing it because you want to."

"My ass!" Gul planted her feet in the mud and started pounding on the back of Hurrrling's hand to get him to let go. "I ain't doing shit with you!"

"Relax, it's not like we haven't done it before."

"And you think I enjoyed it?!?" The Zero was incredulous as she lashed out and punched Huurling in the jaw, making him release her. "I wouldn't have given you the time of day had those bastards not been holding a gun to my head!"

Livid, Huurling drew his sidearm and aimed it at the bridge of her nose. "That's what it's going to take? A gun to your head? I can do that."

"Go ahead," Gul snarled. "I fucking dare...."

Before Gul could finish her sentence, Ritza Xi had snuck up on Huurling from behind and, with moves my praetorian taught her, spun the man around and used her palm to push the Marine's right arm away from her. Simultaneously, her free hand grabbed the pistol and twisted it in the opposite direction. The weapon was instantly wrenched from the PFC's grip, except for Huurling's index finger, which got trapped in the trigger guard and snapped.

Being a Zero in possession of a firearm was cause for instant execution, so Xi let it fall to the ground before kicking it out of reach. Huurling tried to scream out in pain, but before any sound could escape his lungs, Zubi Jenich, another former morale center inmate, threw her forearm in the space between the bottom of the rifleman's helmet and the back of his neck. She then grabbed the top of Huurling's headcover just above his eyebrows and yanked it back, exposing his larynx to Margi Gul, who wasted no time slamming her fist into it with everything she had.

Stunned and unable to breathe, Huurling dropped to his knees with Xi, Gul, and Jenich pummeling him under a furious barrage of blows. They would have almost certainly killed the man had Sergeant Kal-Xati and the rest of her squad not heard the commotion and intervened in time to save him.

It was supposed to be the beginning of a restful weekend. Instead, Gunny Brumit assembled the entire platoon on the parade ground, in the dark, and under the unrelenting deluge of Kanarisian rain. My Marines were not happy to be out there, and I could feel their hostility as I marched up to the formation with the bullwhip I pulled from my platoon sergeant's tent.

Walking up to the head of my unit, I saw my three female Zeros on their knees, hands clasped behind their heads, while a pair of Kal-Xati's riflemen pointed their weapons between the women's shoulder blades. The assistant leader of Fourth Squad, Corporal Sasirai Sahim, had her rifle trained on Huurling, who looked as if he had gone ten rounds in the ring with one pissed-off Quarakai.

"They fucking attacked me!" he yelled at Gunny Brumit. "These Zeros assaulted a Kyperion League Space Marine! The Uniform Code of Military Justice demands we execute them! Now!"

There was panic in Huurling's voice. And urgency. Though it was a futile gesture, he was trying to get someone to silence the Zeros before anyone heard their side of the story. This became even more apparent as he turned toward Kal-Xati and snarled, "I don't understand why the fuck you didn't blow them away when you caught them on top of me!"

Kal-Xati shrugged with cool disinterest. "The lieutenant was pretty clear we're not to execute Zeros without his permission. He was also pretty clear that you were not to try molesting them as well."

"I wasn't trying to...."

"Bullshit!" cried Margi Gul. "You were dragging me to your tent to...."

"Shut your fucking mouth, you slimy little whore!" Huurling snapped. "You're a Zero! Your word doesn't count against a Marine in good standing!"

"I wouldn't make any assumptions about your standing, Marine," I told Huurling as I handed Gunny her whip.

Huurling gulped. "Sir, I'm sorry! I was just...."

I pointed my finger at the errant warrior. "Shut up." Turning to my platoon sergeant, I told her, "Five lashes every time he opens his mouth without my permission."

"Yes, sir," Gunny answered.

Stepping over to the female Zeros, I turned to Xi and asked, "What happened?"

Looking me directly in the eye, Xi said, "I saw this Marine, PFC Huurling, trying to drag Margi to his tent. She was struggling against him and refusing to go, so he drew his weapon to shoot her. Zubi and I disarmed and immobilized him before he could fire."

I gazed upon the other two women, whose eyes were fixed upon the ground. I had yet to earn their trust, so I guessed both expected me to shoot them as Marine regulations demanded.

Turning to Sergeant Kal-Xati, I asked, "What did you see?"

The sergeant shrugged. "Just these three women beating the living shit out of PFC Huurling."

"You didn't see what led up to it?"

Kal-Xati shook her head. "No, sir. I got there too late."

"What do you think happened?"

Kal-Xati glared at her PFC. "I think it went down as these three ladies said it did. They knew attacking a Marine was an instant death sentence, so they had no motivation to assault Huurling unless they had nothing to lose. Their tents are right next to ours, and we've walked through them countless times without issue. These women, and the rest of the Zeros, tend to keep to themselves and stay out of trouble. I don't see them turning on a Marine unless provoked."

I nodded at the squad leader in concurrence, then turned toward the rifleman. "Were you trying to take some liberties with one of my Zeros, Huurling?"

"I...uh...I...no...I,"

"PFC," I told him, "You're going to want to slow down and think about your answer to this question. If you intended to disobey my orders, rest assured that the consequences will be harsh. They won't be nearly as bad as they would have been had you succeeded, though. There's room for them to be much worse, particularly if you lie to me."

Huurling let out a long sigh and hung his head in defeat. "Yes, sir. I did."

"Do you remember what I told you I would do if you violated one of my female Zeros, Private?"

My Marine nodded. "I didn't violate her, sir."

"Only because of incompetence," I reminded him. "Had it not been for this woman's friends, you would have passed the point of no return. As it stands, though, it appears these ladies handed your ass to you. In light of your injuries. I'm thinking I'll forgo the ten lashes I was going to give you and just send your sorry ass to the colonel with a recommendation that he bust you down to buck private and dock half your monthly pay times two."

I watched Huurling's shoulders slump. "Aye aye, sir. What are you going to do to them?"

I looked at my Zeros. "Your victims? I ain't going to do a goddamned thing to them. They've done nothing wrong as far as I'm concerned."

Huurling's face twisted up into an expression of disbelief. "All three of them committed a capital crime! If you let them get away with it, the Zeros will think it's open season on the rest of us!"

I scoffed. "Hardly. I sincerely doubt...."

"I'll escalate this right up the chain if I have to, sir! Those Zeros need to learn they can't touch a fucking Marine!"

I looked over at Gunny, who was shaking her head in disgust. "If he makes an official complaint, they'll execute those girls, sir. It won't matter whether they were right or wrong."

Enraged, I stormed over to Huurling, grabbed him by the breastplate, and pulled him in close so that our noses were just millimeters apart. "You need to realize that once we get in the field, I'll have complete control over you, private. If any harm comes to those girls, I'll see to it you die slow out there."

"We don't have to kill them to get the point across, sir."

"Oh?" I snarled. "I take it you have an alternative solution in mind, then?"

Huurling nodded. "Sixty seconds."

I let out a little laugh. "You want me to call a smoker?"

"Yes, sir. Those bitches jumped me. Caught me while I was off guard. They made me look like I can't hold my own against three civilian girls. I want the chance to show my squad that I can take care of myself, sir."

"You want to save face? That's what this is about?"

"Yes, sir."

I smiled in spite of myself. My praetorian, Nila Chisek, did not need much in the way of sleep. Neither did Ritza Xi. Despite how hard we were training, Chisek had been sneaking away to train Xi in Qılıç Elai, the brutal martial art developed on her home planet of Praminat. Nila reported that Xi was a motivated student and a natural fighter. I already knew from what she had done to four deserters during the mutiny against Captain Briggund that she was a killer, so I was sure she could hold her own against Huurling.

Turning to my Zero, I said, "Huurling here wants to face you in a smoker, Xi. Sixty seconds of hand-to-hand combat. What do you think of that?"

Grinning, Ritza lifted herself onto her feet. "I'd love the opportunity to finish what I started."

"No!" shouted Margi Gul as she jumped up behind Xi. "No! I want this! I was the one that had to put up with his sweaty ass on top of me all those times back at the morale center! I was the one who had to lie there while he used me like a piece of meat! Not you!"

I watched Gul's eyes bore into Slai Huurling. It was as if she were trying to burn holes through the man with nothing but unbridled hatred. She may not have had the martial arts skills as my first choice to take on my wayward PFC, but she was motivated to inflict pain on that man in a way that Ritza Xi would never be able to match. Besides, Huurling was half-beaten anyway.

"If anyone deserves a free pass at this son-of-a-bitch," Gul growled at us. "It's me!"

Gunny Brumit looked my way to see what I wanted to do. I shrugged and said, "She has a point. Give her the chance to make that Marine reap what he sowed."

Chapter 16

Sixty Seconds

Class Zero convicts were slaves. There was just no other way to describe them. They had no rights and were officially the property of the Kyperion League Space Corps. Any Marine could do whatever they wanted to them without repercussions, as long as they left them able to perform their duties when the next work day came around. The edict I issued barring my platoon's Zeros from being mistreated was followed, but never popular. That became apparent as Margi Gul entered the circle we formed for her to face Private Huurling.

"He's going to kill you, you know," snarled Polita Pottoka, one of Huurling's squad-mates. That surprised me. I figured as a woman, she would have been more sympathetic to Gul fighting to keep herself from being raped. "He's going to get away with it, too. You murdering cunt."

I read Margi Gul's file. She was convicted for participating in a bombing campaign on behalf of the Terrakand Liberation Front. She had been identified as the leader of her cell, and it was alleged that her devices had killed scores of the planet's non-native residents. League prosecutors believed her crimes to be so heinous that they declined to execute her. They wanted her to suffer, so they sentenced her to live the rest of her days as a Corps comfort woman.

"Crush her, Slai!" called out another of Huurling's comrades, Nero Solvi. He was Fourth Squad's sapper. "I heard the bitch blew up more than fifty civilians! Men, women, and children!"

"Fifty?" Gul scoffed at Solvi. "By my count, it was seventy-seven. Impressive, for sure, but well short of the one hundred and forty-one I was gunning for."

"You wanted to kill one hundred and forty-one people?" Barone Parsons asked, thinking the number oddly specific. "Why?"

"Because when I was fourteen, Kyperion forces bombed my village, which had NEVER taken up arms against them, and killed one hundred and thirty-seven people." Turning back toward Solvi, she emphasized, "Men, women, and children."

Curious about the math discrepancy, Sergeant Kal-Xati asked, "What about the other four? Was there another vendetta involved?"

Gul glared at her squad leader and shook her head. "My sister and her three little boys count double." Spitting at the mud in disgust, the Zero added, "Yeah, when you indiscriminately slaughter people with bombs dropped from aircraft, you're a hero. When you do the exact same thing with explosives packed into pieces of luggage, you're a homicidal maniac."

"That supposed to make me feel sorry for you?" asked Huurling as he dropped the rest of his armor.

"I don't give a fuck what you feel, you pathetic piece of shit." I was caught off guard by the smile I saw on Gul's face. And the rage in her eyes. She wanted this. The woman was full of pent-up anger, and I could tell she was anxious to take it all out on Private Huurling.

Normally, the platoon sergeant would lay out instructions for the smoker, but Gunny Brumit was at a loss on the rules for this one. A sanctioned fight between a Marine and a Zero had a weird dynamic. Huurling could kill Gul and completely get away with it. For her, it was a fight to the death. To survive the bout, she would probably have to kill Huurling, which would be a capital crime in itself and would result in instant execution. To survive to see another sunrise, she needed to exercise restraint, something her opponent was not bound by. "How do you want to do this?" Brumit asked me.

"I don't care how you do it, Gunny!" Gul answered. "Let's just get it going! I'm tired of this shit! Start the fucking timer!"

Brumit shook her head. "I'm trying to set the rules to keep you alive!"

"Fuck the rules!" the convict barked.

I looked at Huurling. The expression on his face hinted that he would probably have preferred a few boundaries as he realized how enthusiastic Gul was to hurt him. Pride would not allow him to insist on any, though. Trying to sound more confident than he felt, he muttered, "Fine with me. I don't give a shit about rules if she don't."

Gunny sighed and opened the stopwatch on her combat tablet. "All right, then. On your mark...get set..."

The word "go" was drowned out by Margi Gul's screams as she rushed her opponent. The Zero charged him at a dead sprint, which the Marine seemed ready for. He cocked his arm and was ready to plant a haymaker to the woman's face when suddenly, she dropped down, sliding through the mud while kicking upward to connect with Huurling's crotch. She nailed him hard enough to lift him right off his feet and send him careening into the ground.

The instant Huurling landed, Gul leapt to her feet and kicked her opponent in the jaw. Then she broke his nose. Again. Both would have been brutal blows had the Marine been fresh, but he was carrying pretty significant damage from their earlier altercation, making Gul's strikes all the more devastating.

While Huurling tried to lift himself up, Gul attempted to put her boot in his throat. She knew that was his weak point. It would still have been raw from when she throttled him earlier. If she could connect with his larynx again, it could close his windpipe and leave him defenseless. Just like she was when he had his way with her.

But she missed. Huurling rolled away as Gul threw her foot out and her kick caught nothing but air, throwing her off balance. The Marine took advantage of that by using his arm to sweep her remaining leg from beneath her. When Gul came down into the mud, Huurling got on top of her and tried to wrap his arm around her neck. Gul thwarted him by tucking her chin under his forearm and denying him access to her throat. She then used her right hand to grab hold of Huurling's ear in an attempt to rip it off his head.

Huurling screamed in pain and tried to retaliate by reaching over Gul's crown to gouge out one of her eyes. In response, the Zero opened her mouth and sunk her teeth into the private's forearm. Not only did Gul draw blood, she bit a large chunk of meat right out of Huurling's inner arm. The rifleman bellowed in agony and let the convict go, ripping his limb out of her mouth and squeezing the wound to stop the bleeding. As the Marine screeched, Gul leapt onto his back and tried to take another chunk out of his neck.

"Holy fuck!" Gunny Brumit gasped. "She's going to kill him!"

"Should we stop it?" I asked.

"No!" snapped Ritza Xi. "He wanted sixty seconds with Margi Gul, so let him have sixty seconds with Margi Gul!"

"Xi, if she kills him, I'll have no choice but to execute her!"

"Then execute her," Xi told me defiantly. "It'll be better than what she had to go through at the morale center."

Huurling reached back and grabbed Gul by the hair, then swiftly bent over, flipping her off him. The prisoner hit the mud hard but jumped right back onto her feet, leaping into the air and kicking her adversary in the chest.

Shouting out in a combination of pain, surprise, and anger, Huurling swung at Gul with his right arm. She easily ducked out of the way. Had she been a man, she could have counter-punched and connected with the Marine's shattered nose. She knew she lacked the upper body strength to make it count, though, so she retreated to look for an opportunity to use her legs again. Huurling swung at her once more with his left, but once more, Gul avoided getting hit. When her opponent cranked back with his right for a third try, the convict saw her opening and ran in to see if she could put her boot into his crotch again. She did but allowed her opponent to grab her with his left arm. She could not break free before the private's fist smashed into her temple.

It was a knockout blow. Gul's head cranked violently to the right so hard I heard her neck pop. It seemed like the woman's entire body instantly went limp as she crumbled into a heap at Huurling's feet. As the Zero went down, the rifleman clasped his left hand over his right and screamed in pain, having aggravated his broken trigger finger.

I expected the platoon to erupt into cheers as their squadmate finally got the upper hand, but the entire crowd fell silent. Except for Huurling. "You fucking bitch!" he screamed as he pounced on her chest and hit her even harder with his left.

Brumit looked at her tablet. "Fifty-eight seconds!"

Huurling struck Gul again across the jaw.

"Fifty-nine!"

Huurling pummeled her in the eye. Luckily for Gul, Huurling's injured digit was forcing him to punch with his weaker fist.

"Sixty!"

Disregarding the count, Huurling socked Gul in the nose. Then the mouth. He was gearing up to hit her again when Sergeant Kal-Xati stuck the barrel of her sidearm against the private's ear. "Did you not hear Gunny Brumit, motherfucker? Time's up!"

Teetering off his victim, Huurling rolled onto his back and laughed as he gasped for air. "I won!"

No one bothered to congratulate him. Margi Gul had fought hard and earned their respect. Huurling lost it when he continued to pummel the prisoner after she had been knocked out.

"Sir?" Kal-Xati asked as she glowered at her rifleman lying in the mud. "First Platoon has an open billet now, don't they? Didn't they lose a man to one of those soroquids the other night?"

I nodded. "Yeah, they did."

Kal-Xati nodded. "You mind if I transfer this asshole to them? I don't want him in my squad anymore."

I shook my head. "Lieutenant Peeli doesn't share my views on the treatment of Class Zero convicts. Shipping this piece of shit over there would be more of a reward than a punishment. He stays here so he can learn to follow orders. Feel free to fuck with him any way you see fit, Sergeant. Lumuk!"

"Yes, sir?" asked my lumbering giant from Gorsu Qat.

"I want you to pick up the prisoner and carry her to sick bay." Turning to my senior medic, I said, "Sergeant Sotalain, I want you to take care of Gul personally. Make sure she gets put back together right. Like a Marine, Sarge, not a convict."

"Aye aye, sir."

I was watching Lumuk as he entered the ring to get Gul. As he bent over to pick her up, I saw the skin on the back of his bald head open up, spraying blood all over Zubi Jenich, who was standing beside him. Corporal Kyang, my Second Squad sniper, fell to the ground clutching his thigh. A split second later, I heard the report of a single gunshot as my entire platoon threw themselves into the mud.

"SNIPER!"

Chapter 17

OUTCAST

At first, we thought it was a Narman that had taken a shot at us. Had it been the rebels, however, they would not have stopped with Lumuk. They would have kept firing as long as they had targets, and with nearly a hundred of us bunched up around the smoker match, the sniper certainly had no shortage of potential victims. Had they kept pulling the trigger, it would have been a massacre.

With no other rounds fired, it was safe to assume that the only Marine they were aiming for was Akkam Lumuk. That meant the triggerman was probably a Qilkorian trying to cash in the mark they had put on my man.

Lieutenant Colonel Baakarad, the commander of our reconnaissance battalion, came to that conclusion even before I did, and she was *pissed*. Before the medics had even put their hands on Lumuk, she had Camp Vayipar's Officer in Charge on the commlink, ordering him to seize and disarm every Qilkorian on site.

As luck would have it, Captain Skual already had most of the Marines under his command at the Qilkorian compound, helping the Killbillies transfer their growing ubatis into bigger pens. When the order came through to detain the Ransairs, the leathernecks dropped everything, drew their weapons, and took their comrades into custody. "Objective secured," reported one of Skual's sergeants less than a minute after receiving the order.

"Did you get them all?" I heard Skual ask.

"We got everyone here," the sergeant answered. "There are eleven in custody."

"There's supposed to be twelve!" Skual snapped back. "Who are you missing?"

"Their boss," the sergeant told his captain. "Buffy's not here."

"Then where the fuck is he?"

There was a pause while the sergeant questioned his captives. "Nobody knows. He left a few hours ago on that naypeto thing."

I cursed as I watched my medics attend to Lumuk and Kyang. Of course, it had to be Bufort Graym. He was the Killbilly I trusted most.

"Get an urgent inquiry in to Section 615," Colonel Baakarad shouted over the comm-link, interrupting Skual's next question. "Using my authority, I want them to tell me everything there is to know about that son-of-a-bitch before we get to their compound! Pustov!"

"Yes, ma'am!" I heard my company commander respond.

"Grab Tauk and his platoon sergeant and meet me at the Qilkorian camp! ASAP!"

When we arrived, all the camp's Killbillies were lined up on their knees with their hands behind their heads. Captain Skual was there waiting for us. "What do we know so far?" our battalion commander barked at him.

"So far, ma'am," the captain sheepishly answered back. "All we know is that none of these men was the one who shot your Marine. Every one of them was here under the eyes of my troops. They're all accounted for."

"Did you get the report about the missing man yet?"

"No, ma'am, I...."

"Then get on the horn to 615 and ask them where the fuck it is!" Baakarad screamed at him.

Our battalion commander had a reputation as a woman no one wanted to cross. As a Samaari, Baakarad naturally came into the Corps with lots of League connections. Being one of those rare Sammies who was actually good at her job also earned her the ear of many high-ranking Corps officers. When she sensed Skual getting resistance from some Section flunky who did not appreciate being rushed by a training captain, Baakarad made a call of her own. I have no idea who she contacted, but whoever it was got us the dossier on Graym within ninety seconds and reduced the agent Skual had been speaking with into a blubbering mess of apologies.

"That lying sack of shit," I growled over the comms as I read Graym's history. "That motherfucker spent two years with the death squads!"

"That was a long time ago," Buda Grein told me. He was one of the guides we were with when the soroquids attacked. "Buffy went on one tour with them and quit. He said it was evil work. He didn't want no part of it."

"Bullshit," Gunny Brumit snapped. "You get in with an outfit like that, and there ain't no going back. They don't let you. He was probably planted here by those pricks. They like having eyes everywhere they can put them."

"The squads ain't got no eyes here!" Buda insisted.

"Then how'd they know where to find Lumuk?" I asked. The Killbilly seemed at a loss to explain that.

"If your boss didn't pull the trigger himself," Baakarad said. "He likely pointed who-ever did in the right direction."

Hirshel Coopa, the Qilkorian cook, shook his head. "I doubt he did either thing. I been working with that man for ten years, and I ain't ever seen him show anything but disgust for the squads. We ain't Killbillies, ma'am! We ain't like them scumbags!"

"Prove it," said Baakarad.

"How?" asked Buda.

"You're trackers, right?"

"Best in the galaxy," Coopa answered.

"Then help us track down your boss."

Coopa and Buda looked at each other, then at the rest of their people. The entire Qilkorian contingent then began shaking their heads in disagreement. "I'm afraid we can't do that," Buda told her.

"Why the fuck not?" Baakarad demanded.

"We can't track down fellow Qilkorians."

Brumit laughed out loud. "You're so full of shit! Half your folklore is based upon tales of you degenerates hunting each other down!"

"Aye," Coopa admitted. "There ain't no shortage of blood feuds on Qilkoraan. We's not supposed to hurt each other, but we do. Just like everyone does on every other planet. Killing each other is a crime, and we'll be punished for it. Killing a fellow Qilkorian on behalf of a foreigner though, an outsider, is a mortal sin. They won't just punish *us* for the crime; they'll punish our entire family!"

"Look," growled Baakarad as she turned her gaze on Coopa. "You're either with us on this, or you're against us!"

Buda bowed his head. "Then it looks like we're against you."

"Fine," Baakarad said as she drew her sidearm and pointed it at the Qilkorian's head.

"Hey!" Captain Skual yelled at the battalion commander. His affection for his Qilkorians apparently made him forget that Baakarad outranked him. "Put that fuckin' weapon away! The one thing we do know is that none of these men took a shot at your Marines! They're innocent!"

"Are they?" sneered Baakarad. "They just told us they're not on our side. That means they must be the enemy. Maybe if we shoot a couple of them, they'll better understand what they're up against."

"Ma'am," Gunny Brumit said. "I suggest we exercise restraint here. We've been getting our asses handed to us because our own people are changing sides. Many of them no longer believe we're the good guys anymore. It'll be tough to convince them we are if we kill people we know didn't cause us any harm."

Baakarad glowered at Brumit for a moment, then softened her expression as she lowered her weapon. "Captain Skual, lock these men in the stockade until we get to the bottom of this. Tauk, get your Marines ready to go back out on patrol to track down Graym and...."

"You don't have to twack down anybody," came a voice from behind us. "I'm heya, saving you all the twouble." It was Buffy Graym, riding into the compound on his naypeto with his ubati trotting along by his side. They were dragging the body of a morbidly obese human behind them.

"Dat's the guy you's looking fo'," Buffy said as he pointed his chin at the corpse on the ground. "Dat's Woostuh Mikkaine. Puddin'. He's the one that shot you man."

Gunny Brumit walked over and studied the mangled body. It looked like Buffy's ubati got hold of it. Nodding her head, the gunnery sergeant said, "That's him, all right. There ain't no way you're convincing me that he got his fat ass out there in the bush all by himself, though."

Buffy shook his head. "Nope. His squad was out the'e with him. They dead, too. All eight o' them."

"How'd you find them?" Brumit asked, still somewhat suspicious.

"Meit was acting funny," Buffy answered. Meit was Buffy's ubati. "He kept twying to go back to this point in the bush, so I'm thinkin' the'e somethin' suspicious out that way. These guys is Qilkowian like us, though. They's vewy ha'd to find. I was able to get into they genewel awea but couldn't pinpoint they actual position until they fi'ed they weapon. Aftuh that, me and Meit took 'em all out."

"You killed them by yourself?" I asked. I was impressed.

"Well," Buffy told me. "I got one. I ain't no match fo' no eight squad men. Lucky fo' me, ain't no eight squad men that's much of a match fo' no angwy ubati, eithuh."

Grinning like she had caught the camp's Killbillies in a lie, our battalion commander turned toward the captives and said, "I thought Qilkorians weren't supposed to kill other Qilkorians on behalf of outsiders."

"We not," Buffy answered. "It's a capital cwime on Qilkowaan. If any of these men slay those Killbillies fo' you, they family back home be executed with them. It best fo' me to do dis by myself. I ain't got no family."

As Buffy dismounted the naypeto, he said, "This is the man who put the Ma'k of the Tuuk on you' Mawine. It's ovuh. The big man's safe now."

Looking at the contempt plastered upon the faces of the men who used to work for him, Buffy added, "That's a lot mo'e than I can say fo' myself at the moment."

Coopa nodded in agreement. "You sure got that right, you baby-talkin' traitor."

"Is it true that the Qilkorians are the best trackers in the galaxy?" I asked Buffy as I was helping him move his gear into my tent. After slaughtering Akkam Lumuk's would-be assassins, Bufort Graym needed a new home, so I offered him one with my platoon.

Graym nodded in response to my question. "If they's a bettuh gwoup of twackuhs out the'e somewhe'e, I've nevuh hea'd of 'em."

"How are you on the scale of Qilkorian trackers?"

Buffy shrugged. "Bettuh than most. Wo'se than some."

"Is that animals? Or can you track people too?"

Buffy squinted at me. "People awe animals, Lieutenant. Since you in the business of combat, you should know that bettuh than most. You lookin' fo' people in genewal, o' you got someone pa'ticuluh in mind?"

"I got someone particular in mind."

My new roommate let out a long sigh, realizing that my offer to take him in may have come with strings attached. "Who you looking fo'?"

Pulling out my tablet, I flipped it onto holograph mode. After a few keystrokes, I set it on my cot and let it project a rotating, three-dimensional view of a Narman insurgent. "That's Deena Vulk," I told Buffy. "She doesn't look exactly like that anymore. Besides being older, she was injured nine months ago in a firefight with the Marines. The left side of her face was burned up pretty bad."

Buffy barely glanced at the hologram. "What she looks like isn't weally that impo'tant. What mattuhs is what she smell like."

My tracker pointed his thumb over his shoulder towards the ubati standing guard outside our tent. Cupid was with him. "I been twaining Meit to twack things using his nose. He's sma't, so it's been going pwetty good. I was testing how fah they nose can pick up an odah, so I know that if you get me within seven clicks of whoevuh you want to find, we can catch huh. I need something with huh smell on it, though."

"I don't have anything of hers," I told Buffy.

"Then you's out of luck."

I thought of the morning that Jella Duverii was murdered at the summit of Mount Toranad. "I know where she's been, though. I can show you exactly where she was lying."

"How long ago was she the'e?"

I did the math in my head. "About ten months ago."

Buffy laughed. "That's too long. Theys pwabably been all kinds of animals and people walking ovuh that spot. Plus, the wain's pwobably washed it all away."

I shook my head. "There's no rain. It's atop a high summit where it's cold and dry. What little precipitation falls up there is in the form of snow."

"That's bettuh," Buffy told me. "But it still ain't good enough. If I take Meit up the'e, he'd pwobably lock onto the scent of some animal, o' some othuh Mawine that also walked awound up the'e. Getting him to lock onto the cowwect scent is impossible. Did she touch anything? Something that might still be up the'e?"

"She touched the body of a Marine. She rifled through his pockets looking for the keys to her cuffs."

The expression on Buffy's face suggested that might be something with which he could work. "Can you get to that body? To that uniform?"

I sighed. Standard procedure would have been to cremate the corpse, usually in the uniform the Marine was wearing when they were killed. In this case, however, the body may have been evidence. The League's military intelligence apparatus, Section 615, might have held onto it for some sort of forensic analysis. It was a long shot, but I could check if the spooks still had it. "There might be a chance I can get my hands on it."

"How much of a chance?"

"A small one."

"Well, Lieutenant," Buffy said. "It's going to be vewy difficult to find this woman no mattuh what we have. If we don't have something with huh stink on it, it'll be impossible."

I nodded in understanding. "I'll see what I can do."

Buffy nodded. "Good. What do you want this woman fo'? What'd she do to you?"

I trusted Buffy Graym, but not enough to confess the real reason I wanted to get my hands on Deena Vulk. Instead, I told him, "She knows where the aliens are."

Chapter 18

Fresh Wings

The Sitaara Raptor was the workhorse of the Marine Expeditionary Forces. It was an all-purpose transport/assault craft that could clear a landing zone before disembarking a fully equipped platoon of combat Marines. It was reasonably maneuverable for what was essentially a heavily armed taxi, but it was not designed for the aerodynamic acrobatics needed for aerial warfare.

The APAAF (All Purpose Aero-Assault Fighter) was. Also known as the Mar-Sitaara, this new addition to the airborne fleet could do it all. It was a big craft. With one hundred seats in the passenger bay, it was designed to carry more than a platoon of Marines, plus its crew of twenty-three. Not only could the Mar-Sitaara clear an LZ, but it also contained enough ordinance to lay waste to kilometers of enemy fortifications, pushing the B-6227 light bombers into early obsolescence. It was nimble enough to take on Haiv Fighters in intra-atmospheric dogfighting, yet was just as much at home in the vacuum of space where it could defend our Kyperion dreadnaughts or assault their Ghuldari equivalent. The Mar-Sitaara even had warp generators, making it capable of interstellar travel.

I had heard of the Mar-Sitaara at the academy and caught rumors that there was a squadron aboard the *Nebulan Phoenix*. Until the day we left Camp Vayipar, however, I had never actually seen one.

"Is that what I think it is?" I asked Lieutenant Colonel Baakarad as we walked onto the staging field to take charge of our troops.

"I believe so," our battalion commander answered me. "That's our latest and greatest killing machine."

My company commander, Captain Pustov, looked perplexed. "It's supposed to be one of the most secretive, too. What's it doing out here on a milk run back to Narman's Pyke?"

"Picking up a VIP," Baakarad answered. "And those things have been used enough down here that they're not so secretive anymore."

I looked around the landing pad for someone who looked more important than the rest of us. No one stood out. "Who's the VIP they're transporting?"

The colonel betrayed a sly grin. "Me. And you."

"Me?" I asked. "What the hell did I do to rate that kind of ride?"

My question was answered by a squeal rising above the din of troops trying to gather their gear in preparation for their return to base. "TAUK!"

My jaw dropped as I spotted a petite, mocha-skinned woman in a pilot uniform sprinting my way. "Albarn?" I gasped. "Je'Sikka Albarn?"

Je'Sikka Albarn had been at the controls of *Wasp-Three* when it smashed into the beach off the Buvalla Sea. Her spine had snapped on impact, forcing us to carry her all the way to Narman's Pyke while our CO did everything in his power to kill her to keep the cowardice of a Samaari highborn covered up. Mere months later, she was running at me as if nothing had ever happened.

Albarn leapt into my arms, wrapping hers around my neck and squeezing so hard I could barely breathe. "What are you doing here?" I asked her. "How are you walking like that? How did they...?"

"I declined your Red Caste nomination," Albarn told me. "I couldn't bear the thought of sitting on the sidelines for the rest of my life. I want to *be* a pilot, not train them."

"But...but...you would've been taken care of forever! You'd have never wanted for anything ever again!"

"Except for a fucking purpose!" the pilot said as she let go of me and dropped to her feet. "You know, you strive your whole life to achieve heaven, only to realize how boring it is once you actually get there. I'm better off here, Tauk. They fixed my back and got my legs moving again. Then they gave me my choice of assignments. Since I was already Raptor qualified, I requested reassignment to the Mar-Sitaara squadron. I passed quals in nine weeks and earned my SFT designation a month later."

"SFT" stood for Strike Fighter Tactics. It was the highest combat pilot rating in the fleet. Having seen first-hand how Albarn handled a crippled dropship in a super-cyclone, it did not surprise me that she earned her qualifications so fast. Still, I could not believe she turned her back on becoming one of the Kyperion elite. "But the Red Caste...."

Albarn glowered at me, making it clear she did not want to talk about it. At least not in present company. To ensure I did not pursue the topic, she grabbed me by the arm and practically dragged me toward her new ship. "Come on, Tauk!" she said as we marched toward the craft. "You have to check this thing out!"

When we reached Albarn's new fighter, the pilot lovingly patted its hull. "This is the *Niberian Hornet*," she said as if introducing me to a favorite cousin. The APAAF was three times as long as the Raptor transports I was used to, stretching more than fifty meters from nose to tail.

"Inside," Albarn told me, "There're four levels. The lower level is for combat staging and egress. The aft end can disembark two armored fighting vehicles, each capable of carrying forty-three Marines, half a platoon. Also back there are four two-person recon hovercraft and a pair of five-person speeders."

Leading me into the ship, the pilot pointed out the seats my Marines would buckle into, each equipped with heavy restraint bars. "You sure don't want us going anywhere, do you?"

Albarn grinned. "Nope. The engineers designed it not only for Marine safety but for prisoner transport. I can release the troops all at once or keep some trapped in place until the MPs come to collect them. Be glad they're there. Despite the size of this thing, the Mar-Sitaara handles like a fighter. The passengers will be grateful to have something like that keeping their asses in their seats. You'll see on the way back to Narman's Pyke. I'll get a few of you puking."

"I suggest you don't," I said. "Lumuk got shot in the head and is already messed up. The Gs we'll pull joyriding will mess with his concussion."

Albarn lifted her hand and covered her mouth in shock. "Lumuk got shot?" she asked. "Is he going to be alright?"

I nodded. "It could've been a lot worse. Thanks to a bit of luck, not to mention an extremely thick skull, he wasn't seriously hurt. The bullet sliced open the back of his head and rang his bell, but he'll be fine."

Albarn sighed in relief. She had a soft spot for my platoon's gentle giant. When Captain Briggund ordered her left behind during our hike up from the beach, Lumuk carried her in his arms for a dozen kilometers until we could rig up a stretcher for her. "Can I see him?"

"You will soon enough. He'll be embarking with the rest of us."

The pilot squinted at her troop seats. "I don't know if he'll even be able to fit in here."

Leading me up a ladder to the second level, Albarn introduced me to her co-pilot, CWO1 Owen Skaigard. With him was the Weapons Officer, Ratta Dav, and the Flight Engineer, CWO2 Baug Kledyff. "How many crew does it take to operate this thing?" I asked.

"Twenty-three," Skaigard answered. "Four warrant officers, a flight medic and crew chief, three mechanics, four gunners, five sentries, four crew members to maintain and operate the transports, and a drone operator."

"And I take it this is the crew area?"

Albarn nodded. "Yep. For longer trips, this is where the crew and embarked troops can lounge. This level has showers, a galley, a gym, and recreational equipment. For even longer trips, the third level is equipped with enough SAC units to accommodate one hundred and ten personnel."

SAC was the acronym for Suspended Animation Chambers. "Why would you have to put troops on ice in one of these things? I thought they were capable of interstellar travel."

"They are," Albarn assured me. "The Mar-Sitaara can do warp speed, but not at hyperdrive levels. It'll take us a bit longer to get to the more remote outposts than it would the dreadnoughts. To ensure we don't exhaust our supplies in transit, we put embarked troops to sleep for the longer trips."

Looking around the bay, I spotted four robots secured in storage cells along the wall. "I thought droids couldn't work on Kanaris."

The flight engineer answered me. "They're all de-activated," Kledyff said. "We have to keep them completely powered down so the Harnillium interference doesn't drive them nuts. We'll activate them again when we're in space."

That made sense. Having covered the first three decks, I asked, "What's on the fourth level?"

"Stores. Food. Ammo. Workspaces. Propulsion machinery and ordinance magazines."

"Impressive," I told Albarn. "It seems like overkill, though. This's an awful lot of capability for a starcraft just large enough to accommodate a platoon."

The pilot nodded. "It's a quick-strike vehicle designed for special operations forces. It's for when you really want to reach out and touch someone. The intent was to have a platoon of Section 615 commandos permanently assigned to one of these so that they're ready to go when the need arises."

"The intent?" I asked. "They're no longer putting 615 shooters in these?"

Albarn shrugged. "They would if they had 'em. Section 615 has taken some pretty heavy casualties since we've been here. We now have more Mar-Sitaaras than they have commandos. My understanding is that the command's going to assign a couple Recon platoons to one of these for strike force operations."

"Recon platoons?" I asked. "Which ones?"

"I don't know," Albarn told me. "But I'm hoping one of them is yours."

After three months at Camp Vayipar, the battalion's Marines were awarded some well-deserved time off. As the troops were prone to do, they flooded the bars the moment they were cut loose, striving to get their blood alcohol level up past their IQs before pairing up to work off some tension between the sheets. Those who could not find willing partners flooded the morale centers looking for action, though those could hardly accommodate so many men at once. Unwilling to wait for a comfort woman after a dozen others had already used her, some looked for relief elsewhere. Vorat Klenan, a rifleman from Lieutenant Peeli's platoon, decided to cruise for a date among the convicts.

Spotting a familiar face before he even got to the Zero bivouac, Klenan grabbed Ritza Xi's arm as she passed. "Hey," he called out to her. "Ritza! Remember me?"

It had been a long time since Xi had seen Klenan, but not nearly long enough. Ripping her arm from the rifleman's grasp, she snapped, "Get your fucking hands off of me."

"Hey," Klenan protested. "Why the attitude? I thought we were friends."

Xi scoffed. "Friends? You think we're friends?!? After what you did to me?"

"Did to you?" Klenan countered. "I never hurt you! I was always gentle."

"It doesn't matter if you're gentle or not. Taking me without my consent is not something a friend would do."

Klenan looked genuinely offended. "Taking you? What? You make me sound like some kind of rapist!"

"That's exactly what you are!"

"What're you talking about? I was doing you a favor!"

Xi laughed in disbelief. "A favor! How do you figure that was a favor?!?"

"Well, look at you! Nobody wanted you with that fucked up face of yours, but I always asked for you so that you'd still feel desirable! So that you'd think someone still wanted you!"

Xi flinched. Despite being spat from the mouth of a dirtbag, Klenan's words stung. She recoiled from the private and stepped over to a nearby building to look at her reflection in one of the windows.

Sergeant Kyker and his buddies had really done a number on her. There were stitch marks all over her face and forehead. Her right eye would not open all the way, wreaking havoc upon the symmetry of her face. Behind her lips was a mouthful of broken teeth. She had a cauliflower ear and her shattered nose was so bent she could hardly breathe through it. They also broke her jaw, leaving her unable to close her mouth correctly. She constantly struggled to keep the drool from draining out of it.

Private Klenan was right. She was hideous. As Xi stared at her disfigured features, running her finger over her scars, a single tear ran down her cheek.

"Hey, Ritza," Klenan said, reaching out to comfort her. "I'm sorry. I didn't mean it that way. I know you must've been beautiful before those bastards did all that stuff to you. That's why I still find you desirable. Look, baby, there aren't many things around here that we can take pleasure in these days. But maybe we can find a little solace in each other. What do you say? Stay with me tonight."

Xi shivered in disgust and let out a single sob before she could regain her composure. "Not in a million...!"

"Hey! Hey!" Klenan interrupted her. "I didn't mean like we used to! I want it to be different! I want to be there for you! Not me! You! Is there anything I could do for you to make you feel better? To make you feel like a woman again?"

Xi's face softened as she wiped her eyes. "You want to pleasure me? Is that what you're saying?"

Klenan grinned, feeling like he was finally getting somewhere. "That's exactly what I'm saying! Surely, there must be something I could do to make you happy tonight."

"Well, now that you put it that way," Xi told the rifleman. "Maybe there is something you *can* do for me."

Taking Klenan by the hand, Xi pulled him in close and kissed him tenderly on the lips. When she finished, she giggled and led him off into the darkness to a place where they would not be seen or disturbed. I do not know what Klenan did to Ritza Xi, but when I saw her at roll call the following morning, she was the happiest I had ever seen her.

Vorat Klenan, on the other hand, seemed to have dropped off the face of Kanaris. He was never seen or heard from again.

••◄►●◄►••

Chapter 19

Mess Deck Moonshine

The liquid started burning as soon as it passed my lips, making me wonder if I had just taken a sip of battery acid. I wanted to spit it out, but Je'Sikka Albarn was staring at me with a bemused look on her face. I had already watched her do a shot of that vile elixir, so I was not about to give her the pleasure of seeing me gag. So, against my better judgment, I swallowed.

I regretted it immediately. The liquor set my whole throat ablaze and ignited a burn in my gut unlike anything I had ever experienced. I brought my fist up to cover my mouth as I let out a small burp, only to have my stomach contract in an attempt to expel everything I had eaten that day along with the booze. To avoid vomiting all over my guest, I had to gulp that putrid shit down all over again.

Despite my best effort to maintain a stoic expression, Albarn saw how close to retching I came and burst into laughter. "Can't handle it, eh?"

"What the hell is it?" I asked. "It sure as hell ain't the Beru Sukka brandy Gunny Malcolm turned me on to."

Albarn laughed again as she poured herself another shot. "No, it certainly isn't," she confessed. "This is some rot-gut homebrew the mess cooks made up."

"Mess cooks?" I asked. "The people that make up the slop the enlisted Marines eat? What on earth made you think they'd be able to make a palatable liquor?"

After slamming another shot, Albarn exhaled for a solid five seconds before answering me. "The cooks aren't interested in making their hooch palatable," she gasped. "Their only objective is to make it strong. They got grains, starches, and yeast. What they don't have is the time to age it all into something tasty. The grunts they typically sell this shit to don't care about flavor, either. They're only concerned with drinking something that will make them forget what they've been through for a little while."

As a pilot, Albarn had a place to sleep back on the *Hornet*. We could have had our drinks there, but then we would likely have been in the company of her crew. I wanted to talk to her alone, so we were in my tent. Je'Sikka thought I might have had other intentions. Looking around my spartan accommodations, Albarn said, "You know, I was pretty doped up the whole time you carried me through the jungle. I remember very little of that ordeal. I can't recall if I told you anything personal, so if you're planning on getting me drunk and making a move on me later, I just want you to know that I'm not into men."

I grinned. "You told me. It's okay, though. I just wanted us to be alone so we could talk."

"About what?" Albarn asked as she poured me another drink. Apparently, she was looking to loosen me up as much as I was trying to loosen her.

"The Red Caste, for starters," I said as I took the glass from her. "Albarn, you were headed for Easy Street. You'd have been set for life! You'd be living among the Kyperion elite! You'd have had it made! Why the hell did you throw it away?"

Albarn sighed. "Do you know the kind of people that decide whether or not you're worthy of being in the Red Caste, Eamon?"

I nodded. "They're Academy Marines."

"Do you have any idea what they're like?"

I snorted. "Of course I do. I'm an Academy Marine myself. I grew up with them."

"Eamon, those people aren't like you."

She was right, although it was more like I who was not like them. Not anymore.

"After they interrogated me about the crash of *Wasp-Three*, they started questioning my political beliefs, trying to ensure I was ideologically pure. They wanted to know if I was a true believer. They needed to be certain I thought the League was faultless, incapable of error. That meant I had to believe the Samaaris were infallible as well."

I had been holding the glass of mess deck hooch in my hand since Albarn handed it to me, in no hurry to put another drop of it on my tongue. Sensing my hesitation, the pilot snatched it from my hand and drained it all in a single swallow.

"Eamon, those Samaari bastards tried to kill me so I couldn't let slip that one of those highborn pricks chickened out of a combat drop. That was it. It was not because

I did something wrong; it was because I saw one of them in a moment of weakness. They couldn't have a witness out there capable of poking a hole in the myth of Samaari invincibility. I couldn't spend the rest of my life around those people. No matter how cushy it was."

I nodded in understanding. "I get it. Now that I think about it, I don't think I could have either."

"What happened to you?" Albarn asked. "Every Academy Marine I saw was all about the Corps and the Kyperion League. It seemed like all they did was march around the ship, chanting the Citadel Oath to themselves over and over again as if it were some sort of mantra. When they weren't doing that, they'd constantly preach to each other about the evils of the Ghuldarian Empire, or make crude jokes about the League's non-Guild worlds. It was as if they needed to constantly remind themselves of how superior they were and how inferior everybody else was. You're not like that. How'd you manage to come out of the Citadel relatively normal?"

"I'm far from normal," I said as I surprised Je'Sikka by taking the glass from her and pouring myself a drink voluntarily. "When I killed Gori Dravidas...."

Albarn choked. "You killed the Butcher of Deraghun?"

I was surprised that the pilot did not know that. "Yeah, I did. In cold blood. He defeated us, Je'Sikka. He killed three of my closest friends and had me at his mercy. He knew no one would let him leave the blooding fields alive, though. Having made his point that he was still the baddest motherfucker the Corps had ever seen, he decided to let me kill him. He gave me the dagger he was holding and then offered me his throat. I was so enraged about what he did to my friends that I took his blade and opened up his neck without any regard for my honor. What I did was cowardly and against every tenet of fair play I was ever taught."

I paused to down the drink I had just poured. When I was confident I could speak without throwing up, I said, "The Academy trained me from birth. They pounded into my head time after time that honor was paramount. We could not lie. We could not cheat. Our word was inviolable. Without our honor, we were nothing. After I killed Dravidas, though, all they did was lie. They claimed I had beaten the Butcher in a trial of strength and skill, and the Academy Marine came out on top, just as they always did and always will. I was forbidden to disclose that Dravidas got three of ours before I got him. I was ordered to pretend that my dead comrades, the only family I had ever known, had never even existed. Their records were erased from every system they had ever been documented in so if I ever gave anyone their names, they'd just look like figments of my imagination."

I sighed. "They told me my slaughtered comrades had shamed the Corps by falling victim to Dravidas. They said my friends were unworthy of remembrance and that the stain of their existence needed to be expunged from the Citadel's memory. I was ordered to never speak of them again."

After slamming another drink, I handed the bottle and glass back to the pilot. "That was an eye-opening experience, Je'Sikka. It pulled back the curtain and showed me how things worked beyond the Citadel's walls. After a couple of months under Captain Briggund's command, I got a sense of just how diseased the Corps is. It's been rotting for a very long time."

Albarn nodded in agreement. "Do you think we can beat the Narmans, Eamon?"

"The Narmans? Without a doubt. If it were just them, this whole thing would've ended months ago."

"But it's not just them," Je'Sikka reminded me.

"You're right. It's not. They've got alien allies, and to be frank, if we don't take them out before they're reinforced, we're going to find ourselves in serious fucking trouble."

"So you don't think we can win this?"

I shook my head. "No, not really."

"Then what are you doing here?"

"Hunting the woman who killed Jella Duverii."

Albarn's jaw dropped. "Jella's dead?!?"

"You didn't know that, either?"

Albarn shook her head. "I spent three months getting my spine fixed. Another month in therapy. Six more getting SFT qualified. I heard you got hurt, but little else."

"Yeah, well, Colonel Palkrait tried to show us what took out Sirrah's dropship when a patrol returned with a Narman prisoner. We ended up getting ambushed and the captive, a woman named Deena Vulk, executed Jella right before my eyes. Then the bitch shot me."

"I'm so sorry to hear that, Eamon. She was so nice. One of the few things I remember about hiking to Narman's Pyke was Jella's voice. It was the only thing that cut through that drug-induced fog I was always in. Even now, it still narrates my dreams about that march."

116

As Jella's bodyguard, I remembered that, too. Even though Albarn was seemingly out cold, Jella talked to her every chance she got. "Yeah, she was special, alright."

Albarn poured an extra big serving of booze into the glass we had been sharing. Holding it up in the air, she toasted, "To Jella Duverii!" She then downed half the hooch and passed what was left to me.

"To Jella," I said before drinking my share. After catching my breath again, I said, "So, that's what I'm here for. What about you? As a Red Caste nominee and an SFT pilot, you could have had a choice of assignments. Why'd you come back to Kanaris?"

"I came back for you," Albarn told me. "And for Akkam Lumuk. And Gunny Malcolm. You all saved my life. I figured the least I could do was return the favor. After those bastards, my own people, tried to kill me, I really don't feel like I belong among the upper echelon anymore. I feel like I belong with you. My Marines."

I smiled. "I'm glad you feel at home with us, Je'Sikka. I get it. It seems like here is the only place I feel I belong anymore, too. For me, home was the Citadel. Now that's the last place I'd ever feel comfortable at."

"Eamon, can I ask you something?"

"Of course."

"You know, before we discovered we were up against an alien civilization, the League was on the verge of civil war. Now, everyone's kind of come together against a common threat, but it feels artificial. Like it'll come undone when things get tough...."

"It will," I assured Albarn. "Once the masses get wind of how many of their children got sacrificed to Samaari incompetence, they'll go from disgruntled to enraged in short order."

Albarn nodded. "Yeah, that's what I think. Eamon, if that happens, what side are you on?"

I poured the two of us another big glass of spirits. I then drank my half and sighed as I handed the rest to Albarn. "To be honest, Je'Sikka, I have no fucking idea. What about you?"

Albarn waved off my glass, lifting her arm to drink directly from the bottle. Shaking her head, she then said, "I have no idea, either."

Chapter 20

Clues

The man that walked up behind the reception desk at the Military Intelligence Bureau looked familiar. He was a powerful-looking individual despite his lack of height. His head was shaved clean and he was dressed in black fatigues, the trademark uniform of a Section 615 field agent. "Agent Takawa?" I asked him.

The spy flinched as I said his name, then squinted at my face as he tried to figure out who I was. When his eyes suddenly popped wide in recognition, he pointed his index finger at me. "Tauk! Eamon Tauk, right? Holy hell, you were the guy who got shot on Toranad! We didn't think you were going to make it."

"Yeah, it was a rough one. You know, I just talked to the pilot who broke her spine when we crash-landed on this planet in *Wasp-Three*. She was paralyzed but at a hundred percent inside of four months. It took me six."

Takawa shrugged. "She only had her spine that needed to be fixed. I saw the holes that Narman bitch punched in your ass. They'd have had to rebuild all kinds of shit inside of you."

I nodded. "I suppose they did."

"Well, I'm glad to see you made it, Tauk. What brings you here?"

"I'm looking for information on Deena Vulk. The bitch that shot me and killed Jella Duverii."

Takawa's eyes narrowed. "What for?"

"So I can track her," I answered.

"Why are you looking for Deena Vulk? Is that your job?"

"I'm in Recon. My mission is to find the aliens and their equipment. Vulk knows where both are. If I find her, I find the Morghul and their shit."

Takawa sighed. "Deena Vulk is a high-priority target for Section 615 — the highest, in fact. We've been searching for her ever since we were ambushed on Toranad. We've come close to catching her on several occasions, but every time we pounce, it seems like we're always about fifteen minutes too late. We think she's got some Marines on the inside tipping her off about when we're coming."

"Why do you think her mole's in the Marines? Why not Section 615?"

Takawa looked offended. "We don't have conscripts in Section 615, so we don't have field agents defecting to the Narmans in droves. The Marines do."

I nodded. Takawa had a point. "What'd Vulk do before this? What was her job in the colony?"

Takawa shook his head. "I can't tell you that. As I said, it appears she's got people inside of the Pyke. All information on Vulk is now tightly restricted, given out only on a 'need-to-know' basis."

"Come on, Takawa. That bitch murdered my girlfriend and damned near killed me. Trust me. I'm not going to tip her off that I'm coming for her."

"Yeah, well, that's the other reason I'm not giving you anything. You're right. Vulk does know the aliens. She knows who they are, their motivations, and how they're equipped. I need her, Lieutenant, but I need her alive. I don't trust you to deliver her to us that way."

For a second, all I could do was stare at Takawa and blink. He was not being irrational. I would not have trusted myself to bring her back alive, either. "Can I...can I...can I at least get something she may have touched. We have ubatis that can...."

"I'm not giving you anything," the agent told me. "Nothing at all. In fact, I'm also going to tell you right now to stay away from Deena Vulk. Her capture is a Section 615 priority, and it's Section 615 that will pursue this target. Not Recon. If I catch you anywhere near her, Lieutenant, there will be consequences."

"What are you going to do?" I balked. "Arrest me for trying to capture your target?"

"No, Tauk," Takawa told me. "The information that woman has is far more valuable to the mission here than you are. We'll kill you to protect it. Am I clear?"

I scowled at Takawa, knowing nothing good would come from pushing the matter further. As I stood there trying to formulate my next course of action, the Section 615 agent stepped closer and growled, "Lieutenant Tauk! Am I clear?!?"

I nodded. "Crystal."

When I returned to my platoon's command post, my head was still spinning as I tried to formulate a way of getting information on Deena Vulk without letting Section 615 know. I considered having Sergeant Naktada hack them, but I knew that would mean the death penalty for both of us if we got caught. And we *would* get caught.

I was so engrossed in my thoughts that I did not even notice a new Marine standing alone in the corner of my CP until my platoon sergeant pointed him out. "We got a replacement Marine," Gunny Brumit told me, nodding toward our latest addition.

"Already?" I asked. It had only been a week since Ziming Kyang's thigh absorbed a bullet meant for Akkam Lumuk's head. Turning to our FNG, our Fucking New Guy, I asked. "You a sniper?"

The Marine shook his head before rendering me a crisp salute. "Recon Rifleman, sir. Private Luuk Bukki reporting for duty, sir!"

The name sounded vaguely familiar. I felt like I should have known who our new infantryman was, but I was drawing a blank. "Corporal Kyang was our sniper," I told him. "My requisition chit specifically requested a replacement sniper. Why the hell did they send me another ground pounder? You a good shot, Private Bukki?"

"I'm fair. I'm not sure I'm a replacement Marine, though. I got my orders here before I even finished Recon school. They told me you requested me specifically, sir."

"What?" I asked. "I don't remember...."

But then I did. After the light bulb went off in my head, I grinned and pinged the man in charge of my First Squad. "Sergeant Parsons, report to the Platoon CP. You have a new Marine here."

"A new guy?" Parsons asked. "My squad is fully staffed."

"This is the man I reached out to specifically for you, Sergeant. Private Bukki. From Apalashu."

"Oh," Parsons said. It was only a single syllable, but it was enough for me to register the excitement in his voice.

Turning to my platoon sergeant, I said, "Gunny, I hear we may be deploying to the front soon. We just came off a tough training course. Why don't you go find a place to relax for the rest of the day?"

"Yes, sir!" Brumit said, leaving the tent without hesitation. It was not that she was thrilled to be granted early liberty; it was that she knew by my tone of voice what I really meant was, *Get out of sight before you witness something you don't want to see.*

When my squad leader entered the CP, he was out of breath. It appeared he had sprinted there. "Private Bukki?" he asked the new face.

The rifleman nodded. "Yes, Sergeant."

Parsons looked the private over, sizing him up. "Good. Glad to meet you. Where you from, Bukki?"

Even though that was typically the first question anyone asked a fresh report in the Kyperion League Space Corps, the look on Bukki's face registered some apprehension. Parsons' voice suggested he was just asking the new Marine to confirm what he already knew. "Apalashu."

My squad leader's face lit right up. "Really!?! What a pleasant surprise! So am I! What part of Apalashu are you from?"

"Draaga Bluff."

"No shit? Me too!" Parsons was over-acting, playing with his prey. I sensed it, and I could see Private Bukki did too. Pretending to look over some of our navigation gear, I moved closer to the exit to intercept the Marine if he made a run for it.

"Tell me, Private," Parsons continued. "What did you do in Draaga Bluff?"

"I was a cop," Bukki told him.

"Really? I know a few cops in Draaga Bluff. You know Mathu Pulayne?"

Bukki swallowed hard. He did not seem to know how he ended up in my tent, in front of that particular man, but he was beginning to suspect it was no accident. I could see the urge to lie flash across the rifleman's face but he must have guessed we already knew he did. "Pulayne was my partner. How do you know him? Were you a cop, too?"

Parsons grinned menacingly. "No. Actually, according to you guys, I was a criminal. A subversive. A conspirator. A terrorist. Y'all had me pegged as a very dangerous man."

I watched Bukki deflate. He knew he was in trouble and seemed to resign himself to the fact that he was about to be held accountable for past sins. "What did you actually do?" the Marine asked.

"What do you mean by 'actually' do?"

Bukki shrugged. "I assume that Pulayne was the guy who arrested you. If he put you away for subversion, you'd be in the Corps as a convict, not a sergeant. I can only assume the Corps didn't see you as the threat Pulayne did. Why did he think you were so dangerous to him?"

"He set my house on fire as a message to me to keep my mouth shut. He didn't realize my family was inside. That motherfucker killed them all."

The rifleman sighed and nodded sympathetically. "I heard rumors of that, but it happened long before my time there. I will say that's completely in character for him, though. What message was he trying to send by setting your family on fire?"

"To not report him for trying to molest my daughter."

Bukki winced. "Well, Sarge, you've got a pretty damned good reason for wanting to kill Apalashu police officers, then. I'd like to say not every one of us was as corrupt as Pulayne, but that place was rotten to the core. It's why I left when my contract expired."

"Were you on the take there, too?"

Bukki nodded. "As much as I had to be. Look, Sarge, I didn't join the police force to be a criminal, but I learned pretty quick that you either took dirty money on the job or you died in the line of duty. I did what I had to in order to put my partner at ease, but I escaped the first opportunity I got."

"So you think you're one of the good guys?" Parsons snarled.

Bukki scoffed. "No, not at all. I tried to be, but came up short. Real short. I did a lot of bad stuff. Nowhere near the level of trying to molest a man's daughter and then burning his family alive to cover it up, but yeah, I've got a litany of things on my resume that I'm not very proud of. I got away with it all, too. On paper, I was one of the best cops Apalashu had ever seen. So, if you're here to make sure someone pays for what we did on that fucking planet, then do what you have to. It's about time one of us got what we deserved."

Parsons drew his pistol, but that was all. He never even bothered to aim it. I could see a lot of conflict and turmoil taking place just behind my squad leader's eyes. We had gone through a bit of trouble to get Luuk Bukki to Kanaris. It seemed like a waste not to do anything now that we had him. Still, Barone Parsons knew Private Bukki played no part in his tragedy. Any harm my sergeant could have done to him would have been injury inflicted upon the wrong man.

Putting his M88 back in its holster, Parsons cursed before telling Bukki, "You'll get what you deserve, all right. All new Marines on Kanaris are supposed to go through the acclimatization course at Camp Vayipar. I'm going to guess that the odds of you surviving the Satapadaya Front without it are pretty slim, but you're going to give it a go. If you make it, I'll consider you cleansed of your sins. If you don't, you got what you had coming."

Bukki nodded. "Okay. I understand. I'm not complaining, but I have to wonder why you're letting me off the hook. If the Apalashu police murdered my family, I'd have killed every fuckin' one of them."

Barone Parsons marched over to Private Bukki and jammed his index finger into the rifleman's throat, just below his Adam's apple. "I'm not you!" my squad leader snapped. "I'm better than you! And don't you ever forget it, you fucking piece of shit!"

Chapter 21

EXPEDITION

Despite having been invited into my inner circle, Bufort Graym looked ill at ease and out of place. Technically, Buffy was a civilian, so instead of wearing the uniform of a Kyperion Marine, he was clothed in a ragged pair of coveralls that still reeked of ubati shit. He had an encyclopedic knowledge of alien zoology that could have made my Citadel professors look like drooling morons, but the man had little formal education. Coupled with a speech impediment that made him talk like a child, he felt like an idiot trying to keep up in a conversation with Barone Parsons, Ritza Xi, and Dmitri Naktada. Not that I could blame him for that last one, though. Naktada made me feel stupid, too.

"Relax, Buffy," I told the man, trying to put him at ease, "you're among friends now."

"I was among fwiends befo'e," he said back. "Until I bwoke the one inviolable law of my people."

Having taken Qilkorian lives on behalf of outsiders, Buffy was cast out of his community and marked for death. A week later, his face was burdened with a heavy expression suggesting he might have been harboring second thoughts about the unforgivable sin he had committed.

"You did the right thing," I assured the man in an attempt to put his mind at ease.

"Did I?" he asked me. "If I did the wight thing, then why do I feel like such a twaituh?"

"You're no traitor," Naktada said. "In the League's eyes, you're a hero."

"Fuck the League's eyes," Buffy snapped. "I've seen the kind of people the League makes hewoes out of. That ain't the kind of company I like to keep."

I nodded in understanding. Being one of the Kyperion League's false heroes myself, I knew where he was coming from. Waving my arms before the group I had assembled in my tent, I said, "Me neither. That's why I spend my time with these people."

Buffy cast his gaze upon the Marines gathered around him. "And what bwought you all togethuh?"

"A long walk through the Kanarisian jungle," Parsons told him. "It's been Tauk's efforts at getting us freed that really bind us, though. And his word to help us achieve our objectives if we help him achieve his."

"And what ah you' objectives?"

Parsons stuck his thumb out at himself and Xi. "For me and her, it's getting out of here to exact revenge against the people who forced us onto this shithole."

"What about you?" Buffy asked my Technological Warfare Specialist.

Naktada shrugged. "I'm with Tauk because I think he's my best shot at getting my hands on some genuine alien weaponry. The command wants to use Recon as cannon fodder, but the lieutenant's got other ideas that might give us the opportunity to do what we're supposed to."

Buffy turned his attention back to me. "And that involves getting that woman you we'e telling me about?"

I nodded. "If we get her, we figure out where the aliens are." After pausing to let out a sigh, I added, "But we've got some difficulties ahead of us. Section 615 wants Deena Vulk also, and they don't want anyone catching her but themselves. They have no interest in sharing the glory of pulling off a coup like that. They threatened to have me killed if they caught me trying to find the bitch."

"Yet, you' still twying?"

I nodded. "It's the only purpose I have in life at the moment."

Buffy squinted at me and shook his head. "I'm sensing the'e's mo' to this than finding the enemy, Tauk. What else you want this woman fo'?"

"Let me be clear," I said. "I want Deena Vulk because she's the key to learning about the aliens on Kanaris. That's my primary objective. I also need to tell you she murdered the woman I was in love with and damned near killed me too."

It was Buffy's turn to sigh. "So this is a vendetta?"

"No," I lied. "Capturing, torturing, and killing Deena Vulk is not the purpose of my mission. It's just a perk."

"You shuh?" Buffy asked. "I don't do vendettas. It's a good way to get the w'ong people killed."

"I'm sure," I answered. I sounded far more convincing than I felt.

Buffy stared into my eyes for a couple of moments to gauge if I was telling the truth. I did not think he concluded whether I had or not, but he eventually remembered he did not have anywhere else to go even if I was lying. "Okay. If we have to find this woman, we'll find huh. What kind of evidence do you have fo' me?"

"Nothing," I said. "Section 615 isn't going to give anything up on our target."

Buffy shook his head. "I need something, Lieutenant. I can't twain my ubati to sniff out a figment of you' memowy. Is the'e anything you know she touched fo' shuh that may still be whe'e you saw huh?"

"I doubt my memory is capable of that kind of precision," I told Buffy.

"You'd be surprised what the human brain can do," Naktada said. "I can pull some pretty amazing shit out of my head when I focus on the details. Tell me everything you can about the first time you laid eyes on Deena Vulk. What was the first thing you saw of her?"

"Her ass," I answered.

Ritza Xi laughed. "You need to take this seriously, sir."

"I am," I told her. "When I first saw Deena Vulk, she was slung over the shoulder of a Marine corporal. Her head was hanging across his back. Her legs were over his chest, held in place by one of his arms."

"Which arm?" Naktada asked.

"His left."

"What was in the Marine's right hand?"

I had to think hard for a moment to visualize the rifleman as he trudged up to our landing zone. To my amazement, I remembered the answer to Naktada's question. "Nothing. His right hand was resting on his sidearm, ready to drop Vulk and draw it if they ran into trouble."

"Good, good," Naktada said. "What was she wearing on her feet?"

"Boots."

"Detail, sir. We need detail."

"They were black. Leather. They went halfway up her calf."

"And what started where they ended?"

126

"Her fatigue pants. Those were black, also. They had cargo pockets on the side...."

"Black fatigue pants?" asked Ritza Xi. "Like the kind the Section 615 commandos wear?"

I nodded. "Yeah. Like those."

"And her shirt?"

I shook my head. "We were at a high elevation. She was wearing a coat for cold weather."

"Was that a Section 615 issue also?"

"No," I told my Technological Warfare Specialist. "It was civilian. Probably from one of the research teams. She was dressed in a hodgepodge of different items she probably scavenged from Narman's Pyke."

"Did she have armor?" asked Parsons.

"No."

"Weapons?"

"No. She was already a prisoner when I saw her."

"It was cold up there?" asked Ritza Xi.

I nodded. "Freezing."

"Was she wearing a hat then?"

"No. She was wearing a scarf."

"But nothing on her head?"

"She was wearing her scarf on her...."

The image popped into my head clear as day. When I first saw Deena Vulk, I thought our Marines had used her scarf to blindfold her. It was wrapped around her head. The black-and-white checkered cloth came undone when the Marine threw her onto the ground, and then a big gust of wind picked it up and carried it into the brush, well away from where we were gathered. "The scarf," I gasped.

"What about it?" asked Naktada.

"It's probably still there! The Marines apparently didn't want to waste their own bandages to cover the injuries on Vulk's face, so they wrapped her head in her scarf. It came off while they were manhandling her and blew into the woods! It was before we were ambushed, so no one thought to grab it!" Turning to Buffy, I asked, "Would that work?"

"A big piece of cloth soaked with Deena Vulk's blood and then pwese'ved in fweezing tempuhatuhes fo' the last ten months?" Buffy paused as a grin stretched across his face. "It's like fate knew we was coming and saved it fo' us! It's pe'fect!"

The first call I made was to Je'Sikka Albarn, asking if she could give us a lift to Toranad after roll call. The second was to Gunny Brumit, ordering her to have the platoon combat ready before quarters. The following morning, immediately after we were dismissed from formation, all my Marines grabbed their gear and double-timed their way to the *Niberian Hornet*. Adhering to combat deployment protocol, we were airborne within ninety seconds of securing the ingress hatch.

After we cleared Narman Pyke's walls, I addressed my troops. "This may sound like your typical military bullshit, but I give you my word that today's mission may be one of the most important things you will do on Kanaris. We're going to Mount Toranad, people. That was the place where I saw the aliens we're up against. It was where I damned near got myself killed. So, while we're up there, I want all of you to be at the highest level of alertness. Do you understand me?"

"YES, SIR!" screamed my Marines.

"We're looking for a black and white checkered scarf. This thing's been on that mountain for about ten months now. It's probably going to be in rough shape. Whatever you do...Do. Not. Touch. It. You mark its position and call me or Gunny Brumit. This fabric is a critical piece of evidence we need to track down someone we *know* has had contact with the aliens. We want to give their scent, not yours, to Buffy's ubati. Got it?"

"YES, SIR!"

My platoon was displaying very high *esprit de corps*. "Whoever finds the scarf earns themselves a full week of on-station leave, completely off the books. That's seven days of rest and relaxation, Marines. Who wants some of that?"

The deployment bay broke into a round of battle cries that did not stop until we touched down in the same clearing where I had lost Jella. When the hatches opened, my troops disembarked and let Gunny Brumit form them into the line in which they marched off into the woods. When they were out of sight, I asked my platoon sergeant, "You think they'll find it?"

Brumit nodded. "If it's out there, it'll only be a matter of time before one of our people stumbles across it."

It only took about an hour and a half. Lance Corporal Ozi Lichak, Third Squad's corpsman, discovered the fabric entangled in the branches of a barren bush about a half kilometer from where Vulk lost it. When Buffy turned Meit on to it, the ubati buried its nose in the tattered cloth and spent five minutes nuzzling and licking it until it snorted excitedly and started pawing at the ground.

Buffy looked up at me and smiled. "Meit's got it! If that bitch gets within two kilome-tuhs of us, Meit'll let us know. If we come acwoss some gwound she's twead within a week of huh passing by, he'll pick up huh scent and lead us wight to huh! We's gonna get huh, Tauk!"

I reached over and slapped Lichak across the shoulder. "Congratulations! You've earned some time off!"

Je'Sikka Albarn was waiting by the *Hornet* when we returned to the ship. "You find what you were looking for?" she asked.

I did not have to answer her. The smile on my face said it all.

Albarn's nose scrunched up in disgust as Meit ambled past her. "Ugh. My god, do those things stink! Anyway, I hope what you found was worth it."

"Worth what?"

"You didn't tell your company commander what you were doing over here, did you?"

I shook my head, relieved I had angered only Captain Pustov. As hard as he could make my life, dealing with him would be far easier than facing an inquisitor from military intelligence. "No, I didn't. Is he mad?"

Albarn gave me a single nod. "Enraged. Apparently, the Narmans launched an assault on our line opposite the Satapadaya Range. Our forces were damned near overrun. It's an all-hands-on-deck situation, and everyone is piling out of the Pyke to beat the bastards back. Recon was supposed to make up the first wave, but that got stalled due to Beta Company missing an entire platoon."

Shaking my head, I buried my face in my hands. "Of all the fucking times to...."

Albarn playfully patted me on the shoulder. "Relax. Pustov's pissed, but if you get your Marines on board right now, I can guarantee I get you to the staging area before anyone else makes it there."

"Thanks," I told Albarn as I turned to shout at all my Marines milling about the Mar-Sitaara. "Everybody aboard the airship! Now! There's been a development on the front and we're being shipped out immediately!"

Spotting Ozi Lichak running past me, I swung around and grabbed her by the arm. "I'm sorry, Lance Corporal. It doesn't look like I'll be able to make good on my promise to get you seven days of R&R."

Lichak shrugged. "It wouldn't matter if you did. I'm a corpsman. There ain't no way I'm letting my Marines go into harm's way without me."

Chapter 22

TAARLAK

The situation at the front was far more dire than initially reported. Since my platoon was combat-ready, we were ordered to skip our return to Narman's Pyke and proceed directly to the rear operating base at Camp Saepayum, situated on the far bank of the Kula River. The Kula was four hundred and fifty clicks west of the Pyke and the extreme of where the Corps could claim air superiority. Beyond the Kula, as the saying went, flying meant dying.

As we disembarked from the *Niberian Hornet,* we were confronted by a sea of wounded Marines awaiting airlift back to the Pyke. There were hundreds of the poor bastards out there, bloodied, battered, split open, and burned. Many had lost their limbs. Others had lost their minds. One young man turned to me as I passed, his eyes set ablaze by the spark of insanity. "THEY CAME OUT OF THE TREES!" he screamed at me. "FUCKING DEMONS! THEY DROPPED BOMBS ON US! SET US ON FIRE! THEN THEY RIPPED US APART!"

"The Narmans?" asked one of my medics.

"THE FUCKING QUARAKAI!"

The corpsman did not really appreciate what that meant. He had never seen the Quarakai up close and in person. I had, however. I fought them at Narman's Pyke and watched them tear Marines to pieces with their bare hands. The idea of having them sneak up and take us by surprise made my blood run cold.

Despite being two hundred kilometers from the line, Camp Saepayum was quickly descending into chaos. The tarmac was filling with mutilated Marines faster than they could be evacuated. The air was full of the roar of Raptor transports, the moans of the wounded, and orders shouted by non-commissioned officers struggling to sort the bedlam into some semblance of order. We had to scream at each other to be heard over the commotion.

It stopped raining just as Albarn was setting her airship down, and the heat was rising fast, adding to the discomfort of the wounded. Fifteen minutes on the ground, and we were already sweating buckets. Our body odor combined with the smell of spent explosives, blood, and human waste to form a noxious assault on our olfactory senses. The stench of gangrene was so thick I could almost taste it.

The scene before us was overwhelming, and I feared the toll it would take on my Marines. "We gotta get out of here," I told Gunny Brumit.

Brumit nodded in agreement. "Yeah, but where the hell do we go?"

"Tauk!" someone screamed out to me as if to answer Gunny's question. It was Agent Takawa, the man who threatened to kill me if I went looking for Deena Vulk on my own. His demeanor seemed much different now.

"Agent Takawa!" I screamed back. "What are you doing here?"

"Waiting for you!" Lacking time for pleasantries, Takawa got right to the point. "I don't think the Narmans know it yet, but they've almost completely wiped out the Third Infantry Battalion's Epsilon Company! Everyone got hit hard, but those poor bastards were just destroyed! There may be a dozen survivors holding the line, tops! We have to get your platoon there ASAP! If the enemy figures out just how few of us are left there, they're going to pour through that breach and hit us from the rear!"

I nodded. "Why are you telling me this instead of the brigade commander?" I was not used to getting marching orders from spies.

"Colonel Torabor is at the front and a little busy! He's down two battalion commanders and the rest of the officer corps is suffering similar casualty rates! There ain't nobody left to meet incoming troops! The northern flank was my area of operations during my last rotation, so I was asked to lead you there!"

"Aye aye!" I shouted back. "Then lead the way!"

Because nothing could fly past the Kula River, we had to march to the western edge of Camp Saepayum and board ground transports to drive us to the Forward Operating Base at Camp Taarlak, one hundred and fifty kilometers away.

"Rest up!" Takawa told my platoon once we secured a combat crawler in which to leave Camp Saepayum. "This route will take us to Taarlak, but no further. The Corps has combat engineers trying to build a road over the forty clicks separating Taarlak from the front, but at best, what we have is a muddy trail. When this crawler stops, we got a long walk ahead of us. Don't expect any rest when we reach our destination, either. We may have to fight as soon as we hit the trenches."

"Fight who?" asked Gunny Brumit.

"Everyone," Takawa told her. "First off, we're up against the Narmans. Most of them are armed with the same gear we have, but a few of them, the ones who've earned the aliens' trust, are using Harnillium blasters. They're not shooting bullets at us. They're shooting energy beams. Your armor is worthless against that stuff, so don't get yourself killed by a sense of false confidence. By the way, there's an eighty-thousand credit reward for anyone who captures an alien blaster. Understand?"

My platoon cheered upon hearing of the reward. For most of them, that was three years' salary.

"In addition to the Narmans, we're also going to be facing off against Marine deserters. These are our former comrades, people. They have the same equipment and training we do. They know us. They know our organization, our tactics, and the personalities leading us. At this point, there are more of them in the enemy trenches than Narmans. I would love to dismiss these insurgents as pathetic weaklings with no moral center, but that would be doing you a disservice. Those deserters are motivated, Marines. They have hate in their hearts for everything the League holds dear, and they are even more passionate about destroying us than we are about destroying them. Do NOT underestimate your adversaries! Got it?"

"Yes, sir!" my platoon called out in unison.

"This brings us to the Quarakai! These are the things nightmares are made of. They're huge and..." Takawa paused long enough to point at Akkam Lumuk, who stood head and shoulders above anyone else in my unit. "They're taller than that guy! They're also four times as strong! We're learning these creatures have the same intellectual capabilities we do, just not the training. They're like cavemen, but stronger. Fortunately for us, they lack our fine motor skills. Also, as fast and agile as they are in the trees, they're awkward on the ground. It takes a lot of bullets to put one down, but it can be done."

I instinctively reached down to touch the seibara hanging from my belt. Naktada used his connections to ensure every NCO in my platoon had one. I hoped they would be a game changer at the front, doing to the Quarakai what our rifles could not.

"Look," Takawa told my troops. "I'm going to level with you. Quarakai are hard to put down, but you have to do it before they get to you. Once you're in their grip, it's all over. They can rip your limbs off your torso without breaking a sweat. They don't have to use their teeth, but they got a lot of them in that big fuckin' mouth of theirs. They can bite you right in half. These creatures are ugly, too. Between that long snout and those big cat eyes they got, a lot of Marines tend to freeze up at the sight of them. I'll tell you right now, that's the quickest way to die out here. If you hear someone yell, 'Quarakai!' you best start shooting the shit out of them. Any questions?"

Jiani Ghinion, Fourth Squad's armorer, raised her hand and asked. "What about the aliens? The Morghul?"

Takawa shrugged his shoulders. "I've only caught a glimpse of them. As far as the aliens are concerned, your guess is as good as mine."

Camp Taarlak was in even more disarray than Saepayum was. Hundreds of Marines, no longer willing to wait for transport to the rear, decided to walk there. The single road into the forward operating base was flooded with troops struggling to press forward in the opposite direction. "Go back!" many of them called out to us. "There ain't nothing up this road but death! Turn around while you still can!"

They were a ragged lot. Most had lost or dropped their armor and were now clad only in tattered fatigues. Those still able to walk dragged along those who could not. Military police patrolled the crowd trying to weed out the malingerers and send them back to the front. While standing atop our transport as it lumbered through the mob, I watched a trio of MPs attempt to seize a young man they deemed fit to fight. As they dragged their quarry out of the throng, those fleeing the battle set upon the cops and beat them into the mud. The fight eventually ended, but I never saw the MPs get up again. I assumed they were dead.

Five clicks out of Taarlak, the road was too clogged with humanity for the crawler to move any further west. We were forced to disembark and walk.

"Keep them in formation," I told my squad leaders once we were on the road. "I don't want our people getting so spooked by the retreating troops that they try to join them."

"Shouldn't we be grabbing these people and turning them back in the other direction?" Sergeant Kal-Xati asked me. "A lot of them look just fine."

"They'd be more of a liability than an asset out there," I told her. "They need to regroup and reorganize. Right now, none of those people are Marines. They're a mob. If we force them back to the front, we'll likely have to fight them as well as the Narmans."

"That's right," added a woman who emerged from the crowd to greet Agent Takawa. She too was wearing black fatigues of the Section 615 commandos. "By my estimation, a third of our troops went to the other side. The other third cut and run in retreat."

"And the remaining third?" I asked.

The agent glared at me. "They held the line. Or died trying."

"I'm glad to see you made it out, Nala," Takawa told the woman.

"Hi Supai," Nala said. The two agents were close enough to be on a first-name basis. "I'm happy to see you made it in."

Turning to me, Takawa introduced his colleague. "Tauk, this is Agent Nala Biragor. She's the one coordinating intel collection along the front."

Agent Biragor reached out to shake my hand. "Not that there's much intel to collect. I've mainly been...."

"Hey!" interrupted a stray Qilkorian as he passed by. "Anybody here need any Demon Root?"

Buffy Graym pushed the Killbilly out of the way. "Get the fuck away fwom us with that shit!"

"Best to get it here!" the man retorted. "Y'all might be fresh now, but after a couple of weeks out there on the front, you're going to want something to take your mind ...."

Buffy drew his sidearm and pointed it in the Killbilly's face. "Fuck off!"

With his hands up in the air, the dealer backed away. "Okay, man. Okay. I can take a hint."

Agent Biragor sighed. "There's been something of a Kan Qui epidemic sweeping the front ever since the Killbillies showed up."

"There usually is," Gunny Brumit agreed. "That shit pops up wherever they do."

Buffy bristled at Brumit's generalization but found it hard to contradict her. As prejudicial as Gunny's comment was, it was true.

"You were saying, Nala?" Takawa asked, trying to get the conversation back on track.

Agent Biragor's face twisted in confusion as she tried to remember what she was talking about. When it finally dawned on her, she cleared her throat and said, "Intel! Yes. It's hard to come by out there. Our optical sensors can't penetrate the thick vegetation, our audible array can't pick out human voices above the din of the rain and fauna, and thanks to the Harnillium interference, our electronic intelligence capabilities are worthless outside of a four-kilometer perimeter."

"Are you getting any data at all?" Brumit asked.

Agent Biragor shrugged. "Just human intel. Mainly from what we can get out of our prisoners. To be honest, we're not getting a lot of that either. Not even after turning them over to the Killbillies for their 'Qilkorian Light Touch.' The Narmans are turning our deserters into fanatics. They ain't talking."

"So what's the situation on the line now?" asked Takawa.

Biragor nervously licked her lips. "Tenuous. The Narmans came at us hard. They got the Quarakai in close, and while we were preoccupied with those savages, the bastards snuck across No Man's Land. Right before they hit us, the Marines planning to switch sides opened fire on their officers and NCOs, sending the entire front into disarray. It was a bloodbath."

"Did we lose the line?" asked Gunny Brumit.

The agent shook her head. "Our best guess is we outnumber the Narmans by about four to one. After subtracting our dead and wounded, those who defected, and everyone who fled, we figure the enemy reduced our strength just enough to make it a fair fight. Against even numbers, the advantage goes to the defenders. We held the line, but just barely. If they attack with even a tenth of what they came at us with the last time, we're done. They'll walk right through our defenses. The last action was pretty much a battle of mutual annihilation."

"Then we best get to the line as soon as we can," said Gunny Brumit.

"Yes, you best," Biragor agreed.

Taking our leave from Takawa's colleague, my platoon marched toward the forward operating base. It took us a few hours to get there, but when we finally reached Camp Taarlak, we found it far less congested than the road leading out of it. I was actually able to pick a familiar face out of the crowd. "Holy shit!" I exclaimed.

"What?" asked my platoon sergeant.

"I just saw Gunny Malcolm step out of one of the command tents! Keep our troops marching, Shai. I'll catch up. I'm going to go talk to him."

"About what?" Brumit asked.

"About what's really going on at the front!" Before my Number Two could give me another question, I took off running toward where I saw Malcolm disappear.

At first, I had lost the man. No one was to be seen but rear echelon Marines and death squad Killbillies. One of the Qilkorians I encountered wore a necklace fashioned out of human ears. Another had a bandolier hanging across his chest made of tanned human skin. I could only assume he liked his victims' tattoos and decided he wanted to wear them, too.

It took a minute or two to find Malcolm. When I did, I noticed he looked like hell. His uniform was a mess. It was covered in mud and a frightening amount of dried blood. The left arm of his fatigue shirt had been ripped off, and the exposed skin was wrapped in bandages. Whether that was to protect his wounds or cover up the needle marks, I did not know.

As I started fighting through the crowd to get to him, Malcolm passed the man with the tattooed bandolier. "Hey, Sarge!" I heard the Killbilly call out. "You looking for some KQR? You need some Demon Root?"

Malcolm stopped dead in his tracks and turned to glower at the pusher. I thought Gunny was going to plant his fist in the dirtbag's mouth, but instead, he shoved his hand into his pocket and pulled out a bunch of credit coins, dropping them into the dealer's palm. After taking possession of a small bag of Kan Qui Radix from the Killbilly, Malcolm pulled a pinch of tan powder from the batch and snorted it up his nose, not even bothering to hide it. After a second hit, he continued on his way.

I did not bother to follow him. I doubted there was anything useful I could glean from Gunny Malcolm while he was in the throes of a Radix bender. I knew how terrifying his dreams could be. I would never be able to comprehend what abominations his hallucinations might have held in store for him.

Chapter 23

The Front

Biragor told us the Marines had held the line. She said it in the past tense, as if the fighting was over. We discovered while walking to our objective, however, that the situation remained fluid. We could hear the battle raging from a half-dozen clicks away. Judging by the machine gun fire and explosions still reaching our ears, the line was still quite contested.

Three kilometers from our destination, we were stopped by a captain. His left hand was bandaged, and it looked as if he was missing a couple of fingers. His armor was marred and scorched. The right side of his face was peppered with shrapnel wounds. The whites of both eyes had turned red from burst blood vessels. He was flanked by a pair of gruesome-looking Killbillies. "You got any Zeros with you?" he asked me without introducing himself.

There was no way for me to lie to the man as we were all in full uniform. "Of course I do. Why?"

"This is as far as they go," the captain told me. "Turn them over."

I involuntarily craned my head to look at Xi, Jenich, and Gul, my three female Zeros. Having a fair idea of what would happen to them at the hands of the Qilkorians the captain had with him, I shook my head and said, "Sorry, sir. I'm an academy officer. I have the right to hand-pick my platoon, which is exactly what I've done, right down to my Zeros. Each has earned my protection, and I'm not about to turn them over to anyone else to abuse."

The captain scowled. "It wasn't a request, Lieutenant. It was an order. Right from Colonel Palkrait. Our Zeros have nothing to lose, so nearly every single one of them has deserted to the enemy the first chance they got. You can rest assured there are few Narmans more motivated to kill Kyperion Marines than freshly freed Class Zero convicts."

Nodding at my trio of liberated comfort women, the captain then told me, "As for abusing your female prisoners, let me assure you they're at far less risk of being molested under my command than they are under yours. In fact, you best worry about *them* abusing *you*."

"How do you figure that?" I asked.

The captain put a couple of his remaining fingers in his mouth and loosed an ear-splitting whistle. At his signal, a dozen female Zeros emerged from the brush on both sides of the road. They were armed with military-issued M72s in blatant violation of Marine regulations.

Stepping back to address my platoon, the captain said, "You have no doubt seen the chaos on the road leading to Camp Saepayum! Hundreds, maybe even thousands, of Marines abandoned their posts along this line and fled in the face of the enemy! So many so that our entire force nearly collapsed! That ends NOW!"

The captain started pacing up and down my ranks. "I want you men to consider your last visit to Narman Pyke's Morale Center. Think about the women your ugly asses crawled on top of there. Put yourselves in their position! Get inside their heads and imagine what they felt as you used them to relieve yourselves. Imagine how you'd have felt had we confined you to a room and allowed a line of sweaty men to pull a train on your pathetic asses night after night after night! Think of the fantasies you'd be entertaining about what you would do to all the fuckers who abused you if the tables were turned!"

After pausing for dramatic effect, the captain said, "Well, let me assure you the tables have indeed turned, gentlemen! If you flee that battlefield, these are the women you'll be running into on your way back to the rear. I promise you they're every bit as enthusiastic about killing Kyperion Marines as their Narman counterparts are. Especially considering that each of them has been promised a full pardon if she kills twenty cowards."

Strolling over to one of the Killbillies, the captain reached beneath his collar to show us the macabre necklace the man was wearing. "As you can see, some members of our Qilkorian contingent have been collecting the ears of their victims to prove how many deserters they've culled. Anyone care to take a guess at what body part my ladies are collecting?"

As the captain waited for an answer, I scanned the faces of the men under my command. Judging by their expressions, I doubted any of them would ever be visiting the Morale Center again.

Margi Gul, her face still showing the bruises she received during her bout against Slai Huurling, was sold. She broke ranks and walked toward the captain's Zeros. One of Gul's new comrades passed her a rifle and hugged her, welcoming her into the fold. Zubi Jenich was close behind her.

Ritza Xi walked up to me before joining her friends. "Thanks for springing us from that hellhole, Tauk. I owe you one. I promise not to hurt you if we cross paths in the jungle someday."

Smiling at my prisoner, I said, "Thanks, Xi. Good luck to you out there."

Xi nodded and walked over to the leader of First Squad. "You too, Barone. If you have to run, drop my name to whoever catches you, and I'll look out for you like you've always looked out for me. Tell Lumuk to do the same."

Sergeant Parsons wrapped his arms around Xi and hugged her tight. "Will do. You be careful out there, Ritza."

"I will."

As my Zeros separated themselves from my platoon to leave with the captain, Margi Gul turned around and, spotting PFC Huurling among my Fourth Squad riflemen, blew him a kiss. "I hope we see each other soon, sweetheart!"

Despite us practically running to our positions in the final stretch to the Satapadaya Front, the sounds of battle abruptly ceased right before I emerged from the jungle at the defenders' rear. It was a scene of pure carnage as the broken bodies of vanquished Marines littered the trench they were desperately trying to hold. I spotted only two survivors. One was oblivious to us walking up from behind. His hands were wrapped tightly around the double handles of an M456 heavy machine gun, from which hung a feeder belt containing the gunner's last three bullets. From my vantage point, it appeared the leatherneck manning the weapon ran out of enemies and ammunition at nearly the exact same moment.

The other defender saw me coming but was too injured to warn her companion. She was seated with her back against the mound of rocks and mud from behind which the gunner was firing. Her chest plate was shattered, revealing the shredded fatigues she wore beneath it. One of her hands was clasped around her throat as she tried to keep pressure on one of her more severe injuries. A small but steady stream of blood trickled from the side of her mouth. I could tell by the faraway look in her eyes that she would not be with us long.

The injured Marine tried to tell the gunner I was there. Her lips moved like a doomed fish suffocating in the open air, but no sound came from between them. Her comrade remained oblivious to me, scanning No Man's Land with his weapon, quaking in terror.

"Sergeant!" I called out at the standing Marine in a coarse whisper, trying not to startle the man.

Wrenching his head around to look at me with crazed eyes, the man blinked in disbelief and stammered, "Who the fuck are you?!?"

"Reinforcements!"

"Really?!?" the Marine spat, turning his attention back to the field of fire before him. "Now?!? Where were you an hour ago? When my people were still alive?"

"Trying to get here. The mob fleeing the lines slowed us down."

"Whatever," the sergeant said, dismissing my excuse to return to his search for targets.

Activating my commlink, I ordered the rest of my troops up front, telling Jatmika and Xarra, two of my light machine gunners, to set up positions on either side of the M456. When they were ready, I had to pry the sergeant's fingers from his weapon. "We got it now, Sarge. You can let go."

I looked at the breastplate of the Marine's exo-armor to identify him, but his nameplate had been burned off. "What do they call you?"

"D-D-Damon, sir. S-S-Sergeant Jaq Damon."

"Holy Hell," I heard Lance Corporal Jatmika gasp as I directed the platoon's senior medic to attend to the dying female. "Sir, you should take a look at this."

Crawling up to the top of the mound, I peered over the fortifications at the chunk of land separating us from the enemy. It had taken so much ordnance that the once verdant rainforest was reduced to wet mulch and covered with hundreds of mangled

Narman corpses. Judging by the shape the bodies were in, it appeared Damon's M456 was responsible for most of the carnage.

"You truly went through hell here, didn't you?" I asked the sergeant, unable to believe he killed all those people himself. "I'm going to see to it you're awarded the Marine Cross for this!"

"Fuck the cross!" Damon sobbed. "I got kids, Lieutenant! Three girls! You want to show some appreciation for what I did here? Send me home! Let me hug my daughters again!"

I looked Damon over and saw that, though he was rattled, his injuries were largely superficial. "I don't think I can do that, Sergeant."

"Then what the fuck are you good for?" The gunner turned his back to me and walked over to a shallow foxhole. Jumping into it, he sat in the mud and cradled his head between his knees, his body shaking as he wept.

I went to comfort him, but Gunny Brumit held me back. "Don't crowd the man," my platoon sergeant told me. "Give him some room and some time. He's earned it."

No sooner had Brumit finished speaking when a woman's shriek erupted from beyond the berm. Xarra immediately opened fire. "NARMANS!" he screamed to the rest of us. "THERE'S STILL SOME ALIVE OUT THERE!"

Looking up at the commotion, I could see bullets ricocheting off the top of the berm as the enemy returned fire. Sergeant Kal-Xati drew a grenade from her web gear, pulled the pin, and tossed it over the earthworks. Someone out in No Man's Land caught it and threw it back. The canister came sailing in over our heads, bounced off LCPL Qarsi's helmet, then landed in the foxhole Sergeant Damon had just retreated to, detonating before it hit the ground.

The explosion sent one of the gunner's arms flying into the air while launching the rest of him far from where he took cover. The blast should have killed the man instantly, but it appeared Sergeant Damon used up all his luck fending off the waves of attackers the Narmans sent at his position.

When the smoke cleared, Damon was not only on his feet but staggering toward us with his remaining arm outstretched in a plea for help. His jaw was almost ripped from his face, attached to his left cheek by a thin strand of shredded skin and a single tendon. His tongue hung limply from a hole torn through his throat where his larynx should have been. The sergeant's nose was sheered clean off his face, as was one of his eyes. The other dangled from an empty socket by the end of an optical nerve. One brief look at what had happened to the gunner gave me an instant understanding of what drove Gunny Malcolm to score some Killbilly Demon Root.

"MEDIC!" screamed Akkam Lumuk, recoiling in terror as the abomination that was once Sergeant Damon approached him. "MEDIIIIIIIIC!"

Bledyn Marwol, one of my corpsmen, ran forward to help but skidded to a stop before he reached his patient.

"What are you doing?" cried Lukka Saceri as my gunners finally cut down the fighting Narmans. "Help him!"

Marwol shook his head, unable to believe what he was seeing. "I don't know where to start!"

A single shot went off behind the corpsman, sending a bullet into the space between where Damon's eyes should have been. The hero collapsed into a bloody heap, finally relieved of his misery.

Marwol turned to see Gunny Brumit still aiming her sidearm at the mangled sergeant. "What the fuck did you do that for?!?" he screamed.

Brumit returned her pistol to its holster. "You think anyone's capable of putting that man back together, son?"

The corpsman looked in horror at what Damon's face had been transformed into. After a couple of moments, he shook his head.

"Then you end his suffering, Doc."

"MEDIC!" Lumuk shrieked again. In shock, it was a word the giant from Gorsu Qat would scream over and over for the next several minutes.

Hours later, as we ventured out onto the near edge of No Man's Land to ensure no more survivors were hiding among the enemy corpses, I saw Lance Corporal Xarra march over and kick one of the bodies as hard as he could.

"What are you doing?" I asked him.

Shaking his head, Xarra told me, "Wishing I could hurt her even more. That's the bitch who threw the grenade at us."

Buffy Graym, my Qilkorian tracker, approached us from upfield. "She could've gotten away, you know. She was in a depwession a hundwed metuhs to the west. If she cwawled the othuh way, she would've made it all the way to the enemy line. We'd have nevuh seen huh again. Instead, she took huh time cwawling towa'd us. To kill us. She wanted ou' deaths mo' than she wanted huh own life."

Using my foot, I rolled the woman's body onto her side to see the stencil on her shoulder plate. She was a Class Zero convict. The captain who took Xi from me was right. Not only could the Narmans turn our conscripts into traitors, they transformed our Zeros into fanatics.

Chapter 24

War Pork

The position we inherited from Sergeant Damon was surrounded by the dead. It took my Class One convicts three days to strip the bodies of their armor and weapons and place them atop a big pile about a hundred meters deep into No Man's Land. The sickeningly sweet stench of decomposition kept wafting back into our trenches, so Gunny Brumit contacted a special weapons platoon back at Camp Taarlak and had them send up a squad of flamethrowers to set the corpses ablaze. They were still burning when Captain Pustov arrived with the rest of Beta Company. He was not happy to see me.

"I had half a mind to charge you with desertion when the mobilization alarm went off and you were nowhere to be found," Pustov snarled at me when he got to my Platoon CP. "Where the fuck were you?"

"For the most part," I told him, "we've been here, proudly serving as the tip of the spear soon to be thrust into the heart of Narman resistance."

"Don't fuck with me, Tauk. I'm not in the goddamned mood for it."

I let out a little sigh. "My platoon had the opportunity to familiarize ourselves with the Mar-Sitaara fighter transport, so we took it. We were onboard in full combat gear when the call went out, so we were sent right here. Quite honestly, I just assumed you made the call to send us directly to the front."

Pustov shook his head. "It wasn't me. Nor was it anyone from battalion. In fact, no one wants to claim responsibility for it. I can only assume someone from the squadron made a judgment call they don't want to own up to."

"Sounds like something a Samaari would do."

"It certainly does." Pustov paused to inhale deeply through his nose. "That smell. It...it...it smells..."

"It's okay," Gunny Brumit assured the captain. "You can admit it. It smells delicious, doesn't it?"

"It smells like you're having a barbecue."

"It certainly does, sir," said a staff sergeant who stepped into my CP uninvited. "I followed my nose, hoping to diversify my diet a bit. As good as they are, I'm getting a bit tired of popped kryptid. Imagine my disappointment to find that that incredible smell was only war pork." The trespassing Marine's armor showed all the signs of having been in the thick of the recent fighting, but the smile on his face suggested the man had never experienced tragedy in his entire life.

Uncomfortable with the intrusion, Gunny Brumit squinted at the Marine and asked, "Who the hell are you?"

The man held his hand out to my number two and introduced himself. "Staff Sergeant Noir Franq, Gunny. I've heard a lot about you."

Brumit's demeanor immediately softened as she took the staff sergeant's hand and shook it. "Not nearly as much as I've heard about you."

Turning to face the sergeant in charge of Fourth Squad, I could see the look of admiration in her eyes. "Who's Noir Franq?" I asked her.

"Black Francis," she told me. Kal-Xati was a formidable warrior with a fearsome reputation, but she appeared positively smitten to find herself in the same room as Franq. I could understand why.

From the news trickling in about what happened during the Narman offensive, it appeared both sides had nearly wiped each other out. In several places, including where we were stationed, the battle left fewer than a half dozen survivors to tell the tale. In one spot, there was no one left at all. From what the clean-up detail could decipher, it ultimately came down to two people in a knife fight who ended up killing each other. The last two combatants were found embracing one another as if they tried to comfort themselves in their final moments. In the middle of the line, where the fighting was thickest, the difference between winning and losing ended up being Black Francis and his Marines, who snuck through No Man's Land, taking the attackers from behind and killing Narman forces just as they were on the verge of victory.

Franq went around my CP, shaking everyone's hands and brushing off their accolades in a show of genuine modesty. "You're Black Francis?" Captain Pustov asked. "For some reason, I thought you'd be, um, darker."

Sergeant Franq grinned as he glanced down at the pale skin of his hands. "That's a common mistake, sir. The moniker came from my given name being translated into one of the ancient earthly languages. It has nothing to do with my appearance. If it did, they'd have to call me something like Albino Jeff."

When he got to me, Black Francis said, "I'm sorry about barging in, sir. I just had to meet the man who killed Gori Dravidas."

I caught myself blushing, embarrassed about being praised for a fraudulent act of heroism. Shaking the sergeant's hand, I said, "In real life, killing Dravidas did not deserve half the adulation I've received because of it."

Franq nodded in understanding. "Stories of heroics rarely measure up to actual events, sir. I know that better than most. Half the things I'm credited for were done by the Marines under my command, not me. I'm pretty sure the other half never even happened at all."

I laughed. I could not help but like Black Francis.

"Once again, sir, I apologize for the intrusion," Franq said to me, despite Pustov being the ranking officer in the CP. "My understanding is we're to hold the line until we get enough acclimatized troops on the front to try hitting the Narmans back. When our situation stabilizes, I'd like to run a couple of ideas by you about how to break this impasse."

Officers in general, and Academy graduates in particular, rarely sought advice from junior enlisted Marines. Black Francis had more than earned the right to be taken seriously, however. "You got it, Sergeant Franq. Feel free to stop by anytime."

"I will," Franq said, taking his leave after sending a wink to Kal-Xati.

"Whatever you two cook up," Pustov told me after Black Francis was gone, "you better run it by me well before it gets to the execution stage."

"Aye aye, sir."

Pustov gave me a nod. "All right. What do you know about our current situation?"

I shrugged. "Right now, all I know is we're here to hold the line and keep an eye on what's happening on the other side of No Man's Land."

"The Narmans nearly took us, Tauk. Do you know that?"

"I gathered that after seeing the final defender of this stretch of mud get his face blown off by a former Zero."

"General Duuq is not going to let that happen again. Next time, she wants it to be us attacking them. Let's take a walk and get a look at this No Man's Land. Shall we?"

My CP was an underground cement bunker built just behind the trench network. To get to No Man's Land, we had to weave through the Class One convicts rebuilding our defenses and climb the berm where Damon's M456 had been positioned. With a fresh delivery of ammunition, we had the heavy machine gun operating again. I had LCPL Lyra Ninauk, a spotter practicing to fill our open sniper billet, looking for targets beside it.

While looking over the contested ground with a set of optical amplifiers, Pustov seemed relieved. "There's more cover out there than I expected."

I nodded. "Yes, sir. There's a lot of artillery craters to hide in. Not to mention the trees here were so massive that even though they've been destroyed, there are chunks of them on the field that are sometimes two stories tall."

"You think it's possible to get across without being noticed?"

Shaking my head, I answered, "I doubt it. The Narmans have Quarakai in their ranks. They're probably up in the trees, looking down upon the wastes. Also, take a look at the tree line."

Pustov tried for a couple of moments but eventually lowered his optics, glaring at them as if they were not working correctly. "I can't focus. It's all blurry."

"That's not your optics. That's alien camo tech. It's some type of hologram. See that shimmer? It's what I saw them using when I got shot on Toranad. I'm pretty sure they can see us, but we can't see them."

"That's problematic."

"It sure is," Gunny Brumit agreed.

"We need to figure out a way to see what's going on over there," Pustov told us, stating the obvious. "Can we sneak around their flanks by going far to the north and bypassing No Man's Land?"

"Not really," I told the captain. "They can detect our vehicles, so the only way to sneak in is on foot. From what Agent Takawa told us, the wilds are patrolled by Narmans on naypetos with ubatis at their sides. The ubatis will pick up our scent, and there's no way we can outrun a naypeto."

"Maybe we need naypetos," Pustov mused.

"The Qilkorians are working on it," Brumit told our captain. "It'll be months before we have any, though. You have to separate them from their mothers and raise them from the time they hatch. The few we have were captured."

"Then figure out a way to capture some more."

I grinned. "You want us to shift from recon to rustling?"

"I want you to shift into whatever it takes to get us to break that line over there," Pustov said. "Look, in a few hours, you're going to have Class One porters bringing you everything you left at Narman's Pyke. Your ubatis. All the tech stuff Naktada was working on. You'll have the equipment, the animals, and the expertise you need to figure this shit out. I need you, all of you, to think outside the box."

Pustov paused to clip his optics back to his web gear. "It's going to take a lot of creativity to find the solution to this obstacle, Tauk. Let me assure you that our high command is not famous for its imagination. If you can't solve this problem, the general staff will try to do it the only way they know how. They'll play the numbers game, assuming we can absorb far more casualties than the Narmans can."

My captain once more inhaled deeply through his nose. "Tauk, their only concern is victory. They don't care how much more war pork they cook up achieving it."

Chapter 25

BARBALU

If there was one thing about war that would most surprise anyone who had never experienced it, it would be just how boring combat could be. That was especially true along a static front. Two weeks after we arrived in the foothills leading up to the Satapadaya ranges, all the bodies littering the battlefield were burned, the defenses were repaired, and the trenches resupplied in preparation for the next Narman move. The only thing left to do was try to keep our eyes on the savages in case they took another stab at overrunning us.

Not that things never happened. A week into our deployment, my aspiring sniper, Lyra Ninauk, poked her head above the berm to get a look at the enemy tree line. As the top of her helmet crested the mound, her counterpart on the other side of No Man's Land took a shot at her. The bullet struck Lyra in the face shield, snapping her head back and hurtling her off our fortifications. She landed in the trench, flat on her back. She lived, but it was a few days before she recovered full range of motion in her neck.

There were a couple of other minor incidents as well, but for the most part, things stayed quiet. My technical warfare specialist, Dmitri Naktada, spent his time trying to improve upon the anti-magnetic properties of my exo-armor. He actually got it to the point where I could levitate off the ground a few centimeters. Again, it was nothing I could use in the field, but it was an amazing breakthrough. Had the League been able to benefit from Naktada's talents for a few more years, it would have revolutionized Kyperion transportation.

Gunny Brumit spent her days trying to keep my troops busy, knowing idle minds sprung little but trouble. My intel sergeant paced the trenches from north to south, looking for weaknesses along the enemy's defenses. My squad leaders trained their ubatis. Deprived of her star student, my praetorian killed time teaching the platoon's females the martial art of Qılıç Elai, making them just as tough as my men. My Qilkorian tracker studied our local wildlife—the barbalu, in particular.

Barbalu were the monkeys of Kanaris. They were small and mischievous, stealing anything that wasn't tied down. They had an irresistible fondness for anything shiny, and Buffy Graym spent hours spying on them, laughing at their antics.

"You know," Buffy told me one night in the CP bunker, where my staff and squad leaders tended to congregate after the sun went down. "The ba'balu have huge tewitowies. I been watchin' 'em and the same animals that play in the twees above us twavel wight acwoss No Man's Land and play awound the Nahmans also."

"You think they're spying on us?" joked Gunny Brumit.

"Maybe," Buffy answered. "If they ain't, maybe we could get them to spy on the Nahmans."

Dina Tiago, my Second Squad sergeant, laughed. "How you going to get them to do that?"

Buffy shrugged. "You think the'es any way we could put a camewa on one and watch what they do on the othuh side of No Man's Land?"

Gunny Brumit shook her head. "I doubt it. We tend to notice when things are different among the stuff we see every day. I'm certain the Narmans are no different. No matter how small we make the camera, I'm sure someone would notice it sooner or later."

"There's also the Harnillium interference," I added. "The opposite tree line is just over four kilometers away. Whatever the barbalu transmitted would be drowned out and scrambled by the time it reached our receivers."

"Unless we could string up a series of repeater stations across No Man's Land," Naktada said. "Hook them to cables to feed the video back to us so the Narmans can't detect the transmission. You wouldn't even have to go all the way to the other side. You could probably get away with putting one halfway. Obviously, the farther we went, the better it'd work and the farther away we could track the animals."

Brumit was unconvinced. "They'd still spot the cameras. Once they did that, it'd be open season on barbalu."

Naktada stared at my platoon sergeant as the gears in his brain ground around, searching for a solution. "You got a close-up picture of a barbalu anywhere?"

"You should be able to pull one off the AWCP," Barone Parsons said. AWCP stood for the Alien Wildlife Classification Protocol. "That Samaari prick we had in our squad on the hike up here was always messing with that thing. I wonder what happened to that guy?"

"Duum's dead," I told the squad leader as Naktada approached the monitor and opened the database. "According to Gunny Malcolm, most of the Marines in his unit switched sides during one of the earlier battles and massacred the loyalists."

"You mean to say Duum got iced by his own Marines?" Parsons asked sarcastically. "Who'd have thought that'd ever happen?"

"Hey, sir," Naktada called out after finding what he was looking for. "Check out the skin on these things. Their scales are spherical. They almost look like beads."

Standing up to see what my techwar specialist was talking about, I read the caption on the right side of the screen. "There are tiny bones in there called osteoderms."

Naktada excitedly tapped the screen. "I got cameras smaller than those beads! I can also rig up a series of micro solar panels the same size, shape, and color to power the camera and the transmitter! Unlike the Quarakai, barbalu have tails. That's a perfect place to put an antenna!"

I looked at Naktada in disbelief. "You can do that here?"

Naktada shook his head. "No. I'd need to get back to my lab at the Pyke."

"What do you need to make this happen?" asked Gunny Brumit.

"Besides a ride out of town? I don't know." My TWS thought for a moment. "I'd need some specimens. A couple of dead animals to dissect to see how they're built."

"I can do that," Buffy told us.

"Don't get them from around here," I warned my tracker. "We need our barbalu to be comfortable around humans. If they think we're going to kill them, they'll avoid us. Worse, they'll avoid the Narmans we're trying to spy on."

"Twue dat," Buffy told me. "Let me go back with Naktada, and I'll get some fwom awound the Pyke."

I shook my head. "You're a marked man. Remember? You're not going back there without our protection. I don't want the Killbillies getting their hands on you." Turning to Gunny Brumit, I asked, "We got any hunters among our troops?"

Sergeant Demangel, the leader of Third Squad, answered for her. "My sapper's dad was a hunting guide on Portuna before all the troubles started. I'm sure Lichak would be thrilled to go on a little safari around the Pyke."

"Perfect!" I said. "Get him ready to go. What else do you need, Naktada?"

"Is there a veterinarian back in Narman's Pyke?"

I looked to Gunny for an answer but got nothing but a shrug in return. "I don't think so. I'm sure we could cough up a surgeon, though. Will that work?"

"It'll have to," Naktada said.

"How long do you think this'll take you?" I asked.

"I can get the hardware rigged up in a few days. The tricky part's going to be figuring out how to get it into the animal."

Looking at the Marines gathered around me, I motioned to Sergeant Kal-Xati to make sure no one could hear us from outside the door. After she signaled the coast was clear, I pulled Buffy, Gunny Brumit, Naktada, and my squad leaders in close. "We keep this on the down-low, understand? This could be a game-changer if it works. If one of our people defects or gets themselves captured, it could spoil the whole thing before it even gets started."

Kal-Xati turned to me and said, "If this comes to fruition, we're going to need to run a mission out into the NML to lay cable and set up the repeaters. What're we going to tell our Marines we're doing?"

Naturally, Naktada had a solution. "Listening posts. We tell them we're setting up listening posts to intercept Narman communications. That's typically something recon would do, isn't it?"

I nodded at my Marines. "It sure is. To be honest, I'm not sure why we haven't done it already."

"We have," Kal-Xati told me. "Section 615 did it a while back. Most of them got blown to shit when our artillery and those Narman plasma blasters destroyed the forest between our lines and created No Man's Land."

"How do you know this?" Gunny Brumit asked.

Kal-Xati shrugged. "Black Francis told me. That was how he and his Marines learned how to survive the NML."

153

Gunny Brumit looked at me. "Sir, we may want to consider bringing Black Francis into this operation. His people are probably the best equipped to help set up those relay stations."

I nodded. "You think you can convince him to help us?"

"If she can't," Kal-Xati said while seductively batting her eyelashes at me. "Then I can."

A couple of weeks later, we were deep in the forest, far from the eyes of our rank and file, watching Naktada inject cyklatamine into one of the barbalus' staple foods: the Ninda Berry. In addition to my techwar specialist and myself, Brumit, Buffy, and Black Francis were in the audience. So was a surgeon from Narman's Pyke, Dr. Peri Maran.

"How'd you decide which dwug to use to knock 'em out?" Buffy asked.

"Trial and error," the doctor answered. "We started with devothurane, but unfortunately, that killed the little critters outright. Dobrapental had no effect on them whatsoever. On the other hand, they seemed to really enjoy the isoflurane. The bastards could party all night on that stuff. Luratufol just gave them explosive diarrhea, while Nikaflurane made them really aggressive. One of our test subjects got so twisted on that shit that it bit a chunk out of our anesthesiologist's ass and escaped the lab to pick a fight with a couple of ubati pups."

"Sounds like Gunny Malcolm's spirit animal," Brumit said, causing those who knew him to burst into laughter.

"Cyklatamine hit the sweet spot, though," the doctor said after we regained our composure. "Fifteen minutes after ingesting the lucky berry, the animal will start swaying in the trees. Sensing they could fall, it'll make its way to the ground, where its metabolism will slow down so much you can't even detect a heartbeat. The creature is then yours for about forty hours. It only takes us about three to install the camera. We can seal the incisions with suture glue so no one, not even the animal itself, can tell what we've done to it."

"So you've done this successfully?" Black Francis asked.

The doctor nodded. "Repeatedly."

"And it works?"

Naktada smiled. "Like a champ! It has the added bonus of convincing the barbalu we can bring back their dead, so the troop we pulled our subjects from now treat us as some sort of benevolent gods."

"What advantages can that bwing us?" Buffy asked.

Naktada shrugged. "Well, it keeps them from pelting our people with their shit when they get annoyed with us."

On the way to Narman's Pyke, I had spent an entire night under a rain of barbalu feces. That was a benefit I appreciated more than most.

Per a previous message from Naktada, we had been leaving bowls of Ninda berries out for the barbalu every few days. The troop around our position got used to eating them, so they suspected nothing unusual when we offered them the treat. They swarmed our offering as if they had not eaten in weeks, even fighting each other over the spoils.

"My god," Black Francis said as he peered closely at our unruly dinner guests. Barbalu stood about knee-high to the average human and, aside from their tail, looked like miniature facsimiles of the Quarakai. They had feline eyes and scaly skin covered in black, brown, and olive stripes. Their most prominent feature was a long, almost crocodilian snout armed with a wide array of needle-like teeth. "It's hard to believe they evolved a mouth that terrifying just to eat berries."

"They didn't," Buffy told him. "They's omnivo'es. They eat evwything. The pointy teeth ah fo' meat. In the back o'they's mouth, they got teeth fo' eatin' plants and stuff."

Black Francis nodded at the Qilkorian. "Good to know."

About twenty minutes after their feast, Naktada noticed one of the animals looking a bit unsteady as it jumped from branch to branch around us. He pointed it out to the surgeon. "Right there," he told Maran. "There's our patient."

The doctor nodded. "It sure does look that way, doesn't it? I'll go get the surgical tent ready."

As predicted, the barbalu eventually made its way to the ground, where it got sick and collapsed, causing a great deal of grief among its troop. They shrieked at it, hoping for a response. They tried to hold its eyes open as if that would bring it back. They pounded their chests and wailed in distress. It was well over an hour before they abandoned the animal, giving it up for dead. Only when they all left did Naktada collect the creature and take it to Maran.

For the next few hours, we gathered outside the surgeon's tent like expectant parents. Finally, just after sunset, Mara emerged and said, "Congratulations! You're now the proud parents of a brand new bionic barbalu!"

As we cheered in delight, Naktada turned to settle us down. "Now, now, Marines. What we just did is the easy part. If this thing's going to work, we're going to need those relay stations set up."

Turning to address me directly, Naktada added, "That means going out into No Man's Land."

Chapter 26

NML

"You can't lead the mission to set the repeaters," Black Francis told me once we were alone.

Not being in the habit of having enlisted Marines tell me what I could and could not do, I bristled at the man's advice. "What do you mean I can't lead my Marines into No Man's Land? I'm an Academy Marine, Sergeant. We don't conduct war from the rear."

"You've been in the combat zone, what? Not even a month? You don't have the experience to pull it off without getting you and your people killed."

I was insulted. "The Citadel trained me for two decades. If I'm not ready to fight by now, I never will be."

"Okay, how are you going out there? What are you equipped with?"

"Standard combat gear. M72 rifle, M88 sidearm, grenades, and three hundred rounds of ammo."

"How are you dressing your troops?"

That was a stupid question. "For war. How else? Full tactical exo-armor, helmet on, visor down, and sealed to their breastplate. Nothing gets out. No breath. No sound. No scent."

"Right," Francis said, fighting the urge to roll his eyes. "Nothing but the radio transmission as we talk between ourselves, right?"

"Uh...uh...uh..." I stammered, seeing where he was going with this. I suddenly felt very, very stupid.

"You won't make it a third of the way across No Man's Land. They'll detect your electronic emissions and blow you off the battlefield before you make it a hundred meters."

"But when I first met you, you were in armor. Armor that looked like it had seen some shit."

Francis nodded. "That was when the NML was flooded with Narmans in their own shells. Our emissions just blended in with theirs."

That made sense and I was embarrassed I had not thought of it. "Who taught you that?"

"No one," Black Francis answered. "I learned it the hard way."

I bet he did. "What else do I need to know before I lead my Marines out there?"

"Far more than I can teach you in the time we have before you set out. Let me lead this one, Lieutenant. I'm not asking you to stay behind, mainly because I know you wouldn't. Just let me call the shots out there in the danger zone. Allow yourself the luxury of learning from my mistakes until you have enough experience fighting the Narmans to adjust your instincts."

"You think it's possible we'll run into the enemy out there?"

Black Francis shook his head. "Not possible. Probable. The Narmans are watching us just as much as we're watching them. Except, with their camo technology, they're better at it. Much of their activity is concentrated at the edges of our line, and the front doesn't really go any farther north than here. I go out there regularly. I see their tracks, Lieutenant. Those fuckers have probably snuck up within fifty meters of your trench, and you never even knew it."

"In other words, they might be watching us put those repeaters out there."

"It'd be safe to assume they are."

I sighed. "So what would you do?"

"Wait," Francis told me. "Save the mission for a night when the rain is really coming down out there. That'll cover the noise we make as we're going about our business. It'll also make it easier for us to push the transmission cables into the mud and cover them up. Let my people enter the NML first and take positions beyond where you'll be operating. We'll set an ambush for anyone trying to get a closer look at what we're up to. You should dedicate two full squads for this mission. That'll be few enough Marines to make it look like we're just conducting a low-level recon patrol, but enough people to grab the

Narmans' attention and keep them focused in this vicinity. Meanwhile, I'll have a couple of five-person teams run redundant networks to the north and south of here completely off their radar."

I nodded in agreement. Tactically speaking, Black Francis was quite sound for an enlisted man. It made me wonder what else he had up his sleeve. "When we first met," I said to him. "You mentioned you had some ideas about breaking this impasse with the Narmans...."

Black Francis shook his head. "Not now. We need to focus on one thing at a time. There's no sense planning future missions if we don't survive the one right in front of us."

The weather hit us a couple of weeks later. The skies opened up with a deluge I had not seen since leaving the Hot Zone during our march from the beach. As soon as night fell, Black Francis sent his Marines into No Man's Land to intercept any Narmans who dared head our way. Before setting out, I presented my Third and Fourth Squads to Francis for a pre-mission equipment check.

Decked out in black fatigues and with our faces painted dark as night, I had Black Francis himself ensure we were good to go. "You don't want anything with a battery on you, Marines!" he shouted at us. "The Narmans will pick out an RFI signature from anything transmitting a signal and then train one of those alien plasma blasters on your position. You, and everyone within thirty meters, will have the skin melted right off your bodies." Unwilling to take our word we were transmission free, the sergeant scanned all my Marines with an RF receiver before clearing us to go.

"Any Narmans you may encounter out there are going to look a lot like you do," one of Francis's people told us. "The only difference is going to be their face shields. There's a faint red glow where their eyes should be. That's alien night vision tech. If you see red eyes, it ain't friendly."

I knew what the Marine was talking about. I saw it atop Mount Toranad the morning I was shot.

Before we set out, another group of Black Francis's people showed up with a mortar tube and several projectiles I had never seen before. "What are those?" I asked as they began firing them into No Man's Land.

"Diversions," Black Francis answered.

"Why aren't they detonating?"

Francis grinned. "Because they aren't explosives. You'll see what that's all about later."

We gave Black Francis's advance team a two-hour head start before we snuck over the berm ourselves. Leading the way were a couple of Marines armed with crossbows. Behind them were two of my people carrying a spool of shielded transmission line. The Narmans would detect the signal if the repeaters broadcast the barbalu video to us over the air, so it had to be done by cable. "What happens if the animals transmit video in the NML?" Sergeant Kal-Xati asked me, the thought just occurring to her.

"I guess they'll get vaporized, too. They can't transmit in No Man's Land, though. Naktada has that covered."

Following the pair with the spool were about forty of my troops, walking single file, stepping on the transmission line as they went, doing their best to push it beneath the surface of the mud. Bringing up the rear were another fourteen Class One convicts carrying additional line to keep us in business once the cable on the front spool was exhausted.

The torrential rain reduced visibility so much that there was little chance of the Narmans spotting us. In fact, we had such a hard time seeing each other we had to tether ourselves together to keep from getting separated.

We had gone about a third of a kilometer when the first spool ran out. A replacement was brought up by Syrano Lekki, a mobster from Tyannik-4, and Tukku Bleda, a POW from Portuna. Giving them the empty spool and unhooking them from the rest of us, I said, "Get this thing back to the trench and turn it over to Sergeant Tiago. She'll be waiting for it."

"What for?" asked Bleda. "Why don't we just leave it here?"

As a matter of practice, I did not divulge my reasons for doing anything to the convict laborers. I was also irked Bleda felt comfortable questioning what I told him to do. To reset our relationship, I smacked him across the jaw hard enough to knock him off his feet. "You'll take it back because I fucking told you to! Do you understand me?"

Lekki shook his head in disbelief. "How long you been a convict, Bleda?" he asked as he helped his partner back up.

"About a year," the former mobster said, rubbing his cheek.

"That's more than enough time to learn nothing good ever comes from speaking to an officer. Grab your end of the spool and let's get the hell out of here."

As my Second Squad armorer, Sergeant Saceri, connected the laid line to the new spool, Black Francis leaned over to me and said, "The nerve of the convicts these days, eh?"

"Tell me about it," I answered. "If that's the worst thing I have to deal with on this mission, though, I'll take it. You think the Narmans can spot us in this shit?"

Black Francis shook his head. "Pinpoint us? Probably not. Make no mistake, though. They know we're out here and up to something. We just have to make sure we don't leave any clues behind that'll help the bastards figure it out."

"That's why I'm sending the empty spools back."

The rest of the mission proceeded without incident. Conditions out in the NML were so good, and by that, I mean god-awful, that we stretched out all seven spools to place our repeater more than two kilometers away from our trenches. We never spotted the Narmans, and to the best of our knowledge, they never spotted us. Three hours after setting out, we were on our way back to the trenches.

"That was easy," Sergeant Kal-Xati whispered to me as we marched home.

Her assistant, Sasirai Sahim, tried to hush her. "Shhh!"

"Relax, Corporal," Kal-Xati said. "There isn't anybody that can hear me over this rain."

"I'm not worried about your volume," Sahim said. "I'm worried about your sentiment. You're going to jinx us!"

As if to prove the corporal's point, their sapper tripped over something and landed face-first into the mud. Because they were all tethered together, he took a couple of Kal-Xati's riflemen down with him. When he rolled over to see what it was, he found himself eye-to-eye with the body of Tukku Bleda, the convict I had slapped earlier.

"Narmans!" cried Kal-Xati, causing the rest of her squad to drop into firing positions.

Black Francis rushed forward to inspect the corpse. Even in the dark, it was easy to see Bleda had been beaten to a pulp. "This wasn't the Narmans," he told me. "They would've slit his throat."

Jogging around our immediate vicinity in search of clues, I quickly found the empty spool I had sent the two men back with. Grinding my teeth in rage, I snarled, "It was Lekki!"

"Lekki?" gasped Corporal Sahim, shaking her head in disbelief. "Why?"

"Why do you think?" snapped Kal-Xati, switching the safety off on her M72. "The son-of-a-bitch is defecting!"

Barone Parsons walked up beside Black Francis and me. "He doesn't know what we're doing out here, does he?"

I shook my head. "He knows we were laying cable. The only reason to do that is to establish a line of communication to the other side. The Narmans won't know the details of what we're up to, but this'll be enough reason for them to put their guard up. They'll take precautions to keep anything that may help us out of the NML. They might withdraw further back into the forest, out of the range of our relay station. If we don't catch or kill that convict, we could lose our shot at learning what they're doing over there."

Black Francis nodded in agreement. "At the very least, they'll send the aliens and officers to a safer area."

And on the off chance Deena Vulk is over there, they'll send her away with them.

Chapter 27

The Hunt

With the line laid and the relay station set, I did not need my armorers anymore. They were too valuable to have them prancing about No Man's Land looking for Lekki. "Get your asses straight back to the line and tell Gunny Brumit what happened," I told Gyanis and Ghinion. "Tell her I want snipers in the trees, as high as she dares put them, scouring the NML for that piece of shit. They're to fire on sight! Understood?"

"Aye aye, sir!"

Slapping both Marines atop their helmets, I said, "Then get the hell out of here and take the convicts with you! If any of them even hint they're thinking about going on the run, you double-tap them right between the eyes!"

I pointed at Kal-Xati. "Jasirat! You take your squad a couple hundred meters south and fan out! Move forward from cover to cover. Do not bunch up, and do not expose yourselves! If you run into resistance, you break it off and retreat. Unless you spot Lekki among the belligerents. In that case, you fight until that treasonous little prick and all his buddies are dead!"

Black Francis returned with one of his people just as I was getting ready to dismiss Fourth Squad. "My Marines are on the move," he told me. "They're at home out here and more effective in small groups. If you want my advice, keep your people in squad strength. What they lack in experience, they can make up in numbers. If it's okay with you, I'll go with Kal-Xati's squad so they've got someone familiar with the conditions out here. I'm sending PFC Terrus with you."

The look on Kal-Xati's face told me she was more than happy with that arrangement. Had she been anyone else, I would have had Black Francis come with me and sent Terrus with them, but Kal-Xati was the best squad leader I had. She knew she was on a mission and not a date. "Fine. The two of you get going."

As Fourth Squad started to move out, a deafening roar emanated from the enemy tree line, and a blast of pink energy burst from the forest. Almost simultaneously, a massive explosion erupted from the far edge of the NML. A large fire flared up briefly, but it was quickly extinguished by the torrent pouring out of the sky. "I sure hope that wasn't any of your people," I told Black Francis.

Our side answered the attack with a missile barrage that struck the spot from which the plasma burst originated. "It's not," Black Francis assured me. That was our diversion. Those mortars we shot were timed radio frequency transmitters. They're meant to attract the Narmans' attention and coax them into giving away their blasters' positions."

"You think we got 'em?"

Black Francis shook his head. "No. Those blasters are pretty mobile. They shoot, then skedaddle. As far as we can tell, we haven't hit one yet. The intent is to desensitize them to radio signals coming from the NML. Anyway, there're more transmitters out there, so if I were you, I wouldn't get within a click of the enemy tree line. You don't want to be anywhere near those decoys when they get hit."

Incredulous, I shouted, "Isn't it a little late to be telling me this now?!?"

Black Francis shook his head as another explosion went off to the south of us. With a wide grin plastered upon his face, he said, "And ruin the surprise?!? Nah, I don't think so. From my vantage point, I think I told you just in time!"

A little more than a half-hour into our search for Syrano Lekki, gunfire broke out to the south, where Kal-Xati and her squad were operating. Whatever the confrontation lacked in longevity, it made up for in intensity. "Should we go over there and help?" Parsons asked me.

I shook my head, lamenting the fact we were forced into the NML without radio communication. "No. We have to trust Kal-Xati and keep looking for our convict. If we lose Lekki, we could lose everything."

Not long after the shooting stopped, Kumiko Baipa, one of Kal-Xati's riflemen, caught up to us. For someone who had just emerged from what sounded like a very violent firefight, she was all smiles.

"Is everybody alright over there?" I asked her.

"Oh yes!" Baipa panted, out of breath from sprinting over to us.

"Did you get Lekki?" asked Parsons.

Still struggling to breathe, Baipa said, "No! We stumbled upon a Narman patrol! We kicked the shit out of them! We killed four! We took two prisoners! And..." The Marine paused to draw in a deep breath of air. "We captured their fucking hologram generator!"

Parsons' jaw nearly hit the ground. "No shit?"

Baipa was beaming. "No shit! We walked right through it, not even realizing it was there! One minute there was nothing, then the next thing we knew, there were seven Narmans right in front of us! Because the visibility was so bad, they never saw us coming! Our weapons were at the ready; theirs weren't. We got the drop on them!"

"But we heard them firing...." Parsons said.

"Oh, they fired, alright," Baipa laughed. "It was the aiming that they weren't doing much of."

"So, what's Kal-Xati doing now?" I asked.

"She's sending Sasirai...ahem...sorry...Corporal Sahim, Pottoka, and Wat back to the line with the prisoners and captured equipment. The rest of us are going to continue searching for the convict."

"Good. When you get back there, be sure to tell your sergeant...."

I was interrupted by another plasma burst from the enemy tree line. It came from much further north than the other and sailed right over our heads to hit the ground a couple hundred meters beyond our left flank. Right where Kal-Xati's people should be.

Our instincts were to run to the scene of the explosion to help our comrades, but we were stopped by Black Francis's man. "No!" PFC Terrus told us. "That's exactly what the Narmans want you to do! Congregate where the wounded are! Bunch ourselves up so they can kill us all with one shot!"

Appealing directly to me, he then said, "Black Francis was with your troops. He'd have made sure they were all keeping plenty of space between themselves. He'll get the survivors back to the line. We need to do what we set out here to. We gotta find that fucking convict!"

Terrus was right, but it was proving impossible to do in the middle of a maelstrom during the dead of night. Progress was slow in the dark. When the sun rose and the rain eased, it stopped altogether. When conditions improved enough for us to be able to see Lekki, the Narmans would be able to see us. We were made aware of this at the crack of dawn when a single gunshot rang out from the western side of the clearing and put a bullet through the head of PFC Bersad.

Bersad's death sent Parsons, Terrus, and me diving for cover in a large crater. "Everybody keep your heads down!" I screamed at my Marines.

"And get comfortable!" added Terrus. "We're going to be here awhile!"

"How long's a while?" asked Parsons.

"Until nightfall, if we're lucky," answered Terrus. "If we're not, we might be out here until the next deluge opens up."

I shook my head. "No, if we're trapped out here, Captain Pustov will have artillery bombard the enemy tree line, giving us the cover we need to run back to...."

"HOLD YOUR FIRE!" a voice screamed out from the west, a couple hundred meters ahead of us. "I'M ON YOUR SIDE! I'M COMING OVER TO YOU!" It was Syrano Lekki, begging the Narmans for protection.

"What the fuck?" said Parsons as he craned his head to peer above the crater's edge. Spotting Luuk Bukki, the former policeman from Parsons' home planet of Apalashu, crouching behind a massive tree fragment closer to the noise, he asked, "Can you see that prick?"

Bukki shook his head. "No, we're too low."

"I'M COMING TO YOU!" Lekki screamed out again. "WHATEVER YOU DO, DON'T SHOOT!"

Luuk Bukki started laughing as he raised his M72 and aimed it down range. "I see him now! He broke cover and is waving his arms over his head to get their attention!"

"What?" Parsons scoffed. "Was he not paying attention when we were all at Camp Vayipar?"

166

From even further beyond Lekki, we heard someone yell, "GET DOWN! GET DOWN! WHAT ARE YOU?!? SOME KIND OF IDI...!"

The crack of a single gunshot rang out across the NML. It did not come from the Narmans, however. It came from a sniper on our side of the clearing. It was followed by a mortar barrage that obliterated everything within fifty meters of Lekki's position. When the smoke cleared, a yellow flare shot up into the air, fired from our trenches, indicating they had visual confirmation their target was destroyed.

"Fucking moron," Parsons said. "The stupid son-of-a-bitch would have made it if he'd kept his mouth shut."

"You probably don't want to hear this, Sarge," Private Bukki replied as he lowered his weapon. "But I had one of the highest case closure rates in the entire department when I was a cop. Legit closures, too. Not that corrupt shit Pulayne was pulling. You know how I was able to do it?"

"Your unnatural powers of deduction?" Parsons asked sarcastically.

Bukki shook his head. "Nope. I cleared shit tons of cases because, as a general rule, criminals are stupid as fuck."

The private paused to peek around his cover at the enemy line. "That said, the dumbest perp I ever cuffed was a mastermind compared to that fucking drooler."

Captain Pustov waited for the rain to pick up again before he fired a red flare above our heads. Looking over at Parsons and Terrus, I said, "That's our cue. We gotta go."

To make sure everyone else got the message, my squad leader yelled, "Get ready to run, people! On your marks...!"

From somewhere far to the east of us, we heard the faint reports of artillery being fired.

"Get ready...!"

A couple of seconds later, the western tree line began to ripple, then the hologram façade flickered, revealing the devastation behind it. Massive explosions started going off all along the enemy trenches.

"GO!" Parsons screamed.

In an instant, around forty Marines, the combined forces of my two rifle squads and Black Francis's troops, emerged from hiding and began sprinting through the mud toward the safety of our trenches. The barrage continued unabated for more than thirty minutes, the time it took for us to cover the kilometer and a half of killing fields before we reached friendly fortifications. We drew some ineffective small-arms fire from our adversaries, but the plasma blasters stayed out of the fight, something I found interesting enough to mentally file away despite my preoccupation with running for my life.

The artillery fire we laid upon the Narmans was intense enough to convince our adversaries in the far trenches to keep their heads down. There were a few stragglers in No Man's Land willing to pop up to take the occasional shot at us, however. At one point, about three hundred meters from my objective, I heard the crack of a bullet whiz by my left ear. Not long after that, I glanced to my right to see one of Black Francis's Marines, dragging a wounded comrade behind him, take a shot to the spine. I shifted to help him, but before I could take two steps, another bullet finished him off. A third took out his injured buddy.

I nearly collapsed when I hit the trench. Sergeant Parsons did when he reached safety, falling to his knees while he tried to catch his breath. Still, he managed to look at me and gasp, "*Covering fire!*"

I nodded and started yelling at the Marines around us. "On your feet! We got people out there still! They need covering fire! Shoot anything not running in our direction!"

We had landed in First Platoon's sector and Lieutenant Peeli immediately had all his troops cover our retreat. Nearly a hundred Marines started popping rounds off at anything that didn't look familiar. The Narmans, unwilling to take that kind of abuse lying down, returned the sentiment. Unfortunately, Fourth Squad was running back where the exchange of gunfire was thickest.

Sergeant Kal-Xati, one of the fastest Marines I had, was the furthest from us. She was bogged down, dragging her badly burned corporal through the mud behind her.

"Come on, Sergeant!" I screamed at her. "RUN!"

She was already slogging through the mud as fast as she could, but it was not nearly fast enough. Bullets were kicking up spray all around her. It was only a matter of time before she was struck by one of them.

I started climbing out of the trench to help, only to have Peeli's platoon sergeant grab me by the collar and yank me back into the muck. "What the fuck do you think you're doing?!?" Gunny Geros screamed at me. "You give the orders, sir! Not execute them!

You're a lieutenant! Learn your fuckin' job! You shouldn't have been out there in the first place!"

Geros pointed her finger at a trio of her people nearby. "Diyana! Emeron! Lusid! Get out there and help get the wounded back in! I want some fire discipline out of the rest of you! Let the machine gunners make the noise! Everyone else, save your ammunition until you've identified a target!" With that, Gunny Geros disappeared further down the line to direct her troops.

Kal-Xati was almost home when a grenade landed a couple of meters behind her. The explosion knocked her off her feet and blew her against the back wall of the ditch. She hit the ground cursing and scrambled to what was left of Corporal Sahim. "SASI!" the sergeant screamed, slapping her assistant's face. "SASI! OPEN YOUR EYES! WE MADE IT! OPEN YOUR EYES! OPEN YOUR FUCKING EYES, GODDAMMIT!"

One of Peeli's medics ran over to check the corporal's vitals. There weren't any. Looking up at my squad leader, the corpsman shook his head, only to get slapped across the face by my distraught squad leader. "Fix her!" Kal-Xati yelled, reaching for her sidearm. "Fix her, or I'll blow your fucking...."

Parsons grabbed Kal-Xati from behind to save the medic from her wrath, only to have his grip broken with an elbow to the groin and a headbutt to the nose. While Parsons was getting knocked on his ass, another of Jasirat's Marines landed in the trench with a Narman prisoner. "YOU!" she screamed, pointing her pistol at the captured insurgent. "YOU! THOSE WERE MY PEOPLE YOU KILLED, YOU SORRY SON-OF-A-BITCH!"

The prisoner was dazed, wounded, and obviously experiencing a great deal of pain. Whatever discomfort the man was in paled in comparison with what Kal-Xati wished upon him.

Trying to distract her, I ran up to my squad leader and spun her around. "How many people did you lose?"

Kal-Xati let out a single sob. Not out of grief, but of rage. " I don't know! I lost Sahim! And Wat! Pottoka! Probably more! FUCK!"

I looked around at the rest of the Fourth Squad people in the trench. I had a hard time figuring out who else was missing. Except for one. "Where's Black Francis?"

Kal-Xati looked around in panic. "I don't know! He was with us when...."

Sergeant Kal-Xati was a woman of action, not words. She knew how valuable Black Francis was to us, so without asking permission, she leapt out of the trench to look for him. No sooner had she cleared the berm when a Narman bullet drilled a hole through her forehead and splattered the brains of one of my best Marines all over those of us trying to stop her.

Chapter 28

AFTERMATH

Fourth Squad really took a beating during our excursion into No Man's Land. Of the eighteen Marines deployed on that mission, seven were killed in action. Two were wounded. Only five made it back in the same condition they departed in. First Squad lost two of its convicts, Lekki and Bleda, and one rifleman, Krieger Bersad. Parsons' assistant machine gunner and his sapper were wounded.

I was looking at the corpses staged outside the Company Command Post when Black Francis joined me. His right arm and the side of his face were wrapped in gauze. I nodded at him solemnly. "I'm glad to see you made it."

Black Francis returned the sentiment as he stomped his boot down upon a kryptid trying to get to the bodies. "How many casualties did you take?" he asked.

"Fourteen," I told him. "Ten dead and four wounded."

"It's supposed to be the other way around," Black Francis sighed. "Injuries are supposed to outnumber fatalities."

I nodded. "They're supposed to. How about you? How'd your people make out?"

"Three dead. Three wounded."

"That including yourself?"

"Four wounded."

"What happened?" I asked.

"It was that fucking hologram generator. According to our prisoner, all alien technology has tracking beacons in it. It's not allowed to be within one kilometer of our line.

If it crosses that threshold, it sends out a signal that transmits its exact position back to the Narmans so they can blow it to hell before we get our hands on it. Along with anyone within a thirty-meter perimeter." Black Francis showed me his wounded arm. "I was about thirty-five meters away."

"The prisoner's singing?"

"Like a canary," Francis said. "He's trying to avoid being turned over to the Killbillies for interrogation."

"Will it work?"

"Fuck no."

Francis paused to approach the only unburnt female corpse among our KIA. He thought he recognized the body, but her head was too misshapen for him to be sure. "Is that her?"

"Yeah. That's her. Jasirat Kal-Xati." I wondered if he knew she was killed trying to find him. In case he did not, I decided not to tell him. I was sure my sergeant would not have wanted him to know. "You going to be alright?"

Black Francis nodded. "I'll be fine. I'd have liked to have known her better, but I never got the chance. I guess it's best to lose her now than after getting attached, you know?"

I was suddenly hit with the pain of losing Jella Duverii again. My grief would have been exponentially lessened had she perished in the crash of *Wasp-Three* instead of being murdered by some Narman captive two months later atop Mount Toranad. "Sure," I told Black Francis. "I know."

Stepping back to get a better look at all the bodies, I shook my head once again. "Man, that was a pretty goddamned expensive mission. It better have been worth it."

"It will be if those relay stations work as advertised," Black Francis assured me. "If we get a glimpse behind the Narmans' hologram wall, we'll save a hundred times the Marines we lost today."

I spat at the ground just shy of Bersad's lifeless feet. "We fucking better."

We were licking our wounds in the company CP when Pustov entered. Despite our injuries, we all stood up in adherence to Marine protocol. "At ease, Marines," the captain told us. "At ease."

Looking at me, Pustov asked, "How many casualties?"

"Thirteen dead. Eight wounded."

Pustov winced. "It's supposed to be...."

"Yes, sir," I interrupted. "It's supposed to be the other way around. Third Platoon's Fourth Squad has been rendered combat ineffective. We lost the squad leader and her assistant, three riflemen, an assistant machine gunner, and their spotter."

Pustov sighed. Looking me right in the eye, he asked, "Was it worth it?"

"If it works, it will be."

The captain's expression hardened. "Then it better work."

Sitting behind his desk, Pustov clasped his hands together before addressing me again. "So, when will this operation bear fruit?"

I shrugged. "As soon as the barbalu cross No Man's Land. We have a signal transmitting from our trench that reaches the enemy line. If the barbalu are receiving that signal, their cameras won't work.... "

"Why?"

"So the barbalu don't trigger the plasma blasters while crossing over to the Narman side."

"You don't think the Narmans can sense transmissions in their own backyard?"

"They can, but they won't," answered Black Francis. "There's all kinds of devices transmitting behind the Narman lines. The barbalu's transmissions will blend in with all the other electronic noise over there."

The captain nodded in understanding. "Okay. What do we expect to learn?"

Black Francis answered for me. "Everything. We've been getting our asses handed to us because we lack actionable intelligence. If this works, we'll have it. We'll know how many humans we're up against. How many Quarakai. Where their plasma blasters are located. Where the alien tech is. If we're lucky, maybe we'll even find out where the aliens are."

And if Deena-fucking-Vulk is anywhere in the vicinity, we'll find her too, I added silently.

"You're expecting quite an intelligence coup then, aren't you?"

I nodded. "I am."

Pustov turned his gaze upon me. "I'll be presenting the action report on what went down here to Lieutenant Colonel Baakarad in the morning. She's going to kick it up to Colonel Palkrait. He's going to bring Section 615 in to analyze the data. Be prepared. If this works out how you think it will, the spooks will want to take over your operation."

"Don't let them," Black Francis advised. "They ain't done anything out here but fuck shit up ever since we landed on this rock."

"I'm not going to argue with you on that, Sergeant Franq." Captain Pustov might have been the only Marine on Kanaris who called Black Francis by his actual name. "But if we expect them to feed information to us, we can't withhold intelligence from them either, can we?"

"We sure can," Black Francis retorted. "I can guarantee you those pricks are holding back on us. They know a lot more about what we're facing out there than they're letting on."

Our company commander shrugged. "Prove that, and maybe we'll have a leg to stand on. Until then, get your barbalu stuff working and be prepared to show the higher-ups whatever tricks you got up your sleeve."

"Aye aye, sir," we all said in unison.

After a brief silence, Pustov looked at Black Francis and me again. "Thirteen dead. That's a lot. Did we take away any tactical lessons from this?"

Yes, sir," I answered. "Never take convicts into the NML."

Commandant Nilton Tailur was the ranking Section 615 agent attached to the 247th Marine Expeditionary Force. Not willing to chance him falling into enemy hands, he rarely set foot on the surface of Kanaris. When he did, he typically kept himself within the confines of our fortress at Narman's Pyke. Having someone of his stature visit the front line was virtually unheard of, yet there he was, disguised as a gunnery sergeant and flanked by Agent Takawa, Agent Biragor, and a platoon-sized contingent of personal bodyguards. He had come to see our barbalu cameras at work.

"Why are all these hard-hitters here?" asked Sergeant Parsons. He watched the dog and pony show from afar as First Squad had been tasked to guard the outer ring of the commandant's perimeter.

"This's the first look at the enemy position they've ever seen," Black Francis told him. "The plasma artillery, the hologram generators, the Quarakai, it's all there before their very eyes."

"We could have just sent him the video," Parsons countered.

"How?" I asked. "Transmit it? The Harnillium interference won't let us send it any more than four kilometers at best. Put it on a disk? Not going to risk it falling into enemy hands before we have the chance to act on what we've learned."

Sensing the ranking officers were nearing the end of the shameless brown-nosing that always accompanied visits involving people of such high esteem, Gunny Brumit walked up to me and said, "You'd better get in that tent, Lieutenant. You want to be in there before them. Those pompous asses will make your life miserable if you keep them waiting."

Heeding my platoon sergeant's advice, I marched into the battalion's command tent, only to wait another ten minutes for everyone else to get there. Naktada had his projector set up and pointed at a large screen so everyone could see it without being forced to crowd around a small monitor. He was sweaty and fidgeting.

"You nervous?" I asked him.

"Aren't you?" Naktada replied. "Tailur's a guy who can make all of us disappear with the snap of his fingers."

Shaking my head, I said, "He's got an entire machine trying to gather intelligence on the Narmans and their alien allies, but they haven't come up with shit. We have. He needs us now more than he needs his own people. If you want to worry about someone, fret about Section 615's rank and file. They're the ones we're a threat to."

Naktada cast his gaze beyond the tent's entrance, looking at the intelligence agents posted outside, disguised as Marines. "You know, those pricks are supposed to be trained in shit like this. Why haven't they been able to come up with anything on the Narmans?"

"My guess is it's because they're a very insular organization. To get into the intelligence world, you have to be ideologically pure—a proven superpatriot. You have to think exactly like everyone else in Section 615. Ideas running contrary to League dogma are generally viewed with suspicion, so innovative thought is not really encouraged. Without being exposed to much in the way of fresh thinking, our agents find themselves in something of an intellectual echo chamber. They toe the company line and lose their ability to innovate. They just recycle the same old shit they always have. What we've accomplished takes diversity. What inspired you to surgically implant a camera into a barbalu?"

"Buffy telling me they cross enemy lines."

I pointed at Naktada. "Precisely! It was his idea, an idea that he would never have been able to make a reality. You were able to bring it to fruition, but would you have ever thought to do it had Buffy not made the observation that the barbalu travel between our lines?"

My techwar specialist shook his head. "No."

"Exactly," I agreed. "Look, Sergeant, you're a smart guy. One of the smartest people I've ever met, but Buffy will run circles around you when it comes to Kanarisian fauna. And to him, the stuff you do is basically magic. Hell, it is to me, too. As opposite as the two of you are, this breakthrough would never have happened had we not put both of you in the same room."

Chapter 29

Spooks

"What's that?" Commandant Tailur asked, pointing at the device I showed on the screen. It looked far beyond the scope of human technology.

"That would be alien artillery, sir," I answered. "The dreaded plasma blaster."

Tailur looked confounded by its lack of wheels. "How the hell does it move?"

"It levitates. It floats about a half meter above the ground. They're fast, they're mobile, and they don't leave any tracks." Turning my head toward the projector, I said, "Computer, play Video 728."

The screen behind me showed a plasma blaster, a large device with what looked to be an antenna where the barrel should be, emerging from a concrete-reinforced hole cut into the hillside. It rushed to a clearing in the rainforest, unleashed a devastating bolt of pink energy, then retreated back into its underground lair. I let the video play for fifteen more seconds to show how long it took for our artillery to land at the spot from which the weapon fired.

"That's why we've never hit one," I told my high-ranking audience. "By the time we fire back, the blaster's long gone."

"Have we tried hitting the tunnels?" asked a Samaari colonel, showing the gross incompetence for which they were famous.

"No," answered my battalion commander. Arva Baakarad was a Samaari also, but she was an anomaly. She knew what she was doing. "We can't do that without letting the enemy know we can see them. It'll send them scrambling to learn how we knew where the tunnel was. The Narmans may be many things, Colonel, but they're not idiots. If we let them know we're spying on them, it'll only be a matter of time before they figure out how."

Tailur looked intrigued. "What else have you found?"

"Computer...Image 791." At my command, the screen lit up with the picture of a projector about twice the size of a standard Marine battle pack. "Image 333," I commanded, bringing up a photo from higher above that showed a line of them stretching all along the enemy front.

"That's the alien camouflage tech at work. Those are hologram generators. From this side of the NML...."

"What's an 'NML?'" asked the same clueless Samaari colonel.

In spite of myself, I let out a long sigh of exasperation. "'NML' stands for 'No Man's Land,' sir."

"Oh! Yeah! That's right!" the colonel said, starting to blush. "I knew that." Everyone else in the tent was confident he did not.

"Anyway, like I was saying, from our vantage point, all we can see are trees that aren't even actually there. Behind that façade, it looks much like it does here. They have smaller hologram projectors, about the size of a set of optical amplifiers, that can conceal an entire squad and allow them to sneak right up to our lines if they wanted to."

"But they don't?" asked Tailur.

"No. They won't risk having their equipment fall into our hands. If it comes within a kilometer of our trenches, it'll trigger an alarm, and the blasters will destroy it." I paused as an image of Sasi Sahim's burned body popped into my mind. "We found that out the hard way."

"We suspect the Quarakai used them to breach our lines during the Narman offensive a couple months back," Tailur said.

I nodded. "I would assume they did," I answered. "But none were recovered among the Quarakai dead. I would guess they used them to sneak in, but those carrying the devices immediately retreated to the other side once the attack was underway."

Tailur nodded his concurrence. "What else do you have?"

"Image 673." A picture of a man flashed up on the screen. "That's Mailes Ghona. He was the vice governor of this colony until the insurrection. It appears he's in command of enemy forces across the NML. He was the one who attacked us when we reached Narman's Pyke."

"You were one of the *Wasp-Three* survivors?" Tailur asked. He sounded impressed.

"Yes, sir."

"And you were the guy who killed Gori Dravidas?"

I involuntarily diverted my eyes to the ground. "Yes, sir."

Tailur motioned to Agent Takawa, who had been standing along the tent wall during my briefing. When his subordinate arrived, the commandant whispered something into the man's ear before sending him away.

"Has your camera picked up any aliens?" asked an artillery colonel.

"Not yet," I answered. "I suspect they're at fortifications further back. During our mission to put this all into operation, we captured a prisoner who was very chatty. He told us there are a series of three lines going up into the mountains. If we take the trench on the other side of the NML, we'll end up in a trap. We'll be sitting ducks down there while the Narmans pulverize us from higher ground."

Turning toward our Division Commander, Major General Lisi Duuq, Commandant Tailur asked, "Do you have a plan to contend with that?"

Duuq was a consummate desk jockey. Flustered by the commandant's question, she stammered nervously and said, "I...I...I'm not...no. Not yet."

"Then you better get busy making one." The rebuke was mild to the ears, but the implication that Duuq did not have the commandant's confidence reverberated throughout the tent. Technically, Duuq outranked Tailur, but the agent in charge of Section 615 forces on Kanaris knew how to neutralize threats to the mission, whether they be born of malice or incompetence.

Returning his attention to me, Tailur asked, "So what're you going to do with all this? What're our next steps?"

Colonel Palkrait, hoping to land himself in better esteem than the general had, answered for me. "We do nothing right now," he said, "but expand the operation. This front is fifty kilometers long, and we don't have the forces to storm the other side. We've identified a dozen different troops of barbalu crossing back and forth across the NML. We need to put a camera in all of them and map out enemy positions along the entirety of the enemy line. Only when we know where every hologram generator is, where all the plasma blasters are, where all the troops are staged, where all the Quarakai are concentrated, will we be ready to assault the other side."

"And you have plans to expand this operation?"

Palkrait shook his head. "They're not plans anymore, sir. They're missions in progress as we speak."

Agent Takawa approached me after the presentation. "It looks to me like congratulations are in order," he said, despite not looking very happy about it. "The commandant was very impressed by what you've done."

Looking at Takawa with a bit of suspicion, I answered, "And you weren't?"

Takawa shrugged. "No, I was. If I'm being honest, I'm a bit miffed, too. You've accomplished more in weeks out here than the entire 615 apparatus has in months. It's good work. Who came up with this operation? You or Black Francis?"

"The plot itself was cooked up by my team. I just put it in motion. Black Francis helped us execute it. He did very little to develop the mission, but make no mistake; we could never have pulled it off without him."

"How many people know about this?"

I shrugged. "Me. My squad leaders. Black Francis's Marines. All the officers and agents that sat in on the briefing I just gave."

Takawa grimaced. "That's too many. If just one of those defects, this whole thing is blown. Your platoon's in this thick. Having them know is a necessary evil. Black Francis and his Marines spend too much time in the NML. If one of them gets captured...."

"We can't do this without him. He has the experience we need to make it out there in No Man's Land."

"You need to get that experience, Tauk. Fast. I need to pull Black Francis's troops off this operation to limit our exposure."

"The Narmans know he's out there. If you force him to withdraw, they're going to be suspicious. We gotta keep everything business as usual if we're going to maintain the element of surprise."

The agent squinted at me. "You think like one of us, Tauk. I like that."

"I'm not sure if that's supposed to be a compliment or not."

Takawa laughed. "Whatever way you take it is your business. Hey, are you still looking for Deena Vulk, Lieutenant?"

"You think I'd admit to it after our last conversation?"

The agent grinned. "Fair enough. You know, Tauk, Deena Vulk is a high-value target for Section 615 — one of the highest. I'll be frank. If someone other than us catches her, it'll be a huge black eye for our organization. Bigger than the one you've already given us. We can't let you win that race. Since I'm personally in charge of catching her, *I* can't afford to have you get to her before me. That said, after what I've seen today, you might be the one person on Kanaris most capable of netting her. If this thing works out and we break this stalemate, how about you come into the shadows with me? You and your platoon. We'll look for that bitch together. And maybe get our hands on some aliens along the way."

"Assigned to one of those new Mar-Sitaara Raptors?" I asked.

"That's what Tailur told me during your briefing. He thinks you and your team are the right people for that billet."

"Can we get on the *Niberian Hornet*?"

"That's right," Takawa said. "You and Warrant Officer Albarn have some history together, don't you?"

"A little."

"Good. I don't see why we couldn't put that band together again. I'm sure you'd make a great team. She's a hell of a pilot."

"If you pull that off, we have a deal."

"Splendid!" Takawa said while shaking my hand. "Just be aware. Vulk is my mission. I'll be the one giving the orders. Is that clear?"

"Absolutely."

"Then it looks like we have the beginnings of a beautiful relationship. Good luck with your current mission. Stay alive long enough to do some real hunting."

"I'll do my best," I said as the agent walked away, leaving me with the feeling I had just made a deal with the devil.

Chapter 30

PAY DIRT

It took another month to get our operation moving in earnest. Every day, Black Francis's Marines fanned out across the rainforest behind us, where the troops could not see them, offering Nandi berries for the barbalu. Buffy made sure at least one of the fruits was laced with cyklatamine so he could provide an animal to Dr. Maran for modification. At night, Barone Parsons would lead a mission into the NML to set up a relay station. Before long, our combined efforts began to run like a well-oiled machine and took on an assembly line quality.

We collected so much information that there were not enough Section 615 agents to monitor everything. They had to pull some of my trusted people to help. Among them was Dmitri Naktada, who walked into my command post after one of his shifts behind the intelligence monitors with a smile plastered upon his smug face. "I have a present for you."

I grinned and stood up, knowing this was going to be good. "Awesome! And it's not even my birthday!"

Naktada narrowed his eyes at me. "You were born into the Academy. Do you even know when your birthday is?"

"I have the same birthday as the Kyperion Space Corps. Just like all the other cadets do."

"That's what I figured." Naktada typed some commands into the system console on his left forearm and networked his data cache into my projector. He then turned it on and told me to have a seat and pay attention. "I can only show each of these pictures once. After they're displayed, they'll disappear into the ether the instant I close them. Got it?"

"Got it."

After a nod, Naktada said, "Computer, show image 367."

The projector complied and covered my east wall with a picture of a pretty young woman. She had brown hair and green eyes filled with the same rage I saw in them atop Mount Toranad. The photo was obviously of her good side. "You got one of her opposite profile?"

"Do I ever," Naktada said. "Computer, Image 368."

The projector now displayed a horribly disfigured subject. Her face was a mess of scar tissue. Her ear was missing, and there was not enough unburned scalp on that side of her head to grow hair long enough to cover it. The artificial eye in her left socket glowed faintly red. It was undeniably Deena Vulk. "If she was on our side, we probably could have gotten her a cloned eye," I mused.

"It wouldn't have lasted long without a working eyelid," Naktada countered. "Whatever that thing is she's looking out of, I'd bet it's better than her original one. It's alien technology. Not ours. Computer, Video 369."

The footage Naktada called up showed Vulk conferring with Mailes Ghona, the former governor of Narman's Pyke, who we now believed commanded the forces opposing us. "Too bad there's no audio," I told my techwar specialist. "I'd love to hear what those two are talking about."

Naktada looked embarrassed. "Sorry about that, sir. It never occurred to me to add microphones to my barbalu rig. Are you catching her body language, though?"

I nodded. "Yeah, it looks like she's giving orders to him, not the other way around. You think she's the one actually in charge?"

Naktada shook his head. "Nope. Ghona's the one directing troops, taking briefings, and inspecting the fortifications. We've kept pretty good tabs on him. He never seeks her out. She's the one who goes to him."

"She's probably just the messenger, then," I mused. "She's speaking for the aliens. I bet she's their conduit to the front."

"Could be. Computer, Image 370." The projector showed Deena Vulk conferring with a couple of officers. "Our facial recognition identified the troops she's talking to. Both were privates on our side before the last offensive. Apparently, defecting is good for one's career mobility."

I shrugged. "I doubt they're getting paid for that rank."

"Image 371." Deena Vulk eating field rations with another group of troops. "Those people are not in our database. I suspect they're some of the original Narmans. Computer, Video 372."

This footage showed the barbalu's perspective as it scurried across the ground and jumped up into the window of a simple structure some distance off the line. Inside the hut, Deena Vulk sat upon the latrine with her pants around her ankles, wiping her backside. There was no audio, but we could clearly see Vulk mouthing the words, "Get out of here! Now! Go away! Leave me alone, you little pervert! I'm trying to shit!"

"That one's my favorite," Naktada confessed.

I pointed at the numbers spinning around on the bottom right corner of the screen. "Are those what I think they are?"

Naktada nodded. "Yep. They're coordinates. Because of the Harnillium interference, satellite navigation is impossible. The Narmans mapped the surface pretty well from space, however. We can use altitude and surface topography to calculate a pretty precise setpoint for whatever that barbalu's camera is pointed at."

"So, we know exactly where the Narman restrooms are located?"

"We sure do. That's good information, sir. You'll appreciate it if you're storming those positions and are suddenly struck with the urge to drop a deuce. Oddly enough, we've collected much more bathroom video than you'd think. The barbalu seem to entertain themselves a lot by watching us shit. Anyway, this may be my favorite video, but this next one will probably be yours. Computer, Video 373."

It appeared I was watching dawn break across enemy positions. Most of the screen was filled up with visions of sleeping barbalu. At the top left corner of the video, a door opened and Deena Vulk stepped through it, stretching her arms out and yawning as she emerged. "Is that...?"

"It sure is," Naktada said to me. "That's where Deena Vulk stays when she's in town. This particular barbalu almost always sleeps in this exact spot, so I have video of this area at daybreak spanning more than three weeks. If she spends the night on the line, this is where she sleeps. She's there about seventy percent of the time."

Glancing at the numbers at the right, I pulled out my tablet to write them down.

Naktada reached over and ripped it out of my hand. "Don't you even think about it. I put my ass on the line to bring you this information. You're going to burn me if you document it. Her latitude is 48.86534379946667. Longitude is 2.3652672646572626. We're going to sit here until those numbers are as burned into your memory as your own name."

"No problem," I told Naktada. "I can do that. When we're done, though, you're going to find Buffy and teach him those coordinates also. When we get the signal to cross the NML, I want him and his ubati to make a beeline to that position and seize that bitch before anyone else gets their hands on her."

"Aye aye, sir," Naktada assured me. "Any idea when that might be?"

"Soon," I assured him. "It sounds like we've got a bead on every blaster portal along the entire front. We know where their hologram generators are, where the troops are concentrated, where the Quarakai are roosting, and where the machine gunners are set up. We got the same information for most of the second line also. The moment the signal is given for us to charge, all of it goes up in a big, spectacular ball of flame."

"What about that third line?" Naktada asked. "We got any plans on that?"

"Yeah, we got plans," I told Naktada. "We're just waiting until the rain is heavy enough to give us the cover to get another click closer to the enemy. When that happens, Black Francis and Agent Takawa will sneak a set of relay stations so close to the Narman lines they'll be under the tips of the bastards' dicks."

Chapter 31

FNG

There used to be an officer in charge of Black Francis and his Raiders. He was the first to lead Kyperion troops into the stretch of contested turf between Kanaris's opposing forces before it was even called No Man's Land, arriving when the area was still covered with rainforest and wildlife. That unfortunate Samaari was killed shortly after making first contact with the enemy when he accidentally called an artillery barrage on his own position and blew himself up. At least, that was one version of the story. Another was that Black Francis murdered the man after he had gotten half of them killed by friendly fire.

Their second officer fared no better. She lost visual contact with the Marine she was supposed to keep in view as she crawled across the NML and lifted her head too high to get her bearings. An alert Narman sentry made her pay for that lapse in judgment. A third officer stumbled into an enemy patrol and got captured, forcing Black Francis to order one of his snipers to kill their platoon leader before he could give away their positions. After that, the command had trouble finding officers willing to fill that unit's open leadership billet.

The brigade stopped looking for a commander of the Raiders when they discovered Black Francis's platoon did not really need one. In the combined eight weeks they were in theater with an officer at the helm, the Raiders suffered fifty-one killed in action. In the eight months they operated without a platoon leader, they only lost twelve, despite carrying out seven times the number of patrols. Their mission completion rate also improved from sixty-six to ninety-four percent . Colonel Palkrait offered Black Francis an officer's commission just before I reached the front, but he turned it down.

"Too much ass-kissing and bureaucracy," Black Francis told me when I asked why he refused the promotion. "Because of my reputation, I have all the perks of being an officer but none of the responsibilities. Besides, I hate being around those pricks. They ain't worth a shit out here."

Remembering I was a commissioned platoon leader, he added, "Excepting present company, of course."

The operational tempo of Black Francis's Marines was insanely high. While most of our troops along the front sat idle in their trenches, on watch and waiting to repel the next Narman assault, the Raiders were sneaking around No Man's Land. They kept their bellies in the mud, crawling through bomb craters, around shattered tree trunks, and tunneling under obstacles to avoid detection. They put up listening stations, ambushed Narman infiltrators, set booby traps, and kept tabs on enemy patrols.

Black Francis was allowed to hand-pick replacements for the Marines he lost. As a result, he commanded an incredibly tight unit. They were all chummy, with a high *esprit de corps* and a deep distrust of outsiders. Because my troops spent so much time out in the NML with them, the Raiders respected my people and me, but we were rare exceptions. They regarded regular Marines with suspicion, especially after seeing firsthand how easily they could switch sides and turn their weapons on former friends when things got tough. The Raiders thought even worse of Section 615 agents, considering them treacherous in even the best of circumstances.

That was why none seemed happy to see Takawa join them on the mission to set up a relay station far enough west for the barbalu to record video of the enemy's third trench line.

"Oh man," groaned one of Black Francis's squad leaders as he spotted the intelligence agent approaching them in combat gear. "We already got one FNG going out with us tonight! Why the hell are we taking another?"

"If I heard correctly," Black Francis responded. "Agent Takawa's been a field spook for more than a decade. He's also been on Kanaris since Tauk's team reached Narman's Pyke. That hardly qualifies him as an FNG. He's just NFG." NFG was a Marine acronym for No Fucking Good.

Takawa scowled at the Raiders' leader. "You got a new guy on this mission?"

Black Francis pointed his chin at a young PFC to his right who was chomping at the bit to get going. "Duklow just joined us a couple of weeks ago."

The agent looked at the man's shoulder and noticed his rank was outlined in orange. "He's a conscript. Do you trust him?"

"A hell of a lot more than I trust you," Black Francis retorted. "And if you check my file, you'll find I was a conscript, too. If you think Duklow's a problem, though, feel free to sit this out. We wouldn't want you to feel uncomfortable out there."

Takawa's expression hardened. "I'll be fine," he said. They were not going to get rid of him that easily.

"Duklow!" Takawa whispered coarsely. "Get back here!"

Black Francis's newest Raider shot the agent a seething look of contempt, then crawled further to his left, putting even more distance between him and the furious intelligence agent.

"Duklow!" Takawa snapped even louder.

Seeming to come out of nowhere, Black Francis emerged from the darkness, landing on Takawa's back and slapping the hat off his head. Pressing his lips hard against the agent's right ear, he snarled, "Would you shut the fuck up?!?"

"But your FNG's off course! He's dragging us too far south!"

"It doesn't matter! As long as we get this repeater up within a couple hundred meters of the enemy's trenches, we can go a whole kilometer north or south, and it'll not make a damned bit of difference! All you have to do is match his pace, make sure he remains in your line of sight, and keep your trap closed!"

"But it's like he's trying to run away from me!"

"He is! Because if he don't, you'll get his ass killed!"

In the dark, Black Francis could not see Takawa's face turning red, but their heads were so close together he could feel the heat radiating off the agent's cheek. "I wasn't being that loud."

"It doesn't matter! The Narmans set ambushes on the far side of the NML behind hologram camo! We don't know where they are! That's why we don't talk out here! Ever! What do I have to do to get that through your fuckin' head?!?"

After several seconds under Black Francis's unforgiving glare, Takawa diverted his gaze and caught sight of Corporal Dori crouched behind him to his left. She held a combat dagger in her right hand while the look on her face hinted she had been readying to plunge it through the back of the agent's neck if he made another sound.

Letting out a remorseful sigh, Takawa turned his attention back to Black Francis. "I'm sorry."

Francis shook the spook by the neck in fury. "You're what?!?"

"I'm sorry!"

Black Francis let go of the agent. "That's your only warning. Dori's trailing you now. The next peep you make will be your last." With that, Staff Sergeant Franq rolled off Takawa and disappeared into the rain.

Supai Takawa was a man used to meting out discipline. It had been years since he had been subjected to it. Black Francis's correction stung, and as the agent continued crawling through the mud, he grew increasingly furious about what had been done to him. He was especially enraged it happened within view of junior Marines. They tended to talk, and Takawa knew word of the incident would spread through the ranks like wildfire. He would look like a fool.

"I'll make that pompous prick pay for this shit when we get back," Takawa growled to himself.

Or so he thought.

When Narmans emerged from their hologram envelopes, it always looked as if they appeared out of nowhere. One second, Agent Takawa was surrounded by nothing but rain. An instant later, he was confronted by a half dozen enemy infantry, clad in black armor and wearing helmets enhanced with alien night vision that made their eyes glow faintly red behind their visors. "Oh shit!" Takawa gasped.

The Narmans had the drop on the agent, but a couple of Black Francis's Marines had the drop on the Narmans. Trying to stay quiet enough to salvage their mission, Sergeant Korman jumped one from behind and plunged his knife into the sweet spot between his adversary's backplate and helmet, killing him instantly. When the doomed Narman's partner turned to see what happened, Korman unsheathed his blade from the corpse he had just created and jabbed it into the enemy's larynx from the opposite direction.

Dori took out a third and fourth combatant in the blink of an eye, while Duklow stole the life of a fifth. Using his own training, Takawa popped out of the mud and swept the legs from the last, then pounced on him when he hit the ground. More Narmans seemed to appear out of thin air, and while Takawa grappled with his adversary, the Raiders engaged the reinforcements, joined by Black Francis and another sergeant. Despite the Raiders' best efforts, one of the bastards eventually squeezed off a round. The bullet did not hit anybody, but the sound of gunfire effectively ended their operation.

●●-●-●-●-●●

Now that they were exposed, speed became more important than stealth. The Raiders traded blades for rifles and opened fire, cutting down any shadowy figure with glowing eyes behind their visor. They then turned tail and fled back toward friendly lines as quick as they could.

Sprinting through ankle-deep mud was not easy. It was even more challenging when under fire. "SPREAD OUT!" screamed Black Francis as they charged East. "IF YOU CAN SEE ANOTHER RAIDER, YOU'RE TOO CLOSE!"

A half click from where they made contact, a Narman bullet caught Dori in the shoulder and spun her to the ground. "I'm hit!" she cried.

Duklow emerged from her right and, without breaking stride, grabbed her by the neck of her fatigues, dragging her backward through the mud. Ducking for cover behind a fallen palm tree, he pulled his comrade to safety and asked, "Are you okay?"

Dori grimaced in pain, but after rubbing her arm, nodded. "I think so. The bullet went through the muscle. It didn't hit bone."

Sergeant Korman and Black Francis soon joined the pair. "Catch your breath!" Francis ordered. "Quickly! We've been through this before. We're about a half click from where we set the first counter ambush. We have to make it before...."

The Raider was interrupted by Agent Takawa jumping into their midst. "Aaaaaauugh!" the agent groaned as he hit the ground. He was clutching his leg.

"Are you hit?" asked Corporal Dori.

"No, I twisted my ankle when I...."

Sergeant Korman did not let Takawa finish his answer before slugging the agent across the jaw. "You stupid piece of shit! You couldn't keep your mouth shut out there, could you?!?"

Korman was about to hit Takawa again, but Black Francis jumped between them and ordered his squad leader to stand down. After calming his sergeant, he turned to the agent and asked, "Can you keep up?"

Takawa tried to stretch his leg but recoiled in agony. "I don't think so."

Sergeant Korman took a quick peek over their cover but immediately dropped his head back down as enemy bullets splintered the massive log they were hiding behind. "We gotta go, Francis! There's a fucking horde of Narmans bearing down on us right now!"

Black Francis cursed and grabbed Takawa by the collar. "You have to keep up!"

"I can't!" the agent cried. "It's sprained! You're going to have to carry me!"

Korman shook his head. "We can't! He'll slow us down too much! We have to leave him!"

"We can't leave him!" Francis snapped back. "We can't put an asset like that in Narman hands!"

"Then what are we going to do?" asked Dori.

Francis answered her by drawing his sidearm and pumping three rounds into Takawa's chest, leaving him lying motionless in the mud.

"What the fuck!" Duklow gasped. "What are you doing?!?"

Francis turned his weapon on the new guy. "Whatever I have to in order to save our lives! You got a problem with that?"

With his hands up in the air, Duklow shook his head. "No, man! I'm good! I'm good!"

Black Francis nodded at the Raider as he holstered his pistol. "Good. Then let's get the hell out of here!"

Chapter 32

The Phoenix

Three times on the way back to the trenches, Black Francis and his Raiders had to stop and fight long enough to delay their Narman posse. Once they passed the halfway point across the NML, the counter-ambush they set did its job. When the M2117 gunners saw the faint red eyes of the enemy, they cut loose and mowed them down by the dozen. The Narmans dropped into the mud to return fire right where the Raiders wanted them to.

One of Black Francis's Marines fired off a blue flare, and Third Brigade's mortarmen answered the signal. Explosions roared all across the stretch of mud where they pinned the Narmans down and blew them to pieces. After that, the entirety of the Raider platoon broke contact and rushed toward the eastern trenches.

Black Francis was one of the first to reach safety. Despite being gassed, he turned around and screamed at his troops to hurry home. "RUN!" he shrieked at them. "RUN! GET BACK HERE BEFORE THEY REGROUP AND TRY TO FIRE BACK!"

"Take it easy, Sergeant," said a Third Brigade 2nd lieutenant. "You earned it. The Narmans are retreating. You're all safe."

Black Francis looked at the officer as if he was an idiot. "No one's safe until they're all out of the NML, sir!"

One of the nearby Marines tried to jump over the berm to help the Raiders running across No Man's Land. Francis had to lunge to pull him back down. "You're in full combat dress, Marine!" the Raider yelled at him. "You're a radio frequency hotspot! That makes you a plasma blaster magnet! You go out there and you'll get everyone around you killed!"

Turning back to the platoon leader, Francis shouted, "Get on your commlink and tell your Marines to stay in the trenches! If they go out there, they'll be painting targets on themselves and my Marines!"

"I'm an officer. I don't take orders from enlisted...."

Black Francis reached out, grabbed the lieutenant around the throat, and bounced his head off the side of the trench. "Do it right now, or I'll wring your scrawny little...!"

That was all the convincing the officer needed. "Stand fast!" He shouted over the commlink. "Stand fast! Squad leaders! Keep your Marines on this side of the berm! No exceptions!"

As the Raiders began jumping into the trench, Black Francis lined them up against the wall, counting heads. "You have any casualties?" the lieutenant asked, suddenly at Black Francis's beck and call. "Are your people okay?"

Francis did not answer until PFC Omair leapt into the ditch. "That's sixty-eight! Everybody made it!" he shouted, sending off a round of cheers among Marines and Raiders alike. They did not settle down until a Section 615 commander emerged from the crowd and asked, "Where's Takawa?"

The celebration came to a sudden stop. With his head hanging low, Black Francis stepped forward and said, "I'm sorry, sir. Agent Takawa got hit about halfway back. He didn't make it."

"Where is he?" the commander demanded.

The Raider stuck his thumb out and pointed it west. "He's out in the NML."

"We'll need to form a detail to bring back his body."

Francis shook his head. "Not tonight, sir. There's still Narmans out there. Some of them are as good as we are. We'll try to ID the body after sun up. If the Narmans haven't removed it themselves, we can take another stab at it in a couple of days."

"Don't bother!" rang out a voice to Francis's right. It was Supai Takawa, being helped through the crowd by a pair of the lieutenant's Marines. Despite the rain and the agent's black fatigues, the troops could still see blood pouring from the holes Black Francis poked into the agent's chest. More of it was trickling from the side of his mouth.

Despite the life seeping from his wounds, Takawa used his last ounces of remaining strength to point an accusing finger at Black Francis and say, "I didn't get hit by Narman gunfire! I was murdered! By that man!"

Breaking into a violent coughing fit, Takawa sprayed blood over the Marines trying to help him. When he could speak again, he said, "You're going to hang for this! All of you! Seize them! Every fucking one of them!"

The Marines raised their weapons and pointed them at the Raiders, but Francis had already popped the pin on one of his smoke grenades. When it went off, he turned to his troops and screamed, "RUN!"

The Marines and Raiders were in tight quarters, so intermingled neither could fire without hitting their own. Having the benefit of not being bogged down by the armor and equipment the infantry wore, the Raiders cleared the berms before the Marines were even out of the trenches. All but a dozen escaped into the NML while Takawa collapsed in the mud. His commander had to pull him from the fray to get him somewhere with a chance of saving the agent's life.

When Barone Parsons entered my tent, his eyes were as wide as dinner plates. Rousting me out of bed, he informed me Black Francis had defected.

Shooting straight up off my cot, I exclaimed, "What?!?"

"Black Francis went over to the Narmans. I heard he murdered Agent Takawa."

"From who?" I asked.

"From everybody! Word's gone out up and down the line! He's gone, sir. Our plan's probably shot all to hell, also!"

Nodding at Parsons, I patted him on the shoulder. "You heard this on the line?"

My squad leader nodded.

I let out a tired sigh and started getting dressed. "Maybe we'll get lucky, and this just turns out to be a rumor that got legs."

Parsons shook his head. "I've been around Marines long enough to know when something like this smacks of the truth, sir. They're saying Black Francis got away and took the Raiders with him. There is NO way our command wants that news getting out to our rank and file. It'd kill morale."

I slipped my boots on without tying them and stepped toward the door. Cupid, my ubati, got up to join me, but I pointed my finger back at her bed and said, "Stay!"

"Where are you going, sir?" Parsons asked me as I walked out of the tent.

"To get the real deal on this."

The Section 615 command post was slightly over two kilometers from Beta Company's stretch of trench line. I was there in fifteen minutes, greeted by a pair of Kommandos guarding the entrance. "Can I help you?" growled one of them as I approached the door.

"I'm here to see Agent Takawa. I'm Lieutenant Tauk."

"You haven't heard what happened to him?"

"I did," I told the bruin. "I just don't believe it."

"Believe it. He's gone."

"I want to see the body."

"That's not going to...."

"What's going on out there?!?" barked the commander from inside the CP.

"I got someone out here who wants to see Takawa's body!"

"Who?"

"Some Recon lieutenant."

"Tauk?" asked the commander.

"Yes, sir!"

"It's okay. Send him in."

Stepping into the CP, I spotted the commander behind his desk. He directed me toward a door in the back. "He's in the room."

Calling that space a room was generous. It was more like a large closet. Along the rear wall was a gurney, atop which lay a corpse in a body bag. The fallen man was flanked by another pair of Section Kommandos, on post and holding M55 submachine guns diagonally across their chests. They wore armor breastplates, black balaclavas, and shaded combat goggles over their eyes to obscure their identity.

Closing and locking the door behind me, I took two steps to approach the gurney, then unzipped the bag. Staring at the brown-haired, light-skinned man inside, I asked, "Who's this?"

Relaxing his position and lowering his weapon, one of the guards began removing his helmet. "I have no idea," Agent Supai Takawa told me. "A guy some Killbillies caught trying to sneak away from the line."

"That explains his missing ear. You alright?"

Takawa nodded. "I will be. I think Franq might have cracked a couple of my ribs when he shot me."

"Yeah, those M77 vests are thin and easier to conceal, but they don't blunt the bullets' impact like the M82s. They'll keep you alive but make you wish you were dead."

"Ain't that the truth," Takawa said. "So, what's the word on the line?"

"Word on the line is Francis went to the dark side and you to the great hereafter."

Takawa grinned, displaying teeth still stained red by the fake blood capsule he bit into just before he reached our trenches. "So, it worked?"

I nodded. "It worked. The two of you are the talk of the town right now. You guys must have been pretty convincing."

"Convincing?!?" Takawa laughed. "You should have seen us, Tauk! It was a masterful performance by everyone involved! After that, if this war thing doesn't work out, I think we should all become actors! Everybody swallowed it hook, line, and sinker!"

"'Everybody' doesn't really matter," I countered. "Did the one person we needed to convince take the bait?"

"I think so! You should've seen that kid shit himself when Black Francis shot me. Yeah, I think we hooked him."

"So, what's next?" I asked.

"Well, I'm getting a discreet ride back to the mothership under the guise of escorting this piece of shit to his final resting place. I'm supposed to be dead, so we can't afford to have anyone stumble across me at Narman's Pyke, can we? We gotta let this plan you two guys cooked up work itself out."

"This was Black Francis's plan," I told Takawa.

"It's brilliant."

"I know."

Takawa reached out and put his hand on my shoulder. "The three of us make a pretty damned good team, Tauk. Hey, if this works, we're going to be assaulting the Narman trenches very soon. Be careful out there. Survive the offensive and be prepared to do some hunting when I get back. We're going to go get Deena Vulk!"

196

Not unless I get her first.

"Now what?" Sergeant Korman asked. Black Francis's Raiders were gathered in an unusually deep crater located halfway between the Narmans and the Marines, but shielded from both.

"I don't know," Francis answered, perturbed by the question. "If we go back to our lines, they'll hang every fucking one of us."

"Why don't we go to the Narman lines?" asked PFC Duklow.

"If our guys are going to hang us for killing one incompetent spy," Dori answered. "What do you think the Narmans will do to us for killing dozens of theirs?"

"They're desperate for people," Duklow said. "Especially after losing as many troops as they did after that last assault!"

Korman scoffed. "Yeah, I'm sure they'll shower us with hugs and kisses after what we did to them last night. How many do you think we killed, Francis? Twenty? Thirty?"

"A lot," Black Francis answered. "I didn't bother to count, but we iced a shit-ton of them."

"Then those are twenty or thirty troops they'll need to replace!" Duklow exclaimed. "We can't sit out here forever!"

Korman looked at Black Francis. "He's right. We can't."

Francis let out a long sigh. "I know, I know. If we go back, we're dead. If we stay here, we're dead. I guess the Narmans are the only chance we got, even if they're probably going to kill us, too." Black Francis looked at his Raiders. "So, who do I send to parley with these pricks and negotiate our surrender?"

Most of the Marines averted their gaze and looked at the ground. Seeing no one was volunteering, Duklow raised his hand and said, "I'll go."

Francis sighed again. "You think you can make it there in the daylight?"

Duklow looked up at the moisture falling out of the sky. "Yeah, I know how to hug the mud and stay out of sight of our snipers. I can get there."

Black Francis gave the PFC a nod. "Okay. Go. See what you can do. If the Narmans agree to accept us, lead them to our A Rendezvous. If they don't, lead 'em to our B, where we can ambush them. You know where those places are?"

Duklow nodded. "I've been to both a million times since joining you guys."

"Perfect, then," Francis told his Raider. "Get going. We'll see you tonight."

Black Francis and Sergeant Korman watched Duklow crawl away from their position toward enemy lines. When he was out of earshot, Korman turned to his superior and said, "I can't wait to kill that fuckin' traitor."

It was just after dark when Duklow showed up at the A Rendezvous with a dozen Narman troops. That was supposed to mean everything went according to plan, but Black Francis's Raiders ambushed them anyway, disarming the soldiers and having them lead the way back to their positions.

"If you people are on the level, you got nothing to worry about," Francis assured his prisoners. "If you lead us into a trap, however, you'll be the first to die. So, if there's any funny business waiting for us ahead, it's in your best interests to tell me about it now."

When no one stepped up, the Raider platoon moved out with the Narmans up front.

It took them a couple of hours before they reached the Narmans' positions and crossed the hologram wall. Nearly a hundred red-eyed troops greeted them, their weapons unslung and ready to fire if anything went awry. A few of the forces were riding naypetos, and there was a sizeable population of ubatis among the throng. Behind them all stood a levitating plasma blaster preparing to vaporize the Raiders if anyone acted upon unwise ideas.

"Black Francis!" called out a woman from the midst of the troops. She wore a long dark cloak that obscured her entire head. "I've heard so much about you!"

As she approached the Raiders, the woman lowered her hood to reveal a disfigured face dominated by an alien-made bionic eye. "Welcome to the Narman side of the Satapadaya Front. My name is Deena Vulk."

Chapter 33

THE CALM

"Y ou ever eat at Bunhallo's?" I heard Luuk Bukki ask his squad leader as I approached their post. It had been four weeks since Black Francis had gone over to the Narmans, and we were slated to cross No Man's Land the following morning. I tried to get my Marines to sleep, but they just couldn't. Neither could I.

Sergeant Parsons nodded at Bukki's question. "I'm pretty sure everybody on Apalashu has. Four hour wait to get inside. Rude wait staff. Insanely expensive food."

"But worth every credit," Bukki said.

Parsons grinned. "Aye. But worth every credit."

It was odd seeing Parsons and Bukki engaging in civil conversation, considering I had pulled the former cop into my platoon for the sole purpose of serving him to my sergeant on a silver platter. I expected Parsons to kill him for what the Apalushan police had done to his family. Parsons could not bring himself to do it, though. He knew Bukki was not even on the force when the bastards torched his home. To Parsons, slaughtering Bukki would not have been justice. Nor would it have been revenge. It would have been straight-up murder, a line Parsons was unwilling to cross.

"You going to go there while you're on leave?" I asked my squad leader.

"Maybe," Parsons told me. "I got an awful lot of back pay to burn."

"You're going on leave?" asked Bukki.

"Since the high court has vacated Sergeant Parsons' conviction, the Kyperion Space Corps has decided he is entitled to seven months of unused leave."

"You're leaving for seven months?!?" Bukki's jaw nearly hit the ground. "How the hell are you going to come back and do Marine shit after that?"

Parsons shrugged. "I'm not sure I'm going to."

"You deserting?"

"Parsons has been a Class One convict for over seven years," I told Bukki. "Almost eight. Had he re-upped for another enlistment after his first ended, he'd only had to have served five. He's eligible for an immediate discharge. For some odd reason I can't ascertain, though, he's decided to hang around and help us through the assault on the Narman lines."

"Well, you cleared my name and unleashed Section 356 agents on the pricks who framed me and killed my family. It seemed like the least I could do."

"I appreciate it," I told Parsons. "I really do. I wouldn't have faulted you one bit had you dropped everything and left the instant your orders came through. I know you got people you'd like to get to before the 356 agents do."

"Do you know where to find them?" Bukki asked. "The guys who killed your family?"

"A few of them. I got some pretty good ideas about how to get them to tell me where the others are." Parsons paused to yawn and look about his surroundings. "I've learned a lot about inflicting misery out here."

"Talk to me before you leave," Bukki told the sergeant. "I might have some information on who can help you track those sons-of-bitches down."

"Where the fuck's Tauk?!?" The question rose above the low din of the trenches, coming from our south. Gunny Brumit, who was napping nearby, caught it, too. She sprang to her feet and craned her head to see if she could hear it again.

"Tauk!" it cried out again. "You better not be avoiding me!"

Brumit looked up at me and smiled, "Does he have an appointment to see you?"

"Konor Malcolm doesn't need an appointment to see anybody," I told her.

Brumit laughed. "That's the truth. I've seen the man walk into Colonel Palkrait's office without even knocking."

"TAUK!" Malcolm screamed.

"Over here!" I called out.

After hearing my voice, Malcolm recalibrated his bearings and marched my way. As if seeing my former platoon sergeant was not enough of a treat, Ritza Xi was right behind him.

Brumit intercepted her old friend before he got to us and wrapped him in a big bear hug. "How's that candy-ass academy Marine treating you, Shai?" the one-eyed gunnery sergeant asked.

My platoon sergeant slapped Malcolm across the shoulder. "Ah, I've had worse. Actually, if you'd have given him a chance, the kid's got a pretty good head on his shoulders."

"That's what I heard," Malcolm said as he stepped in front of me, went to the position of attention, and rendered me a stiff salute. "In fact, it's my understanding that tomorrow's shindig was something of Tauk's doing."

I returned Malcolm's salute before reaching out to shake his hand. "Actually, it was the effort of my armorer and a Killbilly." Turning to face Buffy, who was lying in the mud at the bottom of the trench, using his ubati as a pillow, I added, "No offense."

"None taken," Buffy replied.

"For fuck's sake, Lieutenant!" Malcolm snapped at me. "Learn to take credit for the shit you accomplish out here! Yeah, your subordinates come up with ideas, but you're the one who gets your Marines what they need to put them into motion!"

As Malcolm lectured me, I watched Parsons walk up to Xi and embrace her. "How are you doing, Ritza?"

"Good," the Zero answered. "I'm going home after this."

"What?!?" Parsons asked. "How?!?"

"I got my twenty deserters. I earned my pardon."

"Seriously?" I asked Gunny. "They're really going to let her go?"

Malcolm nodded. "It looks that way. They took the dirtiest of the dirty and gave them a job no one else wanted to do. Considering how much abuse female Zeros suffer at the hands of male Marines, the command figured hunting down our cowards would be something these women would do with relish, and my god, were they right! The thing is if these ladies knew they'd end up right back where they started when this was all over, they'd use those weapons we gave them to blow away their superiors and join the Narmans the first chance they got. Granting them pardons if they got twenty deserters gave them the incentive to kill who we wanted them to instead of us."

"You don't think the League will renege and fuck them all over again?"

Malcolm shook his head. "The command told me that's the deal, so I'm holding the bastards to it."

"You?"

Gunny Malcolm nodded. "Yeah, I've lost three platoons since I've been here, Tauk. They decided not to trust me with another, so they put me in charge of these killers."

"Holy hell," Brumit gasped.

"Xi!" boomed Lumuk as he barrelled through us to get to our visiting Zero. When he reached her, our big black giant lifted her off her feet and squeezed her so hard she almost popped.

Malcolm sighed. "He's not going over the top tomorrow, is he?"

I shook my head. "Not with us. I temporarily assigned him to the medical battalion. He's going to help them pull our wounded out of No Man's Land."

"Good." Malcolm and Xi stayed with us and talked for more than an hour. We spoke about our march to Narman's Pyke. We discussed what happened to Captain Briggund, the mutiny, and the fight against the Quarakai. We traded stories about what we had done since Malcolm flogged me upon my return to Kanaris.

"I'm proud of you, Lieutenant," Malcolm told me as he stood up to return to his unit. "It's because of you we got this far."

"Me and Black Francis."

"Oh, fuck Black Francis," Malcolm growled. The man was apparently not in the loop. "He's a goddamned traitor. His name's going to end up stricken from our rolls in shame. No, when we take that line tomorrow, you're the one we'll all praise for making it happen."

"Yeah?" I shot back. "What do you think they're going to say about me if tomorrow turns out to be a bloodbath?"

Gunny gave me another grin. "They're gonna make your ass wish you were Black Francis."

After Malcolm and Xi returned to their post, Akkam Lumuk leaned back against the trench wall and smiled sadly. "You okay, big guy?" I asked him as I passed.

Lumuk nodded. "Yeah, sir. It's just that seein' Gunny and Xi made me remember how much I miss Corporal Merik. Without him, I don't think I'd have made it on that walk up here to Narman's Pyke."

I know you wouldn't have.

The giant laughed. "That man tried to teach me how to fight, as silly as that seems."

"It wasn't silly at all," I assured Lumuk. "Had he not done what he had, you wouldn't have been able to save Kalawezi from those soroquids."

"Yeah, but she still died. Eventually."

I nodded. "Yes, she did."

Lumuk shook his head in mourning. "She didn't deserve that. She was a medic! All she ever did was help Marines! Ain't no reason for her to be killed by her own people! She didn't do nothin'! I miss her, too."

"There's a lot of people to miss from that march, Lumuk." Merik. Mardona. Thyster. Jella Duverii.

Jella.

Suddenly feeling my stomach knot up, I patted Lumuk on the shoulder as I took my leave. "Try to get some sleep, big guy. We've got a busy day ahead of us. It starts in a few short hours."

Jella didn't do anything either, I thought as I walked away. *She came to this fucking planet to help her people, and one of them murdered her for it. Well, tomorrow, I avenge her. I make the bastards pay for what they did.*

I fantasized about storming the line the following day. I pictured myself pumping bullets into deserters and Narmans alike, slaying them all in Jella's memory.

Yeah, because that's the kind of thing Jella would have wanted, isn't it? She wants you to slaughter her Narman family members. She would like to see you murder her childhood friends. Lay waste to her teachers and co-workers. Her neighbors....

I tried to shake the voice of my conscience out of my head. In its place, I got the memory of Jella and me on that ledge we spent days on, waiting to be rescued. We were lying naked on the ground one night, and I was thinking about what Gori Dravidas said to me right before I slit his throat.

"There's more to life than just killing."

I must have said it aloud because Jella heard it through her dreams and asked what gave me that epiphany. After I told her those were Gori Dravidas's last words, she said, "He's right, you know."

Jella Duverii spoke to me that night, also. She tried to remind me what I was up against. *Eamon, you came to their home to do them harm. They didn't come to yours. You're fighting them to help the Samaaris mine Harnillium. They're fighting you for their lives. You have a duty to do, and I understand that. I only ask that you do it with honor. I want you to remember some of those people you're going to kill tomorrow are people I once loved, and who once loved me back. They're not the ones who took my life, Eamon.*

I stopped walking and leaned against the side of the trench. I clenched my eyes closed, trying to keep the tears contained behind them. "Deena Vulk," I told her. "Deena Vulk took your life."

That's right. Deena Vulk murdered me. Only Deena Vulk.

"I'm going to kill her," I promised Jella.

I'm gone, Eamon. Killing Deena isn't going to do anything to change that. You don't have to do this for me.

"I'm not doing this for you," I assured her, "I'm doing it for me."

As I strolled past Buffy and his ubati, I asked, "You remember those coordinates I gave you?"

"I do," my tracker said without bothering to open his eyes. "Latitude 48.865343799 46667. Longitude 2.3652672646572626."

"Good."

When I returned to my CP, I called up an unauthorized network link Naktada hooked up for me and punched up the video feed from the barbalu that tended to sleep in a tree just outside Deena Vulk's quarters. There was not much going on in real-time, but when I rewound the footage a few hours and watched again, I saw Deena Vulk enter her room and settle in for the night.

I smiled. In hours, we were going to knock on Vulk's door, the one at the coordinates my Killbilly had memorized, and that bitch was going to find herself on the wrong end of an irate ubati.

Chapter 34

The Storm

Unlike the Marines that would be thrown at the Narmans in waves, we were not wearing armor. We were filling the role left vacant by Black Francis's Raiders. Dressed only in our web gear and black fatigues, we snuck across the NML and waited for the barrage to take out the enemy defenses. Our mission was to let the main assault pass us by but be ready to neutralize any plasma blasters that might have escaped being entombed in their bunkers by our artillery.

An hour before sunrise, a swarm of missiles appeared above the eastern tree line and sailed over our heads. An alarm went off beyond the Narman trenches, but it did not last long enough to make much of a difference. Before the enemy could swing their legs over the side of their cots, three Thundercloud missiles flew into every plasma blaster burrow and blew it to smithereens. The shockwave from the massive blasts caused the hologram generators to flicker just before a second wave of bombing took them out, too.

When the Narmans lost their camouflage, the landscape was transformed in an instant. The illusion of verdant rainforest vaporized into thin air, replaced by barren hillsides stretching fifty kilometers to the south, pockmarked with pillboxes, trench lines, and foxholes. Even though we were expecting that to happen, the contrast was shocking to behold.

Three kilometers to our rear, thousands of Marines began leaping over the berm and flooding into No Man's Land. They were met with a withering wall of machine gun fire from the Narman side of the wastes. These rounds were fired by automated sentry weapons that had not been accounted for and missed by our missiles.

Crouched over to stay out of the line of fire, Gunny Brumit darted over to Second Squad and started yelling orders to Sergeant Dina Tiago. "Get your grenadier on those sentry guns!"

"But if we power up the M44, they'll zero in on our electronic emissions!"

"Then take it out before it hits you!"

With quaking hands, Lance Corporal Abel Biendo attached a guided grenade to his launcher and then pointed it at the sentry gun. The instant he energized it, his target triangulated his position and took aim at him. So did two others. By the time Biendo launched the projectile, all three sentries had opened fire. Biendo destroyed the sentry he was aiming at, but the other two showered his position with thousands of exploding steel rounds in the blink of an eye. They not only killed Biendo, they took out two other Marines who were lying too close to him.

While one of the automatic sentries was still pointed at Tiago's man, Third Squad's grenadier took the opportunity to take her own shot. Having seen what happened to Biendo, Ghear, and Nuuta, everyone in LCPL Premin's vicinity deserted her to flee for safer cover. She fared much better than her Second Squad colleague. Premin destroyed her target and had her M44 de-energized before the remaining sentry could lock onto her. While the last weapon was still pointed south, it was neutralized by a team from First Squad.

As the Marines kept charging, two more waves of missiles lit up the enemy lines. With their hologram cover gone, dozens of spotters in the eastern trenches identified targets and called them out to batteries just beyond the eastern horizon. Once our artillery started receiving coordinates, they joined the party with their own unique blend of Kyperion hellfire.

"When are we going to try to get behind those lines?" asked Barone Parsons.

"Not until that artillery fire dies down!" I answered.

About a click and a half down the line, a plasma blaster appeared from the smoke and opened fire on the first line of Marines approaching enemy fortifications. "Oh, shit!" shouted Sergeant Espiya, my battlefield intelligence specialist, as she slapped me across the helmet. "Do you see that?!?"

I nodded. "Yeah, but it's out of our area of responsibility! Peeli's gonna have to take that one out!"

As I finished my sentence, a second alien weapon floated into a clearing a hundred meters north and fired a burst that struck a unit a half kilometer to our rear. I watched a dozen Marines evaporate before my eyes, weaponry and all. A similar number of infantry on the perimeter of the blast zone were blown to pieces while even more burst into flames, screaming in agony as the armor plates meant to protect them melted through their skin.

"Let's go!" I screamed at my troops as I stood up to run. "That one's ours!"

I expected to be cut down the moment I started moving, but we destroyed the three sentry guns covering our sector, and the Narman plasma blasters were focused on the horde of leathernecks pouring across the NML at our six. Because of the artillery rounds still raining down on the enemy positions before us, the trench's human defenders were nowhere to be seen. I suspected they were tucked away in bunkers deep underground.

If there was a disadvantage to being a Citadel Marine, it was that I was in incredible shape. I was faster than anyone else under my command by far. So, when my adrenaline kicked in as I sprinted for my life across the wastes, I outran my subordinates. I did not realize I was alone until I leaped over the first line of enemy trenches and turned around to start shouting orders. "Oops," I said to myself as I began pulling smoke grenades from my web gear and setting them off to give us better cover.

Arnaud Demangel and several other members of Third Squad were the first to reach me, panting and out of breath. "You still got your grenadier?" I asked the sergeant.

Demangel nodded. "Premin!" he gasped. "Premin! Somebody get Premin up here so we can take out that gun!"

Iggy Nagawo, the medic for what was left of Fourth Squad, ran by us to my right. He was dragging PFC Chieka Vai-Diep across the ground by her web gear. She had been hit by something that had shredded her fatigues and opened up her belly. As Nagawo worked to put Vai-Diep's bowels back inside her, a burst of M2117 gunfire exploded from the hillside above us, killing them both.

"Get down!" my praetorian yelled as she tackled me into the mud from behind just as the Narmans redirected their fire and prepared to shoot at me. Nila Chisek took them out with a single grenade thrown as she rolled off my back. Gorman Riepar, my Second Squad machine gunner, arrived just in time to race up the hillside and occupy the nest my bodyguard destroyed. Not long afterward, I heard Premin blow up the plasma blaster to the cheers of the Marine mob bearing down on us from the east.

The southern blaster fired again. And again. And again.

"Fuck!" shouted Gunny Brumit as she launched herself into the mud at my side. "Can't Peeli get that fucking thing taken out?!?"

"Of course not!" I screamed back at her. "He's Samaari! He's got too much to live for to stick his neck out too far!"

"Should we make our way down there to help?"

I shook my head. "Not until the infantry has this area secured!" Pointing my thumb back at the line of Marines running right for us, I added, "If we leave and something else pops up over here, those people are fucked!"

As it turns out, they were fucked, anyway. Having just completed a four-kilometer sprint through the mud as they crossed No Man's Land, the Marines did not jump over the unoccupied trenches as we did. They jumped into them. Then they stopped to regroup, get their bearings, and catch their breath before continuing on to the next objective. While they were packed like sardines into that big ditch, the Narmans set off a line of canisters buried beneath the bottom of the trenches that saturated the air with a combustible aerosol. A single spark then set off an immense thermobaric explosion, incinerating them all.

There was nothing we, or the second wave of Marines approaching our rear flank, could do but sit paralyzed in horror and watch them burn until the stench of the blaze hit us.

War pork.

We were not wearing the same armor as the assaulting infantry. Hell, we were not wearing any armor at all, so the heat of the fire drove us deeper into enemy territory. Several of my people were too close to the trench when it detonated and were burned alive. Corporal Sara Sarko, one of my snipers, was engulfed in flames as she ran for us, screaming for help. One of my medics tackled her, trying to put her out, but ended up only setting his sleeve alight. My staff medic, Teri Sotalain, helped the corpsman shed his smoldering uniform while Gunny Brumit put Sarko down with her sidearm.

At that point, Narman defenders started emerging from their hiding places. Riepar engaged the first of them with the M2117 while the rest of us dove for cover from which to return fire. Despite the hundreds we lost due to the booby-trapped trench, between the missile strikes, artillery barrage, and disciplined machine gun fire being meted out by Riepar's team, the Narmans seemed overwhelmed and struggling to put up an effective defense. When the inferno up front died down enough for the second wave of Marines to clear the ditch, we overwhelmed the defenders.

While the infantry stamped out remaining pockets of resistance challenging us from the second trench line, Barone Parsons arrived with his squad. "Where the hell have you been?" I snapped.

"We got pinned down out in the NML!" Parsons informed me. "We could've broken through sooner had we not lost our grenadier, but thank god we didn't!"

"Why?!?"

"We'd have probably been in that ditch when it blew!"

Luuk Bukki, the former policeman from Apalashu, shivered. "Did you hear them all?!? That fucking screaming?!?"

"Yeah, we all heard it," I told Bukki. "Put it out of your head! You're going to hear a lot more of it before this shit's all over!"

"What's next?" Parsons asked me.

I pointed up the hill. "The Marines gotta take out the next trench line! Whatever they do, they better not occupy it! The third line probably has the second pre-sighted and is ready to obliterate it!"

"What about us?"

I shrugged. "We don't have armor! They do! The ground pounders are fully equipped, so we let them do the heavy lifting for now! We keep our eyes peeled and look for threats to their rear flank!"

"You think they got that second line prepped to blow, too?" Barone asked.

"It's a definite possibility!" I shouted back. "I'd stay out of it if I were you!"

With a quick nod, Parsons turned his back on me to consolidate his people. I ran north to find Third Squad.

As we set off to locate Demangel's troops, I saw an aircraft clear the eastern tree line, heading our way.

"What are they doing?" asked my praetorian. "They're going to get themselves shot down!"

"It's a drone!" I told Chisek. "They're trying to confirm if we've wiped out the enemy's anti-air capabilities yet!"

Before the craft was halfway across the NML, a plasma blast from somewhere in the mountains far behind the enemy line blew it to pieces, raining debris upon the third wave of Marines now heading across the wastes. I sighed. "It looks like we still got a while before we can depend on air support."

"You know," Chisek asked. "How come these aliens got things like hologram generators and plasma blasters, but they don't have aircraft or artillery? However cool their blasters might be, they can only fire in a straight line! They can't shoot into our trenches!"

I patted Chisek's shoulder. "Trust me, the brass has been wondering about that ever since we got here! It's a good question, but now's not the time to contemplate it!"

As the firefight started dying down in our sector, an infantry captain approached us. "Are you Lieutenant Tauk?"

"Yes, sir."

The captain reached out and shook my hand. "Thanks for taking out that plasma blaster! That fucking thing was doing a number on us out there!"

"No problem, sir!"

"There's another one tearing our asses up to the south!"

"I know!"

"Colonel Palkrait wants you to get down there and blow it!"

"Got it!" I said, turning around to find Gunny Brumit.

When Chisek and I discovered my platoon sergeant, she was crouched just below the second trench line, using a telescopic mirror to see inside it. "Brumit!" I called up to her after she confirmed the ditch was uninhabited. "Gather the troops! We're packing up and heading south!"

"What for?!?" Brumit called back.

"To show that Samaari prick Peeli how shit gets done!"

Chapter 35

'Friendly' Fire

If there was one thing I dreaded about storming the Narman lines, it was coming face-to-face with a drove of enemy ubatis. Bred and conditioned to tear to shreds anything that intruded upon their territory, I knew these beasts were virtually immune to small-arms fire. The creatures were lethal and relentless, so I expended a lot of energy ensuring our artillery officers knew the importance of taking them out in the initial barrage. To drive my point home, I brought Cupid with me and had her stare down the battery commander, drooling, smacking her lips, and growling at the major as I pressed my case.

He got the message. The major put three missiles onto every ubati pen we identified, rendering the beasts a non-entity in the opening salvo. We did not kill them all but got the lion's share. The few remaining survivors fled into the forest and disappeared from the battlefield. Ubatis may not have feared any animal in the Kanarisian rainforest, but loud explosions, crippling shockwaves, and fire were concepts too terrifying even for them.

Our ubatis were a different story. They were more than four kilometers away from where our ordinance was dropped, and though it was still loud, it was just so much thunder to them. Once our troops were on enemy territory, the artillery had to stop for fear of killing more Marines than Narmans. That was when the Killbilles released our own ubatis.

The Narmans tried to turn their last plasma blaster upon our animals, but before they could fire their first salvo into the creatures, Mott Peeli's platoon finally showed up to the party and destroyed it in a spectacular pink explosion. Concluding there was nothing to stop the ubatis from sinking their tusks into them anymore, the Narmans started abandoning their posts in droves.

The Quarakai did not. As we ran toward Peeli's platoon, a small army of them seemed to drop out of nowhere to bar our path. These were the massive gliders I fought at Narman's Pyke months before. They stood more than two and a half meters tall, possessed the strength of seven men, and because of their insane muscle and bone density, could absorb an entire magazine's worth of M72 ammunition before they expired.

M2117 light machine guns were slightly more efficient in taking them out. Lucky for us, Gorman Riepar and Rikkal Tando were on their toes. The two gunners opened fire the moment the Quarakai's feet hit the mud and mowed them down like Angoramese wheat. As effective as those two men were, though, they could not get them all.

Most of my Marines immediately hit the dirt, not wanting to come between the M2117s and their targets. Corporal Liam Kunigas did not have that luxury, however. One of the bruins landed in front of him and instantly had the man in its grip, readying to tear him in two. Fortunately, Gunny Brumit was close by. She ripped her seibara from her belt, deployed the plasma rod, and in one fluid motion, sliced off the Quarakai's arms. Before Kunigas hit the ground, my platoon sergeant struck the monster again through the waist, cutting it in half. She then leapt into the air and decapitated another.

I had forgotten about the seibaras. So had Barone Parsons. After seeing Gunny Brumit make such short work of the Quarakai, though, both of us drew Naktada's creation and rushed in to help Gunny put down the enemy, much to the chagrin of my praetorian, who had lost her seibara in the melee. As a testament to that woman's bravery, Nila Chisek charged the Quarakai anyway, despite her M72 being but a minor distraction to the creatures at best.

Our gunners had slaughtered dozens of Quarakai in an instant. The seibaras did not even dispatch a quarter of that. Nevertheless, they convinced the gliders to retreat and engage an easier target. The survivors started leaping into the trees to get away from us.

Barone Parsons looked at his device in disbelief. "My god. I wish we had these things when they attacked us at Narman's Pyke!"

"Ain't that the fuckin' truth!" I laughed back. I did not relish getting that close to the Quarakai, but there was nothing like having a seibara in hand when the bastards got that close to me.

"Hey!" Parsons called out, his face beaming as if he had just come up with an incredible idea. "You think if we...."

My squad leader's sentence was cut short by a single round that entered his body in the small of his back, severing his spine before blowing his intestines through a fist-sized hole in his gut where his navel used to be. "NOOOOOOO!" he screamed as he collapsed at my feet. His medic dropped everything to rush to his side.

Looking at our six, I spotted Luuk Buuki lowering his weapon from the firing position with a look of shock and horror on his face. "Oh no!" he exclaimed. "Oh no! Oh my god! I'm so sorry! I was aiming at the Quarakai and...."

I looked up the hill, trying to follow Bukki's line of sight. If he had said he was firing at Narmans, I might have given him the benefit of the doubt. The Quarakai were escaping into the branches above us, not scrambling up the hillside. I drew my pistol and pointed it at the head of the former policeman from Apalashu. "Drop your weapon!"

"No! No!" the rifleman pleaded. "It was an accident! I didn't mean to...."

"NOW!"

Bukki let go of his M72 just as Parsons's assistant squad leader rushed in from the former policeman's blind side and clocked him across the jaw. Saili Hermour was also a student of Qılıç Elai, and my praetorian had taught her how to land a devastating blow. She then drew her sidearm and screamed, "I'm going to fucking blow your brains out!"

"WAIT!" screamed Gunny Brumit, causing Hermour to take her eye off Bukki. "We don't know for sure if...."

While the corporal was distracted, Bukki popped off a concealment grenade that enveloped both him and Hermour in an impenetrable shroud of smoke. Brumit and I rushed into the fog, but by the time we arrived, Hermour was lying in the mud, bleeding from her head. Bukki was lost in the crowd of Marines still pouring across the first line of trenches.

"MOTHERFUCKER!" I screamed as I prepared to run after him.

Gunny Brumit intercepted me before I took two steps, spinning me around and shoving me back toward the hill. "You can't go after him!" Brumit screamed at me. "You got Marines to...!"

"CHISEK!"

"Yes, sir!" my praetorian shouted back. She was right behind me, just obscured by the smoke.

213

"Luuk Bukki! You get out there and find his ass! I want him alive if possible! If it's not, you fucking make him suffer! You read me?!?"

"Loud and clear, sir!"

When I returned to Parsons, tears were streaming down his cheeks. They were not from the pain of his injury, though. They were born of frustration and regret.

"WHY?!?" he screamed at me. "WHY?!? WHY DID THAT MOTHERFUCKER WAIT UNTIL NOW TO DO THIS?!?"

I wondered that, too. Then it occurred to me that Bukki just found out the night before that Parsons was going on leave and it was unlikely he was coming back. It was the former officer's last chance to kill his squad leader and make his death look like either a combat casualty or a friendly fire fatality. It was sloppy work, for sure, but Bukki did not have many opportunities left to exploit.

"WHY DIDN'T I KILL THAT PRICK WHEN I HAD THE CHANCE?!?" Parsons screamed as he pounded the ground with his fist. "THAT'S IT! NO MERCY! I'M GOING TO MURDER EVERY FUCKING ONE OF THEM! EVERY! LAST! ONE!"

Despite his agony, Parsons grabbed his medic by the collar. "FIX ME UP, DOC! I GOT SCORES TO SETTLE!"

I cast my gaze upon Lance Corporal Ashwar, subliminally asking him, *Can you do that?*

Correctly guessing the question behind my eyes, he shook his head and pulled a dose of morphine from Parsons's medical pouch. We could have fixed the sergeant's spine. His insides were shredded, though. Ashwar doubted he would have been able to stop the bleeding even if they were in an operating room. It was time to make him comfortable.

Parsons must have felt himself weakening and realized the end was near. He started sobbing hysterically. "They're going to get away with it, aren't they? They murdered my little girls, and they're going to fucking get away with it!"

I grabbed Parsons by the collar. "They're not!" I promised him. "No fucking way! I'll make it right! You understand me?"

"Don't let them off the hook, Tauk." The sergeant was slurring now. The morphine was taking hold. "Fuck 'em all. Every last mother's son of them."

I will, Barone," I assured him, though I had no idea how to make good on that pledge.

214

"You fucking better," Parsons said. Then he died.

The first line was taken with relatively little effort. The second line put up more of a fight but, at least on the flanks, was quickly overwhelmed as well. It was a much different story in the center of the line, about twenty clicks south of where we were. There, the first trench capitulated almost immediately. The second line fought so hard that even our artillery could not unseat them. We tried turning our ubatis on them, but the third and highest line of fortifications blew them all to hell, virtually unopposed.

That was where Black Francis came in.

While the top line was focused on the invaders, the Raiders took it from behind. It was a hard fight, but they eventually gained control of the Narmans' heavy weaponry and turned it on the defenders to their right and left. Once satisfied their flanks were secure, they started firing upon the center line, who now found themselves assaulted from two sides with nowhere to retreat. There was no way the Narmans could hold out long under those conditions.

Once a path was open up the middle, our Marines charged up to the high ground and fanned out. Before long, the enemy was catching hell from all directions. Without their plasma blasters, our adversaries did not even come close to having the forces to stop us.

As the battle wound down, my intel sergeant, Hariana Espiya, approached me. Looking over all the bodies, both ours and theirs, littering the hillside, she mused, "There's not enough."

"Dead?" I asked. "You think we should've gotten more of our people killed?"

Shaking her head, Espiya said, "Based upon the estimates they derived from all the video we processed, we expected more than fifteen thousand Narmans defending these lines. Here at the center, where the fighting was heaviest, we should've had five thousand enemy KIA alone. If I stretch this out across the whole line, I don't think we'll count out five thousand total."

"Maybe they were vaporized by the missile strike."

Espiya shrugged. "Maybe. And maybe the bulk of their forces escaped."

"I don't think anybody could've escaped what we laid down upon those bastards."

"They could've left before the missiles hit."

"You sure you're not just being overly paranoid?"

"It's my job to be overly paranoid," Espiya told me. "I just think we took this hill way too easily."

Taking a step away from my intelligence sergeant, I surveyed all the Marine bodies surrounding us.

"It certainly didn't seem all that easy from my vantage point."

Chapter 36

The Spoils

Luuk Bukki escaped the Narman trenches. Running against the flow of traffic, he even made it across No Man's Land despite my praetorian being hot on his heels. A couple of times, Nila Chisek paused to take a shot at him but had to abort for fear of hitting a friendly Marine. That allowed Bukki to increase the distance between them even more.

By the time Bukki cleared our defensive trenches, he was a quarter click ahead of my praetorian. He disappeared into our maze of earthworks, and Chisek momentarily lost him.

"BUKKI!" Nila screamed in rage. She did not expect him to answer.

Grabbing a nearby Killbilly, Chisek asked, "You see a scared-looking Marine run through here? Dressed in black fatigues like me?"

The Killbilly nodded and pointed his finger to the southeast, sending my praetorian sprinting into the woods. Bukki was waiting for her.

He expected Chisek to enter the forest on the same trail that he had used. My praetorian probably would have taken it had she seen it, but she did not. She blazed her own path, tearing through the underbrush and depriving Bukki of a clear shot. When he pulled the trigger, the bullet was knocked off its trajectory by a low-hanging tree limb. Instead of hitting Chisek center mass, Bukki shot her in the shoulder, spinning her around and dropping her onto the forest floor. As Chisek writhed in the mud, screaming obscenities, Bukki took off deeper into the forest.

The former policeman had to make it to Camp Taarlak, fifty kilometers to the east. Once there, he could arrange a transport off Kanaris with one of the Qilkorian outfits. In addition to filling the ranks of the Killbilly death squads, pushing dope, and taming alien wildlife, the Qilkorians had been smuggling deserters out of war zones for decades. Their prices were high, but Bukki could afford it.

As the assassin sprinted through the forest, he looked for another place from which he could ambush Chisek. Spotting a small ridge in the distance, he made for that, bolting around the trunk of a large tree to get there. When he reached the far side of the massive palm, however, the rifle butt of an M72 smashed him right in the mouth, knocking out a few of his teeth and launching him hard upon his back.

"Well hello, darling!" cooed Zubi Jenich as she spun her rifle around until the barrel was pointing at her victim. "Were you going somewhere?"

"I think he was," said Margi Gul as she stepped from cover to join her friend. "He was in quite a hurry to get there, too! Hey! This guy was one of ours!"

Ritza Xi joined them, relieving Bukki of his weapons while his head was still reeling from the blow he had taken. "Wow. This one's got to be a special kind of coward to run away from a battle we fucking won!"

"Please," Bukki gasped. "I'm not running from combat...I...I...I made a mistake...."

"Oh, you sure did!" Gul told him. "The biggest mistake of your life." Pulling her dagger from its sheath, the Zero thrust it below Bukki's belt, slicing it off and cutting open the front of his pants.

"STOP!" shouted Chisek as she approached the three women. Blood was pouring from the wound on her shoulder, and she was panting from the pursuit.

Xi looked at my praetorian in disbelief. "Don't you dare tell me you're deserting, too!"

"No," Chisek gasped, pointing at the former policeman. "I was chasing him."

"Why?"

"He killed Parsons."

"What?!?" Xi exclaimed. Turning her attention back to Bukki, she shouted, "WHY?!?"

Bukki burst into tears, realizing there was no way out of his predicament. Holding his hands up defensively before his body, he did his best to hold true to his story. "It was an accident! I was aiming for a Quarakai! Parsons stepped into my line of fire! I didn't mean to shoot him! You gotta fucking believe me! Of all the people I had to...."

"Bullshit!" Chisek screamed, startling the prisoner with a menacing step forward. "You murdered him!"

"No! No! I didn't!" Bukki wailed, descending into hysterics.

"Calm down, Nila," Xi told my praetorian. "We're not going to learn anything arguing with him."

Turning to Gul, Xi said, "Go find Gunny Malcolm. He'll help us stake the asshole down, and then we can take our time learning why this piece of shit killed Barone."

"I thought I'd find you here," Black Francis said as he approached my platoon. I was sitting in the mud just outside Deena Vulk's room alongside Buffy Graym and his ubati, Meit. Glancing at the open door to Vulk's abode, the Raider asked, "So, did you get the bitch?"

I shook my head. "Nope. She got away."

Black Francis looked surprised. "I checked her quarters before I turned in last night. She was in there!"

"I think she left me a note." I handed Black Francis the message I found beside her pillow.

"Better luck next time," he read.

"My intel sergeant thinks they might have been tipped off."

"You let somethin' slip?" Buffy asked the Raider.

Black Francis scoffed. "I was on the wrong side of the NML with no direct line of communication to you guys. Hell, I didn't even know you were coming until those missiles started falling. All I knew was to make sure we slept as far away from the eastern fortifications as possible."

The Raider did not seem to take offense to Buffy's implication, but he still offered an alternative explanation. "After all the troops they wasted during that last offensive, they knew they couldn't have stood up to us. Once those plasma blasters were taken out, I spotted a ton of Narmans running for the hills. If I were them, I'd have fled to fight another day, too. Without those big blasters, this line was a lost cause. They're better off drawing us into the jungle and picking us apart one by one while we try to chase them down."

Francis paused to look around the rest of my platoon. Letting out a long sigh, he said, "You look a little lighter in manpower than I hoped you would, sir. How'd you guys make out?"

I shrugged. "Could have been worse."

"Could've been better, too," Corporal Hermour added. She was still beating herself up over not only letting Parsons get shot but for allowing his killer to get away.

"Where's Brumit?" Black Francis asked.

I shook my head. "She's gone."

The Raider covered his mouth in shock. "Gunny's dead?!?"

I nodded.

"How?"

"No idea. We got separated. After the battle, I went looking for her and found her body among a mess of others, Narman and Marine alike."

Shocked, Black Francis sat down beside me. "Who else?"

"Parsons."

"Son-of-a-bitch. How'd the Narmans get him?"

"They didn't. Luuk Bukki did."

Francis's jaw hit the ground. "Why?"

I let out a long sigh. "I can only assume it had something to do with the shit that went down on Apalashu."

A second lieutenant approached us while we were talking. Stepping up to me, he asked, "You Tauk?"

"Yes."

"Colonel Palkrait has everyone looking for you. He wants you to gather your platoon and meet him in G Sector."

I cursed as Black Francis helped me up. "G Sector's a long way away."

"Yeah, it sure is, isn't it?" Francis answered. "I'll walk with you a ways. The rest of my people are in that general direction."

Marching south down the Narman lines, we gawked at the destruction around us. "Pretty epic," I told my Raider escort.

"Yeah, this couldn't have gone any better. We even got that guy who fucked you all up at Narman's Pyke with the Quarakai."

"Mailes Ghona?" I asked, arching an eyebrow. "He's the Narman leader!"

"Yeah, I know. I'd talked with him several times around the trenches. He seemed like a guy who had his shit together. Anyway, I saw a squad of Section Kommandos leading him away in chains. That'll be quite an intel coup."

"It sure will," I said, "You know, this whole thing hinged upon your Raiders taking that third line. If you'd failed, this whole operation probably would have ended very badly, and we wouldn't have had shit. What you managed to do with so few Marines defies comprehension. You did amazing work today."

"Yeah, well, I had help. A lot of it."

"Oh yeah? From who?"

Francis grinned. "That ugly-ass bitch you're so sweet on over here."

"Deena Vulk?" I asked, stopping in my tracks.

The sergeant laughed out loud. "That'd be the one!"

"How?"

Laughing even harder, Francis said, "At first, they put us in the front trenches. Last night, the Narmans got edgy, though. They seemed to feel like something was coming. Vulk got into a huge argument with Ghona himself, saying she didn't want fighters as experienced as the Raiders to get wiped out by the initial barrage if the Marines came across the NML. She had us removed from the first line of trenches and put all the way in back, right where we needed to be! Fucking stupid cunt!"

Seeing me wince at the insult Francis hurled at Vulk, the sergeant stopped laughing and asked, "You alright? You got a look on your face like I just offended you or something."

I shook my head. "No, not offended. More like perplexed. I can think of a million things I could call Deena Vulk that are far worse than what you just did. I'm not sure what she does for the Narmans, but she escaped from us atop Mount Toranad, managed to elude Section 615 for months, and gained the confidence of the aliens. It would never have occurred to me to call her 'stupid.'"

Colonel Palkrait was beaming when he saw us. Too happy to deal with military formalities, he slapped me on the shoulder before I even had the chance to salute. "Goddammit, Tauk! Look at what you've done!" he exclaimed. "We busted the line! We took those blasters out! Not only that, we hit the fuckin' jackpot out here!"

"How so?" I asked.

Captain Pustov approached us with Staff Sergeant Naktada at his side. My techwar specialist was grinning from ear to ear, making me wonder if he had heard about Gunny Brumit. He looked so happy I decided not to break the news to him yet.

"Tell Tauk what you found!" Colonel Palkrait commanded.

"What didn't we find? We got plasma blasters of all sorts. We got the big ones that chewed us up out in the NML! A few of them were sealed in their bunkers by the missiles, but not destroyed. We also got blaster rifles! You know, the ones that blew a hole in your ride when they were evacuating you off Mount Toranad! We got a couple dozen of them! This shit is going to revolutionize Kyperion arms for generations! It's going to put us on par with these Morghul fuckers!"

Naktada reached behind his back, pulled out an alien weapon, and tossed it to me. "We got several of these also. It's a blaster pistol!"

"Give it a try," Palkrait said to me.

The weapon was uncomfortable to hold. It was built for a being with fingers far longer than mine. Though it was a third larger than the sidearm I typically carried, it was about half the weight. I aimed at a nearby palm tree and pulled the trigger, blasting a fist-sized hole clear through it. There was no recoil.

"Why didn't they use these things against us?" I asked.

Naktada shrugged. "They're not designed for humans. They're too big. The damned things are effective to be sure, but their size makes them awkward for us to aim effectively. Unless you're as big as Lumuk."

I passed the pistol back to Naktada. "You going to make a human-sized version?"

"You bet your ass! Give me a few months and fifty manufacturing droids from the Kyperion armory, and I should have enough prototypes to outfit an entire platoon. It'll take me more time to test the damned things than fabricate them."

Our colonel nodded in agreement. "With as fast as those robots and engineering AI work, I would expect our Marines to have a radically different look next year. The biggest delay will be training our troops to use shit like this and refining our tactics to optimize our new technology."

"Did we capture any aliens?" I asked Palkrait.

The colonel shook his head. "Not a one. Didn't even see any. My guess is that the little bitches evacuated out of here so fast they didn't even take their shit with them.!"

"We also got intact hologram generators!" Naktada continued, too excited to hear my question about the Morghul. "We got the big ones they used to generate the tree line, the smaller ones that'll cover a campsite, and the individual ones."

Captain Pustov turned to face Buffy. "We also captured a pen full of domesticated naypetos, already trained and ready to ride!"

As we talked, a column of ragged troops walked down the hill. They were in rough shape. They did not appear to be casualties of the battle but rather victims of prolonged maltreatment. The poor bastards looked like they were starving. "Are those prisoners?" I asked.

Palkrait nodded. "Yeah, but not the ones we took. They were captured by the Narmans."

As the colonel made that revelation, I spotted a short Marine bringing up the rear. It was Mazada Duum. I made a mental note to get word to Gunny Malcolm that the Samaari was alive.

The colonel turned to me once more. "You did good out here, Tauk. Damned good. This never would've been possible without that barbalu trick of yours."

"It wasn't my trick, sir. I couldn't have done it without Sergeant Naktada, Buffy Graym, and Black Francis."

As if on cue, the Raiders arrived on scene. They were dragging along a man with bound arms and a hood thrown over his head.

"Black Francis!" Colonel Palkrait yelled. "Lieutenant Tauk is saying he couldn't have pulled off this little stunt without you! Is that true?"

"Goddamn right, it's true!" The Raider shouted back. He then lifted his hand and slapped their prisoner across the back of the head. "And we couldn't have gotten in here without this piece of shit!"

"Who's that?" asked Palkrait.

Sergeant Korman ripped the hood off their prisoner's head. The young man had been worked over badly. His face was covered in bruises and lacerations, and his eyes were swollen shut. "This'd be PFC Mazen Duklow!"

"Agent Takawa tipped us off this prick was trying to convince our Marines to switch sides and join the Narmans," Francis said. "Because of all the havoc we were creating across the NML, he tried joining our outfit so he could lead us into an ambush. That allowed us to orchestrate the little spate of drama between us and Section 615. It gave us the cred we needed to infiltrate the enemy. Had he not put in a good word for us, the bastards probably would've shot us on sight."

"Amazing work, Sergeant." Palkrait paused momentarily before saying, "You're a natural leader, Franq. You willing to reconsider that offer I made to you a few months back?"

"To become an officer?" Black Francis asked. "I appreciate your confidence in me, sir, but I'm better as an enlisted man."

"Then how about if we promote you to gunnery sergeant?"

Black Francis shook his head. "Nah. Too much paperwork."

"I wish you'd reconsider," I said to the Raider. "I need a new platoon sergeant. I can't think of anyone I'd want more as my number two than you."

Francis grinned and turned toward his troops. "What do you say, Marines? Any of you want to join Lieutenant Tauk's platoon?"

No one spoke up, but I did not take it personally. Black Francis's Raiders did well without an officer at the helm. A few of them had been around long enough to remember the incompetent platoon leaders they had suffered through. None of them wanted to end up in that situation again, and I did not blame them.

"Come on, Marines," the sergeant begged. "There ain't no No Man's Land to patrol anymore. Our mission's done."

"Tauk's going to have a new mission now, too," Colonel Palkrait told the Raiders. "Section 615 has requested he be reassigned to their command. He's going to be shuttled around in one of those new Mar-Sitaara Raptors for long-range insertion and will probably be commandeering some of those freshly captured naypetos to patrol the rainforest on. Not to mention, when Naktada makes those blasters fit into human hands, you'll likely be the first unit equipped with them. And that alien camouflage shit."

That revelation piqued Sergent Korman's interest. "That could be fun. I'm in."

Once Korman took the bait, the rest fell into line, saving me an awful lot of trouble filling all the billets my casualties had opened up. "Welcome aboard, Raiders!"

After a round of celebratory backslaps and handshakes, Black Francis's Marines joined mine, nearly bringing my platoon back to full strength. When the commotion died, Captain Pustov approached me and shook my hand. "We're not leaving you out, Eamon. When we get back to our lines, the colonel and I are putting you in for promotion as well. I expect by the end of the week, you'll be a first lieutenant. Keep this shit up, and I might put captain's bars on your collar after the spooks are done with your ass. I can think of several Samaari company commanders I'd just *love* to replace with the likes of you!"

Pumping Pustov's hand a couple more times, I said. "Thank you, sir!"

"Excuse me, Colonel," Black Francis said as he approached Palkrait. "Like I said before, none of this would've been possible without Duklow, over there. If you're promoting me and Tauk, don't you think we should do something for him to show our appreciation?"

Colonel Palkrait looked over the abused prisoner and smiled. "We should. Hang him."

Chapter 37

A New Phase

"Two hundred thousand credits," Nila Chisek told us once we were all back at my command post.

Black Francis's jaw dropped open. "To kill a convict?!? I could get someone to ice the prime minister for half that!"

"Well, the prime minister doesn't earn the Apalashu underworld billions a year." Chisek winced as she tried to readjust her arm in her sling. "Apalashu is something of a backwater. It's pretty much off the League's radar. The gangsters there make a lot of money. So do the cops. They couldn't believe Parsons earned the pull to get Section 356 involved in his case."

"Parsons didn't," I told her. "I did."

Chisek nodded. "Well, that set off a bit of a panic over there. They want the Section investigators out of their business, and they thought the best way to protect their billion credit enterprise was to invest a couple hundred thousand to eliminate the source of the complaint. No complainant, no case."

I sighed and buried my head in my hands. Bukki might have pulled the trigger, but I was the one who got him killed. Had I left him in the motor pool, he'd have been out of the Corps in a few years and able to at least hold *someone* accountable for the crimes committed against his family. "So now they all fucking get away with it."

My wounded praetorian shrugged. "Not if Ritza Xi has anything to say about it."

"She's got her own scores to settle."

"Well," Chisek mused. "She's taking on Parsons's as well. We know where Bukki stashed his credits. Naktada was able to hack it and transfer it all into a place where Xi can withdraw it. Those fuckers may not realize it, but they just financed their own demise."

Corporal Hermour looked surprised. "How did Xi get the banking information out of Bukki?"

Chisek shuddered. "You don't want to know."

During the weeks following our victory over the Narmans, we were mostly idle. We had to reorganize and replace the Marines we lost. We had to process what we captured. Digest what we had learned. Prepare for the next phase of the conflict.

My platoon was going to be assigned a new mission requiring unique skill sets. While I got sent back to Narman's Pyke to get brought up to speed on the new direction we would be heading, my Marines remained in the foothills of the Satapadaya Ranges, learning how to ride naypetos. While at the Pyke, I took some time to visit Mazada Duum in the convalescence center.

Walking toward the infantryman's cot, I noted all the Marines around me. There were dozens of them; most were former prisoners of the Narmans. Their bodies seemed whole, but it took but a brief look to see how broken they were. They might have had all their limbs, but their minds had been irretrievably mangled, reduced to mush by the horrors they had witnessed. Many sobbed hysterically and continuously, unable to stop. Others wept in silence, staring expressionlessly at the sterile white ceiling of the medical bay while tears streamed down their cheeks.

One young woman returned my gaze with an expression that made my blood run cold. She had the face of an angel and a permanent smile that stretched her lips from ear-to-ear. Her eyes were freakishly maniacal, however, beckoning me to come just a little bit closer, to step within her reach for just a moment. I had never sensed such pure evil in anyone like that before. Fortunately, the nursing staff had sensed it, too. They had her wrists and ankles shackled to the bed rails with a triple set of restraints.

Mazada Duum fared better than most of the patients in that ward. He was not screaming. He was not weeping. He was not catatonic, trying to gouge his eyes out, or cuffed to a gurney to keep him from hurting the others. He was just lying in bed, feeding on all the tragedy in his midst as if replenishing the rage he had always carried within his soul, even before he was captured.

Duum did not look happy to see me. Just surprised. "Last I heard, you were good as dead," he said as I sat by his bedside.

"Old news," I replied. "It was touch and go for a while, but I'm close to a hundred percent now. How about you? How are you faring?"

Duum shrugged. "For someone who's spent months getting starved and tortured by those animals, I'm doing better than most."

"Do the doctors expect you to make a full recovery?"

"Who cares what the doctors say? Even if they say I'll be half the man I was before, that still makes me twice the man of those Narman pricks." There were tears in Duum's eyes — tears of rage. "You know they hate us, sir. HATE us."

"The Narmans? Yeah, I kind of gathered that."

Duum shook his head. "I ain't talking about the Narmans, sir. I mean the aliens."

I winced. "You saw them?" None of the intel I read coming out of our victory even mentioned the Morghul. Section 615 must have been keeping all that to itself.

Duum nodded. "I saw a few of them. They're nasty fuckers. They're the ones that sliced open all those psycho pixies outside the Pyke's front gate. That's a favorite trick of theirs. I watched them do it. It wasn't like they were trying to figure out how we worked, either. They just wanted us to suffer. And be afraid. They're monsters." That was a bold statement, coming from a sadist like Duum.

"You know what else they like to do?" the Samaari asked. "They like to skin us alive. You ever see a man flayed, Lieutenant?"

I shook my head.

The Samaari stared blankly off into space. "I've seen lots. They'll grab about a dozen of us, strip us down, and tie us spread eagle to these upright steel Xs so we can all see each other. They'd leave us that way for hours. We all knew what was going to happen, but we wouldn't know to whom. We'd just hang there, wailing in terror, driving ourselves mad wondering which of us would die that day. After we'd spent hours agonizing over what was to come, the jailor would walk in and pace before us, trying to decide who to cut. That's where I learned to shriek, Lieutenant. I discovered the more terrified you look, the less likely you are to be picked. You see, in a way, being flayed is a sick form of mercy. It takes hours to die, but you eventually do, and your agony's all over. They keep you alive if they feel you're suffering enough watching what they do to their captives."

Duum paused to swallow. "Our jailor was a Mog named Kryndil. He was the one who did the skinning. When he finally decided on a victim, he would start by cutting off their fingernails, slipping the blade behind them and prying them off. Thumb first. Then pinky. Then the rest. Slowly. Methodically. Relishing the screams of the person he was torturing."

Catching me wince at the thought, Duum cracked a grin. We were not friends, so he seized upon the entertainment value of making me uncomfortable. "It's horrible watching men go through that, sir. You know what really messes with you, though? When they do it to the women. There's something instinctual that goes off inside of you, some primordial realization you're not fulfilling your evolutionary purpose to protect your females. It's an extra feeling of futility and impotent rage about the helplessness of the situation."

The Samaari sighed before going on. "After the fingernails are gone, Kryndil slices the skin down each finger, then uses pliers to pull it from the digit. Again, one at a time to ensure we feel every bit of pain they can subject us to. And while the jailor is doing this stuff, his cronies are leering at us with those sickening red eyes they got. If they caught us not watching the horrors that they do, they cut off our eyelids."

"All right, Duum," I told the rifleman. "I get the point. You don't need to go on."

The Samaari glared at me. "Oh, but I do, sir. You need to know what we're up against out there! What happens to us if we fall into their hands! You need to hate them!"

"They killed Jella Duverii, Duum. I already hate them."

"Not nearly fucking enough!" The Marine was so furious at this point he was shaking and sobbing. "They cut us, Lieutenant! Sliced us right down the middle and then peeled us like fucking oranges! They laughed while they did it! It doesn't sound like our laughter, though. They do this weird croaking thing, but they have themselves a ball making us hurt! Sometimes, they would make us eat what they harvested from our comrades! Other times, they made us wear the victim's face like a mask! Send us back to our cells dressed in the skin of our cellmate like a new set of clothes! They're fucking animals, sir! ANIMALS!"

Duum was screaming now. He was highly agitated. "YOU NEED TO GET ME OUT OF HERE, SIR! I NEED TO GET BACK OUT THERE! LET ME GET MY FUCKING HANDS ON THEM! TAKE ME WITH YOU!"

I shook my head. "You're not fit for duty, Duum."

"ARE YOU KIDDING ME?!? I'VE NEVER BEEN FITTER IN MY LIFE! I'M READY TO KILL, SIR! I'LL KILL 'EM ALL! EVERY LAST FUCKING ONE OF THEM! I'M GOING TO TAKE THEIR SKINS! MAKE FURNITURE FROM THEIR HIDES! CLOTHES! SHOES!"

Duum's eyes had gone completely crazed. His volume had alarmed the medical staff, and a trio of nurses was running his way with restraints and a syringe full of sedatives.

"You need to calm down...."

"NO! NO! YOU NEED TO GET EXCITED! WE NEED TO ATTACK THEM, SIR! WITH RIGOR AND FEROCITY! WE NEED TO EXTERMINATE THEM! KILL THEM ALL!"

Duum leapt from his bed and grabbed me by the collar. "I know they broke me, Lieutenant! The Marines know it, too! They want to send me home! Don't let them! Not while I'm like this! If they do, I'll never get myself right again! If they put me back in the field, though, I can fix this! I just have to get my hands on Kryndil! I need to take his skin!"

"You need to settle down, Sergeant!" one of the nurses said as she tried to force Duum back into his bed.

"NO!" he screamed at her. "I NEED TO FIGHT! THEY'RE OUT THERE! WE NEED TO GET THEM! BEFORE THEY TAKE OUR SKIN!"

"Shhhhh," a second nurse said as she arrived. "Nobody's going to hurt you. You're safe here."

"NO, I'M FUCKING NOT! NEITHER ARE YOU! WE'RE ALL GOING TO...!"

As Duum reached out to grab the nurse, I seized his arm and twisted it around his back to keep him from harming her. He screamed out in agony. "NOOOOO! NOOOOO! DON'T HURT ME! LET ME GO! PLEASE! PLEASE! PLEASE! DON'T TAKE MY SKIN!"

I tried to soothe the Samaari Marine. "No one's going to hurt you, Duum. We're trying to help...."

Duum wailed. "STOOOOOOOOP! LET ME GO! I ONLY WANT TO STOP THEM!"

As we struggled to get Duum under control, one of the nurses plunged the syringe into her patient's neck. The effect was almost immediate. The Samaari relaxed as his muscles started going limp. "Oh no!" he gasped. "Don't put me to sleep! They come back when I'm dreaming! *Don't...!*" That was all he got out before he went limp and collapsed in my arms.

I ran into Agent Takawa on my way out of the convalescence center. I was surprised to see him as I had not been told he had returned to Kanaris. He seemed equally surprised to see me at the Pyke's medical facilities. "What the hell are you doing here?" he asked.

"Visiting one of my former subordinates," I answered, still shaken by the encounter.

Takawa nodded in understanding. "He tell you anything?"

I shuddered. "As far as I'm concerned, he told me too much."

I went on to relate to the Section agent what Duum had said to me. When I finished, Takawa nodded at my tale. He did not seem surprised. "They're fucking evil, Tauk."

I shook my head and said, "It can't possibly be that black and white. They've got human allies. If they were singularly driven by an insatiable lust to inflict pain on humanity, they wouldn't be able to attract so many of our Marines to their side. They have to be offering something more than suffering. We've captured deserters. What've they told us?"

Takawa shrugged. "Whatever they think their Killbilly interrogators want to hear. Mostly sob stories about being captured and getting forced to fight us under the threat of being skinned alive. It's bullshit, though."

"How do you know that?"

"For starters, the aliens only flay Samaaris. They're seen as the ruling class, so they're the ones earning all the special treatment. The traitors seem keen to point them out."

I wonder why.

Pulling out his tablet, Takawa asked, "Who were you talking to in there?"

"Mazada Duum," I told him, thinking the agent intended to debrief the patient.

Weeks later, however, I spotted Duum among the replacement troops assigned to Mott Peeli's platoon. Supai Takawa did not just question the Samaari. He recruited the son-of-a-bitch, causing me to seriously wonder what I had gotten myself into when I agreed to join him in the hunt for Deena Vulk.

●●◆●◆●●

Chapter 38

EPIPHANY

"She slipped through your fingers, eh?" Agent Takawa said when he met Black Francis and me at the Section 615 Central Command at Narman's Pyke. It was a few days after our encounter at the convalescence center.

"The video showed Vulk leaving her quarters about an hour before we launched our missiles," Black Francis said. "And she left a note that said, 'Better luck next time.' That bitch was tipped off."

Takawa grinned. "She leaves that note everywhere she sleeps. To toy with us. She also leaves them places she doesn't sleep to throw us off. She's smart like that."

"If she was so smart," Francis retorted, "then why did she keep me and my entire unit together once we 'defected' and post us in the exact spot where we could inflict the most damage? Separating large groups of defectors and making them earn your trust before you assign them to vulnerable areas is pretty basic stuff."

Hearing Black Francis say that out loud jogged my memory. In particular, of something Sergeant Major Maddahor had said in *Wasp-Three* as we approached Kanaris.

Somebody at Narman's Pyke sent off a rocket beacon as we entered the system. Now that we know someone's alive down there, we need to get to them before whatever they're facing does.

I also recalled Captain Mardona's briefing before we left the beach. One of our objectives was to recover a Section 615 asset still on the planet, one nobody could identify.

Though my mental gears started cranking at what Francis said, Takawa shrugged it off. "We put on a damned good show out there, Francis. Duklow was convinced you iced me. Everyone was. There's no better motivation for defecting than a looming capital murder charge. The Raiders were also one of the most feared units prowling the NML. She probably saw the value in keeping a force that lethal together."

"Mailes Ghona didn't think so," Black Francis countered. I could see his mind subconsciously putting the puzzle pieces together, slowly crawling to a conclusion I had already reached. "Ghona tried to override Vulk and put us up front. If he reported that to whoever's in charge of the Narmans, they'll hang that bitch."

"Ghona didn't have the chance to report anything to anybody," Takawa told Francis. "Once those missiles hit, he was too preoccupied with saving his trench line to bitch about Vulk. Unfortunately, he didn't survive the offensive so we're not getting lucky enough for him to report her now, either."

I kept my face expressionless. Black Francis did not. "Ghona's dead?" he asked the agent. "How?"

"It's my understanding he was killed in action."

"Bullshit," Francis said. "Ghona was taken alive. By your people. I saw it with my own eyes."

"Maybe you mistook someone else for Ghona."

"I didn't," my platoon sergeant insisted. "He was surrounded by Section Kommandos. Some buck private with a passing resemblance to the Narman leader wouldn't have warranted that kind of security. I know who I saw. If he's dead, it's because someone executed him after his capture."

Takawa took a seat behind his desk and clasped his hands behind his head. "You're working for intel now, Francis. The official account is that Mailes Ghona was killed in combat. For all practical purposes, that is what happened then."

Despite the look I shot at Francis urging him to drop the subject, he asked, "Why would you execute Ghona? He was at the top of the Narman hierarchy. There is no higher value target than him. He'd have had all kinds of great intel!"

"I told you, Ghona was killed in...."

"You killed him to protect your source, didn't you?" Francis asked. "She's fucking working for you, isn't she?"

"For the last time!" Takawa was losing patience. "We...!"

"Hey, it's cool!" Francis said, holding up his hands. "If you got a great source you have to protect, you've got to protect that source! I get it! I just...."

Takawa sighed. "This is intel, Gunny. We're told what we *need* to know. Nothing more. If they tell me Mailes Ghona died in combat, then I believe he died in combat — end of story. If you were wise, you'd believe it, too. No matter what the fuck you think you saw. Understood?"

Francis gave Takawa a curt nod. "Got it."

"There is something you *do* need to know, though, so let me tell you this unequivocally. Deena. Vulk. Is. Not. A. Section. 615. Asset. Period. We want to catch her. We want her alive so we can use her to find the Morghul. We're going to get her, and I'm charging your Marines to do it."

As Black Francis and I walked out of the intelligence compound, he turned to me and asked, "You buy that shit Takawa's peddling?"

I shook my head. "Nope. Not a bit of it."

"So you think Deena Vulk's working for Takawa?"

"Yep. And I think Ghona's alive, too. He's in some cell back on the mothership, wishing the goons interrogating him would put him out of his misery."

"So, what..why...I...?!?"

Black Francis had a question in there somewhere. He just could not formulate it. To help him along, I asked, "So, why would Takawa want to lead us on a mission to capture a person he does not want to get caught?"

Francis nodded.

"So he can keep an eye on us to make sure we don't succeed."

"Then why send us at all?!?"

"So we can come close to catching her. Takawa wants us to give Deena Vulk credibility. He wants the Narmans to think she's a high-priority target. He wants them to trust her so she can continue to feed us intelligence and hurt the bastards when it counts.

Black Francis put his hand on his forehead as his mind reeled. "Holy fuck! Deena Vulk's a Section 615 asset! What does that mean?"

"It means Takawa doesn't trust us enough to let us in on his little secret and is probably willing to sacrifice us all to keep her safe."

If Deena Vulk was not acting on behalf of the rebels when she killed Jella Duverii, it meant that the Narmans were not the ones responisble for her death, I thought.

The fucking League was.

Chapter 39

Geek Bearing Gifts

N aktada returned to Kanaris aboard a civilian interstellar cargo hauler. Though they were all equipped with a passenger compartment, their main purpose was hauling goods, not people. As I watched it offload on one of the back landing pads on Narman's Pyke, I realized that on this trip, humans were its primary payload. Thousands of them disembarked in chains, dressed in tattered coveralls, and looking dazed.

"Who are they?" I asked Naktada when he finally made his way to where I was, leading an SPS loaded with several large crates.

My techwar specialist looked back at the ragged lot and shook his head. "Inmates from Blinqa-44. My understanding is most of them are insurgents from Portuna."

Taking out my optical amplifiers, I zoomed in on the crowd. I immediately spotted several prisoners who appeared far too young to be combatants. "There's children among them," I told Naktada. "Some look no more than ten years old."

"I try not to think about that," Naktada answered. "We're in a pretty extreme situation, sir. Extreme situations result in extreme courses of action. Word back on Kyper is we may see the Morghul in force soon." The techwar specialist sounded as if he was trying to convince himself of that more than me.

"If the aliens were on this planet in significant numbers, I'd expect we'd have seen a lot more of them already."

"Lieutenant," Naktada said to me. "They're a little freer with information back on Kyper than here. The *Phoenix* detected a signal from Kanaris right after we took the

Satapadaya foothills. It was transmitted into deep space and alien in origin. We have no idea what it said, but the feeling around intel was that it was probably a distress signal."

I shrugged. "Why'd they wait until after we broke their lines to ask for help? Wouldn't it have been more useful had they sent out an SOS after making first contact if they didn't have enough force to overpower us? Not to mention, it's been eight months since we broke their lines. If that really was a distress signal, where's the alien cavalry?"

"There's a lot of stuff we don't know about the Morghul, sir. No one's more cognitive of that than the intel community. All they know is if a large force of them shows up with all their technology, we'll be no match for them. Not yet, anyway. If we're to have a fighting chance against these beings, we need Harnillium. And time."

Raising my optical amplifiers back at the line of Portuna's wretched shuffling across the tarmac, I half wondered if the Morghul were even real. Had I not seen them with my own eyes, I might have suspected they were made up by Section 615 to justify using slave labor to work the mines.

But did I? I saw something for sure, but what exactly?

When I finished looking at the prisoners filing into the colony, I turned my attention back to Naktada. "You look good, Dmitri. Kyper must've agreed with you."

"Thank you, sir," he replied with a grin, seizing the change of subject. Nodding at the crates behind him, he added, "After you've seen what I've got for you, you'll be able to say Kyper agreed with you, too."

When I stepped out from behind the curtain, I felt like I was in a fashion show. Black Francis whistled and clapped in delight. "That is some sweet-looking armor! You say it's packing some new goodies?"

Naktada nodded. "Let's start with a cool little gadget invented by the lieutenant himself." The armorer drew his pistol, removed the magazine, and checked the chamber to ensure there wasn't a round in the barrel. He stood five meters from me, on the other side of my command tent. "You want this gun, sir?"

I held out my hand and snapped my wrist. Nothing happened to Naktada's weapon, but a red dot on my visor followed the movement of my right eye.

"Put that dot on your target, sir. Then pull the weapon in with your fingers."

The pistol flew out of the armorer's hand, sailed across the tent, turned itself around, and slid into my palm, ready to fire. Black Francis was stunned, as were my squad leaders. None of them had ever seen that trick before.

"Whoa," I said, obviously impressed. "That was smooth."

Naktada nodded. "Yeah, I added electromagnetic braking. Now, you don't have to worry about snapping any fingers when you do that."

"Does everyone have this?"

The armorer nodded. "Yep. They sure do."

"Can I still reverse the polarity and launch it?"

"You sure can, and by using that little red dot, you can launch it as accurately as you can shoot."

Walking around my tent, Naktada said, "Harnillium is an amazing power source, particularly as it pertains to magnetism. You know that big iron core at the center of this planet? And virtually every other known world harboring life? The Harnillium-powered magnets in your gloves and boots can now play off that. You can use it to plant your feet on the ground while manipulating heavy metallic objects with your hands. You can reverse polarity and use it to launch yourself into the air."

"Are you telling me we can fly in these suits?" asked Sergeant Korman.

"No," answered Naktada. "But you can now leap about five meters higher than those glider Quarakai that fight with the Narmans. The velocity of that leap is about a third faster, too. Unfortunately, this armor will not do much to help you if you fall into the hands of those damned things. They can still rip you in half if they get their claws on you. It does, however, give you an advantage in both speed and agility. If they catch you in one of these rigs, it's your own fucking fault."

Pacing back toward the other side of the CP, my armorer told us, "These shells are performance-enhancing. As long as your power source is operating, you can run faster, jump farther, lift more, and march longer than you could on your own."

"And if our power sources are not operating?" I asked.

"Then you may as well be wearing a suit made from twenty kilos of lead. It'll become a significant handicap. Your only choice if you experience de-energization is to get out of your shell as quick as humanly possible. The battery pack is the most protected part of this system, though. That's the piece that's completely bulletproof. If you're going to get shot, pray they hit you in the energy cell."

"How well does the rest of this armor perform against bullets?" asked my praetorian.

"Not as good as the old one, Nila," Naktada answered. "In fact, only about half as good. It used to take four direct hits to compromise your shell. This material is more porous to accommodate some of its other capabilities, so this one will only take two."

Everyone in the tent groaned in protest, causing Naktada to raise his hands to quiet everyone down. "You'll be pleased to know that with the camo tech built into this gear, you'll be much harder to hit. Prototype Exo-Armor System 444," the armorer commanded. "Serial Number One. Activate active camo function!"

Naktada's audience collectively gasped. I saw nothing different but heard a faint hum in my helmet. I lifted my arm before my eyes and found it practically invisible, appearing like little more than atmospheric distortion, except for the pistol I was holding.

"The new generation armor is filled with light-bending fibers that take what's visible behind you and project it to the other side of your body. It's not perfect. In a space like this, filled with artificial light and still air, you can make out the lieutenant's outline. Outside, in the dark, fog, or rain, you'll see nothing but a hint of shadow. When utilizing this feature, you'll need to wear a special cloak with the same technology to keep your weapons and other gear concealed. Or stay within a hologram perimeter."

"How are we supposed to see each other out there if we're all invisible?" asked Sergeant Tiago.

"Ultrasonic echolocation," Naktada told her. "A new type of sonar. It'll allow us to see the aliens if they try to sneak up on us in this gear, too."

"I don't remember capturing anything like this when we broke through on the Satapadaya Front," said Sergeant Demangel.

"You didn't," Naktada admitted. "This is true alien shit, here. It might be the reason we haven't seen many of the bastards."

"So, how did we get it?" Black Francis asked.

Naktada shrugged. "If I had to guess, Section 615 has a pretty good source among the Morghul."

Black Francis and I looked at each other, sure we knew who that was.

"There were other things I saw on Kyper," Naktada continued. "They were developing new warp thrusters for our fleet and these massive plasma blasters to replace our dreadnaught missile systems. I could tell by how far along they were on the development curve that we'd had our hands on alien tech intelligence way before we defeated the Narmans at the Satapadaya. Granted, we can reverse engineer damned near anything almost instantly. Some of this stuff we've never gotten our hands on, though."

Tired of holding it, I tried to place Naktada's pistol in the holster on my hip. It would not fit.

Catching this, my armorer smiled. "Yeah, you're not going to be using those anymore," he told me as he walked to one of the boxes he had brought. Pulling what was going to be my new sidearm out of it, he said, "No more bullets, either. Marines, your combat load has just significantly lightened. For as much potential energy as there is contained within a gram of Harnillium crystal, it's amazingly stable. When you put it in close proximity to Nexilium-228, the material that powers our warp thrusters, however, the two react violently and unleash a burst of energy that will burn through the hull of an airship. This is the P662 mini-blaster. Your new sidearm."

Naktada walked over and slapped me on the breastplate even though my camo function was still energized. "Against that, this armor is entirely defenseless."

"There's nothing we can do to mitigate it?" asked Black Francis.

"Against plasma blasts in general, yes, there is a way to neutralize them. You have to generate a field of opposite polarity to cancel it out. The problem is that the process is grossly inefficient. You can significantly reduce the power of a plasma blast but not eliminate it entirely. Even with a protective field, you'll take damage every time you're hit. If they strike you enough times, the plasma will still eventually destroy you."

Stepping closer to my platoon sergeant, Naktada continued. "We can generate a sort of electromagnetic shield that will absorb hits from weapons like these, but the engine required to do it is gigantic. They're working on getting one small enough to fit on a fighter transport, like the Mar-Sitaara, but the most practical application is on our dreadnaughts. My goal is to develop something like that for our shells, but current technology is not even close to being up to the task."

Naktada looked like he was getting ready to say something to me but could not see where I was. "Prototype Exo-Armor System 444. Serial Number One. Deactivate active camo function!"

Suddenly, I was visible again. "So, these shells are voice-activated?" I asked.

The armorer shook his head. "Not for you. These are all tuned to my voice. There's a button on your control console to turn it on and off. All your exo-armor systems and weapons are prototypes tested by me personally. I had to make a couple hundred sets of this stuff. If I had to test them individually, it would have taken me forever to get through them all. It was much easier to call them out by serial numbers and do them in batches."

Once he could see what he was doing, Naktada started slipping weapons into my shell. "The P662 goes where your M88 did but is covered by a flap to keep it concealed. Harnillium is reconstituted by sunlight, so it automatically recharges. This weapon is good for a quarter million shots before the barrel needs to be replaced."

Pulling a futuristic rifle from another crate, he held it up for all to see. "The P-891 battle rifle. Same concept as the pistol, just better balanced for steadier aiming. This one's good for a half-million shots before maintenance is required."

"What's the range of these things?" Sergeant Korman asked.

"In a desert environment with low humidity, this weapon is deadly at forty clicks. Here on Kanaris, with high humidity, rain, fog, and obstacles? You can take a Marine down from about eight kilometers away. That's still much further than you can see in this goddamned place." Naktada finished his presentation by equipping me with a new seibara and a couple dozen smaller grenade prototypes.

"So there you have it, people. The Marines of tomorrow. Each warrior is now entering combat with more capacity than even the most seasoned veteran would have ever fired over their entire career."

"So, how many people can you equip with this stuff?" asked Black Francis.

"All of you," Naktada answered. "I have enough to outfit the two recon teams attached to Section 615. That's us and Peeli's Marines."

My platoon had been folded into Section 615 because we were good. Peeli's platoon was recruited because of their ideological purity. In other words, they were just as depraved as the spies were.

Peeli enjoyed Takawa's confidence and was a true collaborator. My platoon was kept just close enough to the agent for him to keep an eye on us. As a result, mine and Peeli's platoons did not get along very well and rarely mixed without trouble breaking out. No one was thrilled to learn they would be equipped with the same fancy prototype gear as we would.

With his presentation over, Naktada asked, "So what are you going to do with this stuff? What's happened here after the battle at the Satapadaya?"

Black Francis was the one who answered. "A lot of patrols. After the Satapadaya, the Narmans split up and melted away into the jungle. We've been searching for them for seven months. We've made contact with the bastards twice in that time. Other units have gone out into the forest and not come back. We're not sure if they got destroyed by the enemy or joined them."

Dina Tiago laughed. "It should be noted every unit we lost in the rainforest was led by a Samaari officer, so you might think twice about turning this stuff over to Lieutenant Peeli. If he keeps up with the trend, it could all end up in enemy hands."

Silma Hauken, my First Squad target spotter, took offense to that. She was also Samaari. "Of the twenty-seven anti-aircraft blasters removed from Narman service, Peeli's platoon destroyed eighteen. We've only knocked out twelve."

Black Francis nodded in agreement. "Peeli's squad has also suffered twenty-two casualties in the last seven months. We've had six."

"He's just more aggressive," Hauken countered.

"From your viewpoint," said the sergeant who replaced Parsons. "From mine, I would describe him as reckless and stupid."

"Call it whatever you want," Hauken retorted. "But our aircraft are back in the sky because of it."

"That's enough," I cut in, hoping to avoid the interplanetary bickering that plagued nearly every other outfit on Kanaris.

Turning back to Naktada, I asked. "When can you start outfitting the rest of my Marines?"

The armorer shrugged. "Immediately. Have your troops muster at the tech center, and we'll have them hooked up."

Facing my platoon sergeant, I said, "Get everybody there by noon. I want them outfitted by sixteen hundred and on the range by eighteen to get familiar with our new weapons. We'll knock off work by twenty hundred. After that, anyone who can make it to the base club will be treated to drinks on me. Understood?"

My squad leaders cheered in response. They understood.

"You joining us?" I asked Naktada.

"Are you drinking?"

I shrugged. "Academy cadets aren't supposed to imbibe."

Naktada smirked. "Yet you've been known to on occasion. I'll come if you let me buy you a couple of brandies."

"It's also against regulations for me to accept gifts from enlisted men."

243

"Well, thanks to you," Naktada countered. "I won't be an enlisted man for much longer."

Smiling, I asked, "They accepted my recommendation?"

"They did. They took what we accomplished on Kanaris and tested me against some of the best minds of the Kyperion Defense Institute. They're not only making me an officer, they're making me a captain. I'm going to outrank you."

"They're just paying you more," I told him. "It's a technical commission, so you can't be assigned a command position. You still have to follow my orders; only I have to call you 'sir' when I issue them."

Naktada looked horrified. "Please don't call me 'sir.' If you do, I'll bust you in the chops."

I slapped Naktada on the shoulder. "You'll try."

Chapter 40

RIVALRY

The club at Narman's Pyke was a pretty basic affair. Like everything else in the colony, it was built of concrete and stucco. It was a round structure, almost entirely without corners save for the kitchen and restrooms. It was decorated with little besides graffiti, most of which was left behind by the Marines who liberated the Pyke twenty-five months before.

"My god," I said to myself as I thought about that.

"What?" asked Je'Sikka Albarn.

"Do you realize how long we've been here?"

Both she and Naktada shook their heads.

"More than two years," I told them.

"How long have you been heya?" Buffy asked Black Francis.

My platoon sergeant shrugged. "I deployed about two months after the Pyke was liberated. Back then, our main mission was to clear the forest around the walls. Our biggest threats were the Quarakai attacks. And the snipers. They were thick out there. My unit did a pretty good job pacifying our sector, so they sent us out to secure the Nimnaya Valley. Nimnaya was rough. My company was reduced to just a couple dozen Marines by the time it was over. I got promoted from PFC to sergeant during that campaign. All through attrition."

"Ouch," Naktada said.

"Yeah, it was painful, alright. After the valley, they let us recuperate for a couple of months while establishing Camp Saepayum, then stuck us on the north bank of the

Yuddaya River to protect the left flank of the people carving Camp Taarlak out of the forest. That started quiet, but we were close to Narman forces at that point. They figured out we were there pretty quick and started to harass us, but we kept them on the south side of the waterway."

"Were you in the westward press after Taarlak was completed?" asked Espiya, my intel sergeant.

Black Francis nodded. "Yes, we were. In fact, we were one of the first squads to make contact with the main Narman force. We were in the NML before there was a No Man's Land. We got so good at being out there because we literally watched its creation."

As we spoke, I watched Mott Peeli walk in with a couple of his squads and a group of ferocious-looking Killbillies. Buffy's face twisted into an expression of disgust. Sergeant Korman caught the gesture. "You not a big fan of your brethren there, brother?"

"They's not my bwethwen."

"Aren't they from Qilkoraan?"

Buffy pointed to his head with his index finger. "They's simple men. Vewy supastitious and easily misled. They've been duped into believing cwuelty is a vuhchoo."

Spotting Bufort, a couple of the Killbilles waddled out of their way to pass by our table. One of them smiled, showing off a mouth full of rotting teeth. "You still hiding behind these losers, Buffy? You ever going to grow some balls and face us like a man?"

"Move along, gentlemen," I told the pair. "Your party's with Peeli on the other side of the room."

"I ain't no Marine, Tauk," the Killbilly spat. "I ain't takin' my orders from you."

"You're right, Qletus," I replied. I knew his name from our joint briefings with Peeli. "You're not a Marine. You're a civilian—a guest on this planet. I can have you removed from it any time I see fit. And if you threaten any of my people again, I'll have you removed from your very existence."

That might have been the end of the conversation had Black Francis not been feeling so feisty. "Your name's Qletus?"

The Killbilly nodded. "Uh-huh."

"Your parents named you after a woman's naughty parts?"

Trying to stifle a laugh, Nila Chisek nearly choked on her beer.

"Qletus ain't no woman's naughty bit. You're thinkin' clitoris."

The Killbilly's partner started tapping him rapidly on the shoulder. "Naw, man! Naw. Qlitoarus is your mamaw's sister who lives down by Dulali."

"Yeah, dipshit! It is! *She's* the one who got herself named after a lady's naughty bits! What the hell would you know about a woman's body anyway, you sperm-gurgler!"

"I ain't no sperm burglar!"

"That ain't what I said, but what the hell! It still fits!"

"How you figure? I's far too pretty to resort to stealing the stuff!"

"Clayton Vikar would beg to differ."

The second Killbilly's face flushed red. "Naw, man! You know that was an accident!"

"How was that an accident?!? 'Scuse me, Clayton! I slipped, tripped, and shoved your junk in my mouth?!?"

"I was drunk! I stumbled into what I thought was my room! It was dark, and I figured that was my feller lyin' there in bed. Imagine my surprise when I found out it wasn't!"

"Imagine *your* surprise?!?" Qletus scoffed. "Imagine Clayton's!"

That was all we could take. Our entire table lost its shit.

Like most people with significant inferiority complexes, if there was one thing a Qilkorian could not stand, it was being the butt of a joke. It was pretty apparent by the intensity of our hysterics that none of us were laughing *with* the pair of Killbilles accosting us. We were laughing *at* them. This enraged Qletus, who looked at Buffy and snarled, "That shit ain't funny, Bufort!"

"The fuck it ain't!" Buffy replied, gasping for air.

Qletus slammed his fist upon the table. "Y'all shut the hell up!"

Black Francis was laughing so hard tears poured from his eyes, but even while seated, he swept the legs from beneath the Killbilly beside him. Qletus fell to his knees, allowing Francis to grab a handful of the man's hair and bounce his head off the table. My platoon sergeant then seized his dinner knife and pressed it against the bruin's jugular vein.

"Look, ma'am," Francis said, knowing Killbillies generally believed women to be inferior, an attitude that confounded us considering how often they saw female Marines in combat. "You've said you're not taking orders *from* us, so what the hell makes you worthy enough to issue orders *to* us?"

"Let him go, Gunny Franq," Lieutenant Peeli said, stepping up to our table. Unlike the Killbilly, Peeli was someone whose orders Black Francis *was* required to follow. Still, my platoon sergeant looked at me first for approval. It was not until I nodded that he finally let the man go.

Turning to the pair of Killbillies, Peeli pointed to where their platoon was gathering. "Our party's over there. Join it." Being Samaari, Lieutenant Peeli was someone whose words the Qilkorians did not question. They walked away without uttering another word.

"When did you get back, Mott?" I asked the lieutenant.

"Six or seven hours ago," my counterpart answered.

"Any luck?"

Peeli shook his head. "Finding Narmans? No. We better find some soon, though, or my men will be raiding those Portunese miners for sport."

I saw Nila Chisek and Saeli Hermour shudder. When we had taken the Satapadaya, Peeli's platoon grabbed every female POW they could get their hands on and used them to celebrate their victory. When they finished, they turned the women over to the death squads. Their screams permeated the foothills for weeks afterward.

"We saw an anwar, though," Peeli added.

"And you lived to tell the tale?" Naktada asked.

Peeli nodded. "Yeah. Our ubatis sniffed it out before it got close enough to do any harm. Those things are creepy but no match for a pack of Kanarisian war hogs. When are you going back out, Tauk?"

"Next week."

"Us, too. Try to stay out of our way out there."

I spotted Mazada Duum walk into the club and immediately give Akkam Lumuk a sneer of disgust. Having a bad feeling that Duum would be unable to restrain himself from tormenting my giant, I said, "How about you guys try to stay out of our way in here?"

That proved too much to ask. I am not sure exactly how the fight started, only how it escalated beyond our control.

There had always been an unhealthy rivalry between Peeli's platoon and mine. To be completely honest, much of the blame for that fell on my shoulders. For me, Mott

Peeli was a typical Samaari. He was arrogant, impulsive, entitled, and quick to use his connections to avoid being held accountable for his excesses. Not that he was incompetent or cowardly. Quite the contrary, actually. He was an aggressive leader and, even measured against recon standards, was a better-than-average officer.

Peeli was good, but not the caliber of a Section 615 officer. He was short on imagination. The man was also motivated more by greed and personal glory than by a desire to win the war. As long as he got his share of the spoils, he would allow his troops to get theirs, encouraging some of our more unsavory elements to compete for any billet that opened up in his platoon. It was also why so many Killbillies enjoyed his company.

The Marines in Peeli's platoon relished the perks of minimal oversight and distrusted us for not taking advantage of the situation like they were. The Samaari lieutenant not only tolerated his troops' suspicion of my Marines, he actively encouraged it. He warned his people not to mingle with mine, probably to reduce the possibility of us finding out how much they were looting. In turn, I did my best to warn my folks to avoid Peeli's group to keep them from being tainted by the Samaari's moral ambiguity. It was a strategy that worked on the battlefield but not in the club at Narman's Pyke. The quarters were just too close, and the alcohol too plentiful.

I have no idea what the original dispute was, as the brawl's aftermath completely overshadowed what its origins may have been. All I know is at some point, a verbal disagreement between a pair of our Marines deteriorated into a physical altercation. With the underlying tensions between our two units in mind, sergeants from both sides moved in to pull the fighters apart. While they struggled to separate the combatants, one of my squad leaders took a blow to the face that laid him out on the deck, nearly knocking the man unconscious.

Akkam Lumuk, my gentle giant from Gorsu Qat, instinctively jumped in to pull Sergeant Korman out of harm's way. For a moment, the hostilities paused as the Marines wondered what the big man was doing. Despite his reputation for cowardice, Lumuk's size needed to be reckoned with. If he were coming at them with bad intentions, it would have taken half of Peeli's platoon to bring him to heel—or one ill-tempered Samaari with a chip on his shoulder.

As Lumuk bent over to pick Korman up, Mazada Duum burst through the crowd and planted his boot in my rifleman's face. It was a brutal kick that might have killed a smaller man. Lumuk's neck snapped back and popped, blood poured out of his nose, and he collapsed atop the man he was trying to help. "That'll teach you to lock me out of your escape tunnel and throw me to the Quarakai like a fresh piece of meat!" Duum screamed as my giant went down.

It was a cheap shot that enraged my Marines enough to clear the benches. My troops charged Mazada Duum to make him pay for what he had done. Naturally, Peeli's Marines leapt up to defend him. The two sides met on the dance floor and proceeded to annihilate one another. Before long, the melee spread to the rest of the club, destroying everything in its path. Tables, chairs, china, windows, and the occasional member of the club's staff fell victim to the violence, smashed into pieces and strewn across the building's floor.

I had to pull three of my Marines off Duum after I fought through the mob to reach the little prick. Grabbing a handful of the Samaari's hair, I wrenched him to his feet only to have him punch me in the gut on his way up, not realizing I was a commissioned officer. A look of horror washed across his face as he tried to stammer out an apology, then I shattered his nose. Lieutenant Peeli showed up at my side and grabbed the collar of my fatigues before I could hit him again. "Get your fucking hands off of my Marine!"

Batting away Peeli's arm hard enough to break his grip on my uniform, I dropped Duum and kicked him hard enough in the gut to leave him gasping for air. I then shoved Peeli onto his ass. The Samaari looked at me in disbelief, unable to comprehend someone had the nerve to lay their hands on him. "Do you know who I am?"

"You think I care?" I growled back. "Have you forgotten who *I* am, Mott? Huh? Do you think the man who killed Gori Dravidas is going to give a shit what some pampered prick with an exaggerated sense of self-importance thinks he can do to him?"

"Exaggerated?" the lieutenant scoffed as he lifted himself off the deck. "I'll have you know that my family...."

"FUCK your family!" I snarled, poking my index finger hard into Peeli's chest. "What have *you* done, you self-aggrandizing little shit, besides ride on your family's coattails? What have you accomplished here besides looting the battlefield and raping POWs?"

Enraged at the insinuation, Peeli stepped toward me with his index finger wagging as if he was about to give me a piece of his mind. Before he could speak, I grabbed him by the lapels and slammed him against a nearby stanchion hard enough to knock the wind out of him. "Huh, Mott?" I snarled as I held him in place. "I'm waiting! What have *you* done?"

I noticed the fighting had subsided in the club as all eyes focused on Mott Peeli and me. The Samaari caught this, too. "Get your fucking hands off of me!"

"Make me!" I said it loud enough so everyone in the bar could hear the challenge.

Peeli's eyes filled with rage. Physically, the Samaari was no match for me and he knew it. Still, honor dictated he should at least try to break out of my grasp. He did no such thing, though. His arms hung limply at his sides, making no attempt to challenge me. "When my family gets word of this...."

I released Peeli with my right hand and smacked him across the face. It was not meant to hurt the man, but to humiliate him in front of his Marines. It worked. Before the sound of the slap had ceased reverberating off the tavern walls, I heard his troops inhale with one collective gasp.

"Your family?!?" I laughed. "Your family? You ever think you'll get the stones to take care of me yourself, Mott? You're a lieutenant in the Kyperion Marine Corps, for fuck's sake! And you're still calling your mommy to save you? That must be one bad bitch you got there, Peeli! Maybe we should call her to come to Kanaris and lead your Marines!"

For a long moment, Peeli and I just stood there, staring at each other. Finally, I asked, "Are you going to do anything about this, Mott? Huh? Do you have even a smidgeon of self-respect?"

I took Peeli's silence as a "no."

"Fine," I spat, pushing the Samaari officer back onto the ground. Addressing my troops, I said, "All right! The night's over! I want all Third Platoon Marines outside to...."

Something seemed out of place, but at first, I could not put my finger on it. Only after scouring the crowd a couple of times did it dawn on me. All the Qilkorians had vanished. After one more panicked scan of the room, I turned toward Black Francis and asked, "Do you see Buffy?"

Chapter 41

Exile

We found Bufort Graym's body the next day. The Killbillies did not have the time they needed to really make him suffer, so they settled for clipping off his fingers before drowning him in an open latrine pit on the other side of the colony's walls. I was watching the MPs pull the body out of the sludge when Agent Takawa found me. He was furious.

"You have fun last night, Lieutenant?" Takawa snarled.

"Does it look like it?" I answered.

The agent's face turned red as he looked at Buffy's corpse. Shaking his head, he turned to me and said, "What a fucking waste. That was the guy who trained the ubati to sniff out Deena Vulk, wasn't it?"

"It sure was," I said, wondering if the previous night's brawl was deliberately started to neutralize Buffy and his Vulk-sniffing war hog.

"You still going to be able to use the ubati?"

I shrugged. "Probably not." *Not that I would admit it to you if I could.*

Takawa sighed. "I hope what you did last night was worth it. Palkrait's pissed. So is General Duuq."

"Did that pansy report me to his family yet?"

"Peeli? No. I told him if he did, he'd be off this assignment and going back to Captain Pustov."

"And you think that's that?"

"No, I don't, Tauk," Takawa growled at me. "He's Samaari. Those pricks never let anything go."

"You saying I should take him out before he gets me?"

"That's *not* what I'm saying and you know it! The two of you need to make nice and put this shit behind you, but I know that ain't ever going to happen! Not after you humiliated Peeli in front of his entire platoon!" Looking back at Buffy's body, he added, "And, of course, this shit here."

"I can let bygones be bygones," I said. "Just have Peeli send his Killbillies over to see me."

Takawa shook his head. "You stay away from Peeli's Qilkorians, Tauk. I mean it."

"They killed one of my men."

"No!" Takawa snapped, pointing his finger at my face. "They killed one of theirs! The Qilkorians are contractors. They have a different hierarchy and a different set of rules. What happened to this man is Killbilly voodoo shit. It ain't our business what they do to each other out here."

"Do you know they tried to kill one of my Marines?"

"I wouldn't exactly consider Lumuk a Marine...."

I turned my back on Takawa and started walking toward the colony. At that point, I was sure the Killbillies had not just seized a random opportunity to kill Bufort Graym. They had planned it all along. I looked up at the colony's walls and wondered how the Qilkorians got Buffy through the Pyke's heavily guarded gates. I then glanced back at Takawa and realized that they hadn't. Section 615 had to have helped them.

The fuckers set a trap, and I danced right into it.

Doing my best to keep from betraying my suspicions to my commander, I took care to place the responsibility for Buffy's death on whom I thought Takawa wanted me to blame. Turning my head back toward the crime scene, I yelled, "If you value your Killbillies more than your troops, sir, I suggest you advise them to stay out of my way!"

"Yeah, I suspected that would be your attitude," Takawa said as he jogged to catch up with me. "I figured you'd want to kill them on sight."

"I didn't say that."

"Of course you didn't. That would be construed as premeditation at your court martial. You know, there are a lot of Qilkorians to be seen around Narman's Pyke, Tauk. We need to put some distance between you, Peeli, and all the Killbillies."

"You're shipping us out?" I asked.

"I'm not. Palkrait is. He wants me, you, and Peeli off his base. He's pretty pissed about all the damage you people did to his nightclub and concerned that someone lost their life over a bar brawl."

"Buffy wasn't killed over a fight. He was murdered for helping Marines against a Qilkorian psychopath."

"It doesn't matter. Palkrait doesn't want Recon Marines carrying out vendettas on his base."

I certainly could not blame the colonel for that. "So where are we going? Camp Vayipar?"

Takawa shook his head. "Nope. You're to provide perimeter security to one of the Harnillium mining operations. You're going to the Saimsun facility. Way out in the boonies. Peeli's platoon will be based out of Razbauten, which is even further out."

"What about the hunt for Deena Vulk?"

The agent stopped walking and grabbed my arm. "Tauk, we have to have Harnillium to fuel the weapons we'll need to hold our ground against the aliens if they show up here in force. That's our weak point right now. The mines have to run non-stop. The Narmans don't have the manpower anymore to hold a line or threaten the Pyke. They've no choice but to hit us where we're soft. Do things like attack our mines."

Takawa paused to shake his head. "Deena Vulk could be anywhere on this entire fucking planet. It's a big place. We could search this thing for the rest of our lives and never come within a hundred clicks of the bitch. Vulk's smart. I can guarantee they've seen our people mining Harnillium with a desperate sort of enthusiasm. An imbecile could put two and two together and figure out why."

The agent sighed and looked me in the eye. "We don't need to go out looking for Deena Vulk, Tauk. I've got a feeling that very soon, she's going to come looking for us."

I was in the cockpit with Je'Sikka Albarn as the *Niberian Hornet* descended upon the landing pad at the far edge of the Saimsun mining facility. The sight on the ground looked like a scene from some ancient earthly atrocity. Hundreds of people, men, women, and children emerged from a hole bored into the side of a mountain. They were dressed in tattered rags and harassed by scores of Samaari Blue Shirts wielding whips, batons, and electrical prods. Even from a hundred meters up in the air, we could sense the terror of the prisoners below.

"Who are they?" asked Warrant Officer Albarn.

I sighed. "Probably prisoners from Portuna or Terrakand."

"Prisoners?!?" asked Owen Skaigard, the *Hornet's* co-pilot. Using the craft's exterior cameras, he zoomed in on the wretched miners. "Some of them aren't even teenagers yet!"

Ratta Dav, the craft's weapons officer, looked up at the video playing on a monitor above Skaigard's head. She winced as she saw a little girl pulled from the crowd by a couple of Blue Shirts. We could not hear her from inside the *Hornet*, but we could see the kid shrieking in terror as she was hauled away. A grown woman in the throng, presumably the girl's mother, wailed at the guards in a vain attempt to get them to return her child. Another woman held her back, trying to keep her from being punished, too. The Blue Shirts laughed hysterically in response to the miners' distress. Then one ripped off the young prisoner's smock while another unhooked a bullwhip from his belt. "What the fuck are they doing?!?" cried Dav.

"Turn it off," Albarn ordered her co-pilot.

"Turn it off?!? I'm recording it! Someone needs to be held accountable for this shit!" Skaigard protested.

Hanging my head in futility, I said, "Trust me, no one's going to be held accountable for anything. If you try to bump this up the chain, the only thing that'll happen is you'll be branded a troublemaker. At best, they'll reassign you someplace where you won't see stuff like this. At worst, they'll frame you for some crime to discredit you, then sentence you to join the miners. Listen to your pilot, Skaigard. Turn the video off."

The entire cockpit crew turned to look at me in disbelief. "They're torturing children!" the flight engineer exclaimed. "We can't let them get away with that!"

The *Hornet's* crew chief, Chief Petty Officer Qora Guerrogosa, had been around a while. She knew the way things worked in combat zones. "The lieutenant's right," she told the officers. "There's no good that's going to come from exposing this."

"Turn it off," Albarn told her co-pilot, repeating her order. "I'm not telling you again."

Shaking his head in disgust, Skaigard shut down the monitor. "Fucking Samaaris. Why do they feel the need to do shit like this?"

"Because if we're going to beat the aliens, we need Harnillium for our new weapons," I told him, trying to parrot what Naktada once said to me. I am quite sure I was even less convincing. "We're facing an existential threat. We're in an extreme situation, prompting an extreme reaction from the League."

Guerrogosa scoffed. "We've been doing shit like this on Portuna long before there was ever any alien threat. I've never been there, but I bet we're doing it on Terrakand, too. I'm pretty sure the Samaaris provoke these civil disturbances themselves to justify getting even richer off free prison labor."

I made a mental note to keep an eye on Guerrogosa. She sounded very disillusioned. Not that anything she said was factually incorrect. I had a feeling it would not take much to convince her to switch sides. In fact, scanning the faces of the *Hornet's* crew, I did not see anyone who appeared proud to be in the Kyperion Space Corps at that moment. It would not have surprised me had I heard they all defected to the Narmans after we disembarked. At that moment, my biggest concern was that they would leave me behind if they did.

It was a situation that made me very nervous. The Saimsun Mine was to be the *Hornet's* new home. Ours, too. I wondered how many examples of Samaari sadism we could witness before my entire platoon started seriously questioning our mission on Kanaris.

Ratta Dav sounded like she was already wavering in her commitment to our mission. "So we're not going to do anything about this?!?"

"Oh, I'm going to do something, all right," Skaigard promised. "I blew up the video. I got the face and the name of the prick whipping the kid. Once we land, I'm going over there and beating that worthless wad of dick spit to within an inch of his life."

"No, you're not," I told him.

"Why not?" Skaigard snarled. "I'm an officer attached to a military mission. Legally, those Blue Shirts are civilians and under our jurisdiction. I can get away with doing whatever I want to those pieces of shit!"

"Sure, you can," I agreed. "But they can get away with doing whatever they want to the little girl you're trying to protect. If you beat that son-of-a-bitch's ass on her behalf, he's going to be pissed. He'll want to take out his frustrations on somebody. Since he can't do anything to you, who do you think he's going to make pay for what you do to him?"

Skaigard's jaw clenched shut as he ground his teeth together. Furious, he lashed out and punched the side of his control console. "Is this really what we're on this planet fighting for?"

"Yes." It was barely a whisper. It would not have been audible had it not been amplified by the commlink microphone positioned right in front of her lips. Still, it was a powerful statement coming from such a decorated pilot. It implied CWO Je'Sikka Albarn was quickly losing faith in The Cause.

And that was the first time I truly realized that I was, too.

Chapter 42

GHOSTS OF THE ARAD

The Arad was a valley west of the Satapadaya Ranges. The mountains surrounding it were among the tallest on Kanaris. Only the highest storms could pass the peaks to rain upon the depression, making it one of the driest regions on the entire continent. It only experienced precipitation about thirty percent of the time.

In addition to the everpresent rainforests, the Arad Valley boasted a couple of expansive savannahs covered in grass so tall we could only see above it while on the backs of our naypetos. It was while crossing one of these that we got into our first bit of trouble.

Our ubatis sensed it first. They stopped in their tracks and pointed their snouts south, toward whatever was causing them such concern. I looked down at Meit, Buffy's tracking animal, and saw it was not pawing at the ground in agitation. Whatever was out there, it was not Deena Vulk.

"What do you think it is?" asked Black Francis, riding alongside me.

"It could be anything," I answered. "Anwar. Ambush. Aliens. Something we've never even seen before. Whatever it is, we're supposed to be the only friendlies out this way. Send the ubatis over to flush it...."

Before I could finish my sentence, a Quarakai stood straight up to get a better look around. We were all wearing our new armor with its light-bending properties, so while the creature could see the naypetos we were riding, we humans were practically invisible.

"It looks confused," Sergeant Korman said. We were in full combat dress, so we communicated via commlink. Though I could hear Korman from thirty meters away like he was standing beside me, the naypeto I rode upon could not hear me at all. Neither could the Quarakai.

"Of course it's confused," I told my squad leader. "Naypetos are prey to the Quarakai. Our mounts should be running away from that thing. On the other hand, ubatis eat Quarakai if they can catch them on the ground. That thing in front of us probably smells our war hogs and naypetos together and can't figure out what to make of it."

"It probably caught our scent, also," Black Francis added. "All of it together might be too much to compute."

The Quarakai snorted, and a dozen more stood up to look at us. I could see half of them were holding sharpened sticks. They were huge, standing nearly as tall as our naypetos.

"Uh oh," I heard my Second Squad sergeant say. "If I didn't know any better, I'd say that looks like a hunting party."

Our naypetos were getting nervous. It was as if they could sense the Quarakais' intentions and were not happy about it. "I think you're right," I told Tiago. "I'm going to show myself and let them know these naypetos are taken."

It turned out to be a bad move. When I switched off my camo generator, the Quarakai were startled to see me appear out of nowhere. One of them panicked and threw its spear at me. It struck my chest with lethal accuracy, ripping me right out of my saddle and hurtling me to the ground. That triggered an overreaction from my second in command.

"Ubati!" snapped Black Francis, lifting his visor so our beasts could hear him. "Attack!"

Before I could stop them, our alien war hogs rushed into the grass after the creatures who had assaulted me. Realizing what they were now up against, the Quarakai shrieked and fled. They should not have bothered. They were all run down in seconds and ripped to pieces. Their death screeches were so loud our animals could not even hear my calls to break off the attack. I had to patch into my exo-armor's loudspeakers. "UBATI! HALT!"

Buffy had trained our ubati well. The animals instantly broke off the attack and returned to the platoon, taking up posts around the perimeter to guard against any other danger that might emerge. Buva, Corporal Dori's beast, brought an arm back to snack on.

Black Francis ran to my side as the Quarakai wailed in agony out in the grass. "Sir! Are you all right?!?"

"I'm fine!" I yelled back, lifting myself to my feet before kicking the ground in frustration. "They hit me with a goddamned stick, Francis! We didn't have to sick the war hogs on them!"

"They attacked us!"

"They panicked!" I shouted at him. I was pissed, but not at Black Francis. He followed protocol and, procedurally speaking, made the right call. It was I who should have done things differently. Frustrated at my own stupidity, I stomped through the grass toward the sound of the injured Quarakai.

"Wait! Sir!" Black Francis called after me. "I wouldn't do that if I were you! Did you see how big those things were?!?"

They *were* big. Huge. Even larger than the glider species we fought when we first reached the Pyke. Now they were broken. Mauled. Dismembered, ripped open, mutilated, and maimed. After seeing a couple of them, I realized that calling off the ubatis was no mercy. Cursing, I drew my blaster from the holster on my hip and shot the closest one through the head. Unlike the bullets we used on them in the past, the plasma burst from our new weapons killed the Quarakai instantly.

I walked up to another and put it out of its misery. Then a third. As I approached the fourth, Black Francis could see my hand was shaking. "Are you alright, sir?"

"No, I'm not alright!" I snapped as I killed another creature. "Why do we end up annihilating everything we ever come into contact with? Fuck! You know, if the aliens and the Narmans are so evil, why do they have Quarakai allies? Why don't we?"

"You told me we did at one point," Black Francis reminded me. "Back at the Pyke. Isn't there one of those Quarakai that lives by itself on a ledge at the end of our sewage tunnel?"

I nodded as I marched off to find another victim. "Yeah. Tukko. He wouldn't leave that ledge with us, though. He didn't want anything to do with anyone but Jella Duverii. I can only guess what his story was."

"This is about more than these Quarakai, ain't it?"

I nodded while I pushed down the grass in front of us. "How long have you been in the Marines, Gunny?"

"Nine years."

"That long? I thought you said you were a PFC when you got to Kanaris."

"I was. I've been a PFC several times. Been a sergeant more than once, too. I get promoted pretty fast. I just get busted even faster. I have to tell you, sir, this is about the longest I've ever gone without going up in front of the old man and losing my stripes."

"You're on your second enlistment, then? Why didn't you go home after your first?"

Black Francis shrugged. "I guess I didn't have a lot to go back to. There ain't a lot of work on Orbewan. The pay's better here."

"You going to make this a career, then?" I paused as I tripped over a Quarakai leg.

"Yeah, I guess so."

While I looked for the rest of the creature who belonged to the limb, I asked, "Are you going to return home after you retire?"

Black Francis shook his head as if he was not quite sure. "I thought I was, but after seeing what I've seen? No, I can't picture myself being content where I grew up. I'd just be spending my days watching family members waste away in a place where there's not much upward mobility."

"So where would you go?"

Black Francis stopped while he tried to think up an answer. "I don't know."

"Can't you think of a place better than Orbewan?"

The gunny sergeant looked at me dumbfounded. "Nobody's asked me that before."

"Well, can you?"

Black Francis thought for a minute, then shook his head. "No. Now that you mention it, every planet I've been to in the Corps has been just as bad or worse than the world I grew up on."

"Look around this place, Gunny. Beautiful, isn't it? Dangerous as all fuck, but gorgeous. I bet we could transform this planet into something extraordinary if we put our minds to it. We could turn it into paradise. Instead, look at what we've done at the Saimsun Mine. We turned it into a goddamned concentration camp."

"I wouldn't call it that, sir. Concentration camps are the kinds of things the Ghouls would do."

"The Ghuldari? Have you ever fought the Ghuldari, Gunny?"

Black Francis shook his head.

"Me neither. I marched up to the Pyke with a corporal who battled them on Sivma-11, though. Harlund Merik. He respected them. He said 30,000 of them were on that planet, and they fought to the death. Every one of them. You have to be a true believer to fight like that, Gunny. You have to love what you're fighting for. We don't have that. Our grunts are more likely to desert, surrender, or flee in the face of the enemy. I doubt the Ghouls fight as hard as they do to keep some concentration camps running. What are you fighting for, Gunny?"

Black Francis shrugged. "I guess I just don't have anything better to do. You?"

"As far as I can tell, I fight to increase Samaari profit margins."

Francis frowned at me. "You can't tell me that's what's keeping you from going over to the other side."

I hung my head and sighed. "Sometimes it feels like the only thing holding me back from taking up the Narman cause is how certain I am that they have no chance of actually winning."

Two days later, we found a crude fence in one of the savannahs we crossed. Its discovery was pure luck as it was entirely covered by the tall Kanarisian grasses. We were in the middle of nowhere, hundreds of kilometers away from any known settlement, be it Narman or Marine. It should not have been there. "You think it's human or alien?" Black Francis asked me.

"I'm going to guess it's human," I answered. "It looks like pictures I once saw of some ancient Earthly structures."

My gunnery sergeant looked on the other side of the barrier, where the savannah grass was somewhat shorter. Seeing some patches further back where there was no grass at all, he climbed off his naypeto and went to investigate. Francis spent several minutes poking through the vegetation before declaring, "It was a pen. They kept ubatis in here. They haven't been around for a while, though. Nature's reclaiming it pretty quickly."

I nodded. "There's got to be another structure of some sort around here someplace. You see anything?"

Black Francis shook his head. "They wouldn't have put one up in the open like this." Pointing toward the end of the clearing, he said, "They'd have put it in the woods where the canopy could keep it concealed from passing aircraft or satellites."

"You think it's still occupied?"

Before Francis could answer, he tripped over the skeleton of a dead ubati and nearly landed on his face. After seeing what he had stumbled over, he looked at me and shook his head.

Those were not the only bones we came across that day. When we discovered the dwelling a couple of hours later, we were welcomed to the homestead by a line of human skulls stuck atop sticks pounded into the ground. They looked to have been the heads of two adults and three children.

"Is anyone else supposed to be out here?" asked Sergeant Korman.

My intel specialist shook her head. "Just us. This is supposed to be unexplored area."

"Then who the hell did this?" asked the leader of First Squad, Saeli Hermour. "The aliens?"

Seeing something shiny near the hut, Black Francis got off his naypeto and began picking things up off the ground near the abode's entrance.

"What've you got?" I asked him.

"Shell casings," he called back to me. "10 mm. 7.88 mm. There're also holes in the stucco that look like rail gun projectiles."

Francis stuck his head through one of the shattered windows. He pulled it out very quickly. "The remaining bodies are inside, picked clean by the kryptids. There're shell casings in there, too. They look like M72 ammunition."

I nodded. "Well, the mixed ammunition suggests the Narmans inside were fighting Killbillies outside. It looks like the Qilkorians are patrolling this neck of the woods, too."

"You think they're still out here?" asked Sergeant Espiya.

"I hope so," I told her. "I wouldn't mind having an opportunity to settle the score for what they did to Buffy. Tiago!"

"Yes, sir!" The sergeant had been trying to take Buffy's place in handling our animals.

"You think our ubati can track these pricks?"

"I think so, sir," she told me. "But you might want to take a look at Meit first."

I craned my head around the grounds, looking for the animal Buffy raised. I found it by the northern corner of the Narman hut, pawing at the dirt with its left hoof.

"Holy shit," I gasped as I watched the creature. "Deena Vulk's been here!"

Three of our ubatis took up the scent of the Killbillies that had assaulted the settlement. Meit tracked Deena Vulk. At first, I was worried about splitting our forces, but I soon discovered my fears were unfounded. Based on the scent trails our animals had picked up, both targets were treading the same ground.

"You think the Killbillies captured Vulk?" Black Francis asked me as our naypetos struggled to keep up with the ubatis leading us across the high grass of the savannah.

"Maybe," I answered. "It could also be they're trying to track her down." Switching to a channel that only Francis could hear me on, I added, "Hell, for all we know, maybe Vulk and the Killbillies are working together."

I looked back at the swath of flattened grass our naypetos were leaving in our wake. There was no such trail in front of us. "It seems like they're all on foot. If they are, we're going to overtake them pretty quickly. Make sure our people stay alert and prepare for an ambush. If they're walking, we'll overtake them in no time."

I was right. In less than five kilometers, we found the squad of Qilkorians. What was left of them, anyway. Spread out and concealed in the high grass were the bodies of seven humans and twice as many ubatis. The dead animals had holes burned through their boney plates, suggesting whoever killed them had the same types of weapons we did. They had not been cut down by conventional bullets. Before abandoning the corpses, Vulk and her people took anything of use off them. Weapons, ammunition, optics, tablets, everything. It was all gone. The kryptids took the rest. The men's bones were picked clean.

My intelligence specialist, Sergeant Espiya, said, "Well, at least we know the Killbillies weren't tracking Vulk."

"Nope," I replied. "It looks like it was the other way around."

Black Francis lifted a piece of clothing off the ground and showed it to me. It looked like Vulk dipped her finger in one of the victims' blood and wrote upon it, "Better luck next time."

"How long do you think they've been here?" I asked Espiya.

She shrugged. "A few days, maybe."

One of our tracking ubatis let out a squeal, letting us know she had picked up another scent. Pausing to mark the location of the bodies on our tablets, we mounted our naypetos and set off across the grass once more. After a three-kilometer ride, we came across the body of a soroquid, its skull split open by gunfire.

Black Francis shook his head. "Oh man," he groaned. "Can you imagine having to fight those things in this grass? You wouldn't be able to see them until they'd already sunk their teeth into you."

I nodded. "Yeah, without an ubati around to scare them off, you wouldn't stand a chance out in this shit. I'm kind of surprised they got this one."

"It wasn't a 'they.' It was a 'he,'" announced Sergeant Korman. He was standing near the body our animal found. "The kryptids devoured him, too, but I can tell by the holes in his coveralls that one of the 'pedes got him. That's good news for us."

"Why?" I asked as I dismounted and walked over to my squad leader.

"He's still got everything on him. Communications gear, weapons, ammo, tablet...."

Pulling the tablet off the dead Killbilly, I looked it over and handed it to Espiya as she arrived. "Can you hack into that?"

The sergeant shook her head. "No, that's a job for one of our armorers."

"Shit." Our armorers were in Narman's Pyke with Naktada, learning how to maintain and repair our new gear. Letting out a sigh, I said, "We need to get this into one of their hands. Pronto. This will have tracked their movements. There's probably some useful information on this thing about where they've been and what they've seen."

"Not to mention what they learned from the people back at the settlement they took out," Black Francis added. "Does that mean we're heading back to Saimsun?"

I nodded. "I'm afraid so."

I could feel the mood sour among my entire platoon as the news spread we were headed home. As hard as it was living in the field, our "home" was a true horror. We avoided it as much as possible.

Chapter 43

The Pyre

I did not ride in the cockpit of the *Niberian Hornet* on the way back to the Saimsun mine. I saw what the toll of living there had done to Je'Sikka Albarn and her crew, and I selfishly wanted to delay subjecting myself to its horrors for as long as possible. As soon as we were on the ground and the debarkation doors were lowered, we got a scent of what had been going on there. Literally.

"You smell that?" Black Francis asked me.

I nodded. "War pork."

Stepping off the Mar-Sitaara, I was greeted by Dmitri Naktada, who had already been on the ground at the facility for several hours. He stood at the end of the ramp with a haunted look in his eyes, holding a rag over his mouth and nose to fend off the smell. "You got the tablet, sir?" he asked. As brilliant as Naktada was, he never seemed able to wrap his head around the fact that, with his recent promotion, he now technically outranked me. I had given up correcting him for calling me 'sir.'

"It's nice to see you, too, Captain," I told him, handing over the device.

"Sorry, sir," Naktada said. "The faster I crack this thing, the faster I get the fuck out of here."

Normally, when an aircraft landed, the crew would disembark to ensure it was ready for its next mission. I noticed the *Hornet's* team was staying put this time. I punched up Albarn's commlink and asked, "Are you coming out?"

"Negative," Je'Sikka answered back without explanation.

I was going to ask why but caught site of the massive fire raging near the mine's entrance. Putting that together with the smell, I quickly understood why no one wanted to leave. Turning to Black Francis, I pointed to a clearing just outside the perimeter of the landing area. "Have the platoon break out the tents and set up camp there. It should be far enough from the space freighters to keep us from getting blown away if they lift off."

"No barracks?"

"No. Not until I figure out what's happening."

"You're going there by yourself?" Francis asked.

I nodded. "I think I have to."

My platoon sergeant shook his head. "Not alone. Give me a second to get the troops going on their tents, and I'll come with you."

"I'm going, too," said Nila Chisek, her rifle at the ready with the safety off.

When we reached the mine, we were greeted with a vision of pure hell. Blue Shirts were dragging their most sickly miners from the hole they had dug into the mountain, beating their charges mercilessly until they were at the edge of the firepit. The drunken Samaaris would then execute the lucky ones and throw them into the flames. The less fortunate were burned alive.

Aghast at what he was witnessing, Black Francis marched up to the nearest Samaari he could find and grabbed the man by the scruff of his shirt. "What the fuck are you doing?"

The Blue Shirt batted the gunnery sergeant's hand away. "Making room for the next batch of prisoners coming in tomorrow! These scumbags are all used up! They ain't worth a shit anymore!"

As my platoon sergeant argued with the Samaari, Chisek tugged at my arm and directed my attention to a man carrying a half-naked girl toward the inferno. Her back was scored with angry red lash marks that had yet to heal. I recognized her as the child we had seen whipped in front of her mother when we first landed at Saimsun. I pulled out my sidearm and pointed it at the Blue Shirt's face. "Put her down."

The Samaari froze. Two of his comrades, so drunk they were oblivious to what was going on, strolled right past us, singing some marching anthem. They were carrying long sticks with sausages hanging from the ends of them, intending to cook their treats over the pyre. "Sir," the Blue Shirt said to me. "I'm just doing my job."

"Drop her," I growled as two female prisoners passed by me, weeping in grief and terror as they dragged the body of a third to the fire. I had seen one of them before. I watched her on the *Hornet's* monitor when we first arrived. She was restraining the mother of the little girl the Blue Shirt was carrying in front of me, trying to keep her from being flogged, too. She was someone I would see again very soon.

The Samaari did as I told him. He released the girl and let her fall to the ground. She landed on her head hard enough for me to hear her neck snap. That did not kill her, though. The gaping hole in the middle of her chest suggested she had been dead long before she was brought above ground. I looked at the Samaari with an expression of pure rage.

"Sir, I'm not the one who...."

I struck the guard with my pistol hard enough to shatter his jaw. When he hit the ground, I grabbed the man by the hair and dragged him toward the flames as he screamed for mercy. Suddenly conscious of their surroundings, the men with the sausages dropped their sticks and ran to intervene, but Francis and Chisek stopped the Blue Shirts by sticking their weapons in the Samaaris' faces. In return, two dozen guards unshouldered their rifles and drew beads on us.

"Sir, what do you want us to do?" Black Francis asked nervously, realizing we were dangerously close to embarking upon a suicide mission.

"Kill as many as you can," I said without turning around, singularly focused on tossing my Blue Shirt into the inferno.

"Tauk!" screamed a voice behind me. When I refused to acknowledge him, he screamed again. "TAUK!" When that did not work, Agent Takawa drew his pistol and fired a shot over my head.

Without a word, I let go of my Blue Shirt and spun around, reaching for my own weapon. Seeing Takawa already had me in his sights, I did not draw it.

"You best back away, Lieutenant," Takawa said as he took a couple of steps closer to me. "Make no mistake, if you so much as twitch that pistol, I'll blow a hole through your chest ten times the size of the one you must have in your goddamned head! Do you understand me?!?"

Chisek activated her distress beacon to summon the rest of my platoon to our location. Black Francis shifted his aim to point his rifle at the agent. "If you shoot him, I shoot you."

Turning his steely gaze upon my subordinates, Takawa growled, "You're flirting with open mutiny here, Gunny."

As my Blue Shirt scurried away on all fours, desperate to put some distance between himself and the fire, I screamed at Takawa. "And you're committing a war crime! For all the horrors Gori Dravidas was accused of, he never came close to doing something this fucking sick! You're okay with this?!?"

The Blue Shirts could see my Marines running toward us, weapons drawn and ready to fight. Expressions of panic began flashing across their faces as they wondered what they should be doing with their rifles. They did not want my troops catching them with us in their sights, but they knew turning around and taking aim at a mob of angry leathernecks could significantly shorten their lifespans.

Bolstered by the arrival of my platoon, I repeated my question, shouting even louder so that my people could hear it. "Agent Takawa! Are you okay with this?!?"

"Of course I'm not okay with it!" the agent screamed back, cognizant of his hostile audience. "It's evil, son! Evil! If it weren't for all the Harnillium interference, we'd have robots down here working these mines! But we can't, so we have to use prisoners! We need Harnillium! Without it, we don't stand a chance against the aliens! However horrible this shit is, it has to be done for the greater good!"

An older Blue Shirt stood beside Takawa. He had stars on his collar, indicating he was in charge. Sweat was pouring down his face. "Nobody here enjoys this, Lieutenant."

"I could tell by all the singing and celebrating everyone's doing as they feed the flames," Black Francis retorted.

"They're not happy," the commander said. "They're drunk. You think you could do this kind of stuff sober?"

"Go back to your camp, Tauk," Takawa ordered me. "If you care about your people, you'll get them away from here before something happens that none of us can take back. We'll forgive the man you struck as an unfortunate lapse of judgment committed during a moment of passion. The next one will be considered an act of treason. The full force and fury of the Kyperion League will be brought to bear against you and your Marines. Do you understand what that means?"

Had it just been me, I would have killed Takawa right there and let the chips fall where they may. If I did anything to him at that point, I would not just be condemning myself to death. I would be putting my entire platoon at risk of meeting a horrific end at the hands of a demented Killbilly.

I looked at the little girl's broken body on the ground, then at the faces of my Marines. I could see their blood was up. All of them looked disgusted by what they saw. Even Silma Hauken, the only Samaari in my unit, could not believe what she was witnessing. All I had to do was give the order. In an instant, Takawa and the Blue Shirts would exist only in the past tense. And it would be eighty mutineers caught between the Narmans on one side and a half million League Marines on the other.

Full of impotent rage, I turned to Takawa and yelled, "It isn't supposed to be like this!"

The spook nodded. "You're right, Tauk! It's not! But it is, and if the human race is going to survive, this is what needs to be done!"

The senior Blue Shirt addressed his men, trying to dial down the tension before someone other than a condemned inmate got hurt. "Lower your weapons and get back to work. Get this shit over with. No more fucking around. Do what you have to do, but do it humanely and quickly. Go."

Takawa still had his pistol pointed at me. "I believe I gave you an order."

Staring defiantly at the agent, I walked over to the girl's body instead of back to our camp. Lifting her off the ground, I carried her to the fire, getting so close to the flames I could smell my hair burning. Then, as respectfully as I could, dropped her into the pit.

Walking away from the inferno, I spotted a pair of Blue Shirts holding unopened bottles of liquor. "Give them to me," I ordered.

The Blue Shirts looked at their commander, who nodded his approval. After snatching the booze from their hands, I tossed a bottle to Black Francis and another to Nila Chisek. I kept two for myself. Only then did I turn my back on Takawa and, with tears streaming down my face, tell my people, "Let's go."

Black Francis, Nila, and I were all quite drunk when the Blue Shirt sergeant showed up at my tent, asking if he could speak to me alone. After dismissing my Marines, the Samaari introduced himself. "I'm Torma Saad. I'm the unit leader of the man whose jaw you broke."

"Is he going to be okay?" I slurred.

Saad nodded. "He'll be fine."

"That's too bad."

The Samaari sighed. "I'm sorry you had to see that. We're in a rough business, Lieutenant. You especially. I know you've been out in the field for weeks, and I can only guess
how that could wear on a man. You're due some rest and relaxation. I thought I could help
you with that. I came with a little peace offering to show you there's no hard feelings."

"What do you have that I could possibly want?"

The Samaari whistled, and two Blue Shirts entered my tent, dragging a woman inside
between them. I recognized her as one of the prisoners carrying bodies to the fire right
before I popped that pissant Samaari in the kisser. "A man has needs," the sergeant said.
"I figured this might help you clear your head a little about what you saw tonight."

My first reaction was to kill all three Blue Shirts where they stood, but I realized that
would do nothing to help the woman. She was far safer spending the night with me than
she would be with them. I wondered how twisted someone's mind had to be to think that
the best way to get a man's mind off an atrocity he witnessed was to allow him to commit
one himself. Then a realization forced its way through the alcoholic fog in my head to
reach my frontal lobes. The woman was not a treat. She was a test.

For the Samaaris' benefit, I looked the prisoner over lustily. "Thanks. Now, get out. I'll
bring her back to you tomorrow."

After the Blue Shirts left, the woman started quivering. "Please, sir. I saw you at the fire.
I know you're a good man. Don't do this. I'm married and...."

I passed the woman my booze. "Relax. I'm not going to hurt you." After she took the
bottle, I pulled out the cot Buffy Graym once used and set it up next to mine. Quarters
were tight, and that was the most distance I could put between us. "I'm Eamon Tauk."

"I'm Haeli. Haeli Deboara."

Nodding sadly, I asked, "How did you get here? To this fucking place?"

"I'm from Portuna."

"I figured you were either from there or Terrakand. I meant, what did you do to get
arrested?"

A single tear rolled down Haeli's cheek. "I told you, I'm from Portuna. I was born
there."

"And?"

"And what? I don't know what you want me to say. The League's had enough of us.
They're depopulating the planet, rounding us all up and sending us to work camps. I'm
here because I was born Portunese."

I would have found that very hard to believe a couple of years before. Now, however, it did not surprise me one bit. I sat on my cot and dropped my head into my hands.

"You didn't know?" Haeli asked as she sat on the cot I set up for her.

I shook my head. "No. I've never been to Portuna."

"Good for you," Haeli said, taking another sip from the bottle. After she swallowed, she asked, "You're really not going to hurt me?"

"No."

"Can you help me, then?"

"How?" I asked. "What do you think I can do?"

"Get me out of here? Set us free? There's more of you around than there are Blue Shirts. You can take them."

"So can you," I told her. "There're more of you here than us. Far more." I was not an experienced drinker. I was too intoxicated to speak anything but my mind, and I was not in a good place that night. "Look, I can't save your lives if that's what you're asking. As for your freedom, I can't give you that, either. That's something you have to take for yourselves."

"But they'll kill us if we try."

I laughed. "They're going to kill you if you don't. Bullets are a far more merciful way to go than being worked to death."

"But my husband, my boys...."

"Look, ma'am," I said, rolling down to lie on my cot. "I'm too drunk and tired to debate you. If you want your freedom, take it. You have a fresh batch of prisoners arriving tomorrow, swelling your ranks even more. You'll probably outnumber the people keeping you here by a hundred to one. If you rushed us all at once, you could seize our weapons and run off into the jungle. I'm sure there are Narmans lurking about in the forest, keeping an eye on this place. They'd probably swoop in and guide you back to their camps at the first sign of trouble."

Fighting off the urge to drift to sleep, I slurred, "And if you wait for me and my Marines to leave, your odds of success will be even better."

Haeli sat there and stared at me for a moment as my eyes closed. Before I could nod off, she said. "I want to be free. I'm ready to do whatever it takes."

I forced my eyelids back open. "Are you sure?"

The woman nodded at me. "I did everything possible to stay out of the fighting on Portuna. This is where it got me. You're right. If I do nothing, I'll die. If I do something, I'll probably still die, but it'll be quicker. And I'll have the satisfaction of taking a few of those fucking monsters with me."

I felt myself sobering up fast. "Now that we're back here, my Marines will be replacing the Blue Shirts on perimeter patrol. I bet we can find a Narman somewhere in the woods watching this place. They have to be out there. Do you think you can organize a revolt among the prisoners?"

"I don't think I have a choice. I have to."

I stared at Haeli Deboara for a moment before nodding at her. "Then do it. Wait for the Mar-Sitaara, the fighter, to take off and get out of sight, then attack."

"How will I know the Narmans will be ready to help us?"

"You won't," I told her. "They're either there, or they're not. It doesn't matter; the day you fight will be your last day of bondage, one way or the other."

Haeli stared back at me for a moment. "Why are you encouraging me to do this?"

"Because I'm a dead man, and I want to hurt them before I go."

"If they were going to kill you, I doubt they'd have thrown me in here with you."

I laughed again. "When I broke that Blue Shirt's jaw, I revealed my opinion about what they're doing here. To them, I displayed a glaring lack of commitment to The Cause, proving I'm not on board with their program. You're not a peace offering. You're a test. If I take you, I can show I'm capable of being the fiend they want me to be. If I don't, I'm a liability. I bet they're going to examine you after you return tomorrow morning to see if I molested you or not."

Haeli blinked in disbelief. "Then why don't you do what they want?"

"Because I'm not a rapist," I told her. "I want to die knowing that just once in my life, I did the right thing."

Haeli sat in silence for several minutes, lost in thought. Then she stood up and started undressing. "What are you doing?" I asked her.

"What does it look like?"

"You're fucking me?"

The prisoner shook her head. "No. I'm fucking them. And when we're done, you're going to tell me everything you can to help me give these Blue Shirts what they got coming to them."

●●◆●◆●●

Chapter 44

Dissent

When I walked into the office Agent Takawa used at Saimsun, he was with Captain Naktada and livid about what had gone down the night before. "You know, Tauk, I went to bed last night intending to have you and your troops arrested for mutiny. Not by the MPs, either. I was going to have the Section Kommandos deal with you. Let them make you just disappear! Then Captain Naktada here showed me what you found in the Arad Valley. It put me in quite a quandary. On the one hand, I don't think I can fucking trust you to do the right thing out here anymore! On the other, you keep producing for me!"

As I watched Takawa speak, I fantasized about shooting him in the face. Revealing the inner hostility I felt for the man would not have been wise, though. I was on very thin ice. I had to keep him thinking there was still enough of an academy Marine in me to carry out my orders, however heinous they may be. "I take it there was something good on that tablet I turned over?"

Naktada nodded solemnly. He had also seen what the Samaaris had done the night before, and I could feel his discomfort. Takawa had not spent as much time with the armorer as I had, so luckily, he did not pick up on it.

"The tablet belonged to a man named Waldo Kroner," Naktada told me. "He ran the death squad you found."

"Stop calling them 'death squads,'" Takawa spat. "They're contractors."

The captain nodded at the agent. "That device monitored the contractor team's vitals and location. I don't know why, but he left the unit long before they were attacked.

He wasn't fleeing Deena Vulk, the Narmans, or the Morghul. He was fleeing his own people. As we all know, Killbillies are incredible trackers who know how to evade other humans and animals. The only reason those Narmans were able to kill that unit off was the Qilkorians were so focused on finding their boss that they didn't know they were being chased."

"Why didn't the Narmans find Kroner?" I asked.

Naktada shrugged. "They probably didn't even know he was out there."

I nodded. "That makes sense. It looked like the bodies lay where they were killed. It didn't appear the Narmans interrogated them or anything. They just shot them and stripped them of anything useful before abandoning the corpses."

"Uh huh," my former armorer agreed. "That proved fortunate for us. The soroquid that got Kroner wasn't interested in intel, so we got the tablet with all the information the Killbillies gleaned from that settlement they found."

"I take it there was something good on it?"

Takawa nodded. "Only the location of every Narman settlement within fifty clicks of the Arad Valley."

"And the knowledge that some of the aliens live around there, also," Naktada added.

I let that information sink in for a moment. "So when are we going to scoop some of these people up?"

Takawa smiled. "Soon. Since the Killbillies I had patrolling the area are dead, I need to get some more out here."

"For what?" I asked. My voice betrayed my still simmering hatred for the Qilkorian death squads, and I regretted posing the question the instant it left my lips.

Takawa looked at me with renewed disappointment. "To interrogate whoever we capture. No one can get information from a prisoner faster than our Qilkorian contractors. Do you still have a problem with our Killbillies, Tauk?"

"No," I lied, not that it mattered.

Despite passing Takawa's test with the female prisoner the night before, I could sense the agent had lost all confidence in my Marines, and me in particular. We had drawn weapons on the man. My inability to even feign my acceptance of Takawa's methods made us all a significant liability. Not only were we a threat to his personal safety, but our collective disapproval of the Blue Shirts' methods at Saimsun increased the likelihood that at least one of us would expose what was happening deep within the rainforests of Kanaris.

I left that meeting convinced that I was living on borrowed time.

"I got a huge problem with it," Naktada confessed as we returned to the *Niberian Hornet*. "I'm sick of the part I'm playing procuring lambs for the Killbilly slaughterhouse."

I understood where Naktada was coming from, but felt he needed some clarity. Though I knew I was drifting down a perilous path, I had no desire to take him with me. I had already placed my entire platoon in a very precarious situation. "I would hardly call the Narmans 'lambs,' Captain. I spent a little time with Mazada Duum after he was liberated and got a harrowing account of how the Morghul tortured their prisoners."

Naktada stopped walking and turned to face me. "There was video on that tablet you gave me, sir. Would you like to know how the Killbillies found out where all those Narman settlements were? I don't have to tell you about it. I can fuckin' show you. I'm sure what the Morghul did was god-awful, but at least they did it to combatants. Those Qilkorian fucks tortured children, Lieutenant."

I nodded. "Of course, they did. They're Killbillies, Captain. Scum."

Naktada threw his arm out and waved it in the direction where the Blue Shirts had burned all those bodies the night before. "You can't blame the Killbillies for what went down here yesterday. That was the Samaaris who did that shit! You know, the same people that run the whole fuckin' League!"

I dropped my face into my hands and shook my head. "What do you expect me to do?"

"Get off the fuckin' fence! Sir, what I saw last night...well...it got me thinking. What's the League supposed to be about? What's this Cause we're supposed to be defending?"

"We're defending freedom...."

The captain choked on his own spit. "Do the people in that mine look free to you?"

"Equality...."

"Yeah, to be equally poor and hungry if you're anything but Samaari."

I allowed a morbid grin to creep across my face. "Justice."

"Tell me what a ten-year-old girl could have done that warrants working her to within an inch of her life before throwing her screaming into a fire pit right in front of her parents!"

"Protection from the Ghuldari menace...."

"Bitch, please. How many Kyperion citizens are languishing under Ghuldari oppression?"

"On this side of the Haifauna Rift? None that I know of."

"And the people on the other side of the Rift *are* Ghuldari! So none. You ever wonder, if it's so bad over there, why we never hear of the Ghouls seeking asylum within the League's borders?"

"Because they don't," I said. "According to what I was taught at the Academy, the Ghouls are all sheep, too brainwashed to even consider they might find a better life under the League's jurisdiction."

"Like how most of us are standing in a hostile jungle, constantly exposed to summary executions, Killbilly torture chambers, forced labor, and sexual slavery, yet we're still convinced the Ghuldari, the Narmans, and the Morghul are the greater evil?"

"Do you know Gunny Malcolm?" I asked Naktada.

"Only by reputation. We've met, but I've never spent enough time with the man to know much about him."

"He's a junkie. The guy pumps all kinds of shit into his veins to help dull the memories of the horrors he's done in the name of the League. On the way up here, he told me killing soldiers is easy because they're just as much scum as we are. He basically implied that, despite what we always call each other, we weren't really killers. To be a proper killer, you had to ice people who didn't deserve it."

"You telling me he thinks we're not worthy of respect unless we commit a war crime?" Naktada gasped.

"No, not at all. He was trying to tell me he had done things for the League that made him too ashamed to leave it. I had a friend die in my arms whose last words basically implied the same sentiment. He was killed by the mutineers right after we secured the Pyke. He gave his life fighting for the League and passed away regretting he had chosen the wrong side. He told me if he had known he was going to die that day, he would rather have given his life for the Marines who killed him."

"He soured on the League at the end?"

I shrugged. "I wouldn't say that. He soured on our commander. At that point, we didn't know what the Narmans were. We didn't know about the Morghul. Hell, we still thought the Quarakai were just big alien apes. What he soured on was fighting for what was wrong out of nothing but blind allegiance. He regretted not fighting for what was right."

Naktada looked toward the pit where they'd burned the miners. "If he were here today, what side do you think he'd be on?"

"Well, I have a hard time imagining him fighting for the people whipping children in labor camps. Even if they were traitors."

The captain sighed. "You and your platoon drew guns on Takawa. Do you think he considers you a traitor now?"

I nodded, "I'm pretty sure he does. He tried to test me last night. They delivered a woman to my tent for me to use. I think they wanted to see if I hated the people they considered enemies of the state just as much as they do. They figured if I did, I'd display it by forcing myself on that prisoner. If I left her alone, it'd show I had sympathy for her. It would've made me a security risk."

Naktada cursed and looked around nervously to check if anyone was following us. "What did you do?" he asked.

"I bought myself some time."

"You raped her?!?" Naktada exclaimed, aghast.

"Shhh!" I hissed, trying to quiet him down. "Of course I didn't! I was prepared to die before I did something like that! She consented to protect me."

"Sir, I don't think it worked. "

I sighed. "I don't think it did either."

Naktada let out a nervous laugh. "To be honest, I'm surprised Takawa didn't arrange to have you killed in your sleep."

I shrugged. "Initially, I was, too. When you think about it, though, he can't just kill us outright."

"Why not?"

"Because I'm the man who killed Gori Dravidas. Remember? I'm kind of a celebrity. Black Francis is, too. He's a fucking legend. After all the shit he did in the NML, the rank and file lionize him. They'd be pretty pissed to learn Section 615 had us murdered. So would my superiors. We were responsible for breaking the line at the Satapadaya. I don't think Colonel Palkrait and Captain Pustov would tolerate Takawa executing us without a trial. No, if Takawa's getting rid of us, he needs us to die in combat. He's going to lure us into an ambush."

"You think he'll have Peeli take you out?"

I shook my head. "Not a chance. He keeps Peeli close because he's dependable. He has no problems doing Section 615's dirty work. Peeli's a capable officer, but if he puts the two of us head to head in the field, I'll chew that Samaari and his Marines to pieces, and Takawa knows that. He might posture otherwise, but I'm pretty certain Peeli knows it, too."

"He could tip off the Narmans somehow and give them a shot at you."

"Too uncertain," I countered. "They might wipe us out. They might not. And if they fail, I'm going to know who set me up. The last thing Takawa wants is both me and Black Francis coming after him looking for payback, with neither of us having anything left to lose."

"Killbillies?"

I nodded. "That'd be my guess. They're experts at camouflage, unparalleled in field tracking, and equipped with incredible firepower. Not to mention, they've got an insane number of ubatis at their disposal. Without Buffy, we're at a real disadvantage against them in the bush, even with all our toys."

"So, how do you survive a Killbilly ambush?" Naktada asked.

"By not walking into it," I told the captain. "The best way to win a battle is by choosing the opponent you're best equipped to beat and forcing your adversary into a fight where they're grossly outmatched."

"That seems like a solid strategy."

I squinted at Naktada. "Are you in some trouble or something I don't know about?"

"No. Why?"

"Because the way I see things, you're still in good standing around here. I'm the one who's not. Me and my Marines. It sounds like you're rather eager to get neck-deep in the shit I might have to stir."

Naktada sighed. "I joined the Space Corps to be a Marine. Not a butcher. Last night, we didn't burn any of those inmates. We didn't hurt any of those kids. We're wearing the uniform of the entity that did, though, which makes us a piece of it whether we like it or not. I will never be able to live with myself knowing I played a part in something like that, sir. No matter how small a part it may have been. From my viewpoint, the only way to not be part of shit like that is to actively battle it."

"You want to fight the League?" I asked.

"Don't you?"

I let out a long sigh. "To be honest, no. I don't. I can't see how we win against them. Unfortunately, it now appears that the League is about to fight me. That kind of takes away any choice I may have had in the matter."

"You got any plans?" Naktada asked.

"I just now figured out what side I'm on, Captain. Of course I don't. Do you?"

Naktada smiled at me. "Fourteen hours ago, I watched a pair of Blue Shirts toss a boy my nephew's age into a raging inferno while he was still alive. I figured out right then whose side I was on. I had all night to think about this shit. So, yeah, I got a couple of ideas."

Chapter 45

The Narman

I trusted every member of my staff. Black Francis and Nila Chisek were at my side during the inmate cull and were the first to pull weapons on the Blue Shirts. My intelligence sergeant, Hariana Espiya, had to be dragged from the massacre by the leaders of First Squad, Sergeant Hermour and Corporal Tivad. My senior medic, Teri Sotalain, told me she had to talk the three of them out of sneaking back to the mine before dawn and killing Blue Shirts in their sleep. My medic confessed that she had talked them down despite her own desire to join them.

Second Squad was led by Sergeant Tiago and Corporal Kunigas. Tiago wept as she left the inferno. I had never heard Kunigas hide his distaste for the Samaaris for as long as he had been under my command, which was well before we arrived at Saimsun. Sergeant Demangal and Corporal Agha were in charge of Third Squad. Both were Gunny Brumit's proteges and shared her distaste for committing atrocities on behalf of the state.

Fourth Squad fell under the leadership of Sergeant Korman and Corporal Dori. They were former Raiders and fiercely loyal to Black Francis. Whatever he did, they did. We had nothing to worry about from them.

We were all gathered in the *Niberian Hornet's* cockpit as I brought the Mar-Sitaara's crew up to speed on my platoon's situation. Having witnessed their reactions when we first descended into Saimsun, I trusted them, too.

The *Hornet's* co-pilot, CWO Owen Skaigard, was the most vocal in his outrage about the conditions on the ground at Saimsun. He was also understandably leery about the course upon which we were embarking. "Are you telling me that of the eighty-six Marines in your platoon, none of them have reservations about taking up arms against the League? Nobody's got buyer's remorse after what happened?"

Black Francis answered. "I'd have greater concerns if we had more Samaaris within our ranks. We only have one, though, and after having had the brutality of her people thrown in her face the other night, she's having something of an identity crisis at the moment."

"Do you trust her not to talk, though?" Je'Sikka Albarn asked.

Francis shook his head. "Silma Hauken's a good kid, but she's got a big family on Samaar Ghun. What she saw shook her to her core, but was it enough to convince her to turn her back on her kin and fight against them? I don't know. That's a lot to ask of anybody."

"So what are you going to do about her?" asked Albarn.

"Keep her in the dark," I said. "We've got about a dozen troops we're not sure we can count on to switch sides. They might, and they might not. Our plan is to not give them so much as a hint of what we're up to until everything is in motion and it's too late to raise the alarm. After that, we'll give them a choice of whether they want to join us or not."

For a fighter ship's weapons officer, Ratta Dav seemed like an awfully sensitive woman. "What happens to those who decide not to join you?"

I sighed. "The safest thing would be to execute them on the spot. With one exception, all the people I have reservations about are excellent Marines, though. It's just that their ties to their home planets are very strong. I can't guarantee they'd be willing to give up what they were yearning to return to one day. I've fought alongside most of them for more than a year now. I won't repay them for all they've done for me by putting them down like old dogs."

"So what are you going to do?" Dav asked, repeating her question.

"When the mission's over, I'm going to disarm them and turn them loose with their ubatis. That'll greatly increase their odds of making it home again."

Oddly enough, it was that statement that seemed to dispel any doubts the *Hornet's* flight crew had about helping us. It was what assured them they were not throwing their lot in with a group of people just as bad as those they were opposing. After all her subordinates turned to the Mar-Sitaara's pilot and nodded in assent, Je'Sikka Albarn looked me in the eye and said, "We're in."

My Marines and I all let loose a long sigh of relief. We now had a fighting chance. "I suppose you need to talk this over with the rest of your crew?" I asked the pilot. "I think we can strike quite a blow against the League on Kanaris, but long-term, our odds of making it out of this place are not very good."

Albarn shook her head. "We're quite aware of what we're up against, but we don't have to talk to our crew. We've been discussing shit like this since we first landed at Saimsun, and they'll all be in."

Black Francis looked shocked. "You've been talking treason with your enlisted personnel for that long?"

Je'Sikka nodded. "We have. You know, Gunny, we're all Navy people here on the *Hornet*. Don't take this the wrong way, but, with the exception of your armorers, the academic threshold for joining the fleet is significantly higher than it is for serving in the Corps. It has to be. The skill set necessary to keep our ships operating in space is very technical and requires a critical mind. People become Marine officers out of patriotism. Navy officers are usually drawn from a pool of candidates seeking to prove their intellectual meddle. Pilots aren't typically saddled with the ideological baggage you leathernecks have."

As Albarn loosed a sly smile upon us, she said, "If you think the talk between me and my crew has been treasonous, you'd be shocked to learn what I've heard other Mar-Sitaara pilots say after flying missions into these goddamned labor camps."

"Hello, sweetheart," Black Francis purred as he stuck the barrel of his rifle up against the Narman's ear.

The woman was startled and surprised. She was hidden behind a hologram cloak and thought herself virtually invisible. To the contrary, she was staring right at Black Francis and me and still could not make us out. "H-h-how d-d-did you know I-I-I was here?"

"Because this is where I'd be if I wanted to spy on that mine," I told her. We were atop a bluff overlooking the Saimsun facility. She had a perfect view of the entire complex. "I can't figure out how nobody caught you before."

"Blue Shirts are loud," the Narman spy told us. "They march through the bush like they're on safari, trying to flush out game animals. They also don't have ubatis to track us with or armor that makes them damned near invisible. For that matter, neither do most Marines."

"We're not most Marines," my platoon sergeant informed her. "Not anymore. You can consider us Narmans in disguise."

As Francis spoke, I reached over and took the woman's weapons away before turning off my camo generator. "You don't have an ubati with you? Aren't you afraid of soroquids or anwar?"

"Ubatis are good for protection. They're not so good at staying quiet for days on end."

Black Francis plucked a canister off the woman's web gear and sprayed some of what was in it into the air. It had a powerful stench that nearly made us vomit. "Ubati concentrate?"

The woman nodded. "It works just as good as having the actual animal with you. Once they get a whiff of stink like that, nothing wants to get close enough to see firsthand whether there are ubatis in their neighborhood."

"What's your name?" Francis asked.

"I told you enough," the woman said. "I'm not telling you that."

"Then make up a fake one," I told her. "We just want something to call you by."

The woman thought for a moment. "Paipyr."

"Alright, Paipyr," I said. "I know you've got a couple of Quarakai sneaking up on us right now. Call them off. Our snipers have them in their sights, and if your friends get too close, they're going to die." To prove my point, I pulled my sidearm off my hip and fired it into the ground. "As you can see, we're armed with plasma blasters, just like your alien friends. We're not firing bullets like you. If we shoot your Quarakai, we'll kill them."

Paipyr nodded at me, then cupped her hands around her mouth and let out a call that sounded like a laughing dragon. "By the way, they're not my Quarakai. They're not anybody's."

Francis nodded. "We know."

The Narman spy looked at us quizzically. "Do you want something? Usually, I'd expect to be treated harshly if caught by League people."

I shrugged. "First off, I'd like to suggest you pick a less obvious vantage point from which to spy on the base."

"I switch spots every night."

"Yeah, well, avoid this one," Francis advised. "It's too obvious. If you paid attention in boot camp, you'd know that."

"I never went to boot camp."

"No shit?" I asked. "You're a native Narman?"

Paipyr nodded. "Born and raised here." The woman correctly deduced by our silence that neither Francis nor I had ever spoken with a local. "They keep you separated from us, don't they?"

"I guess they do," I told her. "The only people I've ever gotten my hands on have all been Marine deserters."

"That makes sense. It's not in the League's best interest to tell you the real story about what went down here, is it?"

I shrugged. "That depends. What happened at Narman's Pyke from your perspective?"

"The same thing that seems to happen everywhere the Samaaris go. They let their god complexes get the best of them and started treating the rest of us like property."

Cocking her head towards the Saimsun mine, Paipyr told us, "Had it not been for the Morghul, we'd have all ended up like those poor Portunese down there."

"They rescued you?" Francis asked. "The aliens?"

"Eventually," Paipyr answered. "The Marines were hunting Quarakai specimens for our lead zoologist, Dr. Briiz. He didn't want to traumatize our local population, so he sent the troops far away from the Pyke to do it. As luck would have it, the Marines shot some from a tribe allied with the aliens here. When a Morghul boy tried to intervene and stop them, he got killed, too. That drew the aliens into our fight."

"What did they do to you personally?" Black Francis asked. "The Samaaris."

"What didn't they do?" Paipyr answered. "When they realized their excavation robots wouldn't work because of the Harnillium interference, the Samaaris forced us into the mines. They paid the Marine commander to help them meet their quotas. They killed the governor, declared martial law, and compelled us to harvest Harnillium at gunpoint. When someone had the bright idea of making the civilian women take turns staffing brothels for the Marines, it sparked a mutiny that morphed into a civil war. We fled into Morghul territory, not even knowing there was such a thing. Long story short, we joined forces and overthrew the Samaaris."

"No one thought about reporting what was happening to the League?" I asked.

"Why? They knew what was going on. League officials were coming and going off of Kanaris all the time. They didn't care about us. All they cared about was their Harnillium."

None of what Paipyr said surprised me. I sighed and asked, "What are you doing here? In the forest?"

Paipyr looked at me as if I had asked a trick question. "Isn't it obvious? I'm watching you. What are you doing here? With me?"

"Passing you a message," I told her.

"What message?"

"To keep watching. And to be ready to act if something happens. I got a person down there, someone among the miners. If you can help her, she may be able to start some trouble. It'll all be for naught if you can't support them, though. With your help, they can probably overpower the Blue Shirts, raid the armory, blow the mine, and add several hundred motivated fighters to your ranks. Can you do that?"

Paipyr pursed her lips. "We don't have that kind of manpower anymore, not after what happened at the Satapadaya. Quarakai power, on the other hand...."

Black Francis grinned. "The Blue Shirts are armed with conventional rifles, not plasma blasters. They don't have armor, either. If you throw a tenth of those things at the mine that you did at Narman's Pyke, you should be able to roll right over the fuckers."

Paipyr thought about what Francis said for a moment, then nodded. "When do you think this is going to happen?"

"Within a few days," I told her. "After we leave. If they try anything before that, they won't just be fighting Blue Shirts. My Marines will have to fight them, too. We won't have a choice."

The Narman woman nodded at me. "I'll have to run this up my command."

"Is Deena Vulk in that chain?" I asked.

Paipyr winced as if she were surprised I knew that name. "Yes."

"Do you have direct access to the person above her?" asked Black Francis.

"Yes."

"Then go to them. If Vulk gets wind of any of this, those people down there are all dead."

"Deena Vulk is one of the most dynamic leaders we have," Paipyr said, sounding genuinely offended. "No one has more battlefield victories than she does."

"She's got all those victories because Section 615 let her have them," I assured the Narman woman.

Paipyr eyed me suspiciously. "You got proof of that?"

"You want proof?" I asked her back. "Go ahead and tell her there's an uprising brewing among the Portunese prisoners at the Saimsun Mine. Your proof will be the pyre lighting up the night sky within hours of letting that information slip off your tongue."

Chapter 46

NAUTIK

There was a small café near the airwing's maintenance bay at the northeast corner of Narman's Pyke. The place was a true dive. It was dirtier than hell, had walls covered in a golden Kanarisian mold that reeked of stale feet, and served food that tasted as bad as the tavern smelled. Since we were banned from the colony's sole nightclub after tearing it up a few months before, it was the only place we could buy alcohol. The establishment was usually all but empty during prime hours, but when we walked in just past lunch, the only other person present was Chief Warrant Officer Lodai Nautik, the co-pilot of the Mar-Sitaara to which Mott Peeli was assigned.

When Je'Sikka Albarn, Owen Skaigard, and I walked in, we could tell Nautik had been there for quite some time. Despite the early hour, he was already quite drunk. As we stepped through the door, he sneered at us and shook his head in disgust before returning to his booze. We ignored him entirely and took our seats at a table as far from him as we could get.

About an hour after we arrived, Warrant Officer Amella Henne entered the café as well. She was Nautik's Chief Engineer. When she saw us, she also flashed a dirty look our way and turned to walk to the other side of the room. She froze when she spotted Nautik at the bar, however. His face lit up in a broad smile as the two made eye contact, forcing Henne to turn around and invite herself to our table. The three of us from the *Hornet* burst into laughter as she approached.

Nautik did not. "What the fuck, Amella?!?" Henne's co-pilot snapped. "You're seriously going to sit with those shitbirds over me? What the hell do they have that I don't?!?"

"Control over their libidos," she snapped back. "I'd rather slum with them than get groped and slobbered on by you."

I stood up and pulled a chair over to our table for Henne. "We'll try not to get our gunk on you."

"I'd appreciate that," the engineer replied. "I know Albarn and Skaigard are here for pre-op workups, but what're you doing in the Pyke, Tauk? Shouldn't you be preparing your troops for our upcoming mission?"

"I got Black Francis as a gunny sergeant. He can prep them far better than I can. I'm here because a few weeks back, a fucking massive Quarakai chucked a spear at me and knocked me clean off my naypeto. It damaged some of the fiberoptic channels in my breastplate and messed up my camo. I turned it over to Naktada to get it back to a hundred percent."

"You didn't have any spares?"

"Mine's got some extra capabilities."

"Like what?" Henne asked.

I placed the tip of my index finger over my lips. "Top secret."

"Top secret, my ass," Nautik slurred as he stumbled our way, taking the bait. "Who the fuck do you think you are to deserve personal attention from Naktada?"

"He's the man who killed Gori Dravidas," Henne told him.

"I heard that was bullshit!" Nautik announced, grabbing a chair and sliding it between Henne and me before sitting in it.

"Lodai, why don't you go back to the bar before you regret it," Albarn said. "We already got banned from one club on this colony because of this rivalry thing. I'd prefer not to get kicked out of another."

"Fuck you," Nautik snarled.

"Hey!" Skaigard protested. "You're an officer! Show some class!"

Nautik pointed at his *Hornet* counterpart. "And fuck you, too." Then he pointed at Albarn. "And fuck the dyke." Finally directing his finger at me, he said, "And fuck the imposter most of all. I heard from a pretty good source Dravidas kicked the piss out of you."

I nodded. "He did."

The drunk winced. He was not expecting me to admit it. "Say what?"

"Dravidas kicked my ass. He defeated four of us, actually. He killed three of my fellow cadets and could've killed me, too. Instead, he passed me his dagger and offered up his throat."

"And you slit it?"

"Yep," I confessed to Nautik, staring him straight in the eye.

"And they made you a hero for that?"

"They sure did."

"That's bullshit."

"I've never claimed otherwise."

"So you ain't half as tough as they say you are."

I shrugged. "Maybe not, but I'm sure I'm still ten times as tough as you."

Nautik smiled drunkenly while lifting his shoulders so high they almost touched his ears. "You think you'd win a fight against me?"

"I know I would."

The warrant officer scoffed. "Yeah, maybe you'd win the actual battle, but if me and you went to war, I'd waste your ass. Do you know who I am?"

I grinned. That was a question you could always count on a Samaari officer asking. I was amused that, even though he was only a half-Sammy, Nautik posed it like a purebred. "No, I don't know who you are, but I have a feeling you're about to tell me."

Nautik laughed. "You're goddamned right I am. My father's a League senator representing Portisbain. He's the son of a waste management worker. He literally crawled out of the sewer and elevated himself to one of the most powerful positions in the known galaxy. He was elected with eighty-eight percent of the vote for his seventh term. The people of Portisbain love him! My mother's a high jurist from one of the most prominent families of Samaar Ghun. Her family's been running the League's judicial machine since the League was founded!"

Leaning back into his chair and throwing me a smug smirk, he punctuated his bragging with a, "And you don't even know who fucking spawned you."

"So, who are *you*?" I asked.

"I just told you."

"No, you didn't. You told me who your parents are. Both sound like very accomplished people. What they've achieved is very admirable. What've you done that would impress me? Have you gotten anything for yourself, or do you owe it all to mommy and daddy?"

"I-I-I'm..." Nautik stammered, trying to come up with an answer. "I'm a pilot."

Je'Sikka corrected him. "You're a co-pilot. And you've been one for quite some time. It seems like you're struggling to make that leap into the Number One chair."

"You don't know a fuckin' thing," Nautik growled at Albarn.

Our pilot shrugged. "Well, you can't blame me for that. When it comes to the accomplishments of Lodai Nautik, it doesn't seem like there's an awful lot to research."

Nautik's face started turning red. "You think you're better than me?"

Albarn smiled. "You want to compare medals?"

The half-Samaari's face twisted into several indescribable expressions as he tried to formulate a response. Failing, he turned to Henne as if urging her to help defend him. Instead, she only offered him a smug smile showing she was thoroughly enjoying our exchange. In frustration, Nautik pounded his fist on the table hard enough to make our glasses jump. "You all don't know shit about me!"

I stretched my grin even wider. "We know much more about you than we'd like to, Nautik."

Sensing something ominous in my tone, Nautik struggled to cut through the alcoholic haze in his head. "Huh? What're you talking about?"

As if on cue, Dmitri Naktada walked into the café carrying my exo-armor breastplate. Walking over to our table, he set the equipment beside me and pulled up a chair. "There you go, sir. Good as new."

"Thank you, Captain." I pointed at the inebriated airman. "Do you know Warrant Officer Nautik?"

Naktada gasped and then covered his mouth in mock surprise. He had been listening to us through the circuit I had opened on my tablet. "Lodai Nautik?!? The son of Melman Nautik? The senator who won the Portisbain vote by more than eighty-eight percent?!? And of Justice Ama Nautik? The husband to Ariana Bukoal? The father of Gilla, Moel, and little Tipper? Of course I know him!"

The drunkard looked confused. "Really?"

Naktada's expression dropped into something much more somber. "No. Besides your family, the only thing I know about you is you have no idea how your exo-armor works.

Not that you should. You Navy people typically don't wear it. It's the equipment of field Marines who get trained in it at boot camp. It seems to me Section 615 just threw you a shell and told you to put it on. They probably didn't spend much time telling you all it does. Morons."

Only then did Nautik start suspecting that ours was not a chance encounter. "Wait a second. Huh? What is this?"

"In most fighter craft, operations are recorded by cockpit cameras," Naktada continued. "Marine combat operations are recorded by cameras mounted within their breastplates and helmets. If you had come up flying transport craft like a standard Sitaara, you'd have been more familiar with your shell. The League would've wanted you outfitted like the grunts so you could still keep up if you crashed. You were trying to be a fighter pilot, so you were used to being equipped differently. You didn't know the cameras in your shell are always recording. *Always.*"

I could see the gears turning inside Nautik's skull, wondering if he had said anything in some drunken stupor that we could use against him.

"So, Warrant Officer Nautik, when you finish a stressful combat mission and want to take your frustrations out on a Portunese girl at Razbauten, powering down your shell does not turn off your cameras. That's why Marines store them in their lockers when they're off duty instead of throwing them on a chair facing their bunks."

Naktada pulled a video up on his tablet, then set the device on the table so Nautik and Henne could see it. He had the sound turned down enough so the bartender could not hear it, but we all listened in disgust to Nautik bludgeoning the prisoner with his fists as he ripped her clothes off. Henne gasped and recoiled, covering her mouth with her hand in shock. Naktada apologized to her, adding, "Believe it or not, that isn't his youngest victim."

Warrant Officer Nautik was sobering up fast. "I...I...I wasn't the only one! I...."

"No, you're not the only one," Naktada told him. "I'm appalled to say what's going on in that video is the norm at Razbauten. It's not the exception."

"And you're telling me that shit doesn't happen at Saimsun?!?"

I sighed. "My platoon was hand-picked by me. Gunny Brumit sought out people who were mission-oriented and guided by a certain moral code that would keep them from doing shit like this. Peeli chose his people based upon ideological purity and their willingness to loot."

Pointing at the video, I said, "This does happen at Saimsun, but it ain't us doing it. It's the Blue Shirts."

Nautik was sweating buckets. Keeping the pressure on, I asked, "You think your old man will still get more than eighty-eight percent of the vote when those images start circulating around Portisbain? How impressed do you think your wife will be to see this? You think she's going to want you around her daughters?"

"Please. Don't do this," Nautik whispered. "My father's a good man. This'll kill him. It'll ruin my whole family. They didn't do anything wrong. This's all on me."

"Whatever we do with these images is in your hands," Skaigard said.

Nautik nodded in resignation. "I figured as much. What do you want?"

"In two days, we're attacking Narman settlements all over the Arad," I reminded him. "Plus a couple of alien ones. I know Takawa's accompanying your unit. I want to know where they're going."

"I...I...I don't know where...."

We all stood up to leave at once.

"Okay! Okay! Okay!" Nautik cried, urging us to sit back down with his hands. "I don't have the coordinates memorized! They're on the ship!"

"Get them to us," I ordered. "Within the hour."

The warrant officer was close to tears. "That's it?"

"No, that's the beginning," I told him. "After your fighter lands and the Marines are out of sight, you're to shoot your pilot."

Nautik's mouth dropped open. "You want me to kill, Veriilan? H-h-he's my f-f-friend...."

"That's too bad," Naktada said. "If it's any consolation, he deserves it just as much as you do. I got video of him, too."

"B-but I don't think I can! And even if I did, how would I escape?"

"You don't," Albarn told him. "Once Veriilan is gone, you cap your own ass, too. If anyone's left able to fly that fucking aircraft, our deal's off."

"You expect me to die?" Nautik gasped. "I've got children."

"Children who are only going to know you as a kiddie-raping monster if that video gets out," Albarn assured him.

"Your choices are to die to stop even more atrocities from happening," I told him, "or getting yourself hung for the rape and murder of prisoners at the Razbauten mining facility."

Nautik shook his head. "The League would never do that! My father's a senator! My mother's a...."

I cut Nautik off by laughing out loud. "Oh, they'll hang your ass, all right! In public! The League'll have to prove to the masses on all those non-Guild planets that these atrocities were committed by rogue operators, and this was not state policy. I'll bet a year's salary they even get your own mother to throw down the sentence on you just to show everyone that justice is universal."

Nautik put his face in his hands and sobbed. "I'm sorry! I'm so fucking sorry!"

I shrugged. "I don't care."

The warrant officer looked up at us, expecting someone to show at least a hint of sympathy for him. He was wrong.

I pointed at the video still playing on Naktada's tablet. "Look, man, nothing can redeem you after shit like this. You're lost. The best we can do is allow your children to remember you fondly. If I don't have those coordinates in an hour, they're going to know what kind of sadistic creep you actually are. Got it?"

Weeping softly, Nautik nodded.

"Good. Now get the fuck out of my sight. The clock's ticking."

As Nautik stumbled out the door, Albarn turned to her flight school roommate and asked, "Do you think he'll go through with it?"

The flight engineer shrugged. "I don't know the details of what you all have cooked up, but if you ask me...."

Henne stuck her thumb out at the door Nautik just exited. "...that's your weakest link."

Chapter 47

COUNTDOWN

Samaari Blue Shirts were recent arrivals to Kanaris. They did not understand how intelligent the Quarakai were. To the Blue Shirts, the creatures were akin to apes. Having never been attacked by one, the militiamen regarded them as animals and did not fully appreciate the threat they posed. They certainly never considered how effective they could be as spies.

But I did. Every time I saw one near the Saimsun mine, I wondered if it was just passing by or a part of some Narman surveillance operation. When a glider showed up the day before we were to commence our sweep of the Arad Valley, I knew exactly what it was doing there. The Blue Shirts did not.

"Holy shit, Helman!" I heard one of them tell his buddy. "Take a look at the size of that thing!"

Helman sounded just as impressed. "Oh, man! That head would look awesome on my old man's trophy wall!"

"Then why don't you shoot it?"

Helman looked open to the idea. "I wonder if there're any taxidermists on Kanaris."

"I bet the Killbillies know how to mount it," Helman's buddy said. "They're all big hunters."

Helman unslung his rifle. "I bet you're right. Watch this, Mel."

Before Helman could take aim, I snatched the weapon from his hands and backhanded him across the cheek. "Don't even think about it!" I snapped at him. "If there's one around here, there's a hundred of them! They're happy to leave you alone if you don't bother them, but if you harm those things, every member of their troop is going to swoop down here for a piece of your ass! What are there, fifty fucking Blue Shirts down here?"

Mel nodded. "But we have guns."

"It takes about thirty rounds to stop one of them things. Trust me! I've fought 'em!" Slamming the rifle back into Helman's chest, I asked, "Who's your supervisor?"

"Ulrik," Mel answered.

"I'll be paying him a visit about this. If I see you put our lives at risk again, I'll tear you both apart right where you stand! Now, get out of my sight!"

After the Blue Shirts finished tripping over themselves to get out of my way, I looked up at the glider again. It was staring at me. Me, alone. I offered it a nod and watched as it returned the gesture. Then it gave me a thumbs-up and leapt from its perch, disappearing into the canopy.

That was the Narmans assuring me it was game on.

My final briefing with Takawa ran much longer than usual. I had a lot of questions about the mission's details, and he was growing increasingly frustrated about getting bogged down in the minutiae of the operation. "For fuck's sake, Tauk!" the agent groaned in exasperation. "I've got seven other units to prepare! You're an academy Marine! Are you really so unclear on what we need to do here?"

I pointed at my objective on the map, the one I had no intention of getting within a hundred kilometers of. "You're sending me to a place with a high probability of having an alien presence. I just want to make sure there isn't anything else I need to know."

"You know everything we do," Takawa growled impatiently.

"It doesn't feel like I know much of anything at all."

Takawa sighed. "That's because we don't know much, either," the agent finally admitted. "Look, Tauk, I'm going to level with you. You and Peeli drew the two most dangerous missions of the lot. You earned them because you both have all the fancy equipment and...."

Takawa paused as he looked over my gear. "Why did you tape over the grips of your weapons?"

"Extra friction," I told him as my heart skipped a beat. "It keeps them from getting slippery when they're wet. It's a trick Black Francis learned in the NML. You were saying?"

"Oh. I was just saying you've got the latest and greatest gear we have to offer. We gave you the toys, but it's up to you to figure out how best to use them. You're an academy Marine. There's no one better equipped to improvise than you. I have full faith in you, Lieutenant. You'll do fine out there."

Takawa was an excellent actor. I supposed it went with the job. After checking the time again, he said, "We've been over this several times. I have to get going. I'll see you tomorrow afternoon at our rendezvous point." With that, the agent marched out of the briefing room.

When he was gone, I sighed. I still had half an hour to kill. To fill it, I sought out Helman's supervisor and gave him a long lesson on why we should not let our Blue Shirts shoot Quarakai for sport.

I left Ulrik's tent just as the miners changed shifts, stopping at the crossing path to let more than a thousand prisoners pass. Half were going into the mine. The rest were coming out. Haeli Deboara was among those whose time in the hole had ended. She was haggard and exhausted, her hands resting on the shoulder of a young boy to her left and a younger one to her right. Both children looked starved and exhausted as well. I could see their will to live was waning.

When Haeli and I made eye contact, I nodded at her twice, letting her know we were leaving the following day. She nodded once back to let me know she was ready. Haeli then pulled her kids in close, wondering if they were well enough to survive what was to come.

Dmitri Naktada stepped off a Harnillium freighter dressed in Marine fatigues, which made Black Francis nervous. "You stand out like a sore thumb," he told the armorer. "You should've dressed in a Tahnebaht uniform to fit in better."

"Number one," Naktada responded. "Where am I going to get hold of a corporate uniform? Number two, the crew on that ship all know each other. They're going to figure out right away I'm not one of them if I snuck aboard. They'd probably take me for a saboteur. It was better to walk up to the pilot and ask if I could hitch a ride."

I slapped Black Francis on the shoulder. "He's better at this stuff than you are, Gunny." Turning back to the captain, I asked, "How much time do you need?"

Naktada shrugged. "Thirty seconds."

"Good," I said. "I can give you eight hours. You got the data from the tablet we turned over to you?"

"I've never not had it. Who's shell am I pumping this comm circuit program into?"

"PFC Huurling's," I told him.

"The guy who beat up that Zero girl during the smoker at Camp Vayipar?"

"Yep. That'd be the one. You two are about the same size."

Naktada nodded. "Where is he now?"

Black Francis shrugged. "I'm quite sure he's not in the armory where you need to be. Do you have access to it?"

Naktada shook his head. "No, but I'm sure you do. Lead the way, Gunny."

It was approaching midnight when Black Francis and I finished reconciling Nautik's coordinates and Naktada's tablet data to put the finishing touches on our plan. "You think everything's ready?" I asked him.

My platoon sergeant nodded. "Everything but me."

I stopped what I was doing and looked up at Gunny Franq. "You okay?"

Black Francis shook his head. "I will be. It's just starting to sink in what we're doing here, you know?"

"You don't think we can pull it off?"

Francis shrugged. "I figure our odds are about fifty-fifty. Even if we do succeed, though, what will we accomplish? Are we going to bring down the League and fill our future full of nothing but kittens and sunshine until the end of time?"

"All I know is if we go out there and operate according to Takawa's plan, most of us will die."

"We'll never be able to go home again."

"Big deal. I've never really had a...."

I stopped myself from saying it, but not in time for Black Francis to know what I was thinking. "My god," I gasped. "I'm sorry, Gunny. I can't even imagine what that must be like. I mean that quite literally. I've never had a home or a family. I didn't mean to come across as so insensitive, but brother, I can't even begin to relate to what you're turning your back on."

Black Francis held up his hand. "It's fine, sir. No offense taken."

I realized at that moment how little I knew of Black Francis's life outside of the Marines. "Who will you be leaving behind?"

"Parents. Grandparents. A son...."

"Oh, fuck. A son? I didn't know. He must really miss you."

"He doesn't even know me," Francis confessed. "I got drafted right after he was born. Three years into my hitch, his mother hooked up with someone who was around. My boy calls him 'Daddy' now. He doesn't miss me. I sure miss him, though. I always kind of looked forward to seeing him someday. I wouldn't even tell him who I was. I just dream about discovering what kind of man he turns out to be. Maybe what we do will eventually lead to a better life for him."

I leaned back and let that information sink in. "I have to make a confession, Gunny. With all the thought I've put into how to tear the League down, I've never considered what should replace it."

"Nor should you," Francis assured me. "Not yet, anyway. No sense wasting time on shit like that if we end up dying tomorrow. Let's focus on living through the next forty-eight hours."

"I'll drink to that."

Francis pulled a flask from the cargo pocket of his fatigues. "Will you?"

I stared at the container for a moment before saying, "No. Not tonight. Not hours before a mission."

Lodai Nautik had no such qualms. While Black Francis was taking a quick sip of brandy to settle his nerves, the warrant officer was killing his second bottle of homebrewed vodka. By the time he passed out, his blood alcohol content was coming dangerously close to surpassing his IQ.

The next morning, Warrant Officer Nordiq Veriilan had to yank his co-pilot out of his bunk. "Are you fucking kidding me?!?" he screamed at the man. "You're drunk?!?"

Disoriented and confused, Nautik shook his head to get the cobwebs out. "No," he slurred. "I just had a couple drinks before bed."

Veriilan smacked his Number Two across the face. "If Takawa gets a whiff of your breath, he'll have you fucking shot! What's the matter with you?!? You idiot!"

"I'm okay, Nord," Nautik said, trying to reassure his friend. "I can fly! Hell, I can dance!"

Enraged, Veriilan grabbed the drunk under the chin. "What the hell am I going to do with you, Lodai?!? This might be the biggest mission of our lives! The biggest mission in the history of the League! This could be the one where we actually capture an alien! My god, man! Don't you realize that?"

Nautik winced as a tear rolled out from one of his eyes. "I'm sorry, man. I'm sick. I've got a problem." Breaking down into sobs, he wrapped his arms around his friend's neck and cried, "I need help, Nord! Please help me! Don't report me!"

Letting go of Nautik's face, the pilot said, "Shhh. Shhh. Quiet down and pull yourself together. I'm not going to report this. Takawa's going to be onboard the *Space Serpent* in forty-five minutes. You better be there in fifteen so he don't see how you walk. Make sure your helmet's on, too. I don't want anyone getting a whiff of your breath."

Nautik nodded. "I'll be there. It'll be good, Nord. You can count on me."

The *Serpent's* pilot sighed. "I wish I could believe that, Lodai. If the Narmans had air capabilities, I'd be grounding your ass. You understand me? The next time this happens...."

Nautik shook his head. "There won't be a next time, Nord. I guarantee it."

The *Niberian Hornet* lifted off a Saimsun landing pad hours before dawn. Haeli Deboara and her husband were guiding a cart full of Harnillium ore to one of the freighters as we left. "Is that the one?" Daino asked.

Haeli nodded. "That's it."

Placing his right hand over her left, Daino squeezed his wife's fingers tight. With the abuse that his knuckles, as well as the rest of his joints, had taken from continuously swinging a pick axe for days on end, the gesture caused him significant pain. "So, this is going down?"

"Yes," Haeli told her husband. "During the shift change."

Daino nodded. He was terrified of what was to come. He was not so concerned about his own safety, but his boys were weak and fragile, worn down by what they had been forced to do in the mines. They would have been killed days before had Daino not hidden them so well. Even if everything went better than they imagined, it would be a Herculean effort to get his children to safety through the calamity about to unfold. Daino was not in great shape, either. He feared that he would not be up to the task.

Thinking about what they were about to do caused the inmate's nerves to fray, and his hands began shaking with his rising anxiety. To suppress his panic, he soothed himself with the assurance this would be the last day he ever swung his pick, and his final strike would be against the skull of a Samaari Blue Shirt.

Chapter 48

HAMLET

When the *Niberian Hornet* touched down, Je'Sikka Albarn released the troops' drop restraints allowing most of my Marines to leave their seats and start collecting their gear. Eleven of my people remained trapped in place, however. Lance Corporal Idris Jatmika was one of them. "Hey!" she shouted as she banged on the lock bar holding her down. "It's stuck!"

"Mine, too!" shouted Silma Hauken.

"They're not stuck," I told my troops. "Look, I'm sorry to do it this way, but we're no longer Marines of the Kyperion Space Corps. We just can't sit back any longer, watching the League do what it does in places like Saimsun, and pretend we're on the right side of history. We're switching teams. And praying the Narmans aren't any worse than the fiends we're leaving behind."

My trapped Marines' faces all went ashen. "What?!?" gasped Private Sunaipa.

"You heard me. Look, you're all good people. We're not going to hurt you. When this is all over, we're going to give you your naypetos and a couple of ubatis to keep you safe, then send you on your way. In the meantime, you're all going for a little ride. If we meet again on the battlefield, well, we'll both do what we must, but you all deserve better than being executed in cold blood."

Willi Reikjavik, my fourth squad machine gunner, protested. "Fuck the League, sir! Don't you dare leave me behind! I'm with you!"

"Are you sure, Willi? You haven't had a lot of time to think about it."

"Bullshit!" Reikjavik scoffed. "I've been thinking about it ever since we arrived at Saimsun! I don't know what the deal is with the Narmans, but they can't be worse than those Samaari Blue Shirts! If you're giving me a chance to poke holes in those fuckers, I'm with you!"

The machine gunner was convincing. I pulled the manual release on the back of his seat. "I don't have time to brief you on what we're doing here. I need you to stay on the ship."

Walking over to Elia Gyanis, my First Squad armorer, I asked, "What about you? I was really on the fence about whether to bring you in or not. Are you with us?"

Tears were streaming down Gyanis's cheeks. "I got family back on Sumar Agadi, Lieutenant. I...."

I patted the armorer on the shoulder. "It's okay. I understand."

Turning to the rest of my restrained Marines, I said, "If you don't know what you want to do yet, you have a little more time to think about it. When this mission's over, I'm going to ask you again. If you're with us, we'll take you. If you're not, we're sending you back to the Marines."

Naypetos were fast and usually traveled quietly, but they were still animals. No matter how well-trained they were, they could still wander, call out, spook, or even loudly pass gas, giving away our position. The same went for our ubatis. Since our mission depended upon stealth, our beasts remained aboard the *Niberian Hornet*. If we wanted to stay undetected for as long as possible, we had to approach Peeli's objective on foot.

The settlement they were attacking was closer to Saimsun than to Razbauten. We had the time to disembark and make it to the hamlet before the other Marines landed, but we had to hurry, needing to cover about three kilometers to be in place when First Platoon arrived. It was already going to be close, so the last thing we needed was a delay. About two-thirds of the way to our objective, however, that was exactly what we got.

I would have expected most Narmans to run in the other direction after hearing almost seventy-five Marines marching their way while virtually invisible in the latest generation of Kyperion exo-armor. The first one we encountered seemed to be expecting exactly that, however. She stepped out of a perfectly good hiding place to greet us on the trail. Had she not exposed herself, we would have passed right by her without ever knowing she was there.

Dasi Hoa, the rifleman marching point, was so stunned by how calmly the Narman approached us she did not quite know how to react. She stood there as the robed figure strolled up to her as if the Marine was visible as day.

"I thought the main force was approaching from the south," the Narman said. Black Francis and I immediately recognized the voice and pushed our way to the front.

Stalling for time, Hoa said, "It is. We're to take up positions to ensure no one sneaks up on us from the north."

That made little sense and set off the intruder's suspicions. "There's no one to sneak up on you here."

"The private misspoke," I said, approaching the two women. "We're to make sure none of the enemy escapes this way. You must be Deena Vulk."

Sensing something was rotten, the woman took a few steps backward before lowering her hood and showing us her disfigured face. She also revealed her bionic eye, a device I suspected had the same ultrasonic echolocation capabilities we had. "I am. Where's Agent Takawa? Who are you?"

While Vulk's eyes were locked on me, PFC Hoa stepped from between us and casually positioned herself at the spy's flank, ready to intercept her if she ran. Sergeant Korman discreetly pointed his rifle at one of the woman's knees to ensure she would not make it far if she got past Hoa. Vulk missed none of that. "I asked who you are!" she snapped.

"What? You don't remember me?" I asked as I lifted my visor. Like the rest of my troops, my face was obscured by camouflage paint, but my voice was the same as the day she shot me.

Takawa's asset turned to run, only to get pummelled in the nose with the butt of Hoa's rifle. Our point woman nearly knocked the spy out, but not quite. It was Sergeant Tiago who finished the job, kneeling on her chest and smashing the Narman in the face with her fist.

"Fucking bitch," my squad leader growled as Vulk lost consciousness.

•●•❖•◉•❖•●•

It was showtime for Warrant Officer Nautik. The *Space Serpent* was on the ground. Lieutenant Peeli, Agent Takawa, and their Marines were well on their way toward their objective, and Amella Henne's eyes were drilling into the back of the co-pilot's skull, urging him to get going. Three times Nautik's hand had reached for his weapon, and three times he had pulled it back. The *Serpent's* co-pilot had lost his nerve. Not that he ever had much of one to begin with.

Even though she was seated behind him, Henne was watching the man fall completely apart. He had removed his helmet, and she could see the sweat beads rolling down his head through his close-cropped hair. His hands shook so hard he had to grip the ship's auxiliary yoke to keep anyone from noticing. She also suspected he had thrown up in his mouth and forced himself to swallow it more than once during the flight to the settlement.

Veriilan noticed it, too. "You better fucking pull yourself together," he softly commanded his Number Two. "If you don't straighten your shit out, you're going to land us both in the stockade."

"I'm trying," Nautik answered.

"Try harder."

Nautik craned his head around to plead with Henne to release him from his sentence. She glared back at him and furiously mouthed the word, "Now!"

Nodding in resignation, the *Serpent's* co-pilot released his restraints and stood up, placing his helmet back atop his head. Assuming Nautik was leaving to get sick, Veriilan looked in the opposite direction, trying to make it appear he was ignoring the drunk. The man did not see Nautik pull his sidearm, aim it at his head, and then hesitate, trying to force himself to squeeze the trigger.

The weapons officer, however, did. "CAPTAIN!" she screamed, reaching for her own weapon. "LOOK OUT!"

Startled, Nautik swung around and pointed his pistol at Warrant Officer Liira Thaim. Seeing she had a firearm in her hand, the drunkard squeezed the trigger, sending a round boring into her skull right above the bridge of her nose.

Knowing he had passed the point of no return, Nautik swung back around and fired at Veriilan. The bullet struck the restraint bar the pilot was lifting off himself and ricocheted harmlessly into an overhead storage compartment. He could not get a second shot off before Veriilan leapt out of his chair, so he only blew a hole through his target's seat. It was not until he fired a third time that he struck his victim in the shoulder. That bullet bounced off Veriilan's armor and grazed his throat, just missing his jugular vein by a couple of millimeters. The pilot started bleeding profusely, but it was not a lethal wound. The fourth round hit Veriilan center mass, lifting him off his feet and throwing him onto the deck.

At that point, the crew chief was in motion. He had his weapon out and fired off a three-round burst. Two bullets struck Nautik square in the back, while the third hit him in the base of his helmet. None penetrated his armor, but they spun him around, exposing his front to Warrant Officer Henne.

Henne knew their moment had passed. If she tried to finish the job Nautik started, the crew chief would kill her. The best she could do was neutralize the co-pilot to keep him from outing her and thereby, lift herself above suspicion of being complicit in the attack. That could leave her alive long enough to act if another opportunity to take out Veriilan presented itself.

The flight engineer fired six shots in quick succession, missing twice and ineffectively striking Nautik's shell three times. One of the bullets hit the co-pilot in the throat, though, dropping him to his knees as he clutched his neck, choking on his own blood.

"I'm sorry," Nautik gasped as he keeled over onto the deck. "I'm sorry. I'm sorry."

With his right hand covering his own wound, Veriilan rushed over and kicked Nautik's weapon out of reach. He then pointed his sidearm at his comrade's head. "Why?!?" he shouted.

"Th-th-they m-m-made me." Nautik mouthed it more than said it. Then he coughed blood onto the cockpit's deck.

"Who?!?" the pilot barked. "Who made you?!?"

Nautik would have confessed had he been able, but he passed away instead.

In shock, Veriilan turned and looked at his surviving crew, which consisted only of his engineer, flight medic, and crew chief. Addressing the latter, he asked, "Can you operate the guns, Chief?"

"Not really," the chief answered. "I can make them move, but I don't have the formulas to effectively target anything."

"Fuck!" As Veriilan stomped toward his seat, the rest of his crew rushed into the cockpit with their weapons drawn. The pilot yelled at them to get back to their posts. "We got it under control! Assume your battle stations! Get ready for liftoff!" He then turned on his radio as the flight medic worked to stop the bleeding from his neck.

307

"Agent Takawa!" Veriilan shouted into the microphone. "Lieutenant Peeli! Come in! We got a situation here back on the *Serpent*!"

After both men acknowledged his call, the pilot brought them up to speed on what had happened aboard his ship. When Veriilan finished, Takawa unleashed a virulent string of obscenities. After exhausting his comprehensive catalog of curse words, the agent asked, "Is the *Serpent* combat effective?"

Veriilan cast a glance at a couple of the bullet holes that had been drilled into the control panels. Turning back to his engineer, he asked, "Are we?"

Warrant Officer Henne jogged to her console and began punching up diagnostics. After a few minutes, she looked up at her pilot and said, "It appears we are, captain."

Veriilan turned back to the commlink circuit and summoned Agent Takawa. "We're good to go, sir."

"Then get that bird in the fucking air and make sure we don't have any more surprises in the area."

"Should I be looking for anything in particular, sir?"

"Yeah!" Takawa practically shouted at him. "Eamon-fucking-Tauk!"

We were in position just beyond the northern perimeter of the Narman hamlet when the first Marines of Peeli's platoon came into view. "Hold your fire," I told my troops. "They're just scouts."

The three-person advance team scoured the settlement for several minutes but gave no indication of having uncovered us. It was not long before scores of Peeli's Marines began emerging from cover to sneak up to each domicile.

"Stay still," I commanded. "Let the majority get into view. Remember which structure you're assigned to cover, and be ready to kill them when I give the order."

There were seven small domiciles in the settlement. If Peeli's troops followed recon doctrine, eight Marines would be assigned to storm each one. In the center of them all was a long communal hall. It would take twenty to secure that. The platoon's staff personnel would likely hang back and remain behind cover to direct the operation. When I saw our adversaries were in place, I dialed up the platoon network and said, "Get ready to fire in five...four...three...."

Before I could finish, a deafening roar erupted above us as Veriilan's Mar-Sitaara switched out of stealth mode and swooped down on us from behind, having zeroed in on our electronic emissions. "FREEZE IN PLACE!" thundered a booming voice from the vessel's loudspeakers. "IF ANYONE MOVES, WE WILL FIRE UPON YOU!"

Had the *Serpent* possessed a living weapons officer, Veriilan would probably have incinerated us on the spot. Instead, half of Peeli's platoon broke off from their assignments and rushed to take us into custody while the others began breaching the buildings.

For the first time since I met him, Black Francis looked as if he had no idea what to do. "You got any orders, sir?"

I shook my head. "Just keep your wits about you and make sure nothing happens to Naktada."

Chapter 49

Point of No Return

M arine exo-armor was equipped with its own set of restraints. If an arrest had to be made on the battlefield, all an NCO had to do was place the prisoner's hands together behind their back and press a button on the forearm shields near the detainee's wrists. That activated a magnetic field so strong that not even a giant like Akkam Lumuk could break it. Not that he didn't try.

The restraints were so effective that detained Marines did not even have to be disarmed, saving the arresting authority the burden of having to transport the prisoner's gear. The arrestees could carry their stuff themselves. Detained troops were identified by an LED on their right shoulder that glowed red, signifying the person was in custody and magnetically shackled.

Once Peeli's troops were confident we had been rendered harmless, we were forced back onto our feet and marched into the hamlet, which had descended into chaos. Marines had broken into every structure, beating the settlement's inhabitants out into the rain while ransacking the domiciles in search of weapons and intelligence. Others rushed around the site executing the livestock, especially the ubatis that could have caused us real grief had they escaped their pens. About two dozen Narman men, women, and children were herded toward the communal long hall, as were half as many Morghul aliens.

It was the first close look we had ever had of the otherworldly beings. The Morghul were terrifying in appearance. They were tall and lanky, but their muscles were well-defined, suggesting they were very strong. They had oily skin so dark it almost appeared purple when it shimmered in the rain. Most had eyes that glowed red when the light hit them, suggesting they had evolved from nocturnal ancestors. The tops of their heads were larger than ours, hinting they possessed brains with considerable computing power. The lower parts of their faces were narrower than what humans had, containing smaller noses, mouths, and chins than we did. None of them had any hair at all.

As alien as they looked, the Morghul were oddly familiar. I could see a distinct difference between males and females, and their faces expressed emotion just like ours. The ones I saw that night were terrified and held their children close as the Marines beat and pushed them into the long hall. They wailed and cried as Peeli's troops laughed at their grief.

One of Peeli's riflemen drew his sidearm and pointed it at the child of a Morghul he felt was not responding to his commands fast enough. I was shocked to hear the kid's father begging for his son to be spared, speaking flawlessly in our common tongue. The Marine seemed unswayed by the Morghul's pleas and was prepared to shoot them both anyway.

Luckily, Takawa was close by and smacked the infantryman across the back of the helmet before he pulled the trigger. "Not the Mogs," the agent snapped. "We need them. If you want to make a point, kill one of the Narman kids."

The Marine looked at the agent, then at one of the human children. Unable to butcher someone so young, the leatherneck slipped his blaster back into its holster.

After we were forced into the long hall, Peeli had my platoon lined up against the east wall, where his people started disarming us, piling our weapons by the southernmost exit. I tried to stay close to Naktada but got separated as one of the enemy squad leaders dragged Black Francis and me to the center of the formation. Seeing what was happening, Sergeant Korman maneuvered himself closer to our armorer. As we all had our helmets off, Korman leaned toward Naktada and whispered, "Get behind me and try to stay hidden as best you can. I don't want Peeli or Takawa recognizing you."

As I was jostled around, I spotted Deena Vulk on the Narman side of the long hall. I was sure Takawa had seen the woman also, but he seemed to be putting an incredible amount of effort into not noticing her. She was a huge prize, but no one was making any fuss about her capture, removing all doubt she was working for Section 615. They even left her shackled to keep up appearances.

Mazada Duum was also with us, pacing before the prisoners, tormenting the Morghul. He had suffered greatly in their hands and was itching for retribution. When one of the smaller ones called out, presumably for its mother, the Samaari struck it with his rifle, opening a large wound across the alien child's head.

"Leave it alone!" Lumuk screamed at him.

Duum turned around to sneer at Lumuk, then raised his rifle to strike the young Morghul again.

"For the last time!" yelled Takawa as he entered the hall. "Leave the Mogs alone! Duum, you'll get your chance when we finish with them."

The tiny Samaari lowered his weapon and took several steps toward Lumuk. "Maybe I should just knock the fuck out of you, you worthless wad of chicken shit!"

"If you need to occupy yourself, Sergeant," Lieutenant Peeli told him. "Go ahead and beat on the big guy."

A huge smile crept across Duum's face. "Really? How much?"

Peeli shrugged as he stepped in front of me. "Beat the traitor to fucking death for all I care."

"What is that going to accomplish?" I asked Peeli as Duum swung his rifle up and smashed Lumuk across the chin, knocking him down so the vertically challenged sergeant could reach him better.

"It'll keep him away from the Mogs," the Samaari officer told me. Flashing me a smug grin of superiority, he mockingly asked, "What's up with all the camo face paint, Tauk? You're already practically invisible with this cloaking technology we have."

Takawa answered for him. "It's so his people could tell themselves apart from yours. We're all dressed the same. We all have the same gear. The only way to distinguish ourselves is by the names on our shells, which are kind of hard to read during the heat of battle. I thought something smelled funny when I saw they'd taped the grips of all their weapons."

"Please," said one of the Morghul, the same one I heard begging for his child's life earlier. "We are not soldiers. We..." the alien paused as Lumuk started wailing under a barrage of Duum's blows. "We came here to avoid conflict. We are peaceful beings."

"Yeah, well," Takawa responded. "We're not. What's your name?"

"Melki."

"You want to live, Melki?"

The alien nodded.

"Then tell us where we can find the rest of you ugly fuckers."

The alien turned to stare at Duum brutalizing Lumuk, cringing as the giant screamed on the floor of the long hall.

"Yeah," Takawa said. "That's what we do to our own people. Imagine what we'll do to yours if you don't cooperate."

Having tired of beating Lumuk, Duum got up and turned to a couple of his comrades. "Lift him up," the Samaari panted. "I want him on his knees."

It took three men to pull Lumuk off the deck. As they struggled under the weight of the giant, Duum pulled out his sidearm.

"Now," Korman whispered into our tech wizard's ear.

Captain Naktada did not have to say it loud. All he had to do was lean into the microphone contained in the collar of his breastplate and say, "Prototype P662 Circuit. Serial Numbers one-oh-one through two-hundred. Lock."

Duum pointed his pistol at Lumuk's bloodied face and pulled the trigger. Nothing happened.

As the tiny Samaari tried again, Naktada said, "Prototype P891 Circuit. Serial Numbers one-oh-one through two-hundred. Lock."

Realizing his sidearm was not working, Duum reached for his comrade's, yanking it from her holster. That would not fire, either. The rest of the Marines directed a panicked look at the Narman prisoners, who were beginning to realize their captors were without working weapons. Peeli's troops began raising their rifles at the prisoners and squeezing the triggers. Not a single one fired.

"Prototype Seibara Circuit. Serial Numbers one-oh-one through two-hundred. Lock."

No one could hear Naktada effectively disarming Peeli's entire platoon over all the noise in the long hall.

"Prototype Exo-Armor System 444," Naktada continued. "Serial Numbers one through one-hundred. Disengage magnetic restraints."

The red LEDs on my Marines' armor went out, and the tension on our wrists suddenly disappeared. We were free.

"Prototype Exo-Armor System 444," Naktada continued. "Serial Numbers one-oh-one through two-hundred. Full system shutdown."

When energized, Marine exo-systems were performance-enhancing. They made us faster, stronger, and more agile. Unpowered, they were just twenty kilograms of dead weight, which was a big problem for Mazada Duum.

Duum had been tormenting Lumuk from the moment we had all crash-landed on Kanaris. He was shorter, lighter, and weaker than the giant, but he was quick. Lumuk would have destroyed the man had he ever landed a punch on him, but the little Samaari was so fast the lumbering bruin could never connect. With twenty kilograms of extra mass weighing down the Samaari sergeant, Mazada Duum was suddenly not very fast anymore.

When that little red light on Lumuk's armor died, the behemoth grabbed Duum by the collar of his breastplate to ensure he could not get away. Then he ripped the Samaari's helmet off with his free hand.

Mazada Duum immediately realized the danger he was in, and the color drained from his face. As Lumuk cocked his elbow back to wind up his punch, we heard the tiny pissant whimper, "No, Akkam. Please. Don't...."

The blow landed with a sickening thud. Lumuk throttled Duum on the left side of his face, crushing his skull and snapping his neck. The Samaari's entire head buckled under the power of the giant's fist, splintering his orbital socket and popping his eye like an oblong water balloon. I had seen people shot in the head with less damage. The Samaari died instantly, and Lumuk tossed his corpse aside like a broken rag doll. With the scent of blood in the air, Lumuk then turned his attention toward a pair of Peeli's Marines unfortunate enough to be standing within the big man's reach. Thirty years of victimhood began pouring out of the once gentle farmer, and the rage that now propelled him could not be controlled. Not even by Lumuk.

When I was freed, I snapped my wrist to energize the magnets in my gloves. I then pointed my palm toward the table where they had piled our confiscated sidearms. Following my lead, so did the rest of my Marines. In an instant, dozens of weapons with taped pistol grips came flying through the air to our side of the hall. One was drawn right into my hand, which I immediately turned on Lieutenant Peeli before shooting him through his open mouth. I then directed it at Agent Takawa. He froze in place, allowing Black Francis to knock him out with a single blow.

With their armor de-energized, Peeli's Marines never stood a chance. Both sides rushed for black-taped blasters, but with our shells working for us and the armor of our adversaries working against them, we beat Peeli's troops to the weapons by a wide margin. Once we were re-armed, the battle turned into a massacre. The only survivor was Supai Takawa.

"The black tape," I told the agent when he regained consciousness. "Was to tell us which weapons still worked. The face paint was to make us all look alike." I pulled

Naktada front and center and pointed to the name on his breastplate. "Obviously, we didn't want any of you to realize this wasn't PFC Huurling."

"We just made you a captain," Takawa said as he gazed upon the master armorer. "Why would you do this?!?"

Naktada smacked the spy across the face. "Because you're fucking monsters!"

"You still got Henne on call?" I asked my tech wizard.

"Yep."

"Give her the signal."

Turning on the clandestine *Serpent* circuit, Naktada said, "Red Rebel. I repeat, Red Rebel. Prepare for inbound."

Warrant Officer Henne did not know whether to be relieved or concerned about the call she received. The only thing she did know was she had to be decisive. The flight engineer saw what had happened to Lodai Nautik when he hesitated. She knew better than to make that same mistake and die in futility.

The first thing she did was pull up the control panel on her diagnostic console and seal the cockpit doors. Fearing another infiltrator attack, the *Serpent's* pilot already had them closed. No one could have known they were no longer able to be opened from within or without. With cockpit access secured, Henne then inserted a computer virus developed by Naktada into the Mar-Sitaara's operating system. If the ship tried to take off before Henne punched in an override code, the thrusters would lock and shut down, leaving the fighter defenseless on the ground and at the mercy of Albarn and her *Niberian Hornet*. Warrant Officer Henne then drew her pistol and blew away the crew chief before he saw it coming.

The *Serpent's* pilot was already on edge. When he heard the gunshot, he leapt to his feet and spun around to find his engineer pointing her sidearm at the dying crew chief. As Henne had already saved Veriilan's life earlier that day, the first thing that entered his mind was she had just done it again. The next thing to go through his head was a bullet fired from Henne's M88.

The only one left alive in the Serpent's cockpit now was the flight medic, who was unarmed and recoiling against the starboard bulkhead, waiting for her turn to die. "You're okay, Indira," Henne told her. "You're a good person. No one's going to hurt you."

"Then what are you going to do with me?" the petty officer asked, tears streaming down her cheeks.

"I don't know," Henne told her as she retook her spot at the engineering console, punched in the override code to disable Naktada's virus, and activated the red strobe on top of the aircraft to signal to Albarn she had achieved control of the *Serpent*. "I'm not even sure what I'm going to do with me."

"Why did you do this?" Indira asked.

Henne shrugged. "I can't be a part of it anymore. The evil we're doing – I need to try to stop it."

As Indira collapsed in her seat, Henne returned to the clandestine circuit and dialed up Naktada. "Red Rebel over. Mission completed. Proceed with Phase Two."

"Roger that," Naktada responded. "We're on our way."

Chapter 50

A New Dawn on Kanaris

"You down there, Tauk?" Albarn asked as she circled our area of operations.

"I am," I told her.

"Your plan worked?" Albarn sounded surprised. "I was half expecting to have to blow the entire area."

"Well, Plan A shit the bed before it even got started," I confessed. "The Naktada contingency worked like a charm, though."

"Good old Naktada," Albarn said.

"How did you make out with the Killbillies at our objective? Did you give them what they deserved?"

"They got better than they deserved, Lieutenant," Albarn reported. "They died quick. The bastards didn't suffer nearly as bad as they should have."

"How about the loyalists we left on board?"

"They came to a decision quicker than expected. Four decided to stay with us. I released the rest near where we iced the Qilkorians."

"And the body?"

"Petty Officer Farad tossed it out of a cargo portal somewhere over the Arad Valley."

I should have regretted killing Slai Huurling more than I did, but after watching him beat Margi Gul at Camp Vayipar, I could not help but feel he had it coming. "Did you pass by the *Serpent's* LZ?"

"I did. The red strobe is lit, and we counted seventeen crew on their knees outside with their hands on their heads, waiting for us to take them into custody. It looks like Henne convinced them the jig is up."

"Seventeen is a full Mar-Sitaara compliment, minus the cockpit crew."

"It is," Albarn agreed. "How did you make out?"

"Three dead, seven wounded."

Albarn let that sink in for a moment. "I'm sorry, Eamon. You know it could have been a lot worse, right? In fact, it *should* have been far worse."

"I know."

"So, what now, Lieutenant? What are your orders?"

"Proceed to the LZ and have Skaigard take control of the *Serpent*. We'll be there soon."

"Aye aye, Lieutenant. Albarn out."

As soon as my pilot signed off, Melki, the Morghul whose son was nearly killed, stepped beside me and placed his hand on my shoulder. "Sir! Sir!"

Turning to look at the alien, I noticed he had long, freakishly thin fingers. "My name is Eamon, sir. Eamon Tauk."

The alien smiled at me, revealing a mouth full of yellow teeth. "I am Melki. I am what I think you would call an 'elder.' Can I bring something to your attention?"

I nodded, "Of course, sir."

Melki pointed one of those long fingers at Deena Vulk, who was gagged, bound at both the hands and feet, and carried slung over Lumuk's shoulder. "That woman...she is one of us."

I shook my head. "Trust me, sir, she most certainly is *not*. She's a spy, run by Section 615." I motioned toward Supai Takawa, who was being pulled along by a rope tied around his neck. "Turn this piece of shit over to Kryndil. I'm sure he could make that man tell you everything about it."

Melki looked ashamed to learn I knew about the Morghul jailor. "I do not approve of Kryndil's methods."

"Good. I don't approve of Takawa's. Still, if there's anyone on Kanaris that deserves to meet your skin-taker, it's that bitch."

Still unsure of who he was dealing with, Melki changed the subject. "Sir, can I ask you another question?"

"It appears you already have."

The alien looked confused, then realized I was joking. He did not laugh, however. "Sir..."

"You can call me Eamon."

Melki grinned.

I grinned, too. "You smile? Like we do?"

"Not really," Melki said. "I had to train myself in non-verbal human cues."

I nodded. "And I'll have to train myself in yours."

"Eamon, will you allow me to ask where you are taking us?"

"You can ask, Melki, but I don't know the answer to that question."

"Then where are we going?"

I shrugged. "Wherever you tell us to."

The *Serpent* was virtually empty, so we loaded the liberated Narmans, the Morghul, and our animals onto it, then sent it heading for safe haven. Melki boarded the *Hornet* to help us with some unfinished business near Saimsun.

We landed at the mine only to discover it had been reduced to a smoking ruin. The grounds were littered with the corpses of both Samaari Blue Shirts and Portunese prisoners. We spotted the bodies of Tahnebaht management hanging from the trees just beyond the camp's eastern perimeter. "I guess that means the prisoners eventually won," I said to Albarn.

"I guess they did," Je'Sikka answered. "Where do you think they went?"

"I don't know. Wherever the Narmans led them."

As it got dark, we spotted a trio of Raptor transports just our side of the western horizon. With the light as low as it was, we could also see explosions beneath the canopy just below them. I pointed the craft out to our pilot. "There. Did you catch that?"

Albarn nodded. "You want me to engage them?"

"Affirmative. Shoot 'em down."

With the flick of a switch, the three Raptors were destroyed before they even knew we were in theatre. When we got close enough to the conflict, we could pinpoint Marines on the ground by their RF signatures. Albarn wasted them as well. We then directed the escaped inmates they were chasing to a nearby clearing.

I was shocked by how few of the Portunese reached us. I was even more surprised, albeit pleasantly, that Haeli Deboara was among them. She looked horrified, grief-stricken, and exhausted.

"Is your family with you?" I asked as I pulled her aboard.

Panting and sobbing too hard to speak, Haeli pointed to her husband, who was being helped up the loading ramp by Sergeant Korman.

"What about your boys?"

Haeli collapsed at the question, falling into my arms. Nila Chisek rushed beside me to help set her down. The prisoner wailed and shook her head. "They couldn't keep up," she wept. "They couldn't keep up!"

"Did the Marines get them?" I asked, praying we had not killed Portunese children when we bombed the troops pursuing them.

Haeli shook her head. "No," she gasped, heaving so hard she blew snot out her nose. She was so distraught she did not even care. "We had to...we had to...we had to..." She could not bring herself to say it.

Nila Chisek recoiled and covered her mouth in shock. "You killed your babies, didn't you?!?"

The grieving mother clenched her eyes closed, as if she would once again see what she had done if she left them open. "We had to. We couldn't let them fall into the hands of the Marines again! They'd throw them to the Blue Shirts!"

Chisek's reaction was visceral. She could not comprehend what Haeli and her people had done to their own flesh and blood. She was saddened, incredulous, and furious at the fate of the Portunese children. Unable to contain her fury, Nila lashed out. Unfortunately, the target of her misplaced rage was Haeli Deboara.

"How could you?" Nila spat at the despondent woman. I tried to calm my praetorian, but she pushed me aside. "They were your kids! How can you live with yourself after that?!? Why didn't you kill yourselves and go with them?!?"

Haeli suddenly stopped weeping and turned a cold-blooded gaze upon my bodyguard. "You have no idea how badly I wanted to die with them. But I can't."

Unphased, Chisek snarled, "Why the hell not?!?"

"Because if we died with our babies," Haeli snarled back. "There'd have been no one left to avenge them."

The End

Next in Series – The Morghul

Coming November 2023!

Author's Note –

Did you enjoy this story? If so, I invite you to *please* leave a review on Amazon.com! Good reviews not only raise the visibility of an author's work; they massage our fragile egos. It keeps us from priming our muses with absinthe and psychosis.

Also, be sure to sign up for Guerilla Lit, the J.E. Park newsletter, for news, announcements, and information on how to score the occasional free novella!

Epilogue

As Ritza Xi and her two friends crossed the tarmac, heading for their transport to the *Nebulean Phoenix*, she spotted a familiar figure standing by the catwalk. "Did you come to see us off, Gunny?"

Konor Malcolm stepped closer to the women and smiled at them. "Not really. I came to make sure you actually boarded that Wasp and went back to the mothership. I didn't want you getting any weird ideas about disappearing back into the jungle."

"Why the hell would we do that?" asked Zubi Jenich.

"To join Eamon Tauk."

Margi Gul looked confused. "What's going on with Tauk?"

Malcolm felt rainwater getting into his eye socket, so he adjusted the patch to cover it better. "He flipped. The son-of-a-bitch joined the Narmans."

"He what?!" exclaimed Jenich and Gul almost simultaneously.

"You heard me." Turning to Xi, Malcolm said, "You don't look surprised."

Xi shook her head. "I'm not."

"Why?"

"Tauk's a decent man," she told the gunny sergeant. "He could only pretend to be a depraved bastard for you people for so long. It had to happen sooner or later."

Malcolm thought he should react to that comment, but could not bring himself to be genuinely offended. "I guess you're entitled to your opinion as long as you don't get any funny ideas about helping him. I won't have any problems with you as long as you stay out of my way."

"And we won't have any problems with you as long as you stay out of ours." Xi paused for a second, then asked, "You're going after him, aren't you?"

Malcolm nodded. "I am."

"Why?"

"Because those are my orders. I'm a Marine. I don't know how to do anything else but what I'm commanded to."

"That's very sad," Margi Gul told him.

"It is," Gunny Malcolm agreed, extending his mitt to his former subordinate. Gul took it and they shook hands with genuine warmth. "Take care of yourself, Margi."

Jenich passed on the handshake, opting to embrace the gunnery sergeant instead. As they hugged, Malcolm said, "I'd tell you to stay out of trouble, but I'm not going to bother wasting my breath. I know what they're doing on Portuna, and I know you won't stand idly by and let it happen. Be careful out there."

"I will," Jenich promised as she let go.

Xi and Malcolm neither shook hands nor embraced. Instead, they just stood on the tarmac, staring at each other with mutual respect, knowing they would eventually end up on opposite sides of the coming conflict. "I honestly hope we never see each other again, Ritza."

It was a far greater compliment than it sounded. Xi understood what Malcolm meant because she felt the same way. "Me too, Gunny."

An hour later, as the Wasp transport approached their mothership, Jenich looked back at Kanaris through one of the overhead monitors. She felt guilty. "After everything Tauk did for us, I feel like we should be helping him in some way."

"We are," Ritza Xi told her. "There is no better person to fight the League from the outside than Eamon Tauk. He needs help from soldiers, which none of us are. We'd be more of a hindrance to him than an asset. We'll be far more effective taking on the League from within."

Xi reached into her pocket and felt the data chip Elia Gyanis, one of my armorers, passed her after the "loyalist" Marine was rescued from where Je'Sikka Albarn dropped her off in the Arad Valley. On it was hundreds of hours of video documenting the horrors the League inflicted upon the Portunese on Kanaris, all pulled from the cameras of Peeli's Marines. She suspected that when those images started circulating across the more restive worlds chaffing under the Samaari yoke, there was going to be a monumental reckoning.

Xi was planning on delivering some of it to Portisbain personally. She wanted to see Senator Melman Nautik's face when he learned just how depraved his prodigal firstborn turned out to be. She yearned to watch an elite suddenly realize his life would be utterly destroyed by a crime for which he personally bore no blame.

Just like hers was.

•●-◆-●-◆-●•

Acknowledgments

No great task is ever undertaken alone, and this was certainly no exception. There were plenty of people who offered me their encouragement and support in getting this, and the subsequent books of this series, written.

The first people I have to thank is my family. This has been a LONG effort, more than three years in the making. There was a lot of time taken away from my wife and children to get this done. So, to Patrina, Regan, Mason, Carson, Fairen, and Linden, I love you and thank you for your patience, your enthusiasm, and support.

I also need to thank the authors of the Grand Blanc Authors Meetup, who have continually read, critiqued, and listened to my work for five years now. Doug Allyn, Kathleen Rollins, Gloria Goldsmith, Brenda Hasse, Richard Drummer, Jeanie Hunt and anyone else I may have missed, THANK YOU!

And finally, my beta readers! Beta reading is no easy task. It is a HUGE undertaking and requires a lot of time and effort to do. It also requires commitment. You really have to be dedicated to the project to see it through. There is no such thing as casual beta reading and these people are an author's most valuable asset in cultivating a story. So, Rich Sorgenfrei, Matt Shefke, Deann D'Onofrio, and Tim Geniac, thank you so much for your help and invaluable assistance in helping me get this done.

And, of course, to you, the reader, thank you for taking a chance on an unknown author and reading this work. I hope you enjoyed it enough to continue on with the following books in this series.

About the Author

J.E. Park grew up in a suburb of Detroit, MI, where his efforts in seeking misadventures in the Motor City's punk rock scene and pursuing his vices dashed any aspirations in pursuing a higher education. They certainly did not help further his aspirations for a career in politics, either.

After graduation from high school, J.E. Park joined the US Navy and spent the next six years bar-brawling his way across the Far East, gaining the experiences that formed the foundation for his first novel "Tequila Vikings", a tale of a troubled young man navigating the military politics, violence and wanton hedonism woven into the naval culture of the early 1990s.

J.E. Park was a former contributing writer to the now-defunct comedy website Zug .com where he was best known for penning an article on harnessing the hallucinatory experiences of the smoking cessation aid Chantix for recreational purposes, positing that whether a condition is considered a side effect or an unintentional source of amusement depends largely upon the patient's attitude about the whole thing.

J.E. Park currently lives in a suburb of Flint, Michigan with his family where he has successfully used the region's suspect water quality as an excuse to stop neglecting his drinking.

Also By J.E. Park

The Tequila Vikings Series

Tequila Vikings

Olongapo Earp

Neptune's Martyrs

The Eamon Tauk Space Odyssey

Narman's Pyke

Moloch's Garden

The Morghul

Novellas

Acid and Ozymandias: Notes from Skid Row

J.E. PARK

The Nest

She nodded, focusing up on him, even though Arnie grinned at the both of them from the chair where she'd been sitting.

"Well, I don't have to use any of them more than normal, because they fired the coach!"

"Yes!" She grinned, kissed him as he leaned down towards her. His lips felt so perfect on her mouth, his tongue with hers. It was…simply wonderful.

"Now," he said as he broke the kiss. "I've got my happy ending."

She shook her head as she looked up at him. "You need one more piece of jewelry to get a real happy ending."

He shook his head. "I want the cup," he said. "But it won't be worth anything without you to share it with."

And then, he kissed her.

If you've enjoyed

GOING ALL IN

Don't miss

Book 2 in the New York Empires Series

ICING THE PUCK

Out Now!

ABOUT THE AUTHORS

Cassandra Carr

Bestselling author Cassandra Carr writes romance novels and has won numerous awards for them. She's written over sixty works, ranging from short stories to full-length books. Cassandra also writes middle grade books under a different name. Cassandra thinks the best part of her job is writing about people falling in love from the comfort of her own home while others battle daily commutes and cranky coworkers. Information about her books can be found on her website at http://www.booksbycassandracarr.com.

Isabo Kelly

Isabo Kelly is the award-winning author of numerous science fiction, fantasy, and paranormal romances. She also writes best-selling paranormal romance under the name Kat Simons. Her life has taken her from Las Vegas to Hawaii, where she got her BA in Zoology, back to Vegas where she looked after sharks, then on to Germany and Ireland where she got her Ph.D. in Animal Behavior. Now Isabo focuses on writing. She lives in New York with her Irish husband and two beautiful boys, working as a full time writer and stay-at-home mom. For more on Isabo, visit her at her website http://www.isabokelly.com

Stacey Agdern

Stacey Agdern is an award winning former bookseller who has reviewed romance novels in multiple formats and given talks about various aspects of the romance genre. She's also a romance writer. You can find her on twitter at @nystacey. She's a proud member of both LIRW and RWA NYC. She lives in New York, not far from her favorite hockey team's practice facility. Website: https://staceyagdern.wordpress.com/